OF CAGES AND CROWNS

BRIANNA JOY CRUMP

OF CAGES AND CROWNS

wattpad books **W**

wattpad books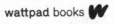

An imprint of Wattpad WEBTOON Book Group

Published in Canada by Wattpad WEBTOON Book Group, a division of
Wattpad Corp.

36 Wellington Street E., Suite 200, Toronto, ON M5E 1C7 Canada

www.wattpad.com

First Wattpad Books edition: November 2022
ISBN 978-1-99025-902-9 (Hardcover original)
ISBN 978-1-99025-903-6 (eBook edition)

Library and Archives Canada Cataloguing in Publication information is available
upon request.

Printed and bound in Canada

1 3 5 7 9 10 8 6 4 2

Cover Design by Greg Tabor
Map of Erydia by Jay Flores-Holz
Images © Arcangel

To my parents,
who read me stories.

To my Papa Crump,
who told me stories.

And to the professors of Craig Hall,
who gave me the space to write my own.

TENGAAR

NARTUK

THE
UPPER
FLOODLANDS

BATYA

NOLAJAN

GAZDA

PALLAE

MAP OF
ERYDIA

PROLOGUE

The Story of Creation

It is said that our world will end the way it began: with fire.

At first, the goddess forged ten daughters, all of them meant to be companions for one another. Things were perfect for a while. They dwelled together in the holy lands and were at peace—until one day, the last of the daughters grew restless.

This girl, Vayelle, didn't fit with the other nine. She was made from a different sort of power than the rest. She didn't find peace in nature or pleasure in worshiping at the altar of the goddess. Despite all that she had, she demanded more from the world. And she wept for things she'd never possessed, experiences that were never meant to be hers.

Out of pity, the goddess offered to create an eleventh daughter, a sister who could be a friend to the girl. But Vayelle declined. Another sister would not satisfy her.

She wanted something deeper. Vayelle wanted what the lions had. What she saw amongst the birds and the wolves and the deer. She wanted affection, protection, and, what is more, she wanted love. A deeper, rooted sort of companionship, unlike any her sisters shared. So, the goddess said that she would form for her a new companion.

And a deal was struck.

Since the love of the goddess and her sisters was not enough, Vayelle could have the love of another, but she would not be allowed to remain in the holy lands—in the direct presence of the goddess. Instead, Vayelle would be cast out. But she would have what she had demanded.

This would have to be enough to sustain her.

The goddess spoke to Vayelle, saying, "Love of this kind comes with risk. Daughter of mine, this creature will have free will, just as all of my daughters do. Perhaps its desires will not always align with your own."

It was then that the goddess forged a man from fire and blood. She named him Erydi. This man, the first of his kind, would be the father of the ten holy nations. The beginning of what would be the end of that first holy place.

And he did have his own will. Much to Vayelle's dismay, he fell for one of her sisters instead. That girl's name was Batya.

Unlike Vayelle, Batya was contented. She saw the world as a glass meant for drinking, and she savored each and every sip. While Vayelle had needed a man to complete her happiness, Batya needed only herself and the goddess. She was the sort that could only ever be loved—and so, Erydi loved her.

Meanwhile, Vayelle was cast out of the holy lands and made to wander the darklands alone. Erydi was not bound to her and although he could have chosen to leave, too, the bargain Vayelle had made with the goddess could not force Erydi's heart toward her. The goddess kept her promise, but Erydi chose Batya.

Vayelle wept our very seas into existence.

When Batya and Erydi were blessed with a child, Vayelle was furious. She broke her vow and crossed into the holy lands. Vayelle begged her other eight sisters for help. She said that together they might convince the goddess to cast out Batya and Erydi. After all, Vayelle had nothing and Batya had everything. The two of them should be the ones to wander the darklands aimlessly. Some agreed with Vayelle out of pity. Others did not.

Vayelle's despair soon turned to bloodlust.

One night, as Batya was sleeping, Vayelle killed her in her bed and stole away her baby. Erydi chased Vayelle for days and finally found her on the very edge of the holy lands—almost into the goddess-forsaken territory of her exile. It was at that moment, just as Erydi reached her, that she slit the throat of the babe. Today, red oak trees bloom where its blood once spilled.

The anger Erydi felt was unparalleled. It rose the Demarti Mountains up from dry, cracked earth. Our land was split because of it. The goddess stepped back from humanity then, her own grief swelling to create the moon and stars. Her heartbreak forged our sun. With her presence removed from the world, everything was cast into shadow and confusion.

Fighting ensued. The other daughters took sides, created alliances. Vayelle struck deals and told lies. Sister turned on sister. There seemed to be no end in sight.

But just as the world was about to succumb to holy fire, the goddess turned her face to her daughters once more. She separated our world. The land was severed into pieces so the fighting might cease. Erydi and Vayelle were cast apart from one another, kept away by the range of mountains he had created with his wrath.

The remaining sisters were dispersed throughout our continent.

This is how the ten counties were created. One county for each of the nine daughters and one for Batya and Erydi's dead child—Gazda. Vayelle was left with nothing but the darklands. This place was a home that could never truly be a home. Her people have been fighting to reenter the holy lands and claim what they believe to be theirs ever since.

But our story of creation doesn't end with Vayelle's fate. We are the chosen people. Our fate is not hers. It is well known that the goddess punished her daughters with shortened lives and worrying hearts, but she did not leave them lonely. Our world was created through the destruction of that first world. Forged from its ashes. To prevent what had happened with Vayelle, Batya, and Erydi, the goddess formed more men and women—all of them unblessed and unmarked by her hand.

Erydi's heartache over Batya and her child did not go unseen and, to soothe that ache, the goddess gifted him a prosperous country. She gave him reign over all ten counties and bid him to take another wife. The goddess promised that the kingdom would flourish under his rule. His throne would always be filled by a mighty queen.

It is written in our texts that when the eldest son of Erydi's bloodline comes of age, the goddess will send him ten girls, all of them goddess-touched with abilities to rival one another. As it is written, so it has always been. It is from this group of girls that the next queen comes.

In that first generation, this promise was a blessing and a curse. How was the son of Erydi to choose who should be queen? Since the mark of the goddess's hand had been left on each and every chosen girl, it seemed that no mere mortal could decide who should be crowned. The choice ought to be left to the goddess, or so the most devout worshipers said. It was because of this that the first son of Erydi formed a competition. *The Culling*. From this fight to the death our next queen will arise.

PART ONE

—

A Game of Crowns

Midsummer
Varos County, Erydia

Ten Goddess-touched Girls Remain

1

I'd only just finished at the pump and was heading back to the house when I heard the crunch of tires on the gravel lane. *Shit.* I had enough sense to dart behind the nearest shelter—the outhouse—but as soon as I was there, my mind went blank.

I'd hidden, but now what? Where could I go with so much open space between where I stood and the main house? And it wasn't like I could really go inside either—what if whoever was in the automobile wanted to go into the house for something? They'd see me. They'd ask questions.

I needed . . . I needed to . . .

My heart plummeted, my insides doing a wicked backflip as I peered out from my hiding spot. Dust rose in a swirling cloud as an automobile headed our way. I scanned what I could of the yard, looking for my brothers.

Bad. This was bad.

Warning bells pealed; red flags waved.

What if they found me? That would almost be worse, because then they'd wonder why I'd hidden at all. Then, if they were anyone important—and they had to be, if they were driving an automobile in Varos of all places—they'd ask about my identification card. Goddess knows, they would see some pretty huge discrepancies if they did.

I was very obviously a blond, seventeen-year-old girl and not the boy my card claimed I was. And that discovery would lead to questions and those questions would lead to examinations. And if they noticed the mark on my hand . . .

The outhouse creaked as I leaned against it, careful to stay in the shadows. The rumble of the automobile's engine died out just as the front door to the house squealed open on unoiled hinges. My oldest brother, Ambrose, shouted a muffled greeting, but the words were lost in the sharp *clack* of the screen door slamming shut behind him as he exited the house.

My other brother, Kace, walked out of the barn to my far left, his brows lifted in surprise at the vehicle parked outside our ramshackle house. He headed toward Ambrose, but stopped in his tracks when he caught sight of me. For a moment we just stared at each other, both of us ensnared by curiosity and fear.

The stillness of the moment died as the man in the automobile called out, "Mr. Benson, I come with a summons."

Kace's eyes widened at the words, and he took off again. I glanced around the other side of the outhouse and then abruptly darted back into the safety of my hiding spot. *A magistrate. There was a magistrate here—on our farm. Only a few feet from me.* Bile rose in my throat and my heart became a caged bird in my chest—the pressure of each beat more valuable and more erratic as I considered every terrible thing that might involve a magistrate.

The distance enveloped the rest of the man's words as he climbed from the automobile and then began to, presumably, explain to my brothers what the hell he'd come for. I dared another look just in time to see Ambrose step forward to take a small bundle of letters from the magistrate's outstretched hand.

The magistrate cleared his throat and pulled a handkerchief from the pocket of his suit. He dabbed at his shining forehead, his voice growing loud with annoyance as he said, "Hot summer Varos is having. If the rains don't come soon, crops will suffer."

I knew exactly what he meant by that: if the crops suffered, the queen's coffers would suffer. You couldn't tithe the dead.

My throat grew tight at the implication. *More than just the crops would suffer without rain. My family could starve or lose the farm.* We relied on our crops to earn enough money to keep us alive. My mother's job as a midwife was rarely paid with coin, and my brothers' apprenticeships in town hardly even made enough to keep the livestock fed—much less put food in our bellies.

In recent years, the government hadn't been as tolerant with their collection of county tithe as they had in the past. And the tithe in Varos would come due in early fall whether we had the money or not.

"I will pray for rain," the magistrate said.

"Seems our prayers are as empty as our pockets these days." Ambrose tucked the letters into the back pocket of his trousers and fiddled with the strap of his suspenders. I winced at his boldness as he continued. "Too much rain and they drown. Too much sun and they fry. Varos always places its bets in extremes. Always too hot or too cold. Too wet or too dry. It's the people who lose every time."

Kace ran a hand through his light-brown curls and said, "Let's pray the goddess sees fit to give us both rain and shine in moderation."

I smiled to myself. The predictability of the response was enough to ease the tension in my body. Kace was nothing if not a kiss ass to government officials.

He was always so good at playing pious when it suited him, but I knew he visited brothels and did all manner of temple-forbidden things. Despite how he acted, I knew he couldn't name half of the Sanctus names or recite any of the official remembrances. But then, neither could I, so I supposed that didn't mean much.

In our defense, Mama wasn't religious at all and hadn't raised us to be. While I was fine being a little heathen, Kace had aspirations of becoming a royal guard one day—and, according to him, they were required to be pious, sanctimonious little shits. I didn't think he needed to practice that, but there he was, kissing ass like it was his job.

The magistrate tucked his handkerchief into his pocket and put his bowler hat back in place. "May the goddess be honored in your harvest."

"May the goddess be honored," Kace returned.

The man turned to leave, but he made it only two steps before Ambrose said, "Excuse me, Magistrate, sir? While I have you here: has there been any official word on when this part of Varos might be moved to higher lands? We've never had water so close to our property before. I worry that with the rains coming we will find ourselves overrun."

Whatever the magistrate said in response was covered by the rumble of the engine as he climbed into the vehicle and started it. *It's bad news.* I could tell by the way Ambrose fiddled with the rolled cuffs of his shirt; the way he seemed to hold himself back from arguing. His hands opened and closed at his sides.

Let him leave, I begged silently. *Let him get away from here before he decides to be curious.*

And what was there to say? Each year the eastern floodlands took more and more Varos territory. The sea was literally washing away our county, bit by bit. And each passing year brought the coastline closer to our farm. If we didn't get the official clearance to move, either to a higher spot in Varos or to a different county, our property would eventually be drowned, and we would be homeless. Hundreds of others had already suffered that fate and the queen had done nothing to save them.

I stayed hidden behind the outhouse as the automobile puttered its way down the path to our house and around the far tree line. Ambrose's back was to me as he watched the man drive away, but once he was gone, Kace turned and met my gaze. He looked pointedly at the letters sticking out of the back of Ambrose's trouser pocket and raised a brow.

Dread pooled in the pit of my stomach, turning my mouth to cotton and my throat into a vise. I didn't want to know what those letters said, and yet, something in me—some deep, instinctual thing—already suspected what they would say. *The Culling.*

Magistrates rarely left the county centers and markets. They weren't errand boys or lackeys. If the queen had sent a letter with this man, then it could only mean one thing: the prince had come of age, and the Culling was beginning.

It was archaic and yet a custom treasured by so many—mostly, I'd imagine, by those it would not directly affect. It was a spectator sport. Something to bring just a touch of excitement to the dreary lives of the Erydian people. The Culling promised the beginning of a new era. A new reign.

Only ten girls in all of Erydia were goddess-touched and capable of fighting in that competition. And I was one of them.

These ten girls would be forced to fight to the death for the Crown. By the end of it there would be nine bodies and a new queen on the throne. The tradition occurred once every thirty or forty years. It was supposed to provide us with a strong queen, one who could guarantee that our country would remain safe from our enemies beyond the mountains.

Or so the temple taught. And, truly, what truth was there in what the temple said? Enough truth to make them right about one thing: the ten heirs were goddess-chosen. All ten girls would possess supernatural abilities. They always did. It was the abilities that made the temple believe that the Culling was the only way to choose a queen. It was also said to be the only way to ensure that the new queen's reign wouldn't be questioned. After all, there was no better opening statement than one coated in the blood of nine other people.

Coated in my blood.

I held my breath, my fingers numb around the handle of the water bucket, as I waited for Kace or Ambrose to call out to me. But I had been forgotten in favor of the letters. By the time the sound of the automobile had faded completely, my brothers were already walking into the house.

Their muttered conversation was turning loud and angry as I ditched my bucket and went after them. The front door was ajar, and I didn't bother to close it behind me as I stepped into the cramped kitchen. Even with the windows and doors open, the summer heat was stifling. The cotton of my dress clung to my back with sweat as I edged toward where my brothers stood by the kitchen table.

"What did he want?"

Ambrose turned toward me. "Don't you have chores to finish, Monroe?"

My blood boiled at his tone. Kace opened his mouth to speak, but Ambrose cut him off. "Don't *both* of you have chores to finish?"

With two opinionated brothers and close quarters, I'd witnessed my fair share of fistfights—I'd *started* my fair share of fistfights—but the look on Ambrose's face said that it wouldn't be wise to push him today. Usually, I'd listen to those cues. We were friends, not just siblings, most days. And I had his back, especially when Kace poked at him and tried to start shit. But I didn't like being spoken to like a child. And . . . I was curious.

Kace and I exchanged a glance. *If we both push him, he'll have no choice but to cave.*

"The rains are coming; we need to prepare," Ambrose said, oblivious to our silent plotting.

"Yes, the rains are coming. But, while we wait, what are the letters about?" I asked.

"Nothing that concerns you." Ambrose nodded to the still-open door. "It's a conversation for later. There are things to be done, and the sun is leaving us."

Kace bristled. "To hell with the sun and rains. Let me see the letter."

A sudden swell of heat pushed at my skin, a warmth that had nothing to do with the stifling temperature of the house. It was a slithering sort of anxiety that I knew could turn to true flame if I willed it. My ability to conjure fire, and the cost of my goddess-given gift, was what pushed me to ask, "Is it the Culling?"

"Chores," Ambrose said. "Now. I'm not arguing with either of you about—"

"If it's the Culling, I deserve to know."

"One of them is addressed to me," Kace blurted. "The magistrate said there was one for each of us."

So, maybe it wasn't the Culling then. That news would probably be directed to the whole family. The government wasn't aware of who was goddess-touched. They wouldn't send a letter to each child in the family just to announce the competition and gather the girls.

12

Ambrose pointed to the door again. "Finish your work, Monroe. Mama will be tired enough without having to cook dinner and tend to your chores too. We aren't dealing with any of this now."

Kace held out his hand. "You aren't the damn king, Ambrose. I don't have to listen to you. Neither does Monroe. Now give me my letter."

That tight coil of power in my gut seemed to relax. The tight chains I'd used to bind it to myself—keep it contained—seemed to unwind at the realization that I might still be safe. If the letter wasn't a Culling announcement, then I had nothing to worry about. But curiosity still prevailed.

"I have plenty of time before Mama's back. I'm sure it won't take me all afternoon to read one letter." I held out my own hand. "If there's one for me, give it here."

Kace smirked, pleased to find the two of us on the same side for once. Without a word, Ambrose brushed past us and out the door.

"Good idea," Kace called after him. "Run from your problems, that's always worked before."

I caught up to Ambrose just before he got to the barn. I didn't say anything as I darted behind him and snatched the bundle of letters from his back pocket. I was already three steps away by the time he realized what I'd done.

"Good goddess, Monroe."

He came after me, but rather than grab for me, he swatted for the letters. I sidestepped him and twirled out of his reach, holding the letters in front of me. Before he could make a second lunge for them, I rotated my wrist and called fire to flesh.

He only had time to yell, "Don't—" before my entire fist was wreathed in flame.

The fire seemed to swell in my chest—pushing out every other thought until I was nothing but flame. I felt alive. Like I was my fullest self when I burned like this.

And it had been weeks. With my mother always around, I'd resorted to small actions—invisible hands to coax the flames in the stove higher, a stray candle lit, or a cup of coffee warmed. I'd learned quickly that siphoning the heat from my veins was a nearly unnoticeable action if I was clever and careful—it was something I could do without upsetting or worrying my mother.

But, goddess, I'd missed the feel of flame on my skin.

Ambrose cursed under his breath.

"They aren't burned. I won't let the fire touch them," I said, rotating the bundle so he could see that the fire was only wreathed around my wrist. "But I could."

"You wouldn't dare."

"Wouldn't I?"

My brother crossed his arms over his chest. "If you burn them, I won't tell you what they say."

"Kace heard the magistrate. He knows what they're about at the very least. He'll tell me." I swallowed. "But I'd rather hear it from you."

We stared at each other for a long moment.

"Fine. Read them then." Ambrose threw up his hands and turned away from me. "You're bound to hear about it anyway."

My fire fizzled out as he continued into the barn without another word. The humor and teasing from earlier dissipated just as quickly.

Ambrose tended to be overprotective, especially where I was concerned, but this—the fear on his face had nothing to do with me. I looked at the letters in my hand. One for Ambrose, one for Kace, and one for me. All of them from the war office.

My stomach bottomed out. *Oh, goddess.*

"Ambrose!" I hurried after him. His back was still to me, his attention on the sacks of grain slumped against the far wall of the barn as I said, "What is this? What—"

"Read it."

I shuffled through the three letters until I found the one addressed to me. The wax of the royal seal cracked under my fingers as I tore the letter open and began scanning the words. Two lines in and I was barely processing them.

The world around me faded, as if I were being sucked into a deep, dark hole in the ground.

This was a declaration of war and a call to action. Drafted. My brothers and I had been drafted. Erydia was going to war against Vayelle—again—and every able-bodied man over the age of seventeen was expected to fight.

"We've barely recovered from the last war and it's been almost twenty years," I breathed.

"I was in the market with Ellora this morning when the announcement was posted. It was all anyone could talk about. The paperboys were yelling it on every street corner. I didn't . . . I didn't think the war office would move so quickly. I figured we at least had a few weeks before we would need to report."

I read the letter again, and then a third time. "It says here we have five days— *You* have five days. You and Kace."

Not me.

Although the letter in my hand held my name, it was addressed to Monroe Benson, the boy. The letter was addressed to the lie my mother had created. I couldn't go to the war office without revealing myself.

"What . . . What will happen if I don't show up?" I asked.

Ambrose ran a hand through his blond hair, mussing the short curls. While we shared the same sun-warmed skin and brown eyes, there was a darkness in his gaze that I didn't possess, a heaviness that came from being the head of our household. It made him appear older than his twenty-three years.

"The magistrate said they'd be investigating any deserters. If you don't show, they could come looking."

"Mama . . . Mama and I will have to run. Or . . ." I swallowed.

Ambrose slipped the remaining envelopes from my hand. He turned back to the sacks of grain as he said, "Let me think on it. Go do your chores."

"Why not let Kace have his letter?"

"Because I know what he'll say. I've been listening to him gush about joining the army for as long as I can remember. I don't have the energy to listen to him talk about it. He heard the magistrate same as I did. He knows there's a war coming. He can have the letter and start planning tonight. Between the concern over you and the rains, Ellora, and Mama," he shook his head, "I have too many things to worry about. I don't have space for his happiness."

"How will we survive if you and Kace are gone and we can't hunt? What will we do about the tithe or the floods or . . . ?"

His expression fell slightly and I regretted saying anything at all. "Chores, Monroe. We'll worry about all of that later."

"But—"

His voice turned sharp. "You wanted to know what the letter said, now you do. There's nothing to be done about it. We can talk tonight. I've got to feed the chickens, and you need to finish dinner and start heating water for the baths. Mama will be home shortly. If she . . ." He sighed. "If she doesn't know about the draft yet, she will soon enough. She'll be upset and I can't— Monroe, I can't . . . I don't want you to be afraid."

"I'm not afraid."

I just want to do something. Anything. I want to crawl out of my skin, to be more than I am. There was always this unspoken assumption in our family that because I was a marked girl and had been hidden away from the world, I couldn't possibly understand or help carry our family's troubles. And it just wasn't true. I was the reason we were in this desolate county to begin with, and I never went a day without blaming myself for it.

All I wanted was to be a part of the solution, but I was once again a part of the problem.

"I'm not afraid," I said again.

His smile was sad. "Well, I'm glad one of us isn't."

I was almost outside when he called back to me. "Monroe?"

I turned, my fingers tight against the chipped paint of the door. "Yes?"

"It's going to be all right." Something in his voice told me that the words were as much for him as they were for me.

I nodded, trying to push down the tidal wave of anxious fire in my blood as I said, "Of course, it will."

2

We were halfway through with the dishes by the time Mama finally arrived home. Ambrose and I stood at the kitchen sink, me washing, him drying. He'd been quiet through most of the evening's chores and all of dinner.

I nudged his hip with mine. "How was Ellora today?"

The corners of his lips quirked up at the mention of his fiancé. Ambrose sighed and placed a dried plate onto the stack next to him. "I was with her when I heard about the war. She . . . She didn't take the news well. I didn't expect her to, and I hate that I can't fix it. I wouldn't leave her if I didn't have to."

"I know that. I'm sure she does too."

"Her father says—"

"Twins!" Mama announced as she came through the door. Ambrose crossed the room and took her midwifery bag from her. She smiled across the room at me. "Both girls, both healthy, and both blessedly unmarked."

I was elbow-deep in dishwater, the black mark on my palm hidden beneath layers of soap, and I still felt the need to ball up my fist. The fire beneath my skin pushed insistently, reaching invisible hands toward the embers in the stove and the rising fire in the hearth.

There was no need to say that. With the prince's eighteenth birthday looming, it was assumed that all of the marked girls were already born. Already into their teens. And besides that, there was only ever one marked girl per county, and I was here in Varos—though it wasn't the county of my birth. So, it could also be assumed that there wouldn't be another goddess-touched girl born here.

But my mother hadn't said it because she'd expected any baby she delivered to be born marked, she'd said it because despite the reality of the situation, my mother relived the trauma of my birth—of my being born marked—with every child she ushered into the world. She saw me in them. Saw my mark on their skin, even when she knew that there wasn't truly one there.

The words were a reminder. And I hated that I was the root of her fear. I hated that my existence was tainted by my looming fate and her efforts to outrun it.

Ambrose caught my eye as he turned back toward the kitchen table and set Mama's bag on one of the empty chairs. "Thank the goddess for that," he said pointedly. *Don't start anything, Monroe*, he seemed to say to me.

"Yes." I sighed. "Thank the goddess."

Mama's honeysuckle-and-mint smell enveloped me as she moved past Ambrose to stand at the washbasin with me. "And thank the goddess for all of you. Seems all the chores are done. Dinner smells wonderful." She tugged at the rolled sleeve of my dress. "You know, I'd like to see you in something other than my old clothes. Maybe come spring, I'll get fabric and we can make you something new."

She must not know about the draft then.

I nodded despite myself.

Mama shrugged out of her sweater and untied her apron, each motion practiced and achingly familiar. The vision of her unlacing her shoes, washing her hands and face, tying back her graying hair, and pulling out her midwifery tools to be sanitized—all of those actions were as familiar to me as my own face.

This was my normal, my sense of peace—and watching her go through the processes of coming home to us made me realize what I was going to miss now that things might never truly be normal again.

Kace opened his mouth like he might tell her about the arrival of our draft letters, but Ambrose stopped him with a well-aimed jab to the ribs.

"There's stew left for you," I said. "And I made bread earlier."

"I doubt there's any bread left after Kace got a hold of it," Ambrose said.

Mama paused by the woodstove, lifting the lid of the pot to examine the vegetable stew warming there. "You know," she said, glancing pointedly at Kace. "Earlier today, someone mentioned to me that the magistrate was making rounds. Did he come by here?"

Ambrose sighed in defeat.

Mama set the lid aside with a soft *clack*. And smiled, tight-lipped, to herself.

Kace had always been a rule follower and if Mama asked a question, he'd answer honestly. It was nice sometimes—especially when you didn't want to be the bearer of bad news—but as siblings it was mostly a curse. Kace was nothing if not a snitch.

Mama grabbed a bowl and began filling it. Ambrose leaned his hip against the wooden kitchen counter and let out a long-suffering sigh as Kace said, "He delivered our draft letters."

My mother's posture turned stiff. "What draft?"

The bowl in her hand fell slack, nearly spilling its contents all over the floor. Ambrose pushed away from the counter and crossed the room in two steps. He took the bowl from her and pulled out one of the kitchen chairs before he guided her into it.

In that moment, she looked eighty, not barely forty-five. "When?"

"We have five days to report," Ambrose explained. "Me, Kace, *and* Monroe."

"Monroe?" Her face drained of color.

"Ambrose said that if I don't show up, they'll send people to look for me."

"It may not be a bad thing," Kace said quietly. "The prince turns eighteen this month. I know we didn't plan for her to go to the Culling, but maybe—"

"No." Mama was on her feet in an instant. "I'm not discussing that. We'll . . . We'll move. I can do my job anywhere. There are always babies to be birthed and mothers to tend to. And I still have the money Philip put away. I'm sure we can rent a place or—"

"What will you eat?" Kace said. "How will you hunt? And how will you explain where you've come from or who Monroe is?"

"I can wear gloves or wrap my mark or," I pulled my hands from the basin and grabbed a towel, "or I could just stay hidden. I've been staying away from town for years. Plus, with another war brewing against Vayelle, everyone will be too busy with their own troubles to worry about one teenage girl. I'm no one."

"You aren't just some random girl, Monroe. You're goddess-touched." Kace pulled out the chair across the table from where I stood and sat down. "That may have worked in the past, but it won't work once the Culling is announced. Our neighbors may not care about you now—they may not question a bandage or any of your other lies—but once the Culling is in session and one girl is missing, there will be a price on your head. The Crown will come looking for their missing contestant."

"We'll deal with that when it comes," Mama said, standing up again. "For now . . . For now I can only deal with one issue at a time. We'll find a way to move. We'll make a new life. Monroe will remain hidden. If anyone asks, all of my sons are enlisted, and I have no daughters. I live alone." She grabbed her bowl from where Ambrose had placed it next to the stove and walked back to the table.

"Monroe should continue to practice her ability," Ambrose said. "She needs to work with it. She's been smart about using it so far. If she uses her judgment and doesn't lose control, she should be fine. But as things are, it wouldn't be smart for her to neglect her training. Not with so many threats hanging over her. Over both of you."

"She isn't going to the Culling," Mama said. "I didn't move all the way to this goddess-forsaken county just so that my baby—*just so Monroe*—could be taken from me. It will not have been for nothing."

"It isn't just the Culling I'm worried about," Ambrose admitted.

Kace leaned back in his chair. "When the Culling is announced and Monroe doesn't show, every abandoned and starving woman in Varos will be fighting to be the one to track down the missing goddess-touched girl. They always offer huge incentives to help track down fleeing girls—with the draft in place and most of the men gone, the stakes will be high. Someone will find you. People will turn on each other for the reward alone. They'll need it to survive. Monroe can't—"

"Then I'll get the necessary papers and go to Vayelle," I said. "They don't believe in the Culling or the goddess."

Kace laughed. "No, you won't. With the war, the border between us and Vayelle will be closed off. No one will be able to get safely through the Suri Gap. And we aren't capable of scaling those mountains. Plus, you're talking about going into enemy territory."

"Vayelle isn't my enemy. They're Erydia's enemy—and right now, that country is safer than this one. They want our land. They care nothing about us."

"You're making assumptions," he said. "You don't know what you're talking about."

Fire heated my blood. "The border isn't closed now, is it?"

"It isn't. Not yet, at least," Ambrose said. "I saw people at the train station earlier today."

"Goddess, would the two of you get your heads out of your asses?" Kace said. "It would take months to get the necessary paperwork to leave Erydia. And that's without a war starting and without a damn mark on your hand. The choice is simple enough, Monroe."

Mama put her head in her hands. "Please, don't argue about this."

"I'm not arguing," Kace said. "I'm simply trying to get the three of you to see reason. Monroe, especially."

I straightened. "What would you like me to do then?"

"I'd like you to give up on outrunning the Culling and do what's best for the family," he said. "I'd like you to stop being a coward."

Mama inhaled sharply. "Kace Benson—"

"I'm not a coward," I said. "I've stayed hidden because it's what *Mama* wanted me to do."

"Maybe the time for hiding is over," Kace said. "Maybe you need to step up and help provide for our family. Ambrose and I have always pulled our weight. We have always made sure you were safe. But that's coming to an end. What will Mama do with Ambrose and me gone, when the rains come and the floodlands expand? When the winter stretch sets in and everything freezes over for months, what will she do?"

Mama shook her head. "What happens to me isn't Monroe's responsibility."

"Yes, it is," Kace said. "It's as much her responsibility as it is mine or Ambrose's. With us gone, neither of you will be able to hunt. The laws surrounding that won't change just because there's a draft."

"There's food in the cellar," Mama argued. "And I'll get money and food from patients."

"When the rains hit and the winter stretch sets in, you won't be able to travel to births either," Kace said. "There goes your food and your income. Ambrose and I will be gone and will have no way to look after you. The money we make in service won't be enough, and you'll starve. If Monroe remains here, she'll starve too. Hell, even if she could make it across the border to Vayelle, she'd still starve. How will she support herself? What will you do if the Vaylish decide to turn you in? You're relying on rumors and naïve hope. Neither will feed you. What will you do, Monroe? Do you plan to stand on street corners and sell your flesh?"

One of the logs in the hearth snapped and sparks hissed against the stone base of the fireplace as I said, "Whatever I plan to do is my decision, not yours."

"Enough," Ambrose said.

Kace shoved a finger in my direction. "If you go to the Culling, Mama will be taken care of. Our family would receive an allowance for as long as you're in the competition. And indefinitely if you become queen. You could save us. All of us. Imagine it, Monroe: a girl from Varos, from the slums, becoming Queen of Erydia. That's the solution, don't you see?"

"You're asking Monroe to put her life on the line," Ambrose said. "You're asking her to join a competition that could end with her death."

"Our lives are *all* on the line," Kace countered. "We're joining a war that could just as easily end in *our* deaths."

Ambrose shook his head. "You're talking as if being a soldier isn't something you've been dreaming about since you were a child. You *want* to serve the Crown."

"Good goddess, Ambrose." Kace gestured to me. "Don't you see? She could *be* the Crown. She could be queen. That mark on her hand isn't going to go away just because Mama refuses to acknowledge it."

"That's enough," Ambrose said. "You can express your opinions, but you aren't going to bully anyone into agreeing with you."

"We're arguing over a threat that doesn't even exist yet," Mama said, her voice drained. "The Culling is a bridge we'll cross when it comes. For now, we need to focus on the draft. Monroe and I can try to sell the farm and—"

Kace cut her off. "If Ambrose and I have to go to war, why shouldn't Monroe have to fight too?"

Ambrose's fist hit the table. "Because war with Vayelle isn't the same thing as a damn Culling, Kace. There will be nine other gifted girls in that arena. It's a glorified slaughter."

Kace shrugged, incredulous. "Monroe can hold her own. She isn't a child. She's seventeen years old and she's marked. She can create fire from nothing."

Even though I had no desire to fight in the competition or claim the crown, I still felt pushed to say, "Kace is right. If I had to go to the Culling, I could—I think I could survive, at least for a while—"

"But should she have to?" Ambrose demanded, not even acknowledging I'd said anything. "Should she have to fight and die for a few stray coins?"

"If it would help keep Mama alive while we're gone, then yes. She should."

The room fell silent.

"Have you seen her practicing behind the barn? It isn't like she doesn't know what she's doing. And it certainly isn't like Monroe doesn't *enjoy* using her ability." Kace nodded to me. "She only pretends to be disinterested because she knows it bothers Mama. She uses it every chance she gets. Every time Mama's back is turned, she uses it."

"Enjoying what I can do doesn't mean I want to die for it," I said.

"Listen to me," Kace said, his attention entirely on me. "You've spent years hiding from who you are and it hasn't changed anything. That mark isn't going to disappear. Your choice is to die running from it or die fighting for it. And you will never outrun the goddess."

I didn't have to look to know that Ambrose rolled his eyes. My brothers ran in different circles and held vastly different friends—and while they argued over a great many things, one of the biggest dividers in our household was the goddess and the temple.

Ambrose saw my mark as a threat.

Kace saw it as our divine deliverance.

I couldn't look at him as I said, "If the border is still open, then I'm going to try to make it to Vayelle." Kace opened his mouth to protest, but I held up a hand. "I've been saving money every birthday since I was little. I'm not sure it'll be enough to buy travel waivers, but—"

"I'll get the papers," Ambrose said. "And the train tickets. I'll get us both safely across."

Kace shook his head in disbelief. "You'll run from the draft?"

Ambrose nodded. "I'm not sending her to Vayelle alone."

Mama sighed. "I'll stay here and tell anyone who comes looking that two of my sons have run."

"You'll starve," Kace said.

She shook her head. "I'm not weak, Kace Benson. I'll remind you that I lived alone on this farm for years with three small children. I kept it running. I kept the three of you clothed and fed. I survived those years on my own and I can survive whatever else is to come. I lost my husband to the last war and I will not lose my children to another. I certainly will not lose my daughter to the Culling. Not if it's within my power to stop it."

3

I woke in the early morning hours to the sound of my mother lacing her boots. The cabin was still dark—even the lanterns in the loft were out—a clear sign that my brothers had both already fallen asleep. It was uncharacteristically cool, a sign that the rains were indeed coming soon.

"Is it the Edwards' baby?" I whispered, thinking of one of the pregnant women on my mother's rotation.

Mama stiffened at the sound of my voice. "No. Agnes Lancaster," she said. "It's her seventh, so it'll likely come quick."

"Did her husband come to take you?"

She shook her head. "They don't have a wagon and he didn't want to leave her. They sent the oldest boy. He's out in the yard waiting. We'll walk. It's not far from here." She finished with her boots and grabbed her sweater by the door.

Before she could protest, I'd slipped out of bed and padded over to the loft ladder. "Ambrose?"

Mama hissed under her breath. "Let him sleep. He's going to Linomi first thing, and he'll need a level head for that."

Just the thought of the massive marketplace sent a chill down my spine. Most in Varos called it the Rat's Nest, and with good reason. Linomi might have been the largest market in our county, but it was also the most dangerous.

Still, it wasn't any less dangerous for Mama to be walking around in the dead of night. I knew my brothers would agree.

His name had barely left my mouth a second time before I heard footsteps and saw the flicker of a lantern through the slatted floor. Ambrose's voice was ragged with fear as he said, "What? What's happened?" His pale face and shaggy head of hair appeared over the edge of the loft opening.

"Mama needs a ride over to the Lancaster farm," I said. "They didn't send a wagon and she shouldn't walk."

"I can take her," Kace called.

"No, I'll do it," Ambrose said. "If I go with her now, I can stop over in town and see Ellora before I go to Linomi. I need to talk to her about the draft and Vayelle anyway."

My mama's clammy hand wrapped around my wrist. "If for some reason I'm not back by the time you need to leave—"

"We aren't even sure if Ambrose can get the papers," I said. "Even if he gets the travel waivers today, we wouldn't be ready to leave for a little while."

"Tomorrow," Mama said. "I've already talked to Ambrose and he says you'll go tomorrow."

"But—"

"I won't risk the borders closing and . . ." She shook her head. "It would be better for you to get out now. Before the Culling is announced and there are too many people looking for marked girls."

There was a thump of boots on wood behind us as Ambrose climbed down the ladder. "Ready?" he asked.

Mama nodded and handed him her midwifery bag. Then she was hugging me. It felt like there was a fist around my heart—crushing me from the inside out. *You will not cry. If you cry now, she won't leave—and she needs to go.* I exhaled a sharp breath, trying to force the raw fear from my bones as I said, "It's not forever. I'll come back."

She sighed into my hair. "No. No, you won't. You'll stay far, far away from here. And you'll live. Live a long and happy life. And you'll die an old woman, surrounded by people who love you just as fiercely as I do." Mama pulled me closer to her and kissed my cheek. "Promise?"

I buried my face in her neck the way I used to as a little girl. In her arms,

I was a child again. I was small and afraid of the swirling darkness that seemed to be blossoming inside of me. A darkness that would one day turn to flame.

I pressed my eyes closed, trying to fight the sudden burning there. "I love you."

She pressed a kiss to my forehead. "Be brave."

Then she stepped away from me and turned to Ambrose. "And you," she said, cupping his head in one of her hands. She pulled him down so she could kiss his cheek. "You'll stay out of trouble and you'll keep her safe."

"Don't worry," Ambrose said. "We'll keep each other safe."

Mama sighed. "Before you go, you tell Ellora Hoffman that I consider her a daughter with or without a temple ceremony. If she needs anything at all, she should come to me. My door will always be open to her."

Ambrose winced. "She may not agree to wait for me. Going off to war is one thing; running away from a draft is another."

"That girl has stuck with you this long and never doubted. Don't count her out just yet," Mama said.

"I'll tell her you said so."

Mama took hold of my wrist and flipped my right hand so that she could see my mark. She ran her thumb across the ink-black patch of skin on my palm. "You keep this hidden and don't make a show of using it. If Ambrose tells you something, you listen to him."

"I will."

Mama hugged me one last time and then held me at arm's length. "This is a beginning for you," she said. "This is your freedom. Fight for it."

I'd never doubted that Lorraine Benson was strong. She'd delivered me with only her mother and my father to help her. When I'd been born marked, she'd lied on my birth certificate and lied to the temple about who I was. She'd given up her old life to get me as far away from the palace—and from possible detection—as she could. My mother had never stopped risking things for me. And she wouldn't stop now.

"There's money hidden under our cot. It isn't a lot, but if you're smart about where you spend it, it should help you to get settled in Vayelle. Don't write to me. Not for a while, at least. Not until the Culling has started and the search for goddess-touched girls has died down. I'll—I'll assume no news is good news."

I didn't cry, not even after they left.

I'd expected to fall apart, but it felt as if my emotions had been stolen from me—like they'd gone away with my mother. The numbness almost made it worse. It would be a relief to cry. To scream and rage. To truly burn from the inside out.

I sat in front of the open woodstove, my hand buried in embers, and tried to calm my racing heart. The pulse of the heat as it turned from spark to flame to inferno was a balm to the ache in my chest. This cold, empty feeling in my chest—was this heartache? *She's gone, and I may never see her again. That was it. That was my goodbye.*

The pain was immense, but no tears fell. It didn't feel real. It couldn't possibly be real.

But it was.

The cabin was silent around me—like a tomb or some mockery of sacred ground. My ability swirled in my veins, pushing against the bonds that held it tight within the cage of my bones. If I dared lean into that darkness, that quiet place of ash and flame, I was afraid of what voice I might hear.

There were certain groups of high priestesses that spent portions of their lives in complete silence—all in hopes of hearing just the barest whisper of what I knew resided in me. If they saw the strange mark on my skin, they'd call me holy. Goddess-touched. The closest thing to a deity that walked our earth. One of ten blessed women. But, sitting in the stillness of my childhood home, I knew I'd trade every ounce of power in my blood to be allowed to stay, or go, or just *exist* without always feeling at odds with the world around me.

Even with the fire now blazing in the woodstove, I could feel the darkness closing in. The goddess was tugging at the threads of my life, and while I hoped she might cut me loose or spin me a new fate, I worried that something worse might be brewing.

This is a beginning for you. This is your freedom.

I hoped my mother was right.

Kace and I ate our breakfast in relative silence, and then he was off to do his chores. I'd expected him to lecture me more about the Culling and my obligations to our family, but he didn't. Nothing good had ever come from Kace being quiet.

Ambrose was the one to stew in silence, but Kace was the sort to choose action. If he didn't get his way, he'd usually try to berate me or tease me until I caved. I'd grown up being harassed over everything from who would get the last bite of birthday cake to which of us could climb the tallest tree. But this wasn't a simple squabble.

There was nothing he could say or do that would sway my resolve. The Culling wasn't an undesirable task I could be dared into doing. It was a fight to the death against nine other supernaturally gifted girls. Whichever girl won the Culling would marry the prince and be crowned Queen of Erydia.

And while Kace was right—I had been practicing with my fire and I could control it—there was no telling what the other girls were capable of doing. My fire might be nothing compared to someone who could see the future or someone who could cause earthquakes.

As far as I knew, there was no real limit to what a goddess-touched girl was capable of. Viera was blessed with poison. While there wasn't a lot of information about how her ability worked, it was clearly powerful. She'd eliminated her competition in the last Culling so quickly that there hadn't even been any official arena trials.

My fire was a strong ability—I believed that. But was it good enough to keep me alive against an equally strong opponent? Abilities could also repeat themselves—and did so frequently—although it had been a few generations since anyone in the Culling had possessed an ability similar to mine. But what if someone had an ability like Viera's? What if there was a girl who had an ability even worse than that?

For my tenth birthday Ambrose had gifted me one of his old history books. I'd barely been able to read it back then, but I'd tried. I'd spent hours skimming those pages and while there had been a lot of information about the Erydian relationship to our neighboring country, Vayelle, and the various laws and regulations that governed the different counties within Erydia itself—I'd been fixated on two chapters in particular: the story of creation and the rules of the Culling.

The first was a story of beginnings and the second was a story of endings. The book made the story of creation seem incredibly dull, but it was the sort of story that most children knew by heart. Ambrose had always been the storyteller in our family, and he could be trusted to recite just about any story from memory. Before I'd been able to read, he'd been my first source of information.

Now that I could read, I could recite both the creation story and the Culling rules from memory, but I still went in search of the book. While Kace went into the market to trade furs and meats from his most recent hunt, I sat at the kitchen table and scanned the dog-eared pages of my least favorite, and most cherished, text.

I don't know why it mattered. The Culling wasn't where I was going. I'd pointed my fate in a different direction, and I would fight to see my chosen path followed through. But I felt an internal nudge to look, to learn, to remind myself why I couldn't go to the Culling.

As I read, fear seemed to linger at the edges of my mind—mingling with a slithering sort of anxiety and the cold realization that my life was now forever changed. And not because of the Culling, but because of a war. It seemed ridiculous that the best-made plans and best-told lies could be undone with one single letter.

Maybe it's a blessing in disguise.

If I got out of Erydia now, then I might never need to worry about the Culling announcement. I would be long gone before the trials even started. Warm air filled my lungs as I inhaled a sharp breath and let it go. A strange sort of peace seemed to envelop me, like the embrace of unseen arms. Hope beat like butterfly wings against my rib cage.

I closed my eyes and pulled the open book to my chest. *Maybe the goddess really will let me go. Maybe my fate will end differently than the rest.*

Within the walls of the arena in Gazda, each goddess-touched contestant would have only the skills that they'd been blessed with. There would be no outside weapons. No other defense.

The book made it sound like there would be some level of physical training involved. Not every goddess-touched girl would come into the competition knowing how to wield her ability. Some would have been training since childhood; others might be like me and might have spent most of their life in hiding.

The ages of the girls would vary, too, since the birth of the prince triggered the appearance of our dormant gifts. Some would be older, closer to the age of the prince, like I was; but they could be younger too. The magic surrounding how we came to be marked and have abilities was unpredictable. The births started with the prince's birth, but they didn't end at any specific point. A goddess-touched girl could be a child. A baby, I supposed. Though the book never mentioned that happening before.

Once the prince was born, the cycle would begin and women all over Erydia would start to give birth to goddess-touched daughters. Some would be born with their marks, like I had been, and others would develop their marks and abilities as they aged. It was unpredictable and strange, but the temple was steadfast in their belief, and their preaching, that the mystery of it all was intentional. We weren't owed sure and fast answers from the goddess.

But even with all of the inconsistencies in the birth and appearance of marks and abilities, one thing always remained the same: we would all meet a similar end.

Girls like me had two choices: kill or be killed. Die or be queen. And when the smoke cleared, only one of us would remain standing. It was the goddess's way. No one had ever escaped it. That was the one thing that the book made desperately clear—there had never been a Culling where more than one girl survived.

Until now.

4

My brothers were both in foul moods. They'd begun arguing before dinner was even on the table, so I'd opted to sit on the front steps and eat in peace. Ambrose had gotten the travel waivers—one for me and one for him. His held his true picture, but false information. Meanwhile, the picture on my card was of a boy around my age. Ambrose had slipped it to me when he'd first arrived home.

"Don't let Kace see," he'd said. "I'll talk to him about it. If he's going to pick a fight, let him do it with me."

The thought of what the waiver meant made me sick to my stomach. I felt like I was standing on the edge of some large canyon. I could either fall or I could fly. That hard-won piece of paper, as false as it was, was my step into thin air.

My brothers' raised voices echoed out into the yard as I set down my empty bowl and reached into my pocket. The picture in the left-hand corner of the waiver was of a boy with a stern expression. I'd never met him before, didn't even know his real name. But when we left here tomorrow, I was supposed to be him.

My hair had grown out over the last year or so, now hanging near my waist. With my summer-tanned skin and blond hair, I looked a lot like my mother had at my age. Her eyes were blue where mine were brown—and I was a little shorter than she was—but judging by the black-and-white prints

I'd once found stashed in her hope chest, our seventeen-year-old selves could have been twin sisters.

I looked a bit more like my brothers when my hair was short, which was how Mama had kept it for most of my childhood. I'd stopped worrying about cutting it after she'd decided it wasn't safe for me to leave the farm anymore. The last time I'd been into town, I'd been thirteen—and things hadn't gone well.

For some reason, I'd wandered into the market temple and had come dangerously close to revealing myself. The altar at the front had been filled with candles and burning incense, and I'd been drawn to those flames.

My chest had felt so warm and being there—in that room—had felt right. As if I were a missing piece to a puzzle, and I'd finally found my place. The distant chants of priestesses had echoed off the high ceilings. The world around me had faded away.

My fingers had nearly been in the flames of those candles by the time Ambrose found me. His hand clamping down on my wrist and yanking me backward had been the only thing to keep me from answering the call of that fire with some of my own.

Once we were outside in the alleyway behind the temple, my soft-spoken brother had almost yelled at me. The fear on his face had brought the world crashing back into vivid focus.

I might have been seen. My mark, my ability, might have been discovered, and I could have been dragged to Gazda to await the Culling. I hadn't been alone in that place.

The rows of stone pews had been dotted with figures slumped and praying. And not all of them were ordinary people.

In the hierarchy of my world, I lingered in a gray area near the top. I was blessed by the goddess but uncrowned. I was seen as an item—a holy object that was meant to be either sacrificed for the betterment of our nation or placed on a throne. High priestesses and acolytes were all trained to be on the lookout for goddess-touched girls. Gifts like ours were hard to hide and rumors in Erydia were difficult to silence. Their job was made easier by the fact that goddess-given abilities could manifest at different ages, sometimes without much warning—leaving marked girls to make careless mistakes that would make their presence known.

Beyond that, there were types of gifted priestesses called videras who could literally "see" a goddess-touched girl. They could sense us from a distance. They were physically blind with black, depthless eyes that had a way of seeing things that no one else could see. They were both legend and myth in Varos. A tale to scare misbehaving children.

What if there had been a videra in the temple that day?

That had been the last time I'd been allowed to leave the farm. I started to let my hair grow out, and I'd become lazy about keeping up a male disguise. Now I wore my mother's old work dresses more often than I wore Kace's ill-fitting trousers and shirts.

I fiddled with the ends of my hair. I bit my lip and closed my eyes, determined that I wouldn't cry over my hair. With everything else going on, it was a silly thing to get caught up on.

But I liked the idea of looking like my mother. Even though I had no female friends my own age, I longed to fit in and be seen as pretty. *Why must I always give something up?* My fire for my safety, this shred of femininity for my freedom.

But even with my hair cut, my face dirtied, and my clothes a size too big, I wouldn't resemble the boy on this waiver. I was thinner than he was, my face too angular. Even in black and white, it was clear that his eyes were dark where mine were lighter. I had freckles on my nose. He had a dimple in his left cheek . . .

The screen door of the house flew open, and Kace came barreling down the front steps, nearly bumping into me as he went. The tight set of his shoulders and the way he clenched his fists at his sides spoke volumes. If there hadn't already been a physical altercation between my brothers, there would be soon.

I abandoned my bowl and the waiver on the steps and went after him. "Kace?" I grabbed for his arm but he yanked away from me.

"Don't."

I stumbled to a stop in the middle of the yard. "It's my life, you know," I called. "If you're mad about me going to Vayelle, you should yell at me, not Ambrose."

He whirled on me. "You have something so many people want, and you're just going to throw it away."

"Goddess, Kace. It isn't a blessing. It's a death sentence. If I could give this damn mark away, I would."

"Liar. Anyone who has ever seen your face when you conjure a flame or stick your hand in the embers of the woodstove knows you wouldn't give it up." Kace shook his head. "You've spent all day fiddling with it. You love it. You love it, and you're robbing yourself of your full potential. Hell, you're allowing Ambrose and Mama's fear—*your own fear*—to keep you from becoming Queen of Erydia. You could change our lives. You could change the world, if you'd stop cowering long enough to try."

Anger boiled hot in my chest, an echo to the fire that pushed against the underside of my skin. The darkness in me seemed to open an eye. It wanted to burn and ruin and fight. I forced it back down.

"I could also be slaughtered in an arena. I could lose my life for a crown I don't even want. I have no desire to be queen of anything. I want to be left alone. I want to have choices, the same way you and Ambrose do."

"The Culling would give you choices."

"No, it wouldn't. Being queen *isn't freedom*. Becoming a murderer isn't freedom. Marrying a stranger and sharing a bed with him isn't freedom. It's a damn prison. At the end of the day, it's my life and it's my choice."

"You're making the wrong one."

"Just because it isn't the choice that you'd make doesn't mean it's the wrong choice." I fell silent. The door to the house creaked open again and I could feel Ambrose's eyes on my back as I said, "Not all of us want to die in battle."

"Your name could be in history books. You could be celebrated, renowned. Think of the power of that, the glory. It's something others can only dream of."

"I don't dream of it. It's my damn nightmare. It's the worst possible thing. Why can't you see that I have no desire to have a Sanctus day named after me? Those days are named for the dead girls, Kace. Not the living. No amount of fame or glory is worth the deaths those girls had."

Kace sighed and shook his head. "When the winter stretch hits and Mama is cold and her belly is empty, remember that this is a choice you made. When the waters of the floodlands continue to rise and we are overtaken, remember that this is something you could have stopped."

Ambrose sat on the front steps of the house, silhouetted by the light flooding out of the open front door. He held an envelope in one hand and a burning cigarette in the other.

"Mama would fuss about that cigarette," I said as I walked out of the kitchen and lowered myself onto the front steps next to him. While I'd sat at the kitchen table and cut my own hair, he'd sat on the front steps and watched Kace saddle one of the horses. Ambrose had said nothing as our brother rode away from our farm.

He'd go into town and calm himself down with the help of a stiff drink. Or he'd pay a few coins to have a stranger help him forget his troubles. Either way, he'd return in a better mood. More than likely, he'd pretend that none of it had ever happened. Kace was the sort that once he'd gotten over something, he considered it to be fixed—your feelings didn't matter.

"Smoking isn't good for you," I said.

"Says the girl who plays with fire." Ambrose brought the cigarette to his lips and muttered, "We all have our vices. And what Mama doesn't know won't hurt her." He drew from the cigarette before he folded the envelope and tucked it into his pocket.

I bumped my shoulder into his, trying to lighten his dark mood. "Aren't you going to compliment me on my skill?"

"Skill with what—?" He glanced my way and froze. "Oh! Wow. You cut your hair."

"Does it look that bad?" I ran a hand over the short locks. The blond waves now fell just long enough to tuck behind my ears. "I couldn't decide if I needed to go shorter. Some boys wear it longer and I just . . ." I shrugged. "I couldn't stomach cutting more of it."

"No, it looks nice." He craned his head and smiled at my handiwork. "The back is a bit uneven, but I can trim it later if you want."

I chewed the inside of my cheek, worrying one of the curls between my fingers as I said, "I figured it would help with the disguise for tomorrow. I mean, it definitely isn't the style for girls."

"Not true. If Ellora is to be trusted, short hair is all the rage right now in Gazda. She says girls are pinning their hair up so it looks shorter."

"Pinning it up isn't the same as cutting it. Plenty of girls pin their hair up—but most don't cut it."

"I've always liked you with short hair," he said. "It reminds me of when we were kids. Everyone used to think you and Kace were twins. Goddess, he hated that."

I nodded thinking of my ninth summer and how annoyed Kace had been when I'd hit a growth spurt and had reached nearly the same height as him. It hadn't lasted long. I'd stopped growing vertically around fifteen and he'd continued. Now he was a little over six feet and I lingered closer to five and a half.

"He was just jealous that everyone thought I was the best-looking brother," I said.

Ambrose laughed at that, deep and loud. "True."

"So how . . . how did you manage to get the travel waivers? Things like that don't come cheap."

"I know some people who work in the business of helping people disappear."

Everyone in Varos played a part in the business of making people disappear. That was why most people lived this far from the capital city of Gazda. Either they'd been born into poverty and couldn't get out of the county, or they'd chosen poverty because the alternative was something far worse.

"That isn't an answer," I said.

He sighed, as if resigning himself to something. "I know some people in the Culled."

My mouth nearly hit the floor. "*The* Culled?" Shock trickled through me like icy water. "Like the rebels?"

He nodded.

The air left my lungs. "Good goddess, Ambrose. What are you thinking? Mama would lose her shit if she knew you'd gone to them. They're traitors to the Crown. They're . . . They're criminals. Mama would— She'd—"

"She wouldn't lose her shit. Not if she thought it was the only way to get you out. She'd have contacted them herself if she'd known how."

I highly doubted that. "Sure, okay, but how did *you* know how?"

He was silent for a long moment.

"You don't just have contacts, do you?" It wasn't really a question.

"Look, I've only attended a few meetings. And I was careful not to be recognized."

I shoved his shoulder hard enough that he rocked to the side. "Kace is lecturing me about keeping our mama safe, while you're literally making friends with the Culled. If you get caught, we'll all die. The Crown will have our heads."

"Mr. Hoffman assured me that it was safe. I told him that I needed waivers to get myself and my younger brother out. He's gotten waivers for tons of other people before. Apparently the Culled does it pretty often. There're a lot of people trying to get out of Erydia, especially with the tithes rising and the borders between counties so guarded. People want better. We deserve better. Vayelle is offering sanctuary, they can see that our government isn't out to help the people. At least not most people. Not our type of people."

I buried my face in my hands. "Mr. Hoffman? Ellora's father is in the Culled?"

"You do realize that trying to run away from the draft *and the Culling* is a criminal offense, right? My head is on the chopping block no matter what. We've already crossed into treason."

"But I didn't choose this. I'm having to be a traitor to stay alive."

"So are they. Think about it, Monroe. They're fighting for all the things we want."

The Culled had existed for years—always in the shadows, always active in the smallest of ways. With tension growing between Erydia and Vayelle again, the group had become more active and more dangerous. My mother was constantly fretting over the list of executions posted in town. Many of those men had been husbands to the women she tended to; some had been the women themselves.

The rebels had chosen their name as a way of changing and reframing our religion's use of the Culling to weed out the weakest goddess-touched girls, leaving only the strongest to be queen. From what little I knew of the growing rebellion, the Culled believed *they* were the people in our world who had been rejected or abandoned by our government. They believed that they had been essentially culled by our government. And they were right.

The Crown looked after themselves and those within the highest wealthy class. The separation of our counties and the waivers necessary to travel from one place to another all contributed to a culling of our people. Only those deemed worthy could have unguarded access to necessities.

"I can't imagine the Culled gave you the waivers for free." I sighed. "What did you give them in return?"

He ran a hand over the top of my head, mussing the curls. "Nothing for you to worry yourself with. It's my job to keep you safe and I'm doing that."

Oh, hell no. He wasn't going to play the protective big brother card—not now.

"What did you give them, Ambrose?"

He shrugged. "I had a few blades."

I rolled my eyes. "You're a decent enough bladesmith, but there's no way any of your knives would earn enough coin to get you illegal documents."

"I . . ." He rubbed at the back of his neck. "Ellora sort of helped out, just a little."

"Well, if her father is in the Culled, I'm sure she did."

He winced and muttered, "I pawned the necklace."

The sound of my hand slapping against my open mouth echoed around the silent yard. I shook my head and hissed, "You took Ellora's promising necklace, and you *sold it*?"

"She gave it to me. She knew— I told her what I needed and she offered it back to me. It doesn't change things between us. I still love her and . . . and when all of this is over, we're still going to get married. Not having a promising gift doesn't change that. She understands."

I lowered my hand to my lap. "Damn it, Ambrose. Why would you sell something so valuable to some stupid rebels? They're all crooks and you know it. We can't even trust that the waivers will work."

"Because you're my sister. And we can trust it."

"What else is there? Clearly, that isn't all you're hiding. There's more."

"What makes you say that?"

I could feel the pulsing heat at the tip of his cigarette. I tugged on the invisible string of the fire until it burned out completely. Ambrose cursed and reached into his shirt pocket to grab a box of matches. He'd only just slid it open when I pushed the flame back onto the end of the cigarette. Ambrose cursed in surprise and dropped the cigarette. Before he could react, I'd dug the toe of my boot into it, crushing it against the stone steps.

"Smoking is a nasty habit."

"Maybe, but it's my habit. And those cigarettes are expensive, you little brat," he said. He pulled out the crumpled box of cigarettes and knocked one into his palm.

"Don't bother," I said as he reached for the matches. "I'll just put it out again."

"You know, on second thought, I think your hair looks terrible."

I laughed. "Tell me what's in that envelope you're hiding and maybe I'll let you have your smoke in peace."

"Monroe Benson, you don't know the meaning of peace."

I held out my hand. "I'm waiting."

"It's nothing."

"It isn't nothing, otherwise you wouldn't hide it."

He reached into his pocket, pulling the folded envelope out. He held it to his chest for a moment. "I didn't keep it from you to hurt you. I just— I knew it would make things worse with Kace. And I didn't know when the right time to give it to you would be. I— Don't be mad."

"I won't be mad." I tugged the envelope from his hands and unfolded it.

All the air left my lungs as I looked down at the hawk and hare crest shining up at me in navy blue wax. My hands shook as I took in the words printed on the top left corner. *Order from the Crown.*

"It changes nothing," Ambrose said. "We were going to run anyway."

Citizens of Erydia:

Upon receiving this letter, all girls who carry a mark and exhibit any unnatural power are to report to their nearest temple for verification. After being assessed by videras, goddess-chosen girls will be transported to Gazda for training, assessment, and Culling. The ten heirs are to report to their local temple no later than noon on Sacrit. Failure to report before the hour and date listed in this notice will result in forcible retrieval. The official Culling of the ten heirs will begin on Sanctus Halletta and will end when nine sacrifices have been made. May the goddess be honored and may she bless our next queen.

Queen Viera Kevlar Warwick

"When?"

Ambrose reached forward and pulled the letter from my hands. "The courier brought it a week ago."

"A week ago?"

"Kace and Mama don't know. I haven't shown it to anyone else. People were talking about the Culling earlier when we were in the market, but I don't think Kace knew that it had been officially announced."

"I've been summoned."

"This letter went out to every family to try to smoke out the goddess-touched girls," Ambrose said. "They don't know about you. No one will be looking, not with a war starting. Everyone is too preoccupied trying to either get out of Erydia before the borders close or they're preparing for the draft. The Culling isn't important right now."

He was right. With the Crown raising taxes and the temples increasing laws and tithes, anyone who could get their hands on the papers to flee our country was trying to. If you didn't live in one of the wealthier counties, then the odds of surviving were slim at best—especially this coming winter if a majority of the men would be gone to war.

Women weren't permitted to hunt or fish. We couldn't use weapons and it was a constant battle to have legal ownership of anything. Thousands of people would starve if they stayed here. Varos would likely become a battlefield, just as it had been during the last war with Vayelle, and the people living here would suffer the most.

Life for most Erydians in the outlying counties had been getting progressively worse. Each year, my mother saw more mothers and babies die. Sickness and starvation killed easily. Two autumns ago, we'd had such a bad outbreak of fever that bodies had reportedly littered the streets in town.

My mother had been saving for years to try to get enough money to get all of us across the border and into Vayelle. The war was over land and religion, and recently Vayelle had seemed happy enough to take in Erydian refugees—there had been rumors circulating since the last war that Vayelle was using refugees from our country, both men and women, to amass a bigger force.

But the people who saw the sport in the Culling weren't here. Their troubles weren't the same as ours. The tribunal of old men that made up the Royal Synod would crown a new queen with or without a war. The announcement letter proved that.

I stood up and paced a few steps away. *Oh, goddess.*

"Sacrit . . ." I tried to calculate the days, but I had no real way of knowing. The calendar pinned to the kitchen wall was over a year old. I turned to look at my brother. "When is Sacrit?"

Ambrose's face was flushed as he said, "Day after tomorrow." He held up his hands in surrender. "You told me you wouldn't be mad."

"I-I'm not mad." I ran a hand through my hair, shocked by the unfamiliar shortness of it. "I just . . ." This made it real. The Culling was happening. That letter meant that if I failed tomorrow and was caught, I'd be forced into the competition. I'd have no second chance to escape. "What if we fail? What if they catch me?"

Ambrose stood up, leaving his box of cigarettes and the letter on the steps as he crossed to me. His hands were a steady force on my shoulders as he said, "We aren't going to fail."

5

We were halfway through the last checkpoint at the train station when the announcement was posted. I didn't see the news for myself, but it carried on the lips of every traveler we passed. There had been an assassination attempt. It had happened during the prince's eighteenth birthday celebration the previous night. It had happened while I'd packed a bag, while Ambrose had helped me fix my hair, while I'd curled up in my cot for the last time, while my mother was still attending a birth—someone had been shooting at the prince of Erydia.

Apparently, he was fine. The gunman was dead. There was no news about who the shooter was or where he'd come from. Standing in line with Ambrose, it was clear that everyone had an opinion. Some said it was the Culled; others said it was Vayelle. I didn't much care who had tried to shoot him. I hated the vile, wicked whisper in the back of my mind that sort of wished they had been successful. What would his death mean for me?

With each checkpoint we passed through, my hope had risen. Each step toward that train was a step toward freedom, but all it would take is one person looking too closely at me and it would be over.

So far, none of the tired old men working the travel waiver stations had cared to peer under my hood or bothered to ask questions. It was a blessing.

Ambrose sidled closer to me in line, careful to keep his voice down as he said, "Up ahead, to the right." I followed his gaze, but the crowd was constantly moving and I saw nothing out of the ordinary.

There were too many possible dangers. With the Culling announcement only recently publicized, there were watchful eyes everywhere. Hundreds of bodies were pressed together in the crowd before us; all were stumbling, stepping on heels, and tripping on travel bags. I wanted to ask Ambrose what I was supposed to be seeing, but I couldn't speak. Being mute was part of the ruse.

All morning I'd been biting my tongue to keep from peppering my brother with questions about the unloading trains of soldiers we saw, the travelers that surrounded us, the smells and noises and myriad shifting colors.

The world around me was so wide and I felt so small in it. Babies cried and people argued over the validity of their travel waivers and the slow creep of the line. Smoke and soot wafted through the rusting steel building and out into the rainstorm beyond. I could feel the pull of the engine fires.

Back before the last war, the train station had been a massive steel aircraft hangar. After the fighting had ceased, Erydia had been left in shambles and the technology—the innovators—behind the rickety contraptions had been suppressed. Planes were a rare, expensive commodity. I knew that a few still existed in Gazda and some of the larger cities, but none existed in these parts anymore.

Now the building had been converted, its high arched ceilings used as a sort of train tunnel and loading area. This train was the only way in and out of Varos. It was also the only station with trains that went through the Suri Gap and into Vayelle. Everyone in the line with us was trying to get on that train. With so much happening around me, I wasn't sure exactly what Ambrose intended for me to see.

"Do you see them?" Ambrose asked. He adjusted the pack he wore as he nodded toward the front of the line. "Up ahead, to the right of the line, just by the gate."

The checkpoint attendant let three more people through the gate and we took a small step forward. My bones ached as that swirling heat in my gut pushed up, my ability bubbling toward a surface I couldn't quite see. I pushed it back down, mentally tethering it to my insides—like my ribs were a prison cell of bone, enough to cage something inherently uncageable.

45

Ambrose kept his tone light as he explained, "There's a man, he's standing by the gate now. Tall. He's got a gun. See him? There's a girl next to him. She's one of *them*."

I saw her.

She wore the navy robes of a priestess, the hawk-and-hare sigil of the queen stitched onto the right shoulder in silver thread. She was young, around my age, maybe sixteen or seventeen, her coppery skin flushed, her hair braided in looping black coils atop her head. She seemed to look at nothing and yet . . . I felt her gaze.

A videra.

Ambrose caught the look on my face and muttered, "Yes, them."

There was a soldier with her, a real bruiser-looking type, with broad shoulders and large hands. Up ahead, he pulled a young girl from the front of the line. A few seconds passed before the videra shook her head and the girl was released, staggering back to her waiting family. The videra's gaze turned to the next group of travelers.

My brother sidestepped slightly, trying to get a better look at what was happening. Maybe they were just offering blessings. I'd read books about priestesses who sold healing elixirs—water taken from the springs of Melloria or minerals gathered from the mines of Freia. Maybe, just maybe, that's all it was.

After all, videras were rare—so rare that they'd been thought to be nearly extinct after the last war. But the push of my ability, as if it were reaching forward toward the priestess, told me differently. There was nothing normal about that black-eyed girl. And if she turned in my direction, even for a moment, she'd know there was nothing normal about me either.

Ambrose must have seen something he didn't like because he grabbed my wrist, his grip nearly painful as he muttered, "Keep your head down. Don't draw attention to yourself."

Fear dug talons into my heart—each breath came fast and faster.

Keeping my head down won't do any good, I thought. Cutting my hair, changing my clothes, it was all for nothing if they're using videras. I might as well unwrap my hand and show my mark to everyone.

A man walked the length of the station wall nailing printed announcements to the cracked wooden beams. As he worked, people flocked to the edges of the building, eager to read the next bit of news. Ambrose and I stayed where we were, moving steadily forward as people left the line.

"Did you hear?" someone said from behind us, speaking to the gathered crowd. "I've just come from the ticket station and they're closing the border. The stationmaster says no one's going through."

A man joined the line again. "The queen has lowered the draft. Every man over the age of fifteen is supposed to report to the nearest pavilion immediately."

"Fifteen?" someone cried. "That's three years below the legal age—"

"And the draft letters said seventeen," a man in front of us said.

Ambrose lowered his head to me. "Keep moving, we're almost there."

There had already been an attack, one person said. An assault on one of the temples near Nolajan. The number of dead varied, depending on the teller. Three hundred, seven hundred, two thousand—it didn't matter how many people had died. All that mattered at that moment was that the transportation between my country and my sanctuary was being cut off.

We're going to be trapped here. I'm going to die.

"The Suri Gap is being sealed," a woman said, her voice high with hysteria.

No. No, that couldn't be happening. I wanted to turn around. I wanted to tell her that it couldn't possibly be true.

I needed it to be a lie. I needed—

"It'll be fine." Ambrose held tight to my wrist. "It'll be fine, Monroe. They won't close the border right away. It'll take time."

We were only a few dozen feet from the train. I looked down at the ticket in my hand. The corners were bent from my grip and the paper was damp from sweat; the words ran in places.

So close.

"It'll be fine," my brother repeated. "It'll be fine, I promise."

It might have been fine before, but back then I'd been trying to fool an exhausted, bored attendant. A videra would know.

I turned to look behind us at the line still forming. Beyond that, the exit to the train station loomed. I gripped Ambrose's sleeve in my hand. *We could turn around and go home. We could leave and maybe . . . maybe they wouldn't come looking for one runaway soldier. But they would come looking for one missing goddess-touched girl. There was no way out of this, was there?*

I couldn't seem to catch my breath.

"We are going to get out of here," he said.

I only shook my head. He was wrong. Despite how close to escape we were, I felt deep in my soul that we weren't going to get out. Dread and fire mingled in my blood—I wished I had a different ability. Even when I wasn't burning, I was ablaze. I knew I attracted attention just by being what I was. And the priestess, *the videra*, she would—

"Deep breaths, Monroe."

Despite the rising frenzy and the rumors circulating about radicals, traitors, and wars, the line continued to move forward. Now we were only a few yards away from the priestess.

I watched through a gap between bodies as a woman, too old to be goddess-touched, approached the priestess, carrying a little boy. The soldier became uneasy. He put a hand on the priestess's shoulder but she shrugged him off. I watched her bow her head and speak a blessing over the child. The mother wept.

Another couple saw the interaction and hurried over, eager to have their own blessing.

"Good," my brother said under his breath. "Maybe that'll keep her busy."

There was noise from behind us as a station guard approached a family a few feet back and asked to see their travel waivers. I tensed, but Ambrose didn't react.

The soldier was shooing away the small crowd that had formed around the priestess. She offered them all blithe smiles and muttered apologies as she moved back to stand near the gate. The man adjusted the gun in his hands.

I was close enough to see the depthless black of her eyes, notice the tiny silver beads braided into her hair. The bangles on her wrists jingled as she lifted a hand and pulled her hood up, so it covered the top of her head and made the royal crest on her shoulder more visible. I felt, more than saw, her look in my direction.

The world turned from dull chaos to needle-sharp in an instant. I held my breath. Ambrose noticed my reaction and stepped forward a few inches, enough to partially conceal me. Three heartbeats passed, and then I felt the videra turn away.

The station attendants continued to examine tickets and waivers. More people passed through the gate and onto the train. The line moved. Only two more groups and it would be our turn.

I focused on the videra.

A station guard addressed the group directly behind us and the sound of his voice so close startled me. The train ticket slipped from my hand.

I cursed under my breath.

Ambrose stiffened next to me as the guard turned in my direction. "Can I see your travel waivers and identification cards please?"

Ambrose was quick to respond. "Yes, sir." He dug in his pocket and produced both of our documents, passing them over to the guard.

The man glanced at them and then said, "Can I help the two of you with anything? Seem a bit nervous."

"My brother just dropped his ticket, that's all."

"Then he'd best find it, eh?"

I nodded, pulled my hood forward, and I crouched down. A large gust of wind pushed through the tunnel of the station, caressing my sweat-damp skin. A cold knot settled in the pit of my stomach as I searched.

There!

The silver edges of the ticket glinted in the low light as it skidded away on the breeze. I leaned forward, onto my hands and knees, reaching for it, but stopped as a boot came down, pinning the paper to the pavement.

I didn't have to look, didn't have to follow the line of those dark-blue robes to know who it was. Without a word, she bent down and felt around the hem of her dress until her fingers found my ticket.

For a moment, the videra crouched there at eye level with me. Those empty black eyes pressed into me like a physical force. She saw what no one else did.

Her lips twitched into the smallest pleased smile before she said, "Ah, there you are."

No.

My brother let out a stunned cry, as if he hadn't seen the videra approach us.

She straightened, those sightless eyes still fixed on me as she said, "We found our girl."

White-hot fear seared me to the spot. The guard with her turned to me. Before I could force myself into action, he'd crossed the space between us and had grabbed my arm. He pulled me to my feet and turned me toward the videra.

"This one?" he said, incredulous.

She nodded. "Let Captain Dellacov know that she's been located."

I tried to pull out of the man's grip, but he held tight. "I've done nothing wrong," I said. "I've got a ticket. I have—I have the papers to get across. Just— Please—"

"She'll cause a scene and worry the other travelers," the videra said. "She should be escorted away. We can't afford panic."

Escorted where?

I turned to look at the videra, but those sightless eyes held no pity. No empathy. "Please just let me go."

"Monroe!" Ambrose called my name and tried to move toward me, but other station guards were already gathering. They blocked his path to me. "Get your hands off him," he said.

"*She* isn't to leave the station," the guard holding me announced. He nodded to my brother. "Neither is he. He'll need to be questioned."

Ambrose shouldered his way past one of the guards. "You have no reason to detain us."

The videra spoke above the murmuring crowd. "She is goddess-touched. That is all the reason we need to keep her here."

Another guard placed a hand on Ambrose's shoulder, halting him in his tracks. "She isn't . . ." Ambrose's voice broke over the words "She's . . . She's my little sister."

"Let go of me." I tried to pull away, but the man held tight to my upper arm, keeping me in place. He turned, pulling me a step farther away from my brother.

The guard spoke to the man working the gate. "Call for the magistrate and Captain Dellacov. We've found the runner. She'll go on the next train to Gazda." He nodded to Ambrose. "Detain him as well."

"I don't want—" Panic rose in my chest, cutting off my words.

The Culling. They are going to take me to the Culling. I'm going to die in the arena.

I met Ambrose's gaze through the group of guards separating us. "I can't."

He took a step toward me. "Take your hands off my sister."

The heat in my blood turned to an insistent flame that pressed against the inside of my skin, demanding to be used. I rallied that unseen force. I could fight. I could use my ability and—

Before anyone could stop him, Ambrose threw a punch at the guard nearest him. The man staggered backward, nearly knocking the videra over. In surprise, the guard holding me loosened his grip and reached for her. I darted toward my brother. Ambrose was still struggling and throwing punches at the guards blocking his path to me. But he was getting tired and there were so many of them.

Sparks danced at my fingertips and I scrambled for the right thing to do. I'd practiced my ability with Ambrose a few different times, but mostly I'd used my ability for practical things. I knew how to light a fire in the stove, but I had no idea how to use it to fight off these men.

Ambrose hit the guard nearest him hard enough to make him fall, knocking down the guard behind him. That was all the opening he needed. His hand caught hold of mine.

"Run!"

We spun on our heels and came face-to-face with a wall of guns. Ambrose let go of my hand and lifted his arms. "Don't . . ." He looked at me then, his gaze frantic as he gauged the distance between those two dozen weapons and us. The guards and the videra were still at our backs. There were guns trained on us there as well.

My brother had always had the answers, had always known what to do and how to help me and what decision was best—but not now. Now he looked afraid.

Someone stepped forward and took hold of my upper arm, pulling me sharply backward and away from Ambrose. My brother followed after me, making it two steps before the guard holding me pressed a gun to my head and said, "You will stand down."

For a moment, I thought he might actually shoot me—and I was oddly relieved. Maybe that would be better, quicker, than the Culling. If I died here, I wouldn't be a killer. I wouldn't have to be a monster. I would just be dead.

But the videra spoke up. "She's valuable." And he didn't pull the trigger. I think, maybe, I hated her the most for that.

"You have two choices," the guard said, addressing my brother. "You will back away from the goddess-touched girl, and we will let you go. Or we will shoot you. Either way, she is going to the Culling."

"It's her fate," the videra said softly, as if she were speaking to a wayward child. "Her service to the Crown is an honor to your family. She is bound for greatness—I can see it." She cleared her throat and I could feel those black eyes still focused on me as she said to Ambrose, "As a gesture of our goodwill to her, we will not kill you."

Ambrose took a step back from me, moving closer to the line of guards behind him. "Truly?" he said.

There was a long silence and then the videra spoke again. "Her fight is not with us, young man."

My brother nodded. "Maybe it isn't, but *my fight* sure as hell is."

There was a loud grunt as Ambrose spun and punched one of the nearest guards. The man's gun went off and the crowd of people that had gathered around us all ducked as the bullet pierced through the thin ceiling of the train station. Ambrose darted forward, trying to get to me, but more guards converged, grabbing his arms and wrists.

The guns turned on him.

I screamed, "Stop!"

The train station grew still as everyone turned their attention to me.

"Please . . . Please stop." I forced my voice to remain even as I said, "I'm fine. I want to go to the Culling. It's my fate and I— I'll face it willingly." I forced myself to reel in my ability, to pull it tight to my spine and control it. I wanted to burn everything. I wanted to turn myself to ash, but instead I straightened and said the words I'd been running from my entire life: "My name is Monroe Benson, and I am goddess-touched."

Anyone who hadn't understood what had been happening did now. Gasps filled the cavernous train station and whispers of the presence of a goddess-touched girl spread like wildfire around us.

Good, let them talk. Maybe if there were witnesses, people to spread the news, the guards would be merciful. Maybe they wouldn't hurt Ambrose.

I knew that if I didn't stop him, he'd continue to fight. He'd get himself killed. And it would all end the same way. I'd still go to the Culling.

"I'm okay," I said.

Someone said something, words I barely registered as hands took hold of my wrists, as someone pulled me back by the shoulder.

The words came again: "Be gentle with her." It was the priestess who spoke. She stepped back, making room as I was hauled away from my brother, from the future I'd been so close to reaching.

Then I was being passed to other strange hands.

Ambrose was yelling to me, "I'll find a way to save you! I won't let you die in that arena. I swear. I swear I'll save you!"

People whispered things as I was ushered away, their words mixing together as fingers reached for me, grasping at my clothes, any exposed skin—

"Goddess-touched."

"Marked."

"Blessed."

"The future queen."

No. I dug my boots into the ground, tried to turn back, tried to take it all back.

But it was too late.

An arm snaked around my waist as I struggled, attempting to fight the way that Ambrose had taught me. I summoned flame. I kicked and thrashed, but the hold was too strong. I couldn't free myself.

When I didn't stop fighting, a cloth was pressed to my nose and mouth. Chemicals burned at my throat as I inhaled, attempted to scream. But I couldn't make a sound. My chest was hot—like fresh coals. Like the heat of the oven on baking days. I blinked, trying to see through an onslaught of tears, past the dark spots in my vision.

I think he was still yelling for me.

I fought back one more time, tried to summon fire to flesh again—I failed. My head swam, dipped down, and then I was sinking, drowning, gone.

6

On a Train

I awoke in a darkened train compartment. For a moment, I didn't know where I was. The memories from the station were shadowy things, difficult to grasp and make sense of.

Ambrose. The videra. The rag pressed to my nose and mouth. The tang of chemicals.

Goddess, I'm going to be sick.

I sat up abruptly, pressing a hand to my mouth to keep myself from vomiting on the spot. Anxiety swirled in the pit of my stomach, mingling with the sudden realization that I was on a train heading toward the Culling. We'd failed.

I sucked in a deep breath and turned to look out the window. Trees. Farms. Waves of green hills and patches of thick pine trees. I had no idea where the hell I was.

My jacket was gone, the fake bandage that had been covering my mark gone with it. My skin stuck to the leather seats with sweat and the walls of the small train compartment were closing in on me with each thin breath I managed.

I'm fine. Everything is fine.

I dug my nails into the flesh of my palms and turned my attention to the train itself. The small space was lit with two gas lamps, the shades crafted from Pallae glass, the cobalt blue tint more vivid than the pictures in the books had made them appear. The thin flames danced against the sconces and made the gray wallpaper seem to shimmer.

There was a second leather bench across from me and, above it, the seal of the royal family—the engraved silhouette of a hawk, wings outstretched, its talons digging into the stomach of a dead rabbit. Underneath the emblem, written in swirling Erydi, was our nation's creed: *The hunters, never the prey.*

A low creak came from beyond the train compartment and I tensed. The door was crafted of dark wood, with frosted glass panels, making it nearly impossible to see anything in the hallways outside.

I let my ability unfurl itself from my gut and reach forward. Invisible hands stoked the flames of the gas lamps, easing them higher, brightening the room. Now the wallpaper appeared blue, not gray.

For a second, my power lingered against the flames of the lamps, as if it was considering what to do, giving me time to consider too. I could break them, burn the flames too high, release the gas—kill myself and possibly everyone on this train.

I looked to the royal crest again. Hunter or prey.

Which am I?

A guard stood watch outside my train compartment, his body silhouetted in the frosted glass. I leaned my head against the window, gazing out at the landscape beyond. The world outside the window was bright with midday sunlight.

All I knew of the other counties in Erydian had come from books—and that information did little to help me figure out exactly where I was. There were farms and trees, rivers and streams. The only indication that we were traveling through other counties came with each massive stone wall we passed. Erydian soldiers dressed in light-brown fatigues paced back and forth on top of the walls, their guns in hand.

Where is Ambrose?

Had the videra really let him go without punishment? I doubted that. No matter what she'd said, my brother had been trying to flee the country with a goddess-touched girl and forged papers. Both of those were top-tier criminal offenses. Maybe they would interrogate him and then ship him off to the nearest war office. He'd be forced to report to the draft. But that was if they were merciful.

Every time I closed my eyes, I saw the way he'd strained against the hold of those guards. He'd yelled promises to me that I knew he couldn't possibly keep. The time for being saved had come and gone. Now it was time to fight or die.

The sound of the compartment doors sliding open startled me and I turned to see a young woman standing in the hall. "Oh, good. You're awake. I was starting to worry. I've come by twice now." She frowned down at me. "We're still a long way away from Gazda. Is there anything I can get you? Food? Maybe a washcloth?"

"Do you know anything about my brother?"

She blinked at me. "Your brother?"

"There was a man at the station with me in Varos—"

"Oh, you mean the one throwing punches?" She shrugged, her slender fingers tightened in the skirt of her dress as she explained, "I assume he's fine. Probably in better shape than any of the guards. I think one of them has a broken nose. He's got a nice right hook, if the guard gossip is to be believed."

"So . . . he wasn't hurt or killed?"

"Goddess, no. Of course not. I mean, I'm sure people had some questions for him, but I think everyone's top priority was getting you on the train before a mob could form. People were already fixated on that videra and then you started talking about being goddess-touched and, well . . ." She sighed. "It was a mess."

Silence settled between us, pulled tight like an elastic band.

"So, can I get you anything?"

I chewed my bottom lip and turned to look out the window again. All the things I'd wanted were beyond my reach now. My mind swirled with too much information, too many worries. The Culling was organized in trials— when would those start? Right away? And who would I fight? How was that decided? The book had said something about there being training and—

"How about a glass of water?" She nudged.

The air left my lungs in a quivering breath and I nodded. "Yes . . . water. Thank you."

"And maybe a tonic to calm your nerves—?"

"No!" I straightened and shook my head. "I don't . . . I don't want to be knocked out again."

She nodded quickly. "Okay. Sure. Just the water then."

I hated the pity written all over her face. *Goddess, what must I look like to her?*

This girl was polished and fresh. Her dark-brown hair was finger-curled, the waves falling elegantly across her brow in the most popular style. She looked like she'd walked out of a fashion magazine, like the ones Kace sometimes brought home from market and hung on the wall. She was almost too pretty, too clean. Her nails were long, the half-moons of them perfectly shaped and buffed.

There was no room in my chest for jealousy, and yet I envied her position in life. We were clearly not the same. What would it be like to be this girl— tall, curvy, beautiful, and allowed to travel the world by train?

"There's nothing else you want?" she asked.

I wanted to be her. At that moment, I wanted to be anyone other than myself.

"Just water," I said.

With another half smile, the girl was gone, leaving me alone in the compartment again. Tears burned at the back of my eyes. *Get it together, Monroe.* The flames in the sconces flickered, dimmed, grew too hot. The heat in my veins swirled. That dark power in me seemed to stretch—take up more space than I was comfortable with. I wanted to carve myself out of my skin.

Moments passed and then the girl was back with a glass filled with water and a small leather bag. She handed me the water and said, "It's a little warm in here, isn't it?"

I nodded and forced that power back down, easing the flames lower. If the girl noticed the flickering lights, she didn't mention it. I drained the water as she turned to close the compartment door.

Her bag clicked open as I set the glass down on the window ledge.

"Here." The girl offered me a small compact mirror and a folded cloth. "I figured you probably don't want to arrive looking like that."

Shame twisted in my gut. *Like that.*

"I also have this." She pulled out a simple cotton day dress and a pair of gray woolen stockings. "The dress might be a little big on you. Still, anything is better than the stuff you have on now, right?"

My dirty clothes were the only piece of home I had left.

When I looked up again, the girl had a hand to her mouth. "Good goddess, that was rude of me."

"No. You're right. I should change. Thank you." I took the cloth and mirror from her and went to work wiping the dirt from my face.

She seemed awfully interested in the guard outside, her attention darting between me and the silhouette at the door. I had expected her to leave, but she stayed standing there, her feet planted side by side and her fingers fiddling with a sculpted curl.

She shifted a bit uncomfortably as she caught me staring. "I'm Uri, by the way."

She held out her hand and took a step toward me. I tentatively shook it. "It's nice to meet you, Uri."

I was about to pull my hand back when she deftly rotated my wrist and smiled down at the mark on my open palm. Instinctually, I yanked my fingers away. Uri didn't comment on my reaction. "You didn't tell me your name."

"Monroe Benson."

"Monroe," she repeated.

Uri settled onto the bench opposite mine and crossed her legs.

She was something else. Uri had a confidence about her that was unlike anything I'd ever seen. It was in the tilt of her head, the way she sat with her shoulders back and her chin held high. Everything about her—the makeup, the forest green dress she wore, her dainty high heels, the perfect set of her hair—was graceful.

"It's awfully nice to meet you, Monroe." Uri leaned forward, propping one elbow on the knee of her crossed legs. "So, you *are* a goddess-touched girl then. I wasn't sure if it was true. Sometimes people lie to try to get to Gazda—you know how it can be. But the videra . . ." Uri chewed her bottom lip. "They aren't the sort to tell tales."

My hand started to sweat around the cool metal of the mirror.

Uri asked, "What can you do?"

Warning bells went off in my head, accompanied by a sharp sense of unease. I lowered the cloth from my face and placed the mirror in my lap. "Why are you doing all of this?"

"Doing what?"

"The mirror, the clothes, the water, *talking to me* . . . ?"

"Just being nice."

"But you don't know me."

Uri folded her arms across her chest. "Are strangers not nice to each other where you come from?"

No. No, they aren't.

When I didn't say anything, Uri shrugged. "Pity."

She leaned across the aisle and grabbed the bag from where she'd left it. After digging around, she pulled out a small silver tube of lipstick. I froze, fixated, as she popped the cap off and, without a mirror, applied a thin, practiced coat of crimson to her lips.

She smacked them together for good measure. "Did I get any on my teeth?" She smiled widely, pausing for me to look. I shook my head and she shot me a tight-lipped smile. "Perfect."

This time her expression seemed laced with something else. Nerves maybe. I waited to see what else she might say, but she only turned her attention back to the guard standing watch outside.

"Do you . . . Do you know anything about the other goddess-touched girls?" she asked.

I shook my head.

Uri's lips twitched and she leaned toward me again, careful to keep her voice low as she said, "Apparently there's a girl from Nartuk who can see the future and one from Fajvurrow who can control people with her voice. And another from Sikari who can control water. My money is on the girl from Fajvurrow. But of course, I don't know what you can do yet."

When I still said nothing, Uri dropped the lipstick in the bag and stood.

"I should probably be heading back now. I've already stayed too long." She grabbed the mirror and cloth, adding them to the bag before she shouldered it, and moved toward the door.

She almost had it open when I asked, "Heading back where?"

"To my own compartment," she answered. "Of course, they don't want us talking before it's started. We might make friends." She winked at me, turned, and slipped through the door. "Oh," she said, turning to look at me once more, "and you can keep the clothes. Consider them a gift."

The guard never even glanced in her direction as she paused, brushed a piece of lint from his uniform, shut the door, and disappeared from sight.

Uri is goddess-touched. And powerful too.

I didn't know what to do with that new information.

Her clothes were a bit too big for me. The dress did hang a little in the shoulders and I was less endowed than she was—but I was as comfortable as I could be in clothes that didn't belong to me. As I dressed, I thought about what I'd seen from her and what it all meant.

I hadn't seen her mark, which wasn't surprising, since the shape, size, and location of goddess-given marks varied. Mine didn't look magical; it mostly looked like someone had taken a piece of coal and smeared it on my palm. But, just like a box of matches, my mark functioned like a striking surface. A good firm snap of my fingers and my skin would spark like a match.

I could wield fire, but what was that against someone who could control others with their voice or read minds? And Uri had waltzed right past the guard standing watch.

Off in the distant quiet of the train, I could just make out the lilt of Uri's voice. Her accent was strange, the syllables stretched in some places and shortened in others. It was different from the shorter, clipped way people in Varos tended to speak. She made Erydi sound foreign, exotic.

I wondered why she wasn't confined in a compartment like I was. Maybe her ability made it difficult to cage her. Or perhaps she hadn't tried to run. It was possible that she'd chosen to come here willingly. And with an ability as strong as hers, she had good reason to.

Meals were delivered to me by maids who didn't speak to me or answer any of my questions. If anyone noticed I was in a different set of clothes, they didn't comment on it. Uri never came back to my compartment, and I didn't bother to try to go in search of her. The guards standing watch at my door were my ever-present reminder that I wasn't permitted to leave.

Imellia Station, Gazda
Sacrit

The train had rocked and swayed all night. While the world outside slept, I was hurtling faster and faster toward my supposed destiny. I wasn't ready for any of it. I didn't know what lay at the other end of this journey. Now, when I needed it most, the chapter on Culling rules was elusive. My mind was scattered between fear and anxiety and a million other small emotions—and remembering what was written in an old book was impossible.

The morning dawned quietly, sinking from night to day with such fluidity that I barely noticed it was happening. We passed county wall after county wall, factory after factory. The landscape changed and trees began to look different. Pines turned to willows. Moss dripped from thick limbs and gulls flew dangerously close to the side of the train. I'd seen creeks and pictures of larger bodies of water, but I'd never passed over anything quite like the massive rivers that ran through the inner counties.

Somewhere, beyond what I could see in the milky morning light, there was an ocean. Gazda was coastal, but I doubted I'd ever see the beaches or the waves. If my memory of the maps served me, the palace was too far inland to give me more than a distant view—if that.

At some point, a guard came to deliver a small tray of breakfast foods and new clothes for the day. The navy blue dress was the prettiest thing I'd ever seen, much less worn. The stitching along the waistband was elaborate, which was a shame since the dark thread was nearly unnoticeable against the fabric of the dress. This was the sort of craftsmanship that would take weeks to do by hand.

According to one of the guards, we were minutes away from the station in Gazda. I was told that when we arrived, I would be escorted to the palace where I would have a meeting with the queen.

What would Viera have to say to me? Would she scold me for trying to run? Would I be punished? I wasn't sure I cared. There was this odd sense of movement around me—like I was standing still but the world as still moving. And I couldn't keep up, couldn't make myself focus on what the next step would require.

I was going to the Culling, yes. But . . . But then what? Could I kill someone?

If you don't, you'll die.

"Are you ready?"

I straightened, only halfway through slipping on my shoes, and found a thin, redheaded young man watching me. He was wearing a gray suit, the fabric heavy and neatly pressed. The shirt underneath was crisp white, the tie a striped pattern of navy blue and silver.

While his clothes were beautiful, all clean lines and sharp angles, his posture was casual, his shoulders slumped, his hands stuffed in his trouser pockets.

There was a handgun strapped to his hip and he had the jacket of his suit hitched up so it was clearly visible. I didn't know if the view of the weapon was supposed to act as a threat or reassurance.

I finished with my shoes and stood, straightening my dress before I looked up at him. He raised an eyebrow and nodded in appreciation as if he didn't notice my cut hair or the way the bodice of the dress hung a bit too loose.

"You look ready enough." He stepped back into the hall and tilted his head back, gesturing for me to follow. "Come along then."

I took a step toward him and then paused. "Excuse me?"

At the sound of my voice, he backtracked so he was standing in the doorway again. "Yes?"

My mouth was dry, the sour taste of the morning's breakfast still lingered. I forced myself to stand straighter. "Who are you?"

"Ah." His mouth spread into a wide smile. It was oddly charming and still inherently unnerving. "Yes. I almost forgot." He stepped forward to meet me, so close that his shoes bumped against mine. His hand slipped from his pocket and snaked forward. "Hugo Dellacov, at your service."

I shook his hand. "Monroe Benson."

"Yes, so I've heard. You're here to participate in the Culling."

When I didn't respond, he stepped backward again, heading for the hall. He was about to leave, expecting me to follow, but I interrupted him. "Mr. Dellacov," I said. "I still don't know who you are."

"You can call me Dellacov. *Captain* Dellacov, technically. I'm apprenticed to the Captain of the Royal Guard. I also have the superexciting job of organizing all of this. It's sort of my first big task since getting the promotion. So . . ." He jerked his head in the direction of the hall. "Hurry it up before you make us both late."

He greeted the guards as we passed, calling them by name. I counted two pairs, one set in front of my door and one in front of a compartment down the hall. I slowed my step, trying to get a look through the frosted glass of that door. When I couldn't see anything, I hurried to catch up with Dellacov.

"Is that where Uri is staying?"

He stopped so quickly I almost ran into him. Dellacov turned around and looked at me, his eyes narrowing as he asked, "How do you know about her?"

I stepped back from him. "She came to my compartment last night."

His lips parted in surprise. "Oh? Is that so?" He didn't wait for my answer, just strolled past me to Uri's door. He nodded curtly to the guards standing watch and then, without a word, flung the door open.

I heard Uri make a sound from inside, a high-pitched yell and what sounded like a muffled curse. Dellacov said something to her, his voice too hushed for me to hear.

She responded loudly with, "Asshole!"

Seconds later, Dellacov came stumbling into the hall pursued by a high-heeled shoe that caught him square in the middle of the chest. Uri followed, hobbling on one heel and one bare foot. She looked like she might actually kill him.

"How dare you barge your way into my compartment without an invitation!" She pulled the other shoe from her foot and chucked it. Dellacov dodged and it hit one of the guards in the shoulder. Uri froze, placed a hand to her chest, and addressed the guard. "I'm sorry, Bolton. I didn't mean to hit you. Please accept my sincerest apologies for any damage done."

Bolton didn't say anything, just stooped, picked up the shoe, and handed it back to her. Uri smiled, nodded in acknowledgment, and then hurled the heel directly at Dellacov's face. He managed to knock it off course but the heel still grazed his jaw, leaving a thin scratch.

Uri bent down and gathered both her shoes, preparing for another assault.

Dellacov cursed, rubbing at his face as he muttered, "You are the most ridiculous, obnoxious, ludicrous, abhorrent—"

"Now you're just listing words trying to sound smart," she said, jabbing a heel in his direction.

"I'm not *trying*," Dellacov said, his voice a bit whiny as he pulled his fingers away to find the smallest trace of blood. "I *am* smart. How could you approach one of the Culling girls? Good goddess, Uriel, it's against the rules and you know it."

Uri's eyes landed on me for the first time. She waved, just the slightest wiggle of her fingers. Dellacov rolled his eyes and snapped his fingers in her face to regain her attention.

Her golden-brown eyes narrowed. "Keep your hands to yourself."

Dellacov snatched one of the heels from her hand and said, "Maybe try keeping your shoes to yourself."

She lowered her voice, but not so much that I couldn't hear as she hissed, "Show some respect or I'll have you demoted."

"Demoted?"

"Yes, demoted," Uri said. "As in knocked down a peg. Put in your place. Brought down from your too-high horse."

"Yes, thank you very much. I know what it means."

Uri made a crude gesture and grabbed the shoe back. Using the wall to keep her balance, she slipped both heels back on and quickly buttoned the delicate top straps. Once she was standing again, she smoothed her blue dress into place and shot me a wide grin.

"Did you sleep well, Monroe?"

"Yes, I slept fine. Thank you."

"Well, I didn't." Uri walked to meet me, both her guards and Dellacov in tow. "I never sleep well on trains. They rock too much. I spent most of the night with my head in a bowl."

"But it was an expensive, pretty porcelain bowl," Dellacov muttered.

"Keep smarting off and I'll make sure your only job is to empty it." Uri turned to face him, her smile that same sly grin it had been when I'd met her the day before. "Do you understand me, Dellacov?" When he didn't acknowledge her right away, her voice rose. "*Dellacov?*"

He pursed his lips. "Yes."

She crooned, "Yes, *what . . . ?*"

"Yes, Your Royal Highness."

Holy shit. Suddenly I couldn't breathe.

Uri saw my expression and looped her arm through mine. She patted my hand consolingly. "I suppose it's time for formal introductions. I'm Princess Uriel Isadora Colette Warwick. But you may call me Uri; everyone of any importance does."

"You aren't a goddess-touched girl then." The words fell out of my mouth, part question and part statement.

Princess Uri started walking toward the exit of the train car, pulling me by the arm alongside her. "No, I'm not. I ended up on a train with you by chance. I saw them bring you past my room. You looked . . ." She trailed off, her eyes settling on the thick metal door leading off the train. She came to a stop and turned to face me. "I wanted to help you. That's all. I apologize for misleading you."

"It's fine," I replied, unsure what else to say.

Princess Uri smiled. "It isn't fine. Queens don't say things like that in response to apologies." She sighed. "We never want to unintentionally condone bad behavior."

She reached forward and adjusted the folded collar of my dress, making the curved fabric lie flat. When she was satisfied, she held me at arm's length and looked me up and down.

Uri smiled. "It's better to accept an apology than brush it aside. Does that make sense?"

I nodded. "I accept your apology, Princess Uriel."

She grabbed my hand and gave it a squeeze. "Uri will do."

7

Imellia Station, Gazda

Sacrit

Dellacov stood with his hand on my arm as Uri and her guards exited the train. "In future," he said, "you should walk at least two steps behind any member of the royal family."

"But Uri—"

"Princess Uriel doesn't have to follow court etiquette. For some reason—and I can't begin to tell you why—people let her do whatever the hell she wants. You, on the other hand, should do what *I* say."

I was far enough back from the door that I couldn't see anything beyond the glare of morning light. Around us, a crowd cheered and Uri, no more than a dark elegant silhouette, waved to them.

She paused on the top step and turned back in my direction. Although the sun was too bright to actually see her expression, I knew she was smiling. Red lipstick would be framing teeth that were perfectly straight, offsetting cheekbones that were high and sculpted, and accentuating a chin that was held at the perfect angle.

If the next queen was meant to be like her, I couldn't imagine myself taking on that role. I didn't have that in me—not in my best shirt and not in this dress. But then again, it didn't come from the clothes.

Even without a goddess-touched gift, Uri was powerful. That commanding presence she wielded so casually was potent enough that, even with her kindness,

I'd mistaken her as an enemy, a rival in the Culling. I was grateful that she wasn't marked.

The princess lingered on the steps, waving and smiling to the crowd gathered in the train station. Dellacov's eyes followed every step she took. His stern expression was gone. It had morphed into an almost dumbstruck admiration.

He saw me looking and grimaced, ducking his head as he muttered, "She's slowing everything down."

Did she know that he liked her? I wanted to ask. I wanted to know if she kind of scared him too. Judging from the heat spreading across his ears and cheeks, I would say she did.

"All right," Dellacov said, "she's off the steps. It's your turn."

I spun to look at him. "Do— Am I supposed to wave too?"

"No," he said, adjusting his cuff links, "in fact I would suggest keeping your head down. I'll keep a hand on your back. We'll walk right through together."

"And when I meet the queen . . . ?"

He shrugged. "You just meet her. There's nothing to it really. Then you'll meet the prince and the Royal Synod. That's the easiest part of the whole Culling. All you need to do is read off a little script and then that part is done." He met my eyes as a thought occurred to him. "Shit. You *can* read, can't you?"

Was he serious?

"Yes, I can read."

He shrugged. "You're from Varos. You honestly can't blame me for the assumption."

"I'm poor, not illiterate."

Outside the crowd still cheered. The tightness in my chest grew to unbearable levels, as if I might burst from my skin and shatter into a million tiny pieces. What would happen if I vomited all over Dellacov's glossy shoes? Uri would probably laugh. He would probably kill me.

Dellacov let go of my arm and rested a steady hand against the small of my back. "The crowd will cheer. Don't stop walking. Don't acknowledge anyone. Just head right for the automobile. You'll see it parked at the end of the walkway."

I had just enough time to square my shoulders and lift my chin before I was ushered out of the train and into the sunlit station. The structure was massive, ten times the size of the little station in Varos. The ceiling was domed stained glass. I focused on the watery pastel patches of sunlight on the sleek tiles of the floor as I walked.

Around us, people cheered and whistled. Guards lined the walkway of the station, creating a man-made barricade to the waiting automobile. *Who had told all these people that I was coming today? Were they here for Uri's arrival?* Surely not everyone in the crowd was here to see me—a random goddess-touched girl.

But they were cheering and chanting something about a new reign and a new crown. I couldn't focus on any one phrase or sound—I only put one foot in front of the other and let Dellacov guide me. His hand was a warm presence against my spine as he nudged me down the steps and off the train.

By the time we reached the automobile meant for me, Uri was already in a separate vehicle. Dellacov moved to shield me as cameras flashed, the bright bulbs hissing and popping as reporters shouted questions to me. "Careful with your skirt as you get in."

I did as he said, paying close attention to where the fabric gaped as I slipped into the backseat. The bench seat underneath me was soft, tan leather and it smelled like lemons and some sort of cleaner. The man in the driver's seat braced a gloved hand on the headrest of the passenger seat and turned to look back at me. He nodded in acknowledgment: "Interregna."

I opened my mouth to ask him what that word meant, but then Dellacov was sliding into the seat next to me. He slammed the door shut behind us. Another guard got into the passenger seat and said, "To Oredison Palace, driver."

The automobile lurched underneath me as the driver hit the gas and I caught hold of Dellacov's arm to steady myself. He settled back against the leather seats, clearly at ease, and glanced my way. "Never been in a car, Miss Benson?"

I shook my head. "It's . . . loud."

And it was. The rumble of the engine had always seemed aggressive from afar, but being in an automobile was like sitting inside the chest of a purring cat. The sound was everywhere and the entire thing seemed to shake with it.

My grip on Dellacov's arm only tightened as we pulled out of the station and onto a busy street. People still yelled at us, their voices muffled by the roaring of the car. Cameras continued to flash, even as the guards in the station held the reporters back from following us.

The driver peered at me from the center mirror. "It's perfectly safe, I assure you."

"It's a short trip, little more than half an hour," Dellacov said. "You can rest if you'd like."

Rest? Was he crazy? How could anyone rest at a time like this—in a thing such as this? I turned my attention to the window on my left. The city beyond was . . . massive. The air left my lungs in a heavy sigh.

I wasn't in Varos anymore.

I'd noticed that we were getting closer to a town—but the last hour or so of my train trip had been filled with anxious pacing and I hadn't truly paid much attention to the world outside the windows. It was a different world from what I'd been raised in.

The streets were packed with buildings made of brick and painted wood siding. Multicolored awnings stretched over sidewalks, which were bright white or swept gray cobblestone. Metal signs hung above shop doors and large picture windows showcased store wares. Paperboys stood on street corners and children milled about, their arms stacked high with books.

School, I realized.

Today was a day that was changing my life forever, but to the people of Gazda it was a regular day. Tonight, the county temple would be filled with families bringing sacrifices for Sacrit. Some families might exchange a small gift like chocolate or flowers, and enjoy a meal together. But for me . . . I had no idea what the next hour would bring, much less the next few days.

I let go of Dellacov's arm and buried my hands in the folds of my skirt, hoping to hide their shaking. My throat burned and I fought to keep my voice steady as I asked, "What . . . What does 'Interregna' mean?"

Dellacov's brows rose. "Oh, it's a title. Sort of a step between princess and queen, I guess. It's what some of the staff will call you while you're in the competition. It's just an honorific."

"And what will happen to me once we reach the palace?"

"Like I said, you'll meet with Queen Viera and King Malcolm, then you'll be introduced to the Synod and to Prince Cohen."

Prince Cohen.

"If you're going to throw up, Miss Benson," Dellacov said, "please be kind enough to aim away from me."

The driver glanced my way. "You do look green. Should I pull over?"

"No." I shook my head. "No, please don't stop."

The automobile fell silent, the only sound the rumble of the engine and the low hum of the radio. We didn't get a very good signal in Varos, so I only knew older tunes and the most recent hits—the songs that my brothers picked up at the local dance hall and would sometimes sing while they did chores. I focused on the quiet crooning of the man as he sang some sort of love song. Every other word was lost to me, but the act of listening was enough to settle the swirling of my stomach.

When I felt certain that I wouldn't be sick, I asked, "When will the Culling start?"

"Not for a week or so," Dellacov answered. "There will be time to discuss all of that."

I pressed my eyes closed, almost relieved at the news. "So, I have some time then."

"The Culling will last a few months. And the first trial isn't for at least two weeks. There will be a dinner and a ball. Some etiquette lessons. It's all very organized, you'll see."

The guard in the passenger seat nodded. "People want to have time to get to know the contestants and find a favorite. Grow attached, you know? It isn't much of a competition if you're all thrown into the arena right away."

Grow attached. As if I was a pet and not a living, breathing person.

Dellacov seemed to sense my unease because he said, "You should focus on your meeting with the queen and on Cohen. Those are the two biggest things happening today."

"What about the other marked girls? When will I meet them?"

"You ask a lot of questions, Miss Benson."

"I don't have a lot of time, Captain Dellacov. And I've been sitting on a train alone for hours and no one has bothered to tell me anything at all. I apologize for wanting to know what's going to happen next."

His lips twitched, almost a smile. "I believe there's some sort of garden party or something. Brunch is usually a tradition on the first day of the Culling. You're the last to arrive, so it'll be a full party."

"Brunch?"

He nodded. "Yes. Dresses and music and probably some sort of official welcome. I haven't really asked much about it. I think Princess Britta is leading the charge. She and Princess Larkin are both sticklers for decorum and Uriel . . . Well, she'll be there because there will be a dessert table."

A girl after my own heart.

The car fell silent again as we drove, and I returned my attention to the outside world. The buildings were all tall, some with as many as five stories. The people walking by carried paper shopping bags and brightly colored boxes. The sky was a vivid blue, the weather so bright and cheery it seemed as if the goddess had chosen to spite me. It didn't seem fair that the world could be so pretty and yet so scary all at once.

The automobile slowed as we turned off a main street and onto a long cobblestone drive lined with dogwood trees. There was a huge stone wall up ahead, and I could see guards standing outside a massive wrought-iron fence.

I sat up a little straighter, trying to get a better view.

Oredison Palace was less like a castle and more like a grand house with sprawling gardens and white sandstone walls. The closer we got, the more elegant the features of the house became.

A drive encircled a marble fountain while two curved staircases led up to a set of oak doors. Tall walls seemed to tower over everything. They were at least eight, maybe nine stories tall. There were too many windows to count, and balconies, trellises, and vines. And guards—there were guards patrolling everywhere. A few of the ones closest to the wall saluted as we entered through the front gates.

The automobile that Uri had ridden in was parked in front of the house and footmen in slate-gray suits and white gloves were already hard at work carrying in trunks and bags. Our driver veered in a different direction, taking us down a separate pathway—past a latticework of hedges and gardens, until we reached a large, tunneled garage partially underneath one edge of the palace.

Footmen, dressed the same as the ones in front of the palace, converged on our vehicle, but Dellacov didn't wait for them to open our door. He got out and nodded for me to follow him.

"Good morning, Mrs. Arden," he called to an older woman who now stood near the palace entrance. "The girl has no luggage, so we'll go straight to meet with the queen and then I'll take her to her bedroom. Please make sure that a bath is run, and that—"

"Enough with your fussing, Dellacov." Mrs. Arden examined her silver wristwatch. She pursed her lips and tugged the white, cuffed sleeve of her blouse back into place. "I know how to run a house. I've been doing it for longer than you've been on this earth."

"Of course." He turned to look at where I still sat, watching him from the interior of the car. "Come along, Miss Benson—between you and Uriel dragging your feet, the Culling will be done and over before you ever even arrive."

"How very unfortunate that would be for me," I muttered.

"What was that?" he asked, his eyes narrowing as he watched me climb out of the vehicle.

I forced a smile. "Nothing."

I followed him up the small set of stairs to the entrance. "Miss Benson," he said, "this is Mrs. Arden. "She's the royal housekeeper and has served as governess to the princesses for the last . . . How long has it been now?"

Mrs. Arden smoothed a withered hand over her calf-length skirt and sighed. "I do believe it's been almost a decade since Uriel ran off the last governess."

Dellacov smiled and pulled the door open for me. "And you've been keeping her in line ever since," he said, ushering me inside ahead of him.

Mrs. Arden followed behind the two of us, her pale-gray eyes examining everything from my choppy blond hair to the slightly too-small pair of matte-black pumps I'd strapped on earlier. We paused at the bottom of a wooden staircase. To one side of the hallway, I could see light shining in from what must have been a kitchen. Fire pulsed from nearby ovens. Pots clacked together and the smell of roast chicken and something sweet wafted through the warm air. There was what appeared to be some sort of hand-cranked lift next to the stairs, presumably for transporting carts of food or other large items. As we stood there, a few maids hurried by—their conversation turning to nervous giggles and girlish whispers as they glanced at Dellacov.

He pretended not to notice them, but I saw how he straightened a little at the attention. Mrs. Arden broke through the moment, her tone sharp as a kitchen knife and said, "Shouldn't she change or . . ." She pursed her lips. "Or at least do something about her hair before—"

Dellacov's hand found the small of my back once more, and he gently guided me toward the stairs. "Unless Monroe's ability is hair growth, which I highly doubt, there is little to be done between now and when we reach the queen's study."

Mrs. Arden only hummed in response, clearly disagreeing with Dellacov's cavalier opinion. "I'll tell Tallis and Juno that she's arrived. They . . . have their work cut out for them."

I didn't know who those people were, but judging by her tone, Mrs. Arden had little faith in their ability to fix whatever she thought was wrong with me.

"They'll see her in the morning," Dellacov said. "Tell them they can train with her first thing."

Then he was pushing me up the stairs toward a closed door at the top. We'd almost reached it when Mrs. Arden spoke up from behind us. "Welcome to Oredison Palace, Miss Benson. And may the goddess be honored."

8

The Queen's Study
Oredison Palace, Gazda

"You're late, Dellacov."

Viera Warwick didn't even glance up from the papers on her desk as I was ushered into her office. The massive cherrywood desk in the center of the room was backlit by a set of huge bay windows that overlooked a sprawling grove of white flowering trees. Far below us, a group of young ladies strolled the pathways between the trees. I wondered if they were goddess-touched too.

I didn't have to wonder about Viera. Even if I hadn't known that she was queen and this was her office, I'd know that the woman sitting across from me was as marked as I was. The power seemed to roll off her in waves. Like smoke, it filled every crevice of the room and seemed to press against my skin. That small, quiet darkness in my chest seemed to recognize the pulsating essence of her ability.

Whatever the goddess had placed in her, sang to whatever was within me. And it was a sickening, slithering sort of feeling, being so close to something so . . . volatile. That was the word. She felt raw and uncontrolled. While my ability had always scraped dull nails against the inside of my bones, it was clear that Viera's power had long ago outgrown the cage of her skin. Everything in me wanted to get as far from her as possible.

Books and papers lined every spare surface and even the lone armchair in the corner was overrun with rolled maps and stacks of paperwork. The wallpaper was a soft pastel purple and there was a vase of white lilies on a stand in one corner. It all seemed so at odds with the woman sitting in front of me. She was buttoned-up—her skirt and long-sleeved blazer set were meticulously tailored to her form. Her black hair, which was laced with strands of silver, had been brushed up into an intricate roll at the base of her neck. And even without a crown, there was no mistaking the power that she held.

Uri clearly favored her mother in that. They shared the same high cheekbones and curly black hair as her mother, but something about Viera was sharper. The lines that framed the edges of her mouth were not from smiling or laughing; instead they pulled her mouth downward into a statuesque sort of sneer, as if she had been born looking down her nose at everyone else. And where Uri's eyes had been molten gold, Viera's were the cool crystal-blue of the sky. Of oceans and depthless seas.

And as she finally turned her gaze on me, I fought the instinct to bolt for the door. The corner of her mouth lifted, just slightly, as if she registered my fear. Then her attention drifted to Dellacov.

"I trust your trip to the border was successful," she said, "and that Uriel was well behaved."

He opened his mouth to respond but paused as the door to the office opened behind us and a middle-aged man strolled in. Viera leaned back in her chair as he circled her desk and came to a stop behind her.

"Don't stop on my account," the man said. "I apologize for my tardiness. I wanted to see that Uri was home in one piece. I hear the new troops were inspired by her visit."

Despite his graying blond hair and sun-kissed skin, he could only be Uri's father. They had the same brown eyes, and it was clear that she'd inherited the king's easy smile too.

Dellacov offered him the same curt bow he'd given Viera upon our arrival and said, "Everything went very well, Sire. We kept a low profile, as you suggested, but I think her presence did lift spirits and helped to remind our men what they're fighting for."

"Yes, well, most men like a pretty face. Speaking of which," his attention swept over me and he smirked, "we found the last one, I see." He looked to Dellacov. "Where was she?"

"Demarti Station," he answered.

The king's expression sobered. "Not heading to Gazda, I take it."

"She was trying to get through the Gap," Viera said. "We had reason to believe the last girl might try to run, and Dellacov had them set up a videra at the station."

"And good thing he did, else we'd be down to nine without a trial. And our enemies would have their hands on a goddess-touched girl." The king snaked an idle finger along the side of Viera's neck as he leaned closer to her and said, "We don't like runners, do we, my dear?"

Viera shrugged away from his touch. "What I don't like is *interruptions*, Malcolm."

They held gazes for a moment.

"We can discuss that later. For now . . ." He turned to look at me. "We should discuss— What is her name?"

I opened my mouth to speak but Dellacov beat me to it. "Monroe Benson."

"And how old are you?" Viera asked.

I swallowed and stepped forward, trying to stand a little straighter as I said, "Seventeen, Your Highness."

She nodded and jotted something down on a piece of paper. "And your ability?"

I dug my nails into my palms. "Fire."

"County of origin?"

I hesitated. "I was born in Gazda, but I was raised in Varos."

Viera leaned back in her chair, the pen going slack in her hand as she stared at me. "Your parents are criminals then? You were raised in a labor prison?"

"That explains the bad haircut," Malcolm muttered.

It felt like someone was carving my heart out with a dull knife.

"My parents moved to Varos by choice. After I was born marked."

Silence fell.

"So, it *isn't* just you then," the queen said softly. Uncertainty gnawed at my chest, but before I could question what she meant, she said, "You come from a family of cowards."

I could have called what my parents did for me a great many things—reckless, dangerous. But I would never have called them cowards. Not ever.

Leaving the county of their birth—a county that was far more privileged than any other county in Erydia—all so they could protect me . . . that wasn't cowardly. It was an action done purely out of love. And I would never shy away from that.

Before I could think better of it, I said, "Trying to save your daughter from dying in the Culling isn't cowardly."

Viera blinked at me. "And is that what you've come to do—die in the Culling?"

The king made a sound at the back of his throat and leaned against the windowsill behind her. "Well," he said, "she certainly isn't cut out to be queen." His smile turned vicious. "Runners don't make good queens."

My teeth cut trenches into my tongue as heat rose in my veins—defiant and angry. I needed to stay calm, to keep myself in check. This was a king. He was a man far more powerful than any I'd ever met.

That dark power in my gut hissed out a growl, smoke on the wind. *The trials will decide who wins and who dies. Forget him. He is nothing. But we . . . we could be everything. Her crown could be ours.*

I swallowed and took a small step back from the desk, wishing I had permission to leave the room. Voices had swirled inside me, both quiet and loud, for as long as I could remember. And yet . . . they had more space here—in her presence. The voice was louder, bolder—two things I wasn't.

Something in Viera's expression shifted slightly and she sat forward in her chair. "Yes, well, let's hope your death is swift. Or, at the very least, entertaining." She pulled a stack of papers toward herself and tapped a manicured finger against the form at the top. "You have . . . Juno Heist and Tallis Elliot as your trainers. They came highly recommended and were chosen with the utmost care. You will also choose an advisor from within the royal court. This individual will serve as an advocate and ally. While your trainers are responsible for helping you perform physically well, it is your advisor who will help you stand out politically and socially. Should you take the throne, this person would become a member of your personal court—an ally and a friend. While your trainers would become the beginning of your royal guard." She glanced up at me, those blue eyes cutting like blades as she examined me from head to toe. "I would choose wisely when it comes to your advisor. You will need all the help you can get."

I bit the inside of my cheek to keep from responding.

"Any questions?" Viera asked.

My throat ached, and I tried to sift through the millions of things I wanted to say and ask. I opened and closed my mouth. *Where is Ambrose? When do the trials start? Who the hell are Tallis and Juno? How am I supposed to choose someone from the court to advise me?*

"We're on a schedule," Viera said.

"When will my family begin to get the stipend for my . . . for me being in the Culling?"

Viera sat back slightly in her chair. "What stipend?"

My heart seized in my chest. "I was told that a stipend or some form of money would be given to my family while I was in the Culling."

"That was if you announced yourself into the Culling willingly. Judging by what Captain Dellacov has told me, that isn't the case. You were caught trying to flee our country."

I couldn't breathe around the terror. No. This couldn't all be for nothing. I didn't lose everything so that my mother could starve—there had to be some bright side to this. Some spark of hope to keep me going, keep me fighting.

"That isn't fair." I inched toward the desk, but Dellacov caught hold of my wrist. I turned to look at him before I spun back to Viera. "But my mother—"

"—should have known better than to try to defy the goddess and her queen," she said. "Now, do you have any other questions?"

Why?

Why deny my family something that was owed to them?

I would die and—

Viera broke through my thoughts. "Don't you have questions about him?"

I glanced to Dellacov. "About who?"

"Cohen." The prince's name sounded like a curse in her mouth. "He's the prize, after all."

If she thinks her son and her crown are the prize, she has it all wrong. My heart was still securely wrapped around my family's troubles as I asked, "Is he kind?"

Viera seemed surprised by the question. "He's—"

"He will make an excellent ruler and a good father to your heir," the king said. "That's all you need to concern yourself with."

Heir. The implications of what it would mean for me to win came flooding in. It wasn't just a crown or a throne. I wouldn't just be made to kill other people; I would be forced to share a bed with a total stranger.

I looked to the queen, expecting to see some sort of understanding or pity—she'd experienced this too, after all—but I saw nothing in her expression but cold boredom. "Any other questions, Miss Benson?"

For a moment, I just stood there looking at her. That power in her seemed to scrape unseen nails along the outer edges of my own ability—as if she were testing the boundaries. I swallowed. "Your Highness, my mother needs—" The words died on my lips as Dellacov's hand tightened around my wrist.

"If there are no other questions, Miss Benson . . . ?" the king said.

The backs of my eyes burned as I whispered, "No, sir."

"Very well." Viera gestured to the door. "You may withdraw."

The room was too hot and my chest was too tight. My heart was going to burst from my rib cage. This couldn't be it. That couldn't be all there was. I would die in the Culling and my mother would starve. After everything, *this* was how it would end?

"Your Majesties, I'm begging you. The rains are coming and my—"

"You may withdraw." Viera had already returned to the papers in front of her.

"Without the extra money, my mother could star—"

"Monroe." Dellacov's voice was sharp with warning.

I turned to leave, but Dellacov's fingers dug into the bones of my wrist, halting me. He bowed low at the waist and then began backing out of the room. I hesitated for only a heartbeat before I dipped into a clumsy curtsy and followed him.

The door to the study had almost closed when I heard Viera mutter, "Pity she didn't die in Varos. She's a waste of time here. The others will eat her alive."

9

Palace Hallway

Sacrit

The two guards standing watch by the door barely looked in our direction as the doors shut and the hallway outside turned quiet. Dellacov said, "Don't turn your back on the queen—or the king, for that matter. It's disrespectful."

"Do you know what happened to my brother?" Before he could lie to me or change the subject I said, "I heard them say your name on the train platform, and Uri knew about him. She said that he'd probably been questioned. Do you . . . Do you know if he's okay?"

If he was, then I knew that Ambrose would take care of Mama. Together he and Kace would find a way to make sure she was fed during the rains and the winter stretch. Dellacov adjusted his tie. "I left him in the station. As far as I know, he was questioned about the travel waivers and then released. I instructed the magistrate not to hold him."

Some small part of me wanted to hug him for that. "Thank you."

"You might be queen one day. I wouldn't want to get off on the wrong foot. Better to play it safe and let him off easy. Anyway . . ." Dellacov cleared his throat. "That went better than I'd hoped."

What had he assumed would happen?

Dellacov nodded down the hallway to our left. "The prince, the princesses, and the Synod are all waiting."

I followed him down wide hallways with wide-planked polished wood floors and pale-green wallpaper. Each corridor we passed through was covered with oil paintings in ornate golden frames and large windows with thick white crown molding. Maids darted about, placing fresh flowers in vases and opening curtains.

The doors to some of the rooms we passed were open, exposing plush sitting rooms, an elaborate state dining room, spiral staircases, electric lifts, and what appeared to be a massive private library. It was a mixture of a house and an office. Each room was immaculately styled for function, but not comfort. The sitting rooms held stiff chairs and couches; even the sunlight veranda seemed untouched. It was as if no one lived here.

There was a silence in the palace broken only by the soft whispers of maids and the occasional shifting of an item as they cleaned. While the palace itself had electric lighting in some rooms and gas in others, I could still feel the pull of fireplaces and the occasional candle. I focused on that, let it soothe the festering anxiety in my chest.

"Hurry it up, Miss Benson."

Dellacov was a few steps ahead of me, his pace far faster than my distracted one. I did as he asked, nearly jogging to get back into step with him. We went up one more set of stairs and then down a long corridor on the southern end of the palace.

"One second." Dellacov stopped at a set of heavy wooden doors and pushed one open.

I craned my head to see inside the cramped little office. There was one tiny window, a large metal filing cabinet, a carved desk, and a wooden banker's chair. Dellacov didn't even bother turning on the light as he opened a drawer and pulled out a set of keys. He riffled through them until he found the one he was looking for, and then he joined me in the hall again.

"This is to your room," he said as he pulled the office door shut behind himself and handed me the key. "After we meet with Cohen, I'll escort you there so you can change your clothes. Come along."

Two shorter hallways later and we were faced with a set of glass-paneled doors that opened into what appeared to be a little auditorium. Wooden benches and tables were staggered on platforms and arranged in a half circle that looked down onto a dais. Inside, around a dozen people mingled.

"This is the Synod Chamber," Dellacov explained. "It's where most laws and policies are discussed. Should you be crowned queen, you would spend a lot of time here."

I followed him into the arena and began the descent toward the dais. All conversation in the room seemed to fizzle out as everyone took notice of my arrival. Middle-aged men moved from the shallow steps to make room for us as we passed. A few even offered me slight bows.

"Interregna." A man with salt-and-pepper hair met us at the base of the stairs and offered me a smile that was just a bit too tight. He clasped his hands behind his back and looked down his nose at me, like I was a misbehaved child. "We had begun to wonder when you might grace us with your presence. The newspapers have had quite a time with your story. *Runaway Goddess-touched Girl Found by Videra*: that headline will sell papers. Everyone loves an underdog, Miss Benson; nobody loves a coward."

Who the hell is the man? "I'm not a—"

"Speaker of the Synod, Raveena," Dellacov said. "I trust that everything is in order."

The Speaker nodded, his eyes still narrowed on me. "We're still waiting for a few people, but the contract is prepared. Once the prince arrives, we can get on with it."

Dellacov nodded to a short line of chairs at the center of the dais. "You can sit here while you wait." I did as he suggested and sat in the nearest chair. The eyes of everyone in the chamber seemed to press in on me, but I forced myself to focus on my breathing.

Ten candles were spaced evenly on the circular walls of the room, and I let my ability sift through those flames. My fingers flexed against the fabric of my skirt as I fought the urge to pull flame from wick.

On the far wall, the projected square of light flickered black and white, spotting and seeming to quiver against the screen. A man stood by the camera and tinkered with a roll of film. My attention shifted to a small table to my left and a caged microphone that stood near it.

While Dellacov seemed certain that reading ability would get me through this, I wasn't entirely sure. I could imagine at least a dozen ways for me to make a fool of myself.

The click of heels announced the presence of someone new. A young woman rounded the back corner of the platform, coming from a door at the rear of the chamber. At first, I thought it was Viera. The girl was thin, with the same heart-shaped facial features and an engrained posture that reminded me a little of Uri. But unlike Viera, this girl seemed to be in her early twenties. She carried weight in different places—making her curvy in all the areas where Viera was sharp.

She was halfway through adjusting the folds of her dress when she caught sight of Dellacov and headed toward him. He bowed as she reached him, but she waved him off, her smile turning from polished to teasing as she said, "I thought for sure my sister would have beaten the decorum out of you by now." This, more than the thick dark curls or the regal bearing, linked her to Uri.

He ran a hand over his red hair, combing it away from his face as he muttered, "Goddess knows, she tried."

The girl's smile grew as she caught sight of me over his shoulder. "You must be Monroe." She bypassed Dellacov and walked to the edge of the dais. Her eyes were the color of the sky as she peered up at me. "I'm Britta Warwick. I'm the oldest. It's wonderful to finally meet you."

My heart seized in my chest and for a moment, I floundered. How was I supposed to greet her? I glanced at Dellacov. He'd bowed to her. When he said nothing, I stood and did what I assumed you were supposed to do when in the presence of a princess: I curtsied, badly.

To her credit, Britta tried to hide her smile. "Oh no, don't do that. You should never curtsy to me, I'm only a princess. As a goddess-touched girl, you're more or less my equal. The only person you should bow to is the queen or the king. And that would only be on the fanciest of occasions."

Dellacov walked to stand next to her. "*We're* on schedule, but none of the others have arrived yet."

Her smile faltered. "Did you and Uri get separated on the trip back?"

"No, she got back to the palace when we did."

She blinked at him. "Then where is she?"

He shrugged.

"You left her alone, *by herself*?"

"I was a little busy. I'm sure her guards are with her."

"If you give her an inch, she'll take a mile." Britta shook her head, but humor danced in her eyes. "Now that Uri's free, we might never see her again." She climbed the steps of the dais. "Let me tell you a secret, Monroe. I may be the oldest, but no one listens to a word I say." She lowered herself into the chair next to me and crossed her legs at the ankles.

"That isn't true," Dellacov said. "I listen to you."

"You work here, Dellacov. We pay you to listen. That hardly counts. Anyway . . ." She turned to look at me. "Let's talk about you. This is a big moment. I assume you've already met with my parents, but in a few minutes, you'll be introduced to the Royal Synod, my sisters, Larkin and Uri, and my brother, Cohen."

Dellacov reached into his vest pocket and checked his timepiece. "Any idea where Larkin and Cohen are?"

"Larkin was training with Kinsley earlier, but she should be here on time. I reminded her first thing this morning. As for Cohen," she shrugged, "he should be getting here any moment. Uri probably forgot."

Dellacov snapped the cover shut on his watch and tucked it away again. "No, she knew it was today. She told me she wanted to grab a scone from the kitchen and then she'd be here."

"Maybe she decided to ditch."

He shook his head. "You know Uriel likes being a spectacle too much to *not* show up for this."

Britta hummed in response. "You must have been very distracted to have let her out of your sight. Tell me, how much trouble did she cause with the troops? She begged to go, but I told Father it was a bad idea."

"She behaved."

"I'm sure she was thrilled to be free for a few days. Away from Mother's scowls and Mrs. Arden's lessons. And Uri always shows just the right amount of thigh to keep the men feeling . . . inspired."

Dellacov's face heated, his ears turning scarlet. "She didn't do that. She was friendly, but there wasn't anything inappropr—"

"I'm kidding, Hugo. Calm yourself. Besides, I'm sure neither of you was upset to be stuck together, in a cramped tent, for days at a time. *Blessedly unsupervised.*"

"Nothing happened."

"I never said anything did."

"Actually," I said, "she *did* throw a shoe at him."

Britta laughed, a loud, full sound that matched her smile perfectly. She clapped her hands together with glee. "Good goddess, did she really? I honestly shouldn't be surprised."

I nodded. "See that cut on his jaw? It isn't from shaving."

Britta leaned forward as if she could see the small gash from her seat. "Brilliant. Cohen is going to love that."

Dellacov shook his head. "Enough about Uriel, tell me about the assassination attempt. Is everyone all right?"

"We're all fine," she said. "It was scary, but the guards handled things quickly. They killed the gunman and cleared the ballroom in record time. The only one hurt was poor Captain Thomas."

Dellacov blanched. "Captain Thomas was injured?"

She glanced toward the door as a few more men, presumably Synod members, filtered in. "Yes. But he's fine. I mean, fine enough. Not dead. He took a bullet to the knee. Anyway, he was already so close to retiring, I think he's talking about not returning at all. That would put you in charge, wouldn't it? You leave for a holiday with my sister and come back Captain of the Royal Guard, that would be quite a promotion. Some would suspect quid pro quo, but I know better."

"It wasn't a holiday." He bristled. "And nothing happened between us. We were—"

The corner of her mouth pulled up into an amused smile. "I'm sure Mother or Father will talk to you about it soon."

The back door to the chamber opened again to reveal a bone-thin girl with stringy black hair and sallow skin. She looked almost ill, but her eyes were the same clear shade of brown as Uri's. She moved with a quiet sort of grace, as if she were a dancer. This girl wasn't objectively pretty, but she shared enough of Viera's delicate features that she could only be the middle sister.

"Larkin," Britta said as she approached our line of chairs.

Larkin wrinkled her nose at Dellacov. "You look positively green, Hugo. Did watching Uriel throw herself at commoners make you sick?"

"Don't be crude," Britta said.

"What?" Larkin said. "Her reputation doesn't matter as much as yours or mine. You know as well as I do that father didn't send her to visit the troops because she's a skilled military strategist. He sent her because he assumed she'd—"

"Larkin, this is Monroe Benson. She's the last of our goddess-touched girls," Britta said. "Monroe, this is my sister, Larkin. She's . . . a joy."

Larkin eyed me up and down. "I saw in the papers that you had a bad haircut, but I hadn't realized just how bad it was. And you're a blond too." She settled into her chair and sighed. "My brother has a thing for brunettes."

Britta sat up a bit straighter in her chair and nodded to the doorway at the top of the stairs. "Oh look, there's Uri."

I followed her gaze and sure enough, Uri was standing in the doorway to the room. She was deep in conversation with a young man I didn't recognize. A few people with cameras came in after them and the guards with her made sure they gave her space.

For a moment, she just stood there chatting with the stranger. They laughed and she touched his shoulder. A few feet away from me, Dellacov shifted a bit. Uri must have noticed him because she paused midconversation and shot him a sidelong look. He pretended not to see, but it was clear from the way his ears heated that he had.

So, that boy must be Dellacov's competition then.

He was taller than Dellacov, and Dellacov looked to be nearly six feet. His features were young but charming, caught somewhere between being a boy and a man: a confident smile, clean-shaven face, flushed skin, and dirty-blond hair that was combed away from his face.

He wore a light-gray suit and black tie, the fit streamlined and tailored like Dellacov's. The only thing that marked him as anyone important was the sapphire-encrusted tie clip and the white rose pinned to his lapel. With the distance, I couldn't tell much more about him.

I watched the two of them, Uri and this boy. She smiled and laughed at something he said. It occurred to me that, as a princess, Uri probably wasn't allowed to just marry whomever she wanted. She would probably end up betrothed to some fancy nobleman or something. Maybe this was him.

That would explain the look on Dellacov's face.

Before I could ask, Britta leaned back in her chair and sighed. "Oh, good, Cohen is with her."

I registered the name slowly, like I was hearing it underwater. *Cohen*. Her brother, the prince and future king—it was amazing how that information impacted my perception. Nothing about his features changed, but this knowledge made me reinterpret everything.

The way he stood, with one hand in his trouser pocket and the other fiddling with his watch chain, had seemed casual before; now it seemed nervous. I noticed then, the way his eyes danced around the room, never pausing on anything in particular—until they did pause. *On me.*

Oh goddess. The air left my lungs, and I felt the candles around me sputter slightly as that darkness in me seemed to narrow its focus from the flame to the young man standing a few yards away from me.

Cohen's eyes were oddly heavy, full of questions and worries. I could feel him picking me apart, scanning my face and my body for any sign that I was who he was looking for. With his mother stepping down from power, Cohen would be in line for the throne and would marry whoever won the Culling.

For him, this was about finding that girl. Just then, as he looked at me, I knew he was trying to decide if I were that person. I was the last of the girls to be brought to Gazda. He'd seen all the others. Where in that lineup did I fall? Was I as pretty as the last girl? Did I want to be?

Uri said something to him, and his attention snapped back to his sister. The smile he gave her wasn't as genuine as it had been before.

Nervous. The prince was nervous.

Finally, he gestured to the dais and Uri nodded.

Dellacov met them halfway and clapped Cohen on the back. The two boys exchanged a few words and the prince seemed to relax. Uri reached us before he did. She bypassed Larkin and went directly to Britta. "I've been gone two weeks, and you aren't even going to come meet me at the train station?"

"I've been playing host to the goddess-touched girls—something you wouldn't understand since you've been touring the counties."

Uri settled into the empty chair on my other side, leaving a space between Britta and me for Cohen to sit. She gestured to me. "I've played host to Monroe. And I've done a good job of it too. Haven't I, Monroe?"

I nodded, my attention still glued to the prince. He'd started to make his way down the stairs toward the dais again. With every step, I could see more of his features—a little curled cowlick toward the front of his head that he kept trying to smooth into place, a dimple in his left cheek, broad shoulders, just the barest shadow of facial hair—as if he hadn't shaved that morning. Up close, Cohen wasn't just handsome, he looked . . . nice. Normal, even.

He stopped and smiled for a few of the reporters. After a few seconds, he'd reach us. Britta caught hold of his wrist as he made to walk past her to his seat.

"You're crooked." She used the lapel of his suit to pull him down to her level and she tugged the tie back into place. "Better."

Cohen kept his full attention on his older sister as he said, "I met with mother before I came here. She was in a particularly foul mood."

Uri crossed her legs and muttered, "Goddess, when is mother not in a foul mood?"

Britta leaned over Cohen and me and hissed, "Careful with your words, Uri. And uncross your legs, you know what Mrs. Arden would say."

"She's always in a foul mood too."

"Yes." I could hear the slightest hint of an accent in Cohen's voice. It was like the slow drawn way Uri spoke; more noticeable than Britta, Larkin, and Dellacov's accents, but regionally the same. "When I left, she and father were arguing about the draft. And about poor Thomas stepping down. Father wants to put Dellacov in his place, but Mother is against it."

Uri sighed. "I heard one of the maids talking about how he smelled like whisky this morning at breakfast."

"Who?" Britta asked.

Uri glanced to her sister. "You know who."

Cohen nodded. "He was drinking from a flask when we trained earlier. She's terrible to him and he—" Cohen seemed to realize he had an audience. "He's relieved that the Culling is starting. The Synod is too. New, stable leadership is what we need right now."

"Father is a lush," Larkin said, her voice mild. "You can dislike Mother, but at least she's sober during Synod meetings. The same can't be said for Father."

"I suppose that's true." Britta said softly. After a heartbeat of silence, she gestured to me. "Cohen, this is Monroe. She's from Varos."

He looked at me again, his blue eyes softening ever so slightly. He hesitated before offering me his hand. "It's nice to meet you, Monroe."

I took his hand. Before I could say anything else, he pressed a kiss to my knuckles and let go of my hand. For a moment, I just stared at him, breathless. My entire body felt like it was tingling, and I wanted to move, to release this bubbling tension in the pit of my stomach. I wondered what it would feel like to have those lips other places.

Not the time and not the place. Goddess, Monroe. Get your shit together.

His eyes narrowed for an instant and he opened his mouth, like he was going to say something else, but he stopped himself. After a second, he said, "I trust your trip was uneventful."

The swirling warmth in my chest was doused in frigid water.

I wondered if he knew I'd tried to run away. Did he know that I'd been forced to come here? That they had drugged me, hauled me away from my brother, stolen my chance at freedom—and now I sat here, waiting to join a competition that could lead to my death. It was a stupid thing to ask.

Cohen's face warmed and he leaned back in his chair, his mouth a tight line as he fought against an embarrassed smile. "Go on," he said, nodding to me. "I realize now how ridiculous that sounded. Feel free to tell me."

"My trip was far from uneventful," I said, pressing my palms into the folds of my dress. That ink-black mark was why I was here. This wasn't a fairy tale or one of the dog-eared books I'd pored over growing up. I hadn't been brought to this palace so I could meet and marry a prince; I'd been brought here to fight and probably die.

There was no happily ever after in this. Not for me.

Cohen was still looking at me, waiting for me to say something else. I forced a smile, trying to tell myself that it wasn't this boy's fault. My being here wasn't his fault. *But he's the prize. He's what will happen to me if I somehow survive this.*

I said, "It was nice of you to try to make this seem less weird."

"It is incredibly weird, isn't it?"

"Very."

Silence fell between us, but it wasn't as awkward as I'd expected it to be.

Slowly, like ants marching across the kitchen floor, more men and women with cameras began filtering into the room. They crowded toward the front of the chamber, snapping pictures of us and talking to one another.

Guards that I'd barely registered before moved to stand between the waiting press and the dais. Anyone who wanted to say or do anything would have to come through them.

Cohen's knee was bouncing, shaking his chair and mine. He smiled and pointed to the reporter nearest us. "Give them a smile. This'll be on the front page tomorrow."

I did as he asked, turning to look at the same reporter he was. We smiled together and I tried not to visibly cringe as they snapped picture after picture.

"Soften your mouth a little, it's a bit forced—the smile, I mean. Try to relax," Cohen advised, never breaking his own practiced smile. He glanced sideways at me, watching my face as I did as he'd asked. "Just a touch more."

Britta was smiling too, her expression as rehearsed as Cohen's. After a few minutes of smiling and looking around at the different cameras, Cohen lifted a hand and Dellacov moved forward. He walked toward the rows of press, shooing them away.

I leaned over. "Do you have to smile like that all the time?" I asked, trying to keep from being overheard.

"You mean because I'm a prince?" Cohen shrugged. "It's different for everyone, I guess. Smiling just makes me seem more approachable. More like someone the people can trust."

"And are you?"

He made a distracted little sound, his attention on his open pocket watch.

"Approachable," I added. "Are you approachable? Can the people trust you?"

He tucked the small silver timepiece back into his vest pocket and met my eyes. "I think so. But I guess it doesn't matter what I think." He gestured to the rows and rows of growing media. "It matters what they think. And—" Cohen stopped midsentence and raised his brow in question as Dellacov climbed the steps of the dais.

"The last of the Synod has just arrived," Dellacov said quietly. "Synoder Raveena will begin the ceremony shortly."

Cohen nodded and turned to me. "Did Hugo explain the teleprompter?"

"Yes. I'm just supposed to read off the slides."

"There will be things you'll have to fill in, like your full name and your age. You'll also have to say where you're from and your ability. But there are places for you to add that information. It isn't difficult. Don't be nervous."

"They said something about a contract?"

Cohen chewed his bottom lip. "Oh. It's just a promising ceremony. A priestess will perform it. I'm sure you've attended one before. It'll be just like that. We'll say a few words, I give you a gift, and we sign our names to seal it. Easy."

"We're being promised to one another. Like engaged?"

A small smile tugged at his lips. "It's a formality, Miss Benson. Nothing is set in stone until after the Culling. It's just a public way of acknowledging your place in the palace. You'll all hold the position of my fiancé until . . . until the Culling is finished. And then one of you will become my wife. And queen."

So I would be his fiancé until I died. Or won the Culling.

My voice was empty as I said, "You'll be engaged to all ten of us then."

"For now, yes."

I watched as the Speaker of the Synod climbed the steps of the dais carrying a large candelabrum with ten black candles. The metal was some sort of polished bronze, with thick chains that seemed to encircle each candle, as if tying them in place. He set it down on the table to our right and turned to look at the blue-robed priestess following at his heels.

Just as he opened his mouth to speak to the gathered crowd, Cohen leaned over and whispered in my ear. "Are you certain about this?"

I turned to look at him, surprised. "Is it a choice?"

"No. I guess it isn't. I just thought I'd ask. I've asked all the other girls."

"And what have they said?" I dared a glance up at him, watched his face change from indifferent to almost sad.

"There were a couple of girls who were excited to have the opportunity to compete for the crown."

"And the rest?" I prodded.

"The rest . . . the rest of them were scared."

"Good to know I'm not alone."

10

Synod Chamber

Sacrit

"Welcome, brothers, royals, priestesses, and press." Synoder Raveena's voice echoed over the high ceilings of the chamber, bringing the room to silence. "Today marks the arrival of the last of the goddess-touched girls and the beginning of a new Culling. Before winter solstice, we will have a new queen."

There was a spattering of applause, mostly from the reporters standing against the far walls. He cleared his throat loudly, indicating the need for silence, and gestured to the candelabrum on the table next to him. "At this time, we will light the nine candles—one for each of the previously announced girls. The final candle will be lit after today's ceremony. At that point, all ten will remain burning until the Culling has drawn to a close. High Priestess Dreher, if you would do the honors."

The priestess walked forward with a long match. I felt the flame spark and then ignite as she scraped it across the striking paper. The hiss of that fire seemed to engulf my senses as the Synoder began to read from the projector at the back of the room.

"Aviana Blair, Tengaar County, gifted with cloaking. Elodie Ketar, Messani County, gifted with mind reading. Joslyn Griffin, Sikari County, gifted with water. Kinsley Raveena, Gazda County, gifted with foliage. Tessa Kent, Pallae County, gifted with air. Grier Jennis, Fajvurrow County, gifted with voice control. Nadia Reese, Batya County, gifted with healing. Vivian

Wade, Nartuk County, gifted with premonition. And lastly, Heidi Larson, Nolajan County, gifted with terror incitement."

As he read off each name, home county, and goddess-given ability, the priestess lit one of the tall black candles. I tried to focus on the words, but the sudden urge to throw up was all-encompassing. This was real. It was happening.

I hadn't cried yet. Not about any of this. But suddenly, it took every ounce of my self-control not to cry in front of a room full of strangers.

Reality snapped back into vivid clarity as Cohen stood up and turned to me. For a moment, I only stared up at him, unsure what was happening. Then he offered me his hand. "It's our turn."

His fingers were warm in mine as he led me over to the table. The Synoder had stepped away, leaving only the priestess and the burning candles. A tall chalice of water steamed from where she'd doused the match. Cohen left me on one side of the small table while he crossed to the other, leaving the priestess to stand between us.

"Interregna Benson," she said, bowing her head in greeting. "Prince Cohen." The nine flames on the candelabrum flickered as the priestess focused her full attention on me. Her wrinkled skin was nearly translucent, the blue of her eyes clouded with age. "Welcome to the Culling."

She turned from me and back to Cohen. He cleared his throat and took half a step forward, garnering the attention of everyone watching. He'd clearly done this enough times that he no longer relied on the projector to get the words right.

"Today you are witness to the initial joining of two souls. The documents signed today, and the gifts bestowed, are representative of a promise between Monroe Benson and myself. Should she win the Culling, we will marry and rule together. These documents are binding and will be witnessed by each of you, as well as a high priestess. Like any temple-blessed engagement, this promise will be legally binding and can only be dissolved through death. On behalf of my mother, Queen Viera, and my father, King Malcolm, I would like to thank each and every one of you for your loyalty and faithfulness during this next season. While we do not yet know who our next queen will be, I am confident that the goddess has sent ten equally worthy candidates."

As he finished speaking, the priestess placed a cold hand on my elbow and ushered me forward a step. The microphone was positioned between where Cohen and I stood, and the woman gestured to it before she retreated behind the table again. My breathing turned quick as I scanned the gathered crowd before my eyes found the flickering screen of the projector.

Cohen moved a little closer to me, drawing my attention back to him. The smile he gave me was soft and silently encouraging. Seconds felt like minutes, and I felt tied to him, clinging for dear life to the slight sign of compassion written on his face.

I forced myself to look back at the crowd.

My vision swam, black with sharp dots of white, the flashes of cameras.

The rustle of other people's clothes.

Whispers.

The faint sound of radio static.

A cough in the back of the room.

Focus. Focus, Monroe.

Dellacov stood by the back door, his eyebrows raised in a silent question. He met my eyes and inclined his head toward the bright projected screen a few feet away from him. I took a deep breath and nodded.

It's just reading. I can read.

"My name—" I had to stop, to clear my throat.

I would've paid good money for a glass of water. Someone started snickering. I tried again.

"My name is Monroe Avery Benson. I am from Varos County, Erydia, and I am seventeen years old. It is my honor, given to me directly from the goddess and indisputable by any man, to participate in the Culling. I swear upon my life, and that of my family, that I am genuinely goddess-touched. I present not only a mark but I also possess the gift of . . ."

Admitting that I could control fire felt like breaking a promise to my mother. It felt like a betrayal of who I'd always been. Or maybe, it was a revelation of who I'd always been.

My eyes landed on Dellacov again. Discreetly, he held a hand out and slowly lowered it, palm down. He seemed to say, *Take a deep breath. Slow down.*

"I present not only a mark," I said again, my voice stronger this time, my cadence slower, "but I also possess the gift of fire." The crowd began to murmur and whisper, but I continued to read the script. "The Erydian throne is my birthright, and, for that inheritance, I will fight in the Culling. If I emerge triumphant, I will gratefully accept the crown and all that such a position demands. I also fully accept my engagement to Prince Cohen Warwick. I acknowledge that in winning the Culling, I will be elevating my family and myself into a position of power. A position for which I am prepared."

I swallowed and took a deep breath, trying to get my hands to stop shaking. My mouth was so dry I wasn't sure I could even manage another sentence. Everyone was looking at me, microphones held high, cameras *click click clicking* away at me. I could feel Cohen's heavy gaze on my back. I could hear the queen's words replaying in my mind over and over again.

Pity she didn't die in Varos.

I looked at the last remaining slide, then out into the sea of people before me. Then I said the phrase I'd spent my entire life hating: "May the goddess be honored through my sacrifice and may she bless our next queen."

The crowd seemed to speak as one. "Goddess be honored."

Everything that came after that seemed like a blur. I'd never imagined getting engaged, and I knew very little about what a temple-blessed engagement entailed. From what I'd read in books and talked about with Ambrose, they were expensive since it usually was a family event and required a private session with a priestess. There was usually some sort of gift given from promised groom to promised bride and a feast to celebrate the future of their joining.

Even though price clearly wasn't an issue for Cohen, our engagement was quick and to the point. Everything that needed to be said had already been announced. I was goddess-touched and he was the male heir. All of this just acted as an official documentation of our intention to marry should I win the competition.

It wasn't like most engagements, which were a celebration of love and two people becoming one entity. It was sterile and quick. I was still reeling from having just spoken in front of so many people when Cohen took my hand and slipped a thin gold band onto my left ring finger.

His voice was soft, almost too quiet for the microphone to pick up as he said to me, "Wear this as a symbol of my faithfulness to you, my trust in you, and my gratitude for your sacrifice. Let it remind you of your purpose as you compete in the Culling. May the goddess guide you and protect you. And, if it is her will, may she make you queen."

People applauded as he finished speaking, but there wasn't time for me to digest all that was happening—because then a pen was being placed in my hand and I was guided back to the table. The Synoder Raveena tapped a bony finger against the two dozen stacks of paper, pointing to each line that required my name or initial.

I started to read the contracts laid in front of me, but he stopped me. "We are on a schedule, Interregna. There is nothing written here that you don't already know."

Cohen spoke from beside me. "I can have a copy of it sent to your rooms later, if you want."

But I will have already signed it.

I straightened and looked at the prince. "Is there anything in here about a stipend for my family?"

He nodded. "Your family will receive double the average monthly wage for the duration of your time here."

"Do you promise?"

"Yes, of course."

I signed the papers. I told myself that there was some choice in it, but I knew that with every pen stroke, I was distancing myself from the girl I'd been only days before. And none of this was what I wanted. The ring on my finger fit just fine, but it was heavy on my hand and I noticed the way it caught the light of the candelabrum and the chandelier above our heads.

That tightness in my chest swelled as I wrote the last signature and stepped away from the table. It felt like I'd signed my death warrant. As if the tiny ring on my finger was somehow a cage that was keeping me here—trapped in this place until the day I died. Whether that day would come sooner or later would be entirely my choice. That was, perhaps, my only choice in all of this.

"We'll take one last photograph for the papers and then we're done here," Cohen said. His hand found my arm and then drifted down until it was nestled into the space between my waist and my hip. Even though I could tell he was being careful with the forcefulness of his touch, the weight of his hand on me was like a brand.

The king had said there would be heirs. Children. That if I won, Cohen would be a good father. That would require me to . . . to . . . I was going to be sick.

My ability pressed insistent against the inside of my skin, and I wanted to let it out. I wanted to burn and fester and turn myself to ash. The world was spinning around me and no matter how hard I dug my nails in, I couldn't get a good enough grip to pull it to a stop. I needed a moment—*Just one moment to breathe.*

"Just a moment or two more," Cohen muttered, his face schooled into the same easy smile he'd had earlier. "And then it's over." His fingers flexed against the curve of my hip.

I felt the tug of flame on a match as the priestess made to the light the last candle. My candle.

The irony of it all wasn't lost on me. There would be a flame lit in my name until the day I died. And then, that would be it. When the fire in me was gone, taken away from me in an arena, some random priestess would douse that flame and I would be forgotten. I'd be smoke in the wind.

I inhaled a sharp breath, trying and failing to steady myself. In my peripheral, I saw the priestess step back from the table with a sudden jerk. The crowd gasped and I turned, just in time to see the match drop to the floor.

The nine candles of the candelabrum had gone out seemingly on their own. Now only the tenth candle—*my candle*—burned. Cohen's hand dropped from my waist as he realized what I'd done. Everyone was whispering and staring—and I didn't understand how I'd done it. I hadn't meant to. I'd just been thinking about it all and then . . .

Synoder Raveena dug the toe of his polished shoe into the match on the floor, dousing any last heat—but he wasn't looking at it or at my lone candle. He was watching me—utterly aghast. I lifted my chin and forced a smile.

When I spoke again, my voice was strong enough that I didn't need the microphone. "May the goddess be honored."

11

Synod Antechamber

Sacrit

After my engagement to Cohen, I was escorted into a small antechamber. The press was excited. With my arrival came the official start of the Culling and everyone had a thought or opinion. As Dellacov walked me away from my still-burning candle and the stunned priestess, reporters called out seemingly unimportant questions:

"Did you cut your hair?"

"Any idea who you'll choose as your Culling advisor?"

"Tell us more about your ability!"

"What did you mean when you extinguished the other nine candles?"

Dellacov bent his head close to my ear. "Say nothing."

Once we were in the antechamber and the door was shut behind us, he led me over to an empty armchair and gestured for me to sit. The room was small, little more than a dark parlor or corridor. There were only two chairs and a table holding an electric lamp. Dellacov took the chair adjacent to mine.

"Miss Benson—"

"You can call me Monroe."

He blinked in surprise. "Okay. *Monroe*, the next few days will be packed with information. You will meet with your trainers tomorrow. They'll walk you through how trial participation will be decided and when the trials will take place. You'll train with them a minimum of three times a week, unless otherwise stated. You are permitted to train as often as you would like, but you are required to always be accompanied whenever you leave your room. You are not allowed to approach the press or answer questions without express permission. You will not speak to the king or queen without first being spoken to. You are not to seek them out. At no time should you use your ability outside of the Culling trials or outside of the designated training rooms. You will be expected to attend etiquette lessons at Mrs. Arden's discretion. The last three girls in the competition will each undergo an exam by the royal physician to assess your general health and fertility. Do you have any questions concerning any of that?"

He spoke so quickly that I had questions about every bit of it. I'd already been forming a long list of questions, but his flippant use of the word *fertility* had me derailed. I ran my thumb over the underside of the ring that Cohen had placed on my finger. I wanted to take it off.

Dellacov continued speaking. "We don't expect you to remember all of this information; after all, etiquette and rules are not your main focus. Your chosen advisor and your two trainers will be here to assist you should you need anything. They will form your court, but I am also at your disposal. My office is the room we stopped by on our way here. It isn't far from where the goddess-touched girls will be staying. I can be easily summoned should the need arise. However, I feel confident that Tallis and Juno are more than equipped to help you with anything you may need."

I swallowed down the millions of other questions bubbling toward my lips and asked the most important one. "When will the first trial pairing be announced?"

"Three days from now, on Sanctus Halletta, at the Commencement Ball. The trial will take place exactly two weeks from then."

I opened my mouth to ask another question but stopped as I heard a knock at the door. Dellacov stood up just as Cohen stepped into the antechamber. He ran a hand through his hair, mussing the dirty-blond waves, and sighed. "Well, that went well enough. You've got everyone talking with that little candle stunt. Uri was nearly dancing with excitement. She loves a rule breaker."

Dellacov sighed. "I was just giving Miss Benson—Monroe—the rundown of the bigger rules and Culling procedures."

The corner of Cohen's mouth twitched up, and it was almost a better smile than the one he'd given the cameras. It was boyish and completely at ease. "Yeah, Hugo does love a good rule book. He's been studying up on all this for months. Has he told you all the rules concerning me?"

I shook my head.

"We hadn't gotten there yet," he said.

Cohen nodded to the Synod Chamber behind him. "Well, why not break a few of them right away and let me escort Miss Benson to the garden for brunch? You've been summoned by the queen."

"Summoned?" Dellacov asked, worry furrowing his brow.

"She and Father must have come to a decision about Thomas's replacement. You might be in line for some congratulations, if my suspicions are correct and she plans to promote you to full Captain."

Dellacov started to argue, but Cohen only pulled out his pocket watch and flipped it open.

"My sisters have already headed to the garden. At this rate, there isn't even time for Miss Benson to freshen up. I'll deliver her straight there. I can explain some of the other Culling rules as we walk. I may not be able to quote the rule book like you can, Hugo, but I can convey the general idea." He turned to me, his brows raised in question, "Shall we?"

"Cohen—"

The timepiece in his hand snapped shut. "It'll be entirely boring, Hugo. Nothing to write home about. It's a walk, in broad daylight. And we're engaged now, so even the temple would say we don't need a chaperone."

"The Culling rules would state otherwise."

"If you don't tell my mother, I won't. I, for one, don't think Miss Benson is the sort to snitch." He held out a hand to me. "Let's go before you're unfashionably late."

I made to stand up, but Dellacov lifted a hand to stop me. "I don't want you stirring up trouble, Cohen."

"Making my mother wait on you a second longer than she wants to will cause far more trouble than our walk to the garden. Besides . . ." Cohen stepped forward and again offered me his hand. I took it and let him pull me to my feet. "I won't walk her all the way; I'll just set her on the right path."

Dellacov didn't argue after that. He left through the door we'd entered by, while Cohen and I went through a side door that took us down two flights of stairs and out onto a sunlit corridor. We didn't touch or talk during the entire walk. To my surprise, the silence between us wasn't uncomfortable or heavy, it just existed.

Cohen seemed to be just as deep in thought as I was. He worried his bottom lip between his teeth, a nervous action he stopped anytime he saw me noticing it.

I cleared my throat. "Did you say you were going to tell me more about the rules?"

That slight smile returned, pulling his features from thoughtful to teasing in a split second. "Do you want me to tell you more rules?"

"I want to know everything I can."

"Rule number one is that we aren't supposed to be alone together. You can check that off your list as one you've broken."

"What is rule number two?"

"We aren't supposed to touch or kiss or . . . or do anything else. According to the temple, that ring means we're spiritually joined, but the physical joining is supposed to wait."

My face flushed with the implication of what his "anything else" meant. I looked down at the gold band on my finger. I hadn't really looked at it before. It was pretty, just the thinnest line of gold crowned with three tiny bluish white stones.

Cohen cleared his throat, suddenly turning sheepish. "Opals. That's the type of stone. I gave each of you a different stone or I tried to. Uri reads the gossip magazines and stones correlating with birth months are all the rage. Opal was yours, I thought. But then Dellacov said your travel waiver and identification cards were both completely fake so maybe that's wrong . . . ?"

"I was born the second month of autumn on the sixteenth day."

He smiled. "The day was wrong then, but the month was right."

"What did the card say?"

"Well, for starters, it said you were a boy."

An odd warmth filled my chest at the teasing in his voice. "What did it say about the day?"

"I think it had the fourth. I just knew I needed something with opals in it. My father suggested I give each of you the same ring—that's what he did for his Culling—but I thought that was weird. A little impersonal. When Uri suggested the stones, I thought it might help make it a little more . . . human. You'd each get a ring, but it would be your *own* ring."

I looked down at the ring again. "I've never seen my birthstone before. I always thought that it would be the same shade of blue Pallae glass but . . . it isn't even similar now that I can see it in person."

We both fell silent again.

After a moment, he said, "I can't imagine this is easy for you. It's . . . It's probably scary. How are you doing?" I tripped on my own feet, and he caught my elbow to steady me. Cohen looked as flustered as I felt. "I'm sorry. I didn't mean to— Whatever I did, I didn't mean to."

I pulled away from him, putting distance between us again. "It's just . . ." *No one had asked. No one had cared at all about how I was.* Looking at this boy, with his sun-kissed skin and freckled nose and bright blue eyes—goddess, he was handsome and everything I thought a prince would be. But I had no idea if he could be trusted with my truth. Any slight shadow of vulnerability seemed too much to risk.

But something in me seemed to ease. I wasn't sure if it was his resemblance to Uri or his strange kindness, but I felt like I knew him. This interaction between us felt old. Ancient and familiar. And dangerous.

"It's just, *what*?" he asked. "I— I'm not a contestant in the Culling, Miss Benson. I'm not out to get you. We aren't enemies. In fact, we're the opposite. We're bound to be married and that isn't something I take lightly. Anything . . . *Anything* you say to me stays between us. That's a promise.

And one I've given to all the girls. I intend to have a friendship with my future bride. Plus, I'm not a fan of lies. Not when they can be avoided."

Silence lingered between us, heavy and thick as smoke.

My throat constricted as I whispered, "I'm homesick. And I think . . ."

He stopped walking and I stopped too. "I'm listening."

But I was in a palace full of strangers. Even with Cohen's promise—which I believed was genuine—there was no telling who else could hear me. "I think I can make it to the garden on my own. It's . . . It's just through those gates up ahead, isn't it?"

I could already hear string instruments playing and the soft hum of conversation. For a long moment, Cohen said nothing and then he nodded. He took a step back from me and bowed at the waist. "Very well then." He turned on his heel and headed back the way we'd come. He'd almost turned the corner when I called after him.

"Prince Cohen?"

He turned at the sound of my voice.

"Thank you for walking with me," I said. "And for asking about me."

"I'll see you later, Miss Benson."

12

The West Garden

Sacrit, three days before Sanctus Halletta

I followed the music, strolling past groves of lemon trees and the outer wall of a hedge maze. The sounds of the gathering were muffled by the greenery, but the tone was light, the murmur of conversation punctuated only by the tinkle of glass and the scraping of chairs on stone.

I'd just passed a second arch of greenery when someone called my name. I turned around to find Uri leaning over a balcony railing, two floors up. She waved. "Wait and I'll walk with you."

The princess disappeared from the railing, and I settled against a stone pillar to wait for her to come downstairs. My attention was on the tiny silk bows on the straps of my shoes when I heard a soft *thump*. A familiar high-heeled shoe skidded across the cobblestone path in front of me, followed closely by its twin. I looked to the second floor in time to see Uri hitch up her dress and swing her leg over the edge of the balcony.

I opened my mouth to yell something—anything—but stopped as she hissed, "Relax. I do this all the time."

Using window ledges, overhanging branches, and large trellises, Uri scaled the wall down into the garden. She grinned wickedly as she jumped down the last two feet, her hands dramatically flung into the air, as if she were an acrobat finishing a particularly challenging flip. She winked at me as she walked to her discarded shoes.

"Close your mouth, Monroe. You look like a dying fish," Uri said as she tugged on her heels and straightened her dress into place. "Damn," she said, examining a spot just above her knee where her tan stockings had torn.

"So, you . . . you do that a lot?"

"What, climb the walls? Weekly, if not daily." The princess looped her arm through mine. "Cohen and Dellacov taught me. That's the southern corridor and there are rarely any guards there." She tugged me farther down the path, toward the swelling music and quiet chatter. "Come on or we'll be later than we already are."

"I didn't realize that princesses—"

"Were so unrefined? Oh, they aren't. It's just me. Larkin is a stick-in-the-mud, and Britta would never be caught dead climbing—"

"I was going to say, that I didn't realize princesses could be so normal."

"Oh, Monroe, if you think that's normal, we're going to get along just fine."

Uri and I rounded the final curve of the garden and emerged into a large courtyard. Tables and chairs had been arranged in a semicircle around the base of a massive water fountain. The carved statue in the middle was of a past goddess-touched queen, water sprouting from her outstretched hand. The sight of it had me scrambling to remember the name of the girl they'd said had an ability like that.

Tessa or Joslyn. Heidi? Something that starts with a V? Goddess, there are too many names to keep up with. And it wasn't like I was really paying all that much attention to the list at the time. I'd been getting engaged to a damn prince I didn't even know and . . .

Whatever conversation had been occurring before my arrival died out as at least a dozen pairs of eyes swiveled my way. The heat soared to new heights, pushing at the cage of my chest. That dark thing inside of me seemed to gnaw at the bones that held it securely in place.

Uri grinned at the attention.

"Monroe, Princess Uriel. Welcome!" Britta smiled from her table across the small courtyard from us and patted the empty chair next to her. Without a word, Uri made a beeline for the other princess, dragging me along with her.

The goddess-touched girls remained silent as we arrived at the edge of Britta's table.

With a flourish, Uri pulled out the lone empty seat and gestured for me to take it. I started to protest, but she said, "You sit here." She guided me into the chair with a firm hand on my shoulder. "Britta can make the necessary introductions. I'm going to hunt for pie. I heard Cook made something with meringue. I'll bring us both back a piece and we can gossip."

"Uriel," Britta scolded, her voice little more than a whisper. "You could at least try to disguise how terrible you are."

But Uri was already gone, her steps light as she headed for the dessert table. I straightened in my chair and glanced to the two girls sitting with me.

They both looked to Britta. The princess stood, lifting a flute of champagne with her. "Ladies," she said, letting her voice carry over the soft orchestra music playing in the background. "This is Monroe Benson. She is the last of the goddess-touched girls to arrive. I trust you will all give her a warm welcome." She paused and then looked to me, gesturing to the circle of girls. "Monroe, this is the rest of your Culling pool. I'm sure they can each introduce themselves as necessary."

A few girls nodded in response, but no one approached the table.

Britta leaned toward me. "How are you holding up?"

The lie was easy this time. "I'm doing great. I'm excited to be here. It's an honor."

The goddess-touched girl next to me was picking at her fingernails, her attention still clearly on me. The other, a slender strawberry blond with eyes the color of juniper leaves, blatantly stared at my mark. She was pretty, but younger than the rest of us, maybe in her early teens. I buried my mark in the skirt of my dress.

"Do you mind?" Britta said, nodding to my hand. I froze, expecting her to ask about my gift, but instead she said, "I've enjoyed seeing the pieces

Cohen has picked for each of you. It's wild to think that my baby brother is old enough to be marrying anyone."

I lifted my left hand, and she took it, carefully rotating my fingers so that she could see the gold band and the opals gleaming there. "It's pretty." *It's beautiful. And terrible.* "You're an autumn baby. How old will you be next?"

"I'll be eighteen." *If I make it until then.*

She let go of my hand. "This must be quite a change for you—all of you—having to come here, to a strange city so far from your home," Britta said.

What is there to say to that? Yes, you're right. It is a change. Yes, it's something I had to do. It wasn't my choice. This ring, no matter how pretty and shiny, isn't my choice.

Uri returned and dropped a plate piled with five pieces of various pies on the table and then reached for an empty chair nearby. A guard stepped forward to help, but she shooed him away and hauled the chair over herself.

"Uriel Warwick," Britta said as her sister plopped down in the chair next to mine. "Please tell me you don't plan to eat all of that by yourself."

The younger girl only offered me a fork in answer. I took it and watched, amused, as she stabbed at a chunk of crust. "It is exactly *none* of your business how much pie I plan to eat, sister." Uri lifted a forkful of lemon meringue to her mouth and mused, "Anyway, this would be a lot more fun if we could talk about what we all *want* to talk about."

"Which is?" Britta asked.

She finished chewing and used her fork to gesture around the courtyard. "All they care about is seeing what each other can do. Or, well, I'm assuming that's all you care about. If I had to fight to the death, I'd be itching to know more about my competition. A boring old list can only tell you so much. Personally, I would want to know how I might die."

Britta pursed her lips. "Don't be crass."

Uri only stabbed at her pie again. "But it's true. That's what they're here to do. Who can blame them for wanting to know what they're up against?"

Britta shook her head and spoke to me. "I apologize for my sister."

"Don't apologize for me, Britta. Monroe likes me. We're friends."

Before I could register what she'd just said, Britta was talking to me again. "Hugo probably already told you this, but you aren't permitted to use your ability outside of the training rooms and the arena. The consequences for doing so would be harsh."

Uri rolled her eyes and spoke through a mouthful of chocolate cream. "I don't know who makes these stupid rules—"

"I'm not sure either," Britta responded curtly. "Someone far older and wiser than us."

"Someone dead, probably," Uri muttered.

"Regardless, I'm sure you'll be the first to break them."

Uri snorted. "Well, someone's got to."

"No, no they don't *have to* do anyth—"

"Agree to disagree."

The eldest princess let out a long-suffering sigh. "Goddess save us."

There was a long silence during which Uri ate the rest of the first piece of pie. She prodded at the next dessert, this one bright with congealed strawberries and what appeared to be crushed pecans. She frowned and glanced across the table to the strawberry blond. "You know, Heidi, if you keep staring like that, your eyes may just shrivel up in the sun."

Heidi turned her attention from me to Uri. It was a heavy sort of stare. It made me want to move, to get as far away as possible. Uri didn't even flinch at the attention, only took another bite of her pie.

I half expected Britta to scold her sister yet again, but she only shook her head and called for a second glass of champagne.

Heidi said, "I was just admiring Monroe's hair. It's an unusual choice—cutting it. She'll stand out in the competition, that's for sure."

My chest burned and I dug my fingernails into my palms to keep from reaching up to touch the wayward curls. Her tone was all innocent curiosity, but I knew what she was implying.

Erydian girls kept their hair long, the style indicative of their purity and, subsequently, their worth. Our magistrates and priestesses often punished women by cutting their hair.

"I quite like Monroe's hair," Uri said. "I was thinking of cutting mine to match."

Britta nearly choked on her drink.

Uri slid the plate of half-eaten pie toward me and looked to the other marked girl at our table. "Aviana, don't you think I'd look splendid with my hair short? I have just the cheekbones for it."

Aviana's eyes darted up from her nails. She blushed and muttered, "Yes, of course. You'd look great."

Uri twirled a piece of long dark hair around her finger. "Thank you. I know I would."

"How modest of you," Britta muttered against the rim of her glass.

"Monroe and I could start a trend. Couldn't we?" Uri turned to me, expectant.

"Definitely."

"*Definitely*," she repeated. "And I already pin it up most of the time. Having it cut would save my ladies time in the mornings. They could use their time in other ways and I could sleep in."

Heidi pushed herself away from the table. "It was lovely to meet you, Monroe."

Our table fell silent as Heidi walked off. Uri leaned over and whispered to me, "You could take her. Her ability is being scary or something lame like that. I don't know. *Anyway*, the most horrendous thing about her, as far as I can tell, is her bad attitude."

Britta looked ready to burst. "Uriel, for the love of all that is good and holy in our world, would you please just—"

"See, even Britta can't disagree." Uri pushed the plate of pie toward me. "Eat up."

At her insistence, I took a bite of pie and did my best not to smile as Britta said, "People can say what they want about you, Uri, but you sure know how to keep a party interesting."

"Oh," she said, crossing her legs. "I wouldn't have it any other way."

Palace Bedroom
Two days before Sanctus Halletta

I didn't like my palace bedroom.

There was so much open space here—several feet separated the bed and the vanity, the dresser from the main door, the bathing room from the walk-in closet. It was elegantly decorated, with pale-lilac-colored bedding and goose-feather pillows. The furniture was all a soft cream color and the rug covering the dark hardwood floor was plush. There was a fireplace with two comfy-looking armchairs facing it. If the circumstances of my being here were different, it would be the sort of place where I might curl up to read a book or take a nap.

But there was no warmth to the room—it was all empty walls and bare surfaces. Nothing in the room indicated that anyone had slept here in ages. Maybe it was the sort of room they reserved just for the Culling. If that were the case, then it was likely the last person to sleep in my bed was very dead. Goody.

Who needed so much space? And why was the bed so large and cold and . . . lonely?

Since the moment I'd been born, I'd shared a bed with my mother. There was something soothing about having another heartbeat so close. The silence where her rhythmic breathing should've been was palpable.

That first night was the worst. It felt like a million tiny needles were being stabbed into my chest. Each inhale was harder than the last, and I knew that if I stayed lying in that darkness, I would cry. The backs of my eyes burned and fear coated my tongue in ash.

Before I'd been dropped off here by a palace guard, Uri had given me a little printed card with a list of all the goddess-touched girls' names and their abilities. I'd spent most of the night drowning beneath the weighty covers, trying to memorize those names.

Aviana Blair – Cloaking
Elodie Ketar – Mind Reading

Joslyn Griffin – Water

Kinsley Raveena – Foliage

Vivian Wade – Premonition

Tessa Kent – Air

Grier Jennis – Voice Control

Nadia Reese – Healing

Heidi Larson – Terror Incitement

In swirling ink at the bottom of the card, Uri had written *Monroe Benson – Fire*.

Heidi had been at brunch, but I didn't quite understand what her ability was. Some of them were a little more abstract than mine. Like Nadia's, which was listed as healing. What did that mean? Same thing for Aviana. What was cloaking?

I read the names repeatedly until I couldn't bear to look at them anymore—until they were a quiet, meaningless chant in the back of my mind. At some point in the night, I gave up on sleep and took up residence in the deep, cushioned window seat opposite the bed.

As the morning dawned, I still sat there and watched as long fingers of sunlight threaded between the buildings of Gazda. I must have finally dozed off at some point because I was jarred awake by a loud knock at my bedroom door. Before the sleep could dissipate enough for me to make sense of the world around me, a man and woman were already making their way into the room.

The woman spoke first. "Good morning, Monroe."

She was petite with light-brown skin and black hair that she had pulled into a slick braid. Loose strands of it curled slightly around her ears, softening the sharp cut of her jaw and the smoke-gray powder she wore around her eyes. The makeup looked more like war paint than the feminine gloss I'd seen the other girls wearing.

I liked it.

The man set a tray piled with what appeared to be breakfast down on the dresser by the door and rubbed his hands together. It was a nervous gesture, like he was looking for something to do. Wiping damp palms on my lacy nightgown, I turned to face them.

My throat was so tight it ached as I said, "Good morning."

"I'm Juno." After a long moment, he walked over and offered me his hand to shake. "I'm one of your trainers." I took his hand in mine, but our hands barely clasped before he was pulling away from me. I followed his gaze to my mark.

I instinctively closed my hand. "I have control of it."

The girl, who I knew must be Tallis, set a glass of orange juice next to the tray of food and turned to look at me. She held a folder against her chest, almost like a shield. Something about her stance didn't make her seem afraid though. Instead, she seemed like she was bolstering herself, preparing for some unseen battle.

Tallis and Juno exchanged glances, and she grimaced. "Are you going to start, or am I?"

He gestured her forward. "Oh, by all means."

She sat on the edge of the bed, facing me. "Okay, so, I'm Tallis Elliot and this is Juno Heist. We're your trainers for the duration of the Culling." She opened the file on her lap and flipped through a few pages. "Your ability is fire, correct?"

I nodded.

"And you're from Varos County?"

"Yes."

"Perfect." She looked up at me and grinned; it made the harsh lines of her face soften. "Okay," she continued, "so I think we should start with introductions." Her eyes darted sideways. "Juno . . . ?"

Juno crossed his arms over his broad chest and said, "Like she said, I'm Juno Heist. I'm twenty-five and I come from a little town called Minden. That's in Sikari County. I joined the military about six years ago and have been training for Culling placement for the last three years." There was a long pause and he looked at Tallis.

"That's it?" she said, her tone teasing. "No interesting hobbies?"

He rolled his eyes but conceded. "I . . ." He scratched at the back of his neck. "I have four younger sisters."

Tallis set the folder down and stood up, grinning like she'd just won a prize. "My turn!" She clapped her hands together. "All right, so as I said earlier, I'm Tallis Elliot. I'm from Dakolt—you've probably never heard of it; don't feel bad, no one ever has. My mother died when I was a kid and my father is an overseer for one of the bigger mines on the north side. I'm an only child. I thought the idea of working in a dark mine sounded like hell and marriage didn't sound much better, so I applied to advise in the Culling. I tested well so now I'm here." She glanced sideways at Juno. "Fun fact: Juno isn't nearly as much of a hard-ass as he'd like you to think he is."

He frowned. "That isn't fair. I didn't give a fun fact about you. I gave one about myself."

"Missed opportunity," Tallis said. "Now Monroe knows two fun facts about you."

Juno sighed and turned to look at me. I wondered what he must think. *She's a waste of time here . . .*

Tallis reached into her folder and produced a little card like the one Uri had given me the day before. "This is a list of all the other goddess-touched girls and their abilities. You probably saw some of them yesterday in passing, but over the course of the next few weeks, you'll have plenty of time to get to know them more closely. I would suggest we focus on the biggest threats— which for you would be water, air, and probably foliage."

"And terror incitement," Juno added. "Heidi is young, but her ability could be detrimental if not taken seriously."

My hand tightened around the card as I tried to match the names to abilities without looking. So, Joslyn with water, Tessa with air, Heidi with terror incitement, and—

"Why Kinsley?" Both of my trainers seemed surprised by the question. "Foliage doesn't sound like something I would struggle with. I mean, I don't know how it works, but couldn't I just burn through whatever she makes? It's just plants, right?"

Tallis nodded. "True. But Kinsley won't be a threat just because of her gift, at least not all on its own. She's a threat because she's the most trained. Her father is the Speaker of the Synod. She was raised in the palace and has had access to the training rooms for most of her life. She'll be a threat because she knows the etiquette and the rules better than any of the rest of you."

"I don't think for one second that she'd win in a trial against you," Juno said. "Your ability is more destructive and, if we can make sure you have a good handle on it, it'll knock her out quickly. She'll be one to watch outside of trials though."

"How developed is your ability?" Tallis asked.

I shrugged. "I can light candles and fireplaces . . ."

"Can you create fire from long distances?" Juno asked.

I hesitated. "No."

Tallis jotted something down in the folder. "We'll need to work on that. What can you do?"

"I can throw it."

Her eyes darted up to me. "Throw it?"

"Yeah. Not super far, but my older brother would sometimes have me practice with it. I also know a little bit of hand-to-hand fighting. Just basic self-defense stuff."

"That'll come in handy," Tallis said. "We'll be focusing on that too. The trials are sometimes just as much body against body as they are ability against ability. You need to be strong and knowledgeable. And fast. We'll help you with all of that."

"We've devised a training regime for you. You'll meet with one or both of us at least six times a week, with the odd day being used for either trials or full-day etiquette lessons."

"Or to rest," Tallis added.

Juno leaned across her and grabbed another piece of paper. He handed to me. "That's your schedule. Someone will be here to escort you to the training rooms every morning at seven. We'll work for three hours and then you'll come back here to change clothes. Breakfast will be held in the royal dining room at ten most every morning, but you can choose to take meals in your room if that's preferable. Our scheduled afternoon time in the training room is from three to six. The first days of the week are yours to do with as you want, since that's when the trials will be. We don't like to schedule things on top of those. The same goes for weeks without trials: you are free to spend your time as you'd like—just be mindful of where you are and how you interact with the other girls.

"But you must be escorted at all times. If we can't go with you, request a guard."

Tallis said, "Dinner is always served in the royal dining room unless otherwise noted. It'll start at seven thirty. Curfew is nine o'clock. After that, you are to be in your room with the door locked until one of us comes to fetch you the next morning. If you have any questions, it's all laid out in black and white there."

One glance at the piece of paper they'd given me and I knew there was no way it would answer all of my questions.

Juno cleared his throat. "Let's start with the hand-to-hand. How much experience do you have?"

I opened my mouth, but hesitated.

When I was fourteen years old, Ambrose had started to teach me to defend myself. Varos was large, full of empty landscape and close enough to the Vayelle border that it held a lot of dangers. With the rainy season, the flash floods, and the winter stretch, it wasn't uncommon for strangers to wander onto our homestead. They came looking for help, for a place to stay, but their intentions weren't always so savory.

Once, when my brothers were off hunting and my mother was with a patient, I'd stumbled upon an Erydian soldier in our chicken coop. He had been half dead and soaked to the skin. I hadn't known what to do or how to protect myself—not that I needed protecting from him.

I'd never been taught to use a gun, but I could have figured it out if I'd needed to. Kace wouldn't have hesitated; even Ambrose, who was one of the most compassionate people I knew, would have dealt with him swiftly. But I couldn't do it.

So, I'd helped the soldier into the house. I'd put him in my cot by the hearth and I'd waited for someone to come home.

Ambrose had been furious when he'd found me sitting by the door, unarmed and alone with an unconscious stranger. A stranger he'd insisted could have killed me. A stranger who could tell others about me—a young girl living in a house where there were only boys registered. What if he'd seen my mark?

If my mother hadn't arrived, Ambrose probably would have shot the boy himself.

Mama had made sure he got back to his unit. After that, Ambrose decided it was time for me to learn to protect myself. If I wouldn't use the gun and I didn't want to kill someone, then I would at least learn to disarm. At the end of the day, if my back was to the wall, I could use my ability to protect myself.

But clumsy kicks and jabs and twists wouldn't be enough in the Culling. And although I'd said I knew some things, Juno would probably be disappointed if he knew just how little I could do.

As if she sensed my thoughts, Tallis said, "Anything is a step in the right direction."

"I know when to go limp and I know how to use my size to my advantage. He taught me to fake one way and hit another. Just small things."

Juno nodded. "We can work with that."

Tallis stood up. "Okay. So, we'll start training tomorrow. Today, you have a dress fitting for your Culling wardrobe. There will be an etiquette lesson at noon tomorrow to help you prepare for the royal dinner and for the ball on Monday. Both of those events will include the other girls and the royal family. Then the first of the trial pairings will be announced at the ball. We'll have two weeks of training, the trial, and another trial announcement soon afterward."

That was assuming I wasn't in the first trial and that I didn't die.

"Before we leave," Juno said, "we need to discuss your court advisor. Building a personal court is important. You'll have Tallis and me, but you'll need someone who can have your back politically and socially. Someone with inside knowledge or some sort of sway."

Tallis flopped back onto the bed. "Someone in the Royal Synod would be good. Or maybe one of the princesses."

Juno shook his head. "Britta isn't taking advisees. And I've heard rumors that Princess Larkin will be working with Kinsley."

Tallis nodded. "Aviana's already secured one of the royal guards. That'll come in handy."

"What about Princess Uriel?"

Tallis and Juno both turned to me.

He shook his head. "She's far too young. You don't want a sixteen-year-old helping you with this."

Tallis nodded in agreement. "And Uriel holds no real sway in the palace. She's a wild card."

A wild card who climbs from second-story balconies and throws high-heeled shoes at palace guards. If anyone would know how to play the game and win, it would be Uriel Warwick.

"I want her as my Court Advisor. I'm seventeen and expected to win the Culling and become queen. I don't see why a sixteen-year-old princess wouldn't be more than qualified to help me do that. Wild card or not."

Juno's eyes narrowed as he considered. "It'd be a mistake to ask her. You'd be better off—"

"I want Uri."

After a long second, Tallis said, "I'll have the invitation sent tomorrow. If she says no, we'll reconvene and choose someone else." Juno looked like he wanted to argue, but Tallis caught his gaze and shook her head.

"Whatever you want, Monroe." He sighed. "After all, it's your life."

The words were sharp-edged, but not mean. He could push the issue, force me to choose someone else, but he was letting me do this—even if he believed it was a mistake. In that instant, faced with his uneasy compliance, I wanted to take it back, to tell him to pick someone else for me, but Uri was the right choice. I knew it in my bones.

13

The Queen's Sitting Room

Two days before Sanctus Halletta

The trainers all had a meeting to attend that morning, so Tallis and Juno left me to eat my breakfast in relative peace. I bathed and put on one of the linen dresses from my closet. It was robin's-egg blue with a cream-colored collar stitched with tiny yellow flowers and trim that ran parallel to the buttons down the front. The swish of the skirt around my calves was different from the heavy pinafores and patched cotton I was accustomed to wearing. The soft, cool material made butterflies flutter in my stomach. I felt . . . pretty in it. And feminine in a way I hadn't in a very long time—if ever.

By the time I'd finished tugging on my stockings and lacing the leather oxfords, there was a sort of energy in the air around me. The thrum of anticipation and fear mingled with a strange sort of nervousness that had nothing to do with the Culling. My reflection in the mirror revealed that I was thin and pale, and that even with the front sections of my hair pulled back and tied with a ribbon, I still looked out of place.

The glint of that golden ring caught the light of the sun as I twirled, admiring the way the dressed fanned out around me. What would Cohen think of me? I squashed that idea and shoved it down, down, down—right next to that dark power inside of me. They could remain locked there together, never to see the light of day.

Who cares what Cohen would think? He's just some boy—or man. Prince. Fiancé. Whatever he was, he was the least of my concerns.

A knock sounded at the door and I hurried to open it, ready to get out of that room and away from my own thoughts—even if it meant seeing the other goddess-touched girls. The guard in the hall was middle-aged and broad-shouldered, with auburn hair and freckles. He barely looked at me as he said, "I've been sent to take you to a dress fitting."

He didn't say anything else to me as we made the long walk across the palace. At first, I tried to remember all of the twists and turns, but it proved fruitless—there was no way I would be able to learn how to get from place to place here. Everything looked the same: all too clean and too empty and too fake.

The sickly sweet smell of fresh flowers permeated the air, mingling with the tart scents of wood cleaner and tile wax. We saw almost no one and those we did see were maids—and they were careful with where they placed their eyes. Had they been told not to look at me? I wanted to ask the guard, but he was avoiding my gaze too. And clearly, he wasn't interested in conversation.

When we finally reached our destination, my feet were starting to ache in my new shoes. The guard abandoned me outside a set of stained-glass doors. Inside, I could hear the hum of feminine voices, punctuated occasionally by a sharp trill of laughter. I recognized Uri's voice before I'd even pushed the door open.

As soon as she caught sight of me, she was on her feet. "Monroe!" She abandoned the little table she'd been sitting at by the window and met me at the door. "I was just thinking about you." Her hand wrapped around my wrist.

"About me?"

She nodded and pulled me over to where she'd been sitting. I could feel the curious eyes of two other goddess-touched girls as I took the empty chair across from Uri's. The princess caught me looking and said, "That's Aviana," nodding to a girl with warm brown skin and dark-chestnut hair. "And Tessa."

Tessa offered me a timid smile from her place by the fire. She was perched on the very edge of a plush settee, her pale fingers fiddling idly with the end of her bright-red braid. She had a spattering of freckles and pale-blue eyes, and although her lips with thin and her chin was a little too angular, she was still pretty in her own way.

Aviana was different. Although she didn't smile at me, her brown gaze wasn't challenging. Her round cheeks and long lashes made her appear younger, even though she had the body of grown woman. And she was tall. Even as she sat in an armchair in the corner, I could tell that she was all legs. The lush green of her dress matched the silk scarf she'd used to tie up her dark hair.

Looking at Aviana made me jealous in the same way that looking at Uri always sort of did. It wasn't a negative kind of jealousy, but more admiration. I was pretty—with clear, suntanned skin and blond hair—but I wasn't beautiful. I didn't know how to release the tension in my shoulders, how to strip away the anxiety from my heart and don any inkling of confidence.

Cohen must have hoped that he'd end up with someone like her. That girl was queen material—wife material. *How can I change to be more like that?*

Stop. I forced that thought away. I didn't want to change. The Culling was so all consuming there was no energy left to put toward my appearance or trying to be anything more than I was. *Why should I change to fit a mold that I don't want? Why should I learn to want something that would cause me to have to change?*

I turned my attention toward Uri, suddenly wishing that I hadn't taken the time to look too closely at the other two girls. Being around other young women my age was hard. Did it always feel so . . . tight? So tense?

Air and cloaking.

That's what I should be focusing on, not their appearance.

I cleared my throat. "What were you thinking about me for?" I asked.

Uri leaned back in her chair. "I was thinking that I wanted some company. I'm here all day. Britta was supposed to play host to all of you while you came for your fittings, but she's planning the dinner. And Larkin is too good to help with any of this. So, I'm just stuck sitting here until all ten of you show up. It's dull as hell. Kinsley is in with the seamstress now. And then it'll be Aviana's turn and then Tessa's and then yours." She grinned. "So, you're essentially my hostage now until you've been fitted—isn't that grand?"

I laughed. "And what do plan to do with me?"

She smiled and reached into the pocket of her pastel-yellow dress and produced a little cardboard box. "I think we should play cards."

A Game of Cages and Crowns—it was familiar. The object of the game was to protect your goddess-touched card at all costs. There was only one prince card in the draw pile, and you wanted to get it, since it would "unlock" the cage card that sat between the players and the crown card. There were three goddess-touched cards in the pile, and you needed one of those to claim the crown. So, the object of the game was to draw in hopes of getting a goddess-touched and a prince card to unlock the cage and crown respectively, but every time you drew a card, you risked getting a trial card or even a death card, which would knock you out of the game right away.

It was the sort of game that got your heart racing because you were always one bad draw away from either victory or death. The first player to get through the cage and get the crown would win the entire game. It was a game I'd played a lot growing up, but it had never held quite as much significance as it did now.

I watched as Uri dealt seven cards to me, including one goddess-touched card, and then set aside another seven cards in front of the remaining empty chair at our table. "Who are those for?"

"Oh." She glanced up at me, half her attention still on setting up the game. "Cohen's coming." She nodded to a large grandfather clock in the corner. "He's three minutes late, but he'll be here. He's got to be fitted for a new suit. When he arrives, I'll have two hostages.

"You know," she added, her nose wrinkling in displeasure. "I don't think Cohen is the worst-looking boy I've ever seen, but I certainly wouldn't want to have to marry him."

"It's a good thing you aren't in the Culling, then," I said.

"Oh, Monroe. The goddess knew the world couldn't handle that."

I eyed a door on one side of the room. I could hear soft conversation coming from the room, and I wondered what the seamstress and Kinsley could be talking about. She was raised here, and her father was the Speaker of the Synod. Tallis and Juno were right in saying that her familiarity with the palace gave her an edge. But I found it difficult to really be afraid of her. Kinsley's ability sounded weak in comparison to some of the other girls'. If it were left to the two of us in the arena, I'd win.

A shiver ran down my spine at the ease of that thought. Uri saw the reaction but didn't comment on it. "We should team up against Cohen," she said, holding up her own hand of cards, gold-and-black edges gleaming. "You and me. If we both aim our attack cards at him, he won't stand a chance."

"But that's against the rules," Aviana said. "Cages and Crowns is supposed to be played player against player. It's a mock-up of the Culling."

Tessa nodded in agreement. "And even if the two of you both gang up on Cohen, you'll still end up enemies in the end. There's only one crown card and you both need it to win."

"Why are we talking about ganging up on me?"

I turned to see Cohen standing at the door to the sitting room. He offered us all a curt little nod of his head. Uri spun in her seat and shot him a wide smile. "Because we're playing A Game of Cages and Crowns." The prince opened his mouth, but she said, "And before you can argue, you're stuck in line behind Kinsley, Tessa, Aviana, and Monroe. So, unless you have something better to do, you might as well play."

Cohen walked to the lone empty chair at our table and looked down at the pile of cards she'd dealt him. "What if I have something better to do?"

Uri nodded to the empty seat. "You don't."

He sighed but obeyed.

For a moment it was quiet as the three of us all examined our cards. Mine weren't terrible. I had a few attack cards, and the draw pile was large, meaning that the chance of drawing a bad card was smaller.

Cohen chewed his bottom lip and took his time arranging his cards into some sort of order. Up close, his eyes were a depthless, bottomless blue. The slight stubble that had been on his face yesterday was darker today, and he hadn't slicked his hair into place. Had he even combed it before leaving his room?

Goddess, it was unfair how handsome he was.

"It's nice seeing you again, Monroe." He met my eyes from underneath thick black lashes. "How was your first night in the palace?"

How long had I been staring?

My throat was tight as I said, "It was fine."

He turned to look at the other girls. "And you, Aviana? Tessa?"

They both muttered similar noncommittal responses. The corner of Cohen's mouth twitched, almost a smile. "Tough crowd."

Uri ignored him. "Who's going first?"

Cohen looked to me. "Ladies first." I reached for the draw pile but paused as he said, "You aren't going to play a card before ending your turn?"

"The risk of drawing a bad card is at its lowest right now."

"Do you only make moves when the risk is at its highest then?" Something about the question seemed heavier than a game of cards.

I drew without giving him an answer. The emblem on my first card was of a throne—a king card. The gold swirls and edging on the matte-black card only seemed to highlight the crimson splattering of blood detailing of the seat of the throne. The king was a wild card. Paired with two other wild cards, I would be able to draw from the discard pile.

"Your turn," I said to him.

Cohen laid down an arrow card—an attack—and nodded to Uri. "Draw twice."

She grumbled but did as he said.

The game continued in relative silence for a while, each of us taking our turn to draw or play a card. The shimmering cage card sat between the three of us—open and waiting for someone to risk playing a prince card.

At some point, Uri and I did start to aim at Cohen. Anytime we had an attack card, we aimed it at him. And usually, he was prepared to deflect in some way. Cohen knew how to use one card to make a big impact—while I usually relied on multiple cards or individual plays to get me where I wanted.

Kinsley finished with her fitting just as Uri drew the death card and knocked herself out of the game. She cursed loudly and slumped down in her chair, drawing raised brows from the seamstress as she peered out of the door and gestured Aviana forward.

Kinsley paused by our table, her nose wrinkling at the sight of the game. "Aren't we all too old for a children's game?"

Cohen smiled up at her. "You're never too old for a game of cards, Kins. And I'd hardly call this a game for children—you of all people should know that the Culling, or a game framed after it, isn't child's play."

Something in the pit of my stomach seemed to recoil at the casual use of the nickname. The unease only got worse as Kinsley turned her attention to me. She was polished in the same way the princesses were. But somehow, she was less eye-catching.

There was an odd paradox to Kinsley Raveena. Her black hair was perfectly teased and wavy, her eyes were a vivid shade of greenish brown, and her brown skin was clean and unblemished, but each piece of her seemed a little off. Her lips were overdrawn, and her smile was too tight. Her nose was turned up slightly and, even when she wasn't sneering down at me, I imagined she always looked a little displeased. But what distracted from all of the normal and pushed Kinsley into the exceptional was her mark.

I hadn't noticed it at the garden party—I'd been so preoccupied with Aviana, Heidi, and the princesses—but Kinsley's mark was on her face. Ink-black vines and flowers snaked along the outer left side of her forehead and upper cheek, swooping over the sharp angle of her jaw, and partially down her neck. It was so intricate and so intentionally crafted that I almost thought it might be fake. She looked . . . chosen.

My fingers closed reflexively in my lap.

Kinsley's attention swiveled back to Cohen. "I chose a dress that would match my ring." She held out her hand, displaying the ruby-encrusted silver band glittering there. "Your mother suggested it. She was also kind enough to get her own dressmaker to design it. She's having an entire trousseau made up. Gowns and day dresses and bows." She sighed. "I already feel like royalty."

"Don't get too comfy with the feeling, Kinsley. You may have a closet of pretty clothes, but you don't yet have the crown." Uri tapped a finger against the forgotten cage card between Cohen and me. "I'd like to play another round, so if you don't mind finishing this . . . ?"

Cohen rolled his shoulders and played his prince card. He laid it atop the cage card and slid the two of them over, leaving the crown free to be claimed. The prince drew a card to end his turn and then nodded to me. This was a gamble. If I had a goddess-touched card, the crown was mine to be won. But all I held were wild cards—kings, queens, princesses, and priestesses. He'd stolen my goddess-touched card a few turns earlier.

I scanned Cohen's deck. He had four cards left and one of them had to be the goddess-touched card he needed for the crown—the one he'd taken from me after Uri had stolen his. I laid down three wild cards and nodded to his hand. "I'll take a card."

He handed one over. Still a wild card.

I laid down three more wild cards, including the one he'd just given me. "Another card, please."

This one was a Synod card. Playing it would allow me to look at the top four cards in the deck and change their order. I laid it down and picked up the deck.

"Only the top four," he said, his voice a bit tight.

"I know." The top four cards were duds. And I didn't want to end my turn by drawing and risk him claiming the crown. I gathered another set of three wild cards. This left me with a reserve of two cards—princess and a priestess. Not enough to steal another card.

As I set the three wild cards aside, Cohen pursed his lips and handed me his second to last card. I smiled at the blade card he'd handed me. *Steal a card of your opponent's choosing*. I slid it right back to him. "Okay, prince, I'll have that goddess-touched card now, please."

He frowned and handed it over. I set it down on the crown card with little fanfare, but Uri clapped as if I'd truly just won the Culling for real. Kinsley took a step back, as if she needed distance from Uriel's rampant enthusiasm.

"That's why you should draw cards when it's the safest. Take the risk up front. You may lose some cards, but it won't be the end of you. My older brothers taught me that. You can always win back whatever you lose at the start," I said. "Because I drew and didn't play any of my cards, I had a lot of ammunition to use at the end."

Cohen bowed his head to hide a smile. "Duly noted."

14

Palace Fitting Room
Oredison Palace, Gazda
Two days before Sanctus Halletta

We played three more rounds before it was my turn to be fitted. By then, Uri had been summoned elsewhere, and it was just Cohen and me. We weren't very talkative as we played, but the game was entertaining enough that the silence didn't seem heavy. Despite the lack of conversation, Cohen's posture grew more and more relaxed as the morning dragged on. His shoulders weren't so stiff, and he sort of sprawled out at the table, his long legs always centimeters away from touching mine.

When the seamstress finally stuck her head out the door and found only the two of us, she said, "I can take you both." As Cohen got to his feet, abandoning his splay of cards, she said, "You're just here to try on the suit, is that correct, Prince Cohen?"

He nodded and offered me a hand up. It was like a bumblebee buzzed inside my chest as his fingers wrapped around mine—and I was unnaturally aware of every place where his skin touched me.

It was there and gone in an instant, then he was leading the way into the small side room where a little stool was set up next to a wooden worktable and shelves filled with bolts upon bolts of fabric. The seamstress didn't bother with introductions—she just ushered me over to the stool and had me climb up. I stood there, taking it all in, as she handed Cohen a hanger holding a crisp black tuxedo, white shirt, and black bow tie.

She nodded to a bathroom to their left. "You change while I get started on her." She spun on me, her hands going to her hips as she looked me up and down. "What's your name, dear?"

The seamstress showed me a few different sketches and took my measurements. "I've got a couple of dresses in the shop that won't take much alteration to fit—I'll have someone on it right away. You'll have them all by the end of next week. And the gowns for tomorrow and Sanctus Halletta will be delivered by tomorrow afternoon."

The door to the bathroom room creaked open and Cohen stepped out. I hadn't known the meaning of the word *handsome* before. I was still gaping at the clean lines of the double-breasted jacket with peaked lapels and the firmly pressed trousers when the seamstress nudged my elbow. "Down with you. I'll make the alternations here, Your Highness."

Alterations? Good goddess, he was perfect.

I stepped off the stool to make room for Cohen. He stood up there just long enough for her to fiddle with the hem of the pants and then she had him step down so she could pin the rest. He hadn't bothered to do up the bow tie so it was draped across his shoulders, and the white shirt underneath was only partially buttoned, revealing a hard chest that was more muscular than I'd been expecting.

"Do you like it?"

His voice broke through my daze and I took a sharp step back, nearly knocking over a pile of cloth. My face was on fire. *All hells, please stop staring at him.* "I . . . I'm sorry?"

"The suit. Do you like it?"

"Of course." The words came out a little too fast. "I— It's— You're— You know, I think I should g—"

"Stay. I'll walk you back to your rooms, just let me get changed. Dellacov's got most of the guards helping him prepare for tomorrow's ball—I don't want to distract any of them." The seamstress finished with two more pins and then gestured him away. "Just let me change out of this, and we'll go."

I gathered the abandoned cards into their box while Cohen changed back into the gray slacks and white button-up he'd been wearing earlier. When he emerged from the little tailor shop, his shirttail was untucked and he looked notably more relaxed. He paused as he noted the way I clutched the box of cards in my hand.

"I'll make sure Uri gets her deck back." He walked to where I sat and held out his hand. I handed the box over and watched as he stashed it into his pants pocket. "You ready?"

I stood.

His hair was a mess, the waves having gone from casually unruly to outright chaos when he changed. "You may want to fix your hair," I said as I followed him toward the door. He did as I suggested and ran a hand through it, trying to finger comb it back into order. It only kind of worked.

"Is . . ." I stepped out into the hallways after him. "Aren't we breaking Culling rules? You said yourself that we aren't supposed to spend time together. But this is the second time, third if you count the card game just now, and—"

"I thought you were the type to throw caution to the wind?" He shoved his hands deep into his trouser pockets and began strolling in the direction of my bedroom. "You said to take the risk up front."

"This isn't a game of cards."

He shrugged. "Could've fooled me. There's enough strategy happening in this palace that it might as well be."

I hurried to catch up to him. "I realize that the risk isn't very great for you, but if we're caught breaking Culling rules it could be bad for me. Your mother—*the queen*—has already tried to deny my mother the stipend for me being here. I can't give her any more reason to—"

"Miss Benson," Cohen said, "if you think that you're the only one risking something, you've clearly misunderstood my position in all of this." His voice had turned cold and the use of my last name had my steps faltering.

"I'm sorry."

"I don't want you to apologize. You've done nothing wrong. I'm just . . ." He shrugged. "I'm trying to explain. To be honest. Because you seem nice and like you deserve a little honesty. But if you'd rather I not talk to you or put you in jeopardy, I understand. I won't do it again. I'll have a guard escort you from now on."

You seem nice and like you deserve a little honesty.

"No. I— What is your position in all of this? If I've misunderstood, then explain it to me."

"I almost died a few days ago. I would have died if the guards hadn't acted so quickly. Some stranger shot at me. And it sort of put things in perspective. I knew we were heading toward a war. The tension between Erydia and Vayelle has been mounting for years. Our religious and governmental differences are always causing problems and . . . and the assassination attempt was just the start."

"But why shoot at you? You aren't the king."

"If I'm dead, then the whole thing falls to pieces. Without me, the goddess-chosen queen can't come to power, and there can be no more heirs to continue my family's rule. Vayelle and the Culled—who I know they are supporting—want nothing more than to break us apart. They want to dismantle our government and our traditions. They want the land that they believe is owed to them by a goddess they claim to not even believe in. And that all requires me to die."

"You said you were going to give me honesty, so I'll give you the same. I don't want to die in the Culling. But I'm not the first girl to feel that way, and it's never been stopped on account of the people being directly affected by it. It's been happening for centuries. The process has always been . . . less than savory. And you— Your family has allowed it to continue. Each generation has a chance to end it, end the bloodshed, but you never do. Why? Why not let us live?"

He stopped walking and I did too, suddenly very aware of what I'd just said, just admitted. Extremely aware of the fact that I was in a palace, talking to a prince. *Bad.* This was bad.

Cohen stared at me for a long moment. His lips parted as he chewed on what he wanted to say, tried to piece together a response. Had anyone ever said that to him? Ever made him face the very real consequences of his decision to support the Culling?

"I could die," I said. "I *will* die. So will eight other girls. All of us killed in an arena like it's a sport. And whoever comes out of it—" The feel of his hand threading through mine made me pause.

"You shouldn't talk like that, Monroe. Not . . . Not where my mother and *others* can hear. It's treason to speak against the Culling, in doing so you're questioning the validity of my parent's reign. You question the temple and the goddess." He gave my hand a squeeze, his blue eyes filled with a million unsaid things. Things I wanted him to voice. "I'm sorry that you're scared. I'm . . . I'm really sorry." Rehearsed. The words came out sounding rehearsed and clinical. Like he'd been coached on what to say.

Or like he'd grown up in a palace where everything he said and did was monitored and scrutinized. I pursed my lips and asked, "What is Vayelle so afraid of?" I took a deep breath and tried to speak around what I wanted to say. He'd brought up the attack, so that seemed like safe footing. "Why attack you now?"

What has the rebels scrambling to end the Culling now, to end the Warwick rule now—when they'd never tried before?

"Yes," he said, cutting me off. "I would argue, *on behalf of those who think highly of the competition*, that the recent issues in our kingdom are not due to the practice of the Culling itself but rather stem from the current . . . regime." He nodded to a footman standing outside a closed set of double doors. "I would hope that a new queen would bring about a new era and fix some of the things that are broken."

"But why act now?" I asked again, unhappy with that response.

"I think after what happened when my mother came to power, people are afraid of what another goddess-touched queen might bring. Seeing someone kill everyone in her Culling in one swoop, before the trials could even begin. I mean, it was ruthless. More than that, she wiped out part of the royal family. She proved right away that she cared for nothing and no one. My mother has always been fixated on power and on keeping power."

"Without the Culling—"

"What would the world be like if someone like my mother was allowed to roam free? What would happen if ten girls like my mother—with destructive, earth-shattering gifts—were allowed to live and do whatever they pleased? It's an interesting thought, but a scary one. The past violence of the goddess-touched girls, both in the arena and before it, has left a bad taste in the mouths of many. I'm not saying I agree with them, but as a ruler I think it's my job to look at it from all sides."

I wished more than anything that someone would look at it from my side, prince or otherwise. But I knew what he was saying. Goddess-touched girls, while revered, were also symbols of unchecked power—a power that in recent years had begun to be resented by the masses of starving and begging people.

My gaze drifted to the mark on my right hand. I had looked for Viera's yesterday and hadn't seen it. Even so, I'd felt the waves of power emanating off her. And her ability . . . it was scary. *She* was scary. Her rule had given nothing to Erydia and it was beginning to rot our country from the inside out.

"Does it scare you, knowing that you have the ability to kill other people?" Cohen asked, drawing my attention back to him.

"Everyone has the ability to kill. What scares me is knowing that I'll do it—I'll kill nine other girls if it means I get to stay alive."

Dread settled in the pit of my stomach at the words. It felt like I'd spoken a curse against myself—like admitting that I wanted to live would prevent me from doing so. Anxiety burned like acid at the back of my throat. Fire pushed at the underside of my skin, a soothing sort of warmth that snaked along my bones.

I found that I couldn't look at him as I said, "Having the potential to kill isn't nearly as scary as having a reason to."

"I'm sorry." Again, I could see him warring with the desire to say more, give me more honesty, but he stopped himself. "It's— As you said, it's unsavory. I hate that you're a part of it." Softer, he said, "I hate that *I'm* a part of it."

Uri's words from earlier about condoning bad behavior by brushing apologies aside resurfaced with a vengeance. It wasn't that I didn't believe Cohen was sincere in his apology, but he wasn't moving against the issue. He wasn't prepared to do anything to stop it and that made accepting his words impossible. I wouldn't soothe his guilt, not when I believed he deserved to shoulder some part of it.

He cleared his throat and started walking again. "Can we talk about something else?"

"Tell me about the last Culling."

He tried and failed to hide a smile. "That wasn't really my idea of a topic change."

I said, "I wasn't ready to change the topic."

"If you must know, my mother's Culling was the shortest in the history of the competition. It took seconds. There's always this fancy dinner the evening before the Commencement Ball. Traditionally, the Synod, all ten goddess-touched girls, and everyone in the royal family attends. In past Cullings, there were rules in place that kept almost everyone—even the royal family and the other girls—from knowing what gift a girl possessed. It's a rule I had them change this time. I wanted full transparency, or at least as much as possible. Anyway, my mother is clever and her ability is really scary."

"It's just poison, right?"

He shook his head. "It isn't *just* poison. That would be like saying you *just* control fire. With enough skill, you could do almost anything with that. You could do things that no one else would ever be able to do. It's the same with the queen. She's immune to poison, and she can influence any existing toxins to make them stronger."

"Which means . . . ?" I prompted.

"Which means," Cohen said, "that you and I could touch the same poisoned item and only the person my mother wants to poison will actually fall ill. And it can be the smallest trace too. So, in the case of her Culling, she used something that was in the food. Some people say that she added the poison herself, but I don't think that's true. I think she saw an opportunity and took it. My mother is . . ." He lowered his voice and moved a step closer to me, so our arms almost brushed. "My mother isn't exactly . . . She's . . . Well, my father says she is sick in the head. And maybe he's right. It doesn't really matter. No matter the real reason or exactly how it happened, she killed multiple people within seconds."

If I had felt inadequate before, I felt pointless now. How could I even begin to compete with girls who had abilities like that? The realization that I might die, that I might be here today and dead in a week, rocked me to my very core.

Suddenly, the ground didn't seem quite as steady beneath me. Bile rose in my throat, and I had the distinct understanding that I was on the edge of passing out. The bright lights of the hallway dimmed and I felt, more than saw, Cohen move toward me.

He took hold of my elbow, steadying me. "Monroe?" His grip on my arm tightened when I pressed the back of my hand to my mouth.

The air bit at my lungs as I tried and failed to catch my breath. I forced myself to meet his eyes even as mine burned with tears—I was a dam, near bursting. *Don't cry. Not in front of him.* I took another deep breath.

"I never meant to upset you," he whispered. "I only told you because you asked."

I pulled away from his grasp and leaned against the pastel-colored wall, letting my fingertips trace the lightly patterned surface. *I'm fine. Everything is fine.* The windows across from me were bright with noonday sun. I blamed that brightness for the way my vision swam.

"There was no warning? No one was able to fight her or stop her?" I asked, trying to keep my voice steady. Trying to pretend that I wasn't completely losing it in front of His Royal Highness. "So, she killed everyone in her Culling and won? Just like that?"

He stepped closer to me but didn't try to touch me again.

"I'm listening." The air was hot in my chest. I needed a few seconds, just an instant without those eyes on me. I needed him to talk. "Tell me . . . Tell me more. What happened next?"

Cohen shook his head. "You're upset. Let's talk about something else. About your family or—"

"I want to know more. I deserve to know more."

"During the dinner, my mother sensed the natural bacteria in the food and intensified it to the point that it was deadly. It effectively killed the entire Culling pool as well as everyone in the royal family. Everyone but my father. Over a dozen people dead before they could even leave the table."

I made a sound, no more than a whimper, but mercifully Cohen kept talking.

"There were a few she let suffer. My grandmother and my father's younger sister were among the few who died very slowly." Cohen sighed. "And by law, my father had to marry her and make her queen."

"But she killed his family," I said quietly.

"As I said, she doesn't play by anyone else's rules."

I thought about Cohen and the position he was in. He was going to marry whoever won the crown. Whatever girl—or monster—emerged from this Culling was going to be his problem for the rest of his life. He didn't have a choice in this either.

But that didn't make us the same. He would be king, and I . . . I could very well be dead.

Things grew quiet and I finally calmed enough to look over at him. He was gazing out the window at the city beyond, his face tense with an emotion akin to pain. I wondered how heavy the weight of that crown was.

We were inches from each other. One small movement and I could brush my hand against the back of his. Something in me wanted to, wanted that human contact, but I stayed still. I waited.

After a second, he turned and looked at me too.

"Are you certain about this?" I asked. "Are you sure?" It was his question from earlier but it was heavier, weighed down with the reality of what this competition meant. For me. For him.

He smiled, tight-lipped, but his chin quivered just slightly with the action. For a second, he looked so damn normal—like he could be any other young man. Any other person from beyond these palace walls. Not a prince, just a vulnerable, frightened person. And I saw it. It was just the shadow of something, there and gone so quickly. So fast that I wanted to reach out, take hold of his face in my hands, and tell him to show me again. Trust me enough to let me see it again. But I didn't think Cohen trusted anyone that much. Even if he was giving me honesty—or his version of it.

The prince took a step closer to me, leaving very little space between us as he whispered, "Is it a choice?"

I shook my head. That was the most I could muster. I thought he had a choice. Or it seemed to me like it should be a choice for him. But it wasn't— we were cards and someone else held us, directed us, took risks on our behalf. And while I may see Cohen as someone with complete autonomy, that didn't seem to be the case.

This was its own game of cages and crowns. And I didn't know how to play it. Did I collect cards quickly and risk picking incorrectly and losing, or was I supposed to take a deep breath and focus on what was in front of me? This feeling—the way my heart seized in my chest every time he looked at me—what did anyone do with that? How was I meant to function or focus or do anything more than stare at him?

I was going to die before ever having had the chance to live and now that I was faced with my mortality, I wanted more than my fair share. I wanted a lifetime of love, small smiles, and card games; friendship and laughter and kisses . . . all the tiny things that make your life feel full when you are old and gray and lying on your deathbed. My heart was flung wide open, ready for any small ounce of *life*.

But I would die in an arena without any of that.

Cohen cleared his throat and eased away from me. "I should probably be getting you back to your room. I've already broken about a dozen rules."

"You know," I said as we started walking again, "you never did tell me what you're risking by breaking Culling rules."

"True." He sighed, chewing on his lip as he considered what he wanted to say. After a moment he ran a hand through his hair, further mussing it, as he spoke. "The biggest threat to my mother's rule isn't a Culling girl or probably even Vayelle, it's me." His ears flushed as he said, "A goddess-touched girl can't be queen without a male heir to complete her crowning. My mother's reign is coming to an end and, despite her arguments to the Synod, they will not allow her to stay in power. Tradition is important and a new goddess-touched queen will bring stability and a much-needed change to Erydia. The temple has its checks and balances."

"But her not wanting to step down doesn't mean she sees you as a threat," I said. "You're her son."

"That doesn't matter. We're talking . . ." He lowered his voice further. "We're talking about someone who killed a room full of defenseless people all so she could have the throne. If my father hadn't kept me away from her for a good deal of my childhood, I probably would have been killed years ago. And even with the distance, she tried."

"She hurt you?"

"I had a lot of mysterious bouts of illness as a child; the court physicians always said it was food poisoning, but we all know what sort of poisoning it really was. But I never died. My father always made sure I had the best doctors. But there were a lot of close calls. I think they had Uri because my father wanted to try for another boy, a spare for the heir. But I didn't die, I'm here and ready to be king. And I think I'll be a good one."

"I think you're right."

He sighed and stopped just short of a set of stairs. "I'll let you go on your own from here. It'll be just up those stairs, second hallway to your left, fourth door down, I believe. Your name is in the bracket on the outside of the door, it shouldn't be hard to find. I have a tutoring session—history and geography, boring as hell—so I should be going."

A lump formed in my throat. *Had all the questions and honesty offended him?* "Aren't you going to take me the rest of the way?"

"I thought you said being alone with me broke the rules?"

I turned toward the empty staircase and sighed. "Yeah, but I'm not supposed to just walk around on my own either. I'm supposed to always have an escort."

Cohen's smile was all boyish charm as he muttered, "Pick your poison."

I found myself smiling too as I said, "Your hair is a mess again." I stepped forward and ran my fingers through it—halfway through the motion, I realized what I'd done and sprang back from him. "I'm sorry. I just— It looks like you just rolled out of bed and . . . and with your shirt untucked like that it just looks a little sloppy."

That smile was so big and bright, it filled his whole face. "Does it? My tutors will think I've been getting myself into trouble."

He had been getting into trouble, but I had a feeling it wasn't the sort of trouble he was implying. And as I considered the sort of just-out-of-bed trouble he was talking about, I felt the fire in my blood grow to unthinkable temperatures. There was no way that my face wasn't as bright as a tomato.

For a moment we just stood there looking at each other. It felt like the tension was climbing a ladder in my bones—the awkwardness between us made my toes curl in my shoes and the need to get away became all-encompassing. *I touched him. I reached out and touched his hair and—goddess, what had possessed me?*

I thumbed toward the stairs behind me. "I'm going to go now."

"Yeah, okay." He didn't move from his spot, didn't stop grinning at me.

"I'll see you later." I paused at the sound of my name. He was gripping the railing at the bottom of the staircase, his face turned up toward me. "Yes?"

"Thanks for talking to me."

I nodded and started up the stairs again but stopped. "Hey, Cohen? Would . . . Would you want to be a member of my court?"

His features opened into an expression of surprise so sudden that he couldn't recover quickly enough to disguise it. "Monroe, I can't—"

"It wouldn't be anything official and of course as the Culling went on, I wouldn't actually expect anything from you. It would just be between us. You'd be on my court and, if you wanted me to be, I'd be on yours. We could look out for each other."

"My court?" he repeated.

"Yeah, I mean, maybe you don't have one officially or anything—but maybe you should have an unofficial one. If the queen, if *your mother*, sees you as a threat, then maybe you and I aren't so different. Maybe you need someone to watch your back too. So, if you wanted to have a court, then I'd be on it. If you'd want me to be, that is."

Cohen looked me over, from head to toe. "You mean that?"

I nodded.

"But when the trials start, you'd have to face them alone. I couldn't help you, even if I wanted to."

"I know that."

He swallowed. "Yeah. Yeah, it's a deal."

15

Palace Bedroom

The day before Sanctus Halletta

Sunday was spent training with Tallis and Juno. We worked on throwing the flame farther, working to keep it burning on impact. I'd made a mess and burned a good part of the floor, but my trainers were proud and hopeful. This was their first time really seeing my ability in action, and Juno seemed to think I had it in the bag.

"Casualties for the cause," Juno had said about the multiple burn marks and melted practice dummies. His smile had been wide as he walked me back to my bedroom, and he'd left me with a hearty slap to the back and an order to rest.

I'd arrived back at my room to find a printed card saying that the etiquette lesson scheduled for today had been postponed. With that obligation gone, I slept through lunch.

By the time I finally woke up, the midafternoon sun's rays were creeping along the plush cream rug. I lay there for a long time, just listening to the palace around me. Maids were scurrying around like mice, their steps mixing with the steady pacing of the guards as they periodically strolled the hall outside my door.

I didn't know where the other goddess-touched girls were staying. That morning, I'd heard of few of them practicing in their own training rooms, but I hadn't passed any of them in the hall. I wondered how their first day of training had gone. Were they as nervous as I was? How much control did they have?

I was lucky in a lot of ways. My ability had manifested when I was young. There were some marked girls who might not have developed their ability until a few years ago—it was possible that some might have had even less time than that.

All in all, I didn't think my session had gone as badly as I'd anticipated. And I liked Tallis and Juno. They were quiet and thoughtful, but they gave me good suggestions and, although this was as new to them as it was to me, they seemed confident. And they weren't afraid to have me try something new or make mistakes, which was refreshing.

I was beyond tired though. Running laps, doing core exercises, and pushing my ability to new limits had drained me. Some vital part of myself left like it was fraying. The joints in my knees and arms were jelly, and I was a pile of exhausted flesh. After years of siphoning my ability in little ways, it was an adjustment to conjure fire in large quantities. My entire body hurt, ached in odd ways—and there was a dinner party tonight.

I needed to get up and bathe, but I wasn't sure I could even stand.

Tallis had told me that dinner was at seven. The entire royal family would be there, as well as every goddess-touched girl. No broadcasts though; this first meeting would be private.

While that should have put me at ease, I couldn't stop thinking about what Cohen had said—what if one of the goddess-touched girls tried to kill us all at dinner?

Oh, goddess.

I pushed myself off the bed, made my way to the bathing room, and collapsed onto the edge of the large claw-foot tub. For a while I fiddled with the waterspout—hot to cold, then back again. Over and over, like a pendulum swinging continuously into oblivion. Counting down the seconds, minutes, hours, days, I had left to live. Hot and cold, flipping temperatures with a twist of my wrist.

When the tub filled to the brim, I pulled the silver plug and watched as the water spiraled its way down the drain like a miniature tornado. It was wasteful, using and draining so much water, but I couldn't stop being enamored by it. I wasn't sure how much time had passed while I sat there, running the water and draining it. Fifteen or so filled and emptied baths' worth of time.

I couldn't imagine living like this—with all the necessities, much less so much luxury.

I put my hand under the stream of freezing water, letting the sharp sting of it ground me. My deal with Cohen and the things he'd told me didn't feel real.

Anytime I'd thought about Cohen, about that question, about my answer, I felt like I was back on that dais. The flashing of cameras, the whispering of strangers, the feel of that ring slipping onto my finger—a promise and a prison.

I'd had a morning where I'd felt almost like myself. The training clothes were new, but the loose shirts and snug pants were like what I'd worn at home. I'd felt comfortable enough in the clothes that I'd napped in them. But that night, my appearance was unfamiliar once more. Two lady's maids arrived with the dress from the seamstress. They did their best to shape me into something entirely *other*. Wax strips were applied to my legs and torn away, until everything was smooth and silken. I was polished. Glossed. Painted.

I was told to tilt my head one way, then the other, close my eyes, pucker my lips, smile, lift my chin, don't flinch. One command after another. By the time it was all done, I felt raw and used.

The gown was blush pink with a long tulle and lace skirt, high neckline, and plunging back. I'd seen dresses like this in fashion magazines. In those images, the women wore draped furs and delicate lace capelets; their hair was always perfectly styled to showcase the deep plunging bodice or trailing straps of the back.

Gazing at myself in the mirror, I looked nothing like those girls. What was worse, I felt nothing like them. Yes, the dress was beautiful, with intricate floral appliqués that peeked through the folds of the skirt, but it seemed to wear me.

My hair had been combed and coaxed into soft waves and they'd pinned a silver-and-jewel headband into place, tying it at the base of my neck with a ribbon that matched the pink lace. It was an attempt at something feminine. Something less sharp than I was. But their attempt at femininity did little to mollify the haircut. Neither did the soft pink lip, mascara, and blush they used to cover my face.

The lady's maids had all gathered around and gushed over how pretty it was.

I thought of how elegant Uri always seemed to be, even after climbing from a balcony. I thought of the way Britta had looked at my announcement, how poised she was. Even Larkin had emanated a vivid sort of grace.

There was a tightness to everything and I could feel my anxiety taking over—*how is the lay of the dress, how does my hair look, am I standing straight enough, is it obvious that I am uncomfortable, what if I trip, there is no way I can eat in this thing, pink really doesn't seem like my color, will Cohen like it . . . ? I certainly don't like it.*

Each inhale was ragged and too shallow. And the lady's maids were staring.

Did the princesses do this all the time? Was this what life would be like if I won? Was I going to spend whatever time I had left looking like someone else? Trying to please someone else?

I lied through my teeth when the lady's maids asked what I thought of it. And then I waited patiently for them to leave before I sat down in front of my vanity and took a good long look at myself.

It'd be a lie to say I didn't look beautiful. I'd never seen myself look like this. My skin was smoothed by creams and colored just slightly with a hint of blush. The powders they'd used really did something to bring out the brown of my eyes. But I also looked like a lie. And it seemed pointless. Everyone at dinner tonight had already seen me without makeup and without my hair pinned into place. *Wasn't the dishonesty in this repelling?*

The maids had chosen a pair of T-strap pumps to go with the dress. The heels were taller than the ones I'd worn during my arrival at the palace. I couldn't walk in them—not with the extra height and the added volume of this skirt.

The length of the dress would probably hide whatever shoes I wore, anyway, so I decided that my normal boots would work just fine. Then at the very least, I would feel a little more like my regular self—even with the makeup.

I'd just finished lacing my training boots when Juno knocked on the door. The look on his face when he saw me was enough to push me over the edge. Raised eyebrows, mouth open in shock—

My eyes stung and I had to press them shut to get myself under control again. "All Hells, does it look that bad?"

"No! No. I, uh . . ." He reached out and touched my arm. "No, of course not." His brow furrowed. "I didn't mean to hurt your feelings, Monroe. You look beautiful."

"Your face a second ago didn't reflect that."

"Who cares about my face? This isn't about my facial expression, it's about you." I could tell he was trying to soften his voice, but it came out as an agitated whisper. "You just look different, that's all. I've never seen you so . . ." He shook his head and pressed a palm to his forehead. "Shit, I'm screwing this up. I should have just made Tallis come . . . Monroe, you look great. Beautiful. Totally royal. Kick-ass too. And I'm not just saying that! I swear."

"Really?"

"Really." He looked at me for a long moment, his expression earnest. "*You* could be the next Queen of Erydia."

I looked down at my dress then back up at Juno. I felt like I should say something. He was looking at me with large earnest eyes. He wanted me to believe that I was worthy of the position I was in. He wanted to look at me and see someone who might one day be queen.

I wanted to look at me and see that too.

"Shoulders back, chin up," Juno said.

I did as he said.

He nodded in appreciation. "Tonight, you're the heir to the throne. All of this," he gestured to the dress, "it's all extra. All it does is emphasize who you already are. You are Monroe Benson. You're goddess-touched and you're going to be the next queen." He met my eyes. "Say it."

"Say what?"

"Say that you're going to be the next queen."

I hesitated. "I'm not sure—"

"Say it. Say it and mean it."

I lifted my chin and straightened my shoulders, pulling myself up to my full height. "My name is Monroe Benson, I'm goddess-touched, and I'm going to be the next Queen of Erydia."

He grinned. "Damn right, you are."

I ducked my head, trying to hide the way my cheeks flushed. "Thank you."

Juno shoved his hands in his pockets and shrugged. "It all comes down to this: what do you want these girls to leave saying about you? Because they're going to leave saying something, Monroe Benson. Tonight is your night to intimidate. Don't go into this thinking you've already lost. If you do, they'll eat you alive. You walk into that room like you've already won."

Instead of walking me into the dining room, Juno abandoned me in the hallway outside. We were five minutes late, and he said it would look better if I just went in on my own. I'd agreed with him when he'd said it, but once I was alone in the hall, I regretted letting him go.

I didn't know if I should open the doors and just walk in or if I was supposed to knock. How exactly are you supposed to enter a royal dining room? Was this one of the instances when I was supposed to curtsy?

I reached out and took hold of the silver door handles. I could hear soft chatter coming from the other side of the large oak doors. Someone laughed. There was the tinkling of glass, the clink of silverware.

I could do this. Everything was going to be fine. This was just a dinner, not a trial. This should be easy. *Pretend you've already won.* It sounded simple enough.

Just as I was about to open the door, someone called my name from down the hall. I'd been so focused on what I was supposed to do that I hadn't even seen Cohen and Dellacov approaching.

Before I could even fully register the prince's presence, Dellacov laughed—loudly. "Are you wearing *boots*?"

In my surprise, I'd forgotten about keeping the dress pulled down. I yanked the skirt back into place and took a step away from them. My face felt four shades darker than my gown.

Cohen shot him a look, and he sobered.

"I'm sorry." Dellacov cleared his throat. "Y-you look very nice."

"Hugo, you can leave us." Cohen nodded toward the other end of the hall. "I can take it from here."

Dellacov didn't argue, just smiled at me before sauntering past.

"He acts like I need a babysitter," Cohen said under his breath. "I'm eighteen, not eight. And being promoted to Captain of the Guard has ruined him. His head has never been larger." He sighed as he took me in. "Anyway, are you nervous about tonight?"

"Extremely."

"Me too." He shoved his hands in his pockets and nodded to me, the corners of his mouth turning up slightly as he said, "And you look fantastic. Even with the boots. Ignore Hugo, he's an ass most of the time."

I should have pretended to laugh at his joke, but I didn't. It was hot in the hallway and I felt like every breath I took was too deep, too noticeable. *You look fantastic. Did he mean that?*

I didn't know what to do with him and those blue eyes. Inside that room were nine other girls, all waiting to speak to him, to pull his gaze, to impress the prince. But here he was, standing outside stalling with me.

My heart was in my throat. The blood was too loud in my ears. All at once it felt like everything needed to be adjusted—my hair, the dress, the way I was holding my arms—but I couldn't seem to move.

He scraped his teeth against his bottom lip. "Too bad we can't just play cards instead. Or do . . . well, anything else."

"Isn't this exciting for you? It's your Culling."

He opened and closed his mouth, as if he wasn't sure what to say to that. "I . . . I don't want anyone to die for me. Not you or any of the other girls."

Then why not put a stop to it? Why not just choose someone to marry and end the Culling? What did the temple matter? Why should some old creation story be the deciding factor in what happens to me? What if it was untrue? What if I was just born marked at random and it meant nothing?

The questions were glued to the backside of my teeth, unable to make it past the fence of my lips. I'd come close to saying a lot of it the day before, but now—now I didn't have the guts.

"We should go in." Cohen gestured to the door. "The queen doesn't like being kept waiting. Who should go first, you or me?"

"I'll go." I hated myself for volunteering, but I just wanted to get away from him. Away from those ocean-blue eyes.

Cohen stepped aside so he was out of sight of the doorway. "It wouldn't look good if we were seen together. You know, decorum and everything." He smiled nervously before he gestured to me. "We aren't supposed to be friends."

We were friends?

Was that what we'd decided yesterday?

I nodded, grabbed the handle, and then stopped. My heart was going to beat out of my chest. "Do I bow?"

He shook his head. "No. Just walk in and a footman will show you to your seat." There was a pause, just a heartbeat of space. "And smile," Cohen added.

"So I'll look more approachable?" I whispered, repeating what he'd told me when we'd first met.

He made a sound at the back of his throat and adjusted his tie. "No, because you're prettiest when you smile."

That deep, dark place where I'd tried to lock away any attraction to Cohen Warwick seemed to spark to life—bright and impossibly warm in the pit of my stomach. It was like I'd taken every ounce of fire from the palace and placed it inside my heart. It wasn't painful, just disconcerting—different from

·anything else I'd ever felt. The feeling was enough to make my fingers tense, my breathing hitch.

You're prettiest when you smile.

It was all that I thought of as I pulled the doors open and stepped inside.

16

The Royal Dining Room
The night before Sanctus Halletta

Viera did not smile when she saw me.

Thankfully Cohen was right, and a footman stepped forward to escort me to my chair. The room quieted, the conversation from earlier dying as everyone turned to look at me. Expressions of disappointment danced off the faces of the girls nearest the door and a few toward the back of the dining room craned their heads as if to see around me.

They were waiting for the prince—the prince who had just been talking to me. The prince, who had just told me I was prettiest when I smiled. I clung to that as I hurried toward my chair.

The room remained silent even as I took my seat. There seemed to be nearly a dozen chairs on each side, as well as places for the king and queen at either end. Most of the girls kept their heads down, their attention on their plates or on the skirts of their dresses. But Uri waved at me, her smile equally as nervous as my own. Britta sat on one side of the queen and Larkin sat across the table diagonally from me.

I tried not to flinch as she took me in. Something about her was off-putting, a natural sort of unease that came directly from her being too similar to Viera. Her expressions always appeared calculative and disapproving, as if a negative comment was only seconds away from spilling from her mouth. I hated that I wanted her to like me. But it felt necessary—as if I needed to win over the entire family one by one. First Uri, then Cohen . . .

You're prettiest when you smile.

You look fantastic.

Nope. Not happening. I was here for the Culling. I was here to compete for my life. Whether or not the prince liked me didn't matter. *Get your shit together.*

Aside from Cohen, I was the last person to arrive. His empty seat was across the table from mine, about three chairs down. This put him next to the queen, directly to her right, where I'm sure she liked to keep him. Four of the girls on my side of the table were goddess-touched; the other five sat opposite me.

There were small folded cards positioned in front of each of our plates, our names and hometowns scrawled in beautiful cursive. I took a moment to drink in the sumptuous décor of the dining room, noting the tall windows, midnight blue velvet curtains, and elaborate floral arrangements. The table was set with more silverware than I'd ever seen—two forks, two spoons, two knives, more than one silver-edged plate, an empty wineglass, and a tall glass filled with water.

One single place setting could buy enough timber to rebuild my family's house.

I was once again filled with a bone-deep dread. This room, with its beautiful wallpaper and silver-lined corridors, felt wrong. It was almost sinful, seeing so much wealth in one place—when just miles away, people in my community were starving.

I took a moment to scan the name cards closest to me.

Aviana

Nadia

Vivian

Elodie

Grier

Cloaking. Healing. Premonition. Mind reading. Voice control.

Kinsley sat directly across from me, her warm skin and floral mark emphasized by the red of her dress. She knew exactly how to highlight her features to make herself look entirely exotic—as if she were a mystery that was begging to be solved.

Inadequacy gnawed at my inside once more.

Kinsley saw me looking and smiled to herself—as if she knew she'd won the game already. I wasn't the only person admiring her; Heidi was looking too. The makeup her lady's maids had applied hadn't done much to disguise just how young she looked. As she watched Kinsley, I saw the carefully crafted confidence in her crumble. Her shoulders slumped slightly, and she made a point not to look that way again.

Kinsley was hard at work—her game was one of intimidation. She ran her fingertip along the rim of her china plate, repeatedly; all the while, she examined each girl. Each opponent.

No one met her eyes. Everyone who glanced her way did so for only a moment. And judging from the shadow of a smile on her face, this was exactly what Kinsley wanted.

I did not like this girl.

I focused my attention on the name cards. Heidi was from Nolajan. I recognized the place automatically, recalling the countless stories my brother had told me. It housed Prythine Market—a place that was rumored to be one of biggest in the country, similar in size to the Deca Market here in Gazda.

Ambrose went into Prythine every few weeks to sell goods from the Varos blacksmith's shop. I used to beg him to take me along. I swore that I'd hide my mark. No one would know. I could avoid the temples, not speak to anyone. But the risk of running into a videra was too great.

Ambrose had always left me standing on our front step, near tears.

He would always return with stories for me and a handful of aster flowers for the kitchen table—my favorite. The small white blossoms grew along the main road leading from our homestead. Ambrose had made a habit of picking them, so the tin pitcher on the table was always full and the mantel of our hearth always littered with dried petals. The gifts he brought home from Prythine were always meant as an apology, but they also served as a reminder of how trapped I was—forever a prisoner within my mother's cage of safety.

But not anymore. Now I was in a different cage.

Joslyn smiled when she saw me looking, her brown skin flushing as she fiddled with the pearl necklace at her throat. I didn't smile back at her. I didn't want to look at any of these girls—knowing that, in the days to come, I would either kill at least one of them or I would die trying.

Uri broke the silence. "Well." She grabbed her empty wineglass and lifted it a few inches from the table. "I already need a drink, and Cohen isn't even here yet."

The king snorted in response, his cheeks already rosy. "I second that."

Cohen had taken most of his features from his father. They were both fair-skinned with dirty-blond hair. But the king had given his golden-brown eyes to Uri and Larkin, while Cohen and Britta had gotten Viera's blue ones. Even with the physical similarities to Cohen, the king looked washed-out. Tired.

Tormented, even.

At Uri's suggestion, Malcolm lifted his own glass and snapped his fingers. One of the footmen stepped forward with a bottle of wine prepared to pour the drink.

Without saying a word, the queen lifted her hand and the footman retreated.

"Goddess, you're a witch," the king muttered as he set down his wineglass and leaned back in his chair.

As if on cue, Cohen walked in, shattering the moment. Viera's attention moved from her husband to her son. The prince didn't seem at all concerned with the fact that he had kept everyone waiting. He was all arrogance and charm as he walked to his chair next to the queen.

Cohen had almost taken his seat when his mother reached out her hand to him. He paused and then slowly straightened. For the first time, I saw something akin to dread touch Cohen's face.

The expression was there and gone in an instant. Then he was smiling again. He held his mother's gaze as he took her hand and kissed the black onyx ring she'd offered.

Viera smiled and pulled her fingers away, keeping her voice low as she said, "You shouldn't have kept me waiting."

"My apologies." Cohen remained standing. "It won't happen again."

"Of course not, my love." She nodded, as if she didn't believe him.

Cohen took that as permission to sit and he did so quickly. Once he was seated, Cohen turned and looked down the long table at the gathered girls. For a brief—perhaps entirely imagined—second, Cohen held my gaze. I lifted my head and squared my shoulders. Met his eyes.

My name is Monroe Benson, I am goddess-touched, and I will be the next Queen of Erydia. As much as I didn't want the throne, I wanted to believe that it was possible. I wanted to survive.

Cohen smiled, brilliant and sincere, and spoke to the table at large. "Please forgive me, ladies. I'm sorry to have kept you waiting."

"Yes, yes," Uri said, clearly bored. "Now that Cohen is here, we can get on with it." She lifted her wineglass again. "I want red." She glanced sideways to her mother. "*And* Her Majesty will take some as well. Yes, Mother?"

"Yes, we've waited long enough. Let's begin."

At that, the footmen burst into action, bringing covered trays of meats, potatoes, casseroles, soups, and different breads. It was more food than I'd ever seen in one place. The dishes seemed to go on forever, spreading across the table like a brightly colored quilt.

The girls around me reached forward, using silverware to carefully add slices of ham and scoops of corn to their plates. No one spoke, but the mood was more relaxed now that everyone had something to occupy themselves with.

I was about to make a plate too when I caught sight of Kinsley. She hadn't moved to touch the food. Instead, she only smiled smugly to herself, her fingertip still running around the silver edge of her plate.

Cohen hadn't moved to make his plate either. He caught my eye and shook his head, the movement so slight I almost missed it. Quickly, I pulled my hands back from the food and folded them in my lap.

Slowly, one by one, the other girls at the table stopped too. Lifted forks clattered against plates as each girl pulled her hands away from the table.

The queen was smiling, a tight-lipped, pleased smile. Her eyes were on the girl next to me, who had her fork in her mouth. Aviana froze, noticing the queen's sudden attention too late.

The lethal stillness stretched on for what felt like eons but must have only been seconds. I couldn't take my eyes off Viera. She was looking directly at Aviana, her head tilted to one side, just slightly, like a cat examining a cornered mouse.

Cohen's voice was sharp, a plea. "Mother—"

The queen lifted a hand, cutting off anything else he might have said. She was still looking at Aviana—who had started foaming at the mouth. The girl convulsed. Her golden skin blanched as she sputtered and coughed onto her plate.

Instinctively I sprang back, sliding my chair into the girl on the other side of me. Aviana's brown eyes were wide, panicked. Her fingers found mine on top of the table and squeezed, hard, as she bent at the waist and vomited all over herself. Before I could do anything, she fell facedown onto her plate of food.

I watched, horrified, as her mark, a thin black line that ran between the base of her wrist and the crease of her elbow, faded. It disappeared like snow melting in the sun, until there was no trace of it. Her short fingernails dug into my skin one last time and then she grew still.

She stopped breathing.

Dead.

She was dead.

There was absolute silence, a silence so deep that I was certain no one in the room dared to even breathe. After a long moment, Cohen stood up. The only sound was that of his chair scraping against tile.

I pulled my hand away from Aviana's, letting her fingers drop to the table. The world was frozen. Even Kinsley had stopped playing with her plate.

Uri still held her wineglass in her hand, inches from her mouth. Slowly, she lowered it to the table. I watched her turn to look at her father, her brown eyes wide as she waited for him to help. For him to do or say something.

Viera watched him too.

Around me, the other girls all had their heads lowered, their eyes downcast—afraid to draw attention to themselves. I glanced around the table. There was a dark challenge in Viera's gaze as she looked to her husband. As if this were all a game, and we were merely easily abandoned cards.

Britta was staring at Cohen, her expression pleading. He met her eyes as she pressed her lips together and nodded to his chair, without words asking him to take his seat, to cave to their mother.

Viera looked up at her son. "Come now, Cohen. That's one less girl for you to busy yourself with."

Cohen gripped the edge of the table but he didn't sit. He schooled his face, lifted his chin, and met his mother's eyes. "The goddess chose them. All ten of them. It wasn't your place to—"

The queen cut him off. "The goddess didn't want that one anymore." Her voice was light, cheerful even, as if they were discussing the weather and not the dead girl next to me.

Cohen's eyes darted to Aviana, then to me, before they landed back on his mother. "This is not *your* Culling."

She nodded and looked to the king. "No. It isn't." Her finger lazily drifted around the semicircle of marked girls sitting before her. "If it were, they would all be dead."

There was a pause.

"Dinner is over," Cohen said, addressing the rest of the table. "Go back to your rooms. I'll have food sent up to you."

Chairs scraped as girls prepared to leave.

Viera tapped her fingernail against her wineglass and very quietly said, "I'll kill the next person to stand."

All movement at the table ceased.

Uri still watched her father, her face bloodless. He didn't look at her; he stared only at the queen. At the black onyx ring she wore.

Britta cleared her throat. "Mother, perhaps it would be best if—"

"Remove the girl and notify the family," Viera said. "We can announce her death tomorrow at the Commencement." She clicked her tongue. "Such a waste of a young life."

She lifted a hand and gestured for the waiting footmen to step forward. They removed the body quickly and cleared away her plate. They cleaned the floor and covered the stained tablecloth until the empty chair was the only proof Aviana had ever even been there to begin with.

"Now," Viera said, "perhaps one of you can tell me what happened?" She scanned the table, pausing on each of us as she waited for a response. "What was her mistake?"

Kinsley spoke up. "The queen always begins dinner. No one eats until she does."

"An archaic rule that none of the other girls were aware of," Cohen said through gritted teeth.

He shot Kinsley a look and she met his gaze, unsmiling.

"That is correct, Kinsley," Viera said, ignoring Cohen entirely.

The queen reached out and took hold of her fork, twisting the glinting silver object between her fingers. We waited. The king still stared openly at his wife; the haze of alcohol faded from his gaze as he waited to see what she might do next. I wondered what it must be like for him to sit here, across from the woman who had taken everything from him during a dinner not so different from this one.

Viera's eyes darted a coy glance in Cohen's direction. "Take a seat, darling, so that we can have our dinner. I'm simply famished." She stabbed a roasted potato and popped it into her mouth.

The prince stood for a second longer, just looking at the queen. She only watched her husband as she chewed. The older man looked to his son, then to his queen. He still said nothing. Did nothing to stop her.

Britta's voice was so soft, I almost didn't hear her as she whispered, "Please."

The word wasn't meant for the queen.

Slowly, Cohen lowered himself back into his chair. He didn't touch his food. No one did, not after what had just happened. The idea of putting anything in my mouth was enough to make my stomach churn.

Britta angled her shoulders so that she was facing all of us and made a show of cutting and eating the steak on her plate. She smiled encouragingly at the girl next to her, Grier. Britta waited until the other goddess-touched girls nearest her had started eating before she leaned forward and spoke to Cohen.

They both sat on either side of the queen, so I knew they couldn't be saying anything too worrisome, but their expressions were stern. Their mother pretended not to even notice them talking across the table.

It was clear that Britta wanted Cohen to eat. He said nothing as she spooned a helping of roasted green beans onto his plate alongside a piece of grilled fish. The prince didn't move to touch the food she had given him; he only drained his wineglass and gestured for the footman to refill it.

The girls around me ate, quietly picking at their plates and whispering to one another. The conversation was dry—the unseasonably hot weather, the upcoming holidays, the taste of the food. No one said a word about their marks, or their abilities, or the fact that Aviana was now dead.

Kinsley and I seemed to be the only two who weren't talking. She ate slowly and daintily, cutting the chicken on her plate with a practiced grace. Clearly, she'd eaten at the queen's table before and was familiar with how meals functioned. I wondered how she'd ended up here, and why she was so obviously comfortable looking at Cohen.

I wondered if they had a history.

Clearly, she hadn't spent her life hidden away—not with a mark like hers. Not in Gazda. She would have been called blessed. Worshiped and revered by the more religious of our country. This was something she'd been prepared for. The evidence was in how well she carried herself.

And if Kinsley was comfortable at the queen's table, I didn't doubt she was also comfortable wielding her ability. I'd had one day in the palace training rooms—how often had she been here, or somewhere else, training for the Culling? I wondered what that would mean for me and the other girls. The years I'd spent suppressing my ability had cost me valuable time.

I pushed a piece of meat from one end of my plate to the other. I just wanted to get out of the room. The food had grown cold and the conversation around me kept stopping and starting.

The king, who'd been silent for most of the dinner, was growing louder the more he had to drink. He'd moved on from wine and was drinking something stronger. Joslyn, one of the girls sitting next to him, kept having to lean farther away from the table to get away. He'd told her how lovely she was no less than five times, and his eyes hadn't left her chest since we'd started eating.

Uri kept shooting the girl apologetic looks and trying to draw her father into conversation. He barely paid her any mind, which seemed to be the typical reaction she received. Even the other goddess-touched girls seemed more eager to speak to Britta or Larkin than Uri. The other princesses could get them things—connections, power, respect—but Uri offered them nothing.

Knowing this only solidified my desire to have her on my court.

Cohen still hadn't touched the food. This was his personal rebellion, I realized. She could make him stay here, but Viera couldn't force him to eat.

He lifted his glass and one of the footmen stepped forward to refill it. Cohen's face was slightly flushed, and it made him look younger. I didn't know how much he'd already had to drink—two glasses, maybe three. Uri and Britta were exchanging glances down the length of the table, both trying to calculate how much wine their brother had actually had.

Before the footman could reach the table, Britta held up a hand. "He'll have water, please."

Cohen smiled, a challenge to his older sister. "Wine."

Britta frowned and shook her head. "I think we should retire for the evening. It's been a long day and you seem tired—"

His hands hit the top of the table with enough force to rattle the cutlery as he leaned forward and said, "I'm not five years old, Britta. I don't need you to mother me—" He stopped short as he caught sight of her stunned expression.

Britta dipped her head as hurt flashed across her face. "I'm sorry. I just . . ."

Cohen eased back into his chair. "I-I didn't mean to snap at you."

She was trying to protect him from himself.

I knew that—I could see it in the stiff way she held her shoulders. I could see it in the way she flinched as the queen set her napkin on her plate and stood. Britta, Larkin, Uri, and the king all stood too. One by one, everyone at the table got to their feet. Everyone except for Cohen, who leaned back in his chair and smiled up at his mother.

He couldn't give less of a damn if he tried.

The danger of what he was doing made my blood turn to ice.

But the queen didn't say anything else. She just turned and left the room, Larkin following at her heels like a watery shadow. With one more refill of his liquor, the king was gone too, leaving just the princesses, Cohen, and the goddess-touched girls.

Britta cleared her throat and folded her hands in front of her. "Thank you all for coming tonight and for showing restraint with one another. Tomorrow begins the competition. You will have the morning to do as you please, but tomorrow night you will be presented to Erydia and to your chosen courts. I know I speak for everyone in the royal family when I say we are incredibly excited to see what each of you has to offer the Crown." Britta smiled, pausing long enough to scan the room. "I am simply overjoyed to be here, amongst you, Erydia's finest. May the goddess be honored and may she bless each one of you as you compete in the Culling."

There was a chorus of "goddess be honored" but I didn't join them. I still looked at Aviana's empty seat. The footman hadn't done a very good job of cleaning her chair. The white fabric was stained yellow—she'd wet herself.

Cohen repeated the words last, his voice loud and annoyed. Uri shot him a look, but Britta only nodded once to us and turned to leave. She paused only long enough to whisper something to one of the footmen and then was gone.

Uri patted Cohen on the back and walked past him. "All right, ladies." She waved her hands in a sort of shooing motion. "Show's over."

17

The Royal Dining Room
The night before Sanctus Halletta

I lingered by the door of the dining room, trying to discreetly size up my competition. My hands still shook, and I swear I could still feel Aviana's fingers gripping mine. Her death had happened so quickly.

"There's only nine of us left now," Joslyn said as she hurried down the hall toward her bedroom. Nadia walked a few paces behind her. She was petite, with wide-set dark-brown eyes and small sullen lips that she chewed incessantly. It didn't matter that Nadia was lovely, with skin the color of honey and brown hair that was braided into an intricate updo; it was obvious she didn't see herself as a threat and that made her easy to overlook.

Maybe it was a ploy, a way to put us at ease. There was no way to know.

I examined the faces of the others, trying to see them for who they were—but it was difficult to see past what they were *to me*. I knew how much my appearance had changed because of the new clothes and the makeup, and it left me wondering how much of *any* of this was real.

Uri was still in the dining room and I wanted to wait and ask her about being on my court. I wasn't sure if she'd received the invitation from Tallis yet, but I thought I could at least find out if she was open to helping me. So, I stayed longer than the rest, waiting for the princess to come into the hall.

Eventually, everyone but Kinsley left. The fact that she'd hung back when all the others had gone made me nervous. I had a reason to wait, but Kinsley was just staring at me—her attention heavy and uncomfortable. When she saw me looking, she grinned, but it wasn't a friendly gesture. I didn't smile back.

Why was she still here?

After a long stretch of uncomfortable silence, Kinsley headed down the hall in my direction, as if she were going to pass me and leave. But she stopped, leaving only a few inches of space between us, and tilted her head at me, those eyes running a race from the top of my head to my—

"Nice boots. Did you dig them out of the garbage yourself?" The smile on her face grew when I didn't respond. "Clearly," she continued, "you're in over your head here. Let me assure you, no amount of makeup or frills is going to disguise the Varos trash that you are. Why don't you make things easier on the rest of us and go drown yourself?"

I followed her gaze to where my black boots were peeking out from my dress.

"You know," I said, trying to keep my voice steady, "no one's ever won the Culling by being a bitch. I hope your ability is more impressive than your insults."

She snorted and shook her head. I thought for a second that she was going to walk away, but she didn't; instead she leaned in, shoving me against the wall. Her fingers dug into the skin of my wrist as she spoke directly into my ear.

"*You*," she said, her breath hot against my neck, "you'll be dead in a few weeks and I'll be queen. Maybe we won't even burn your body; we'll just leave it out for the birds."

She shoved me again, hard enough that my head hit the wall. My vision swam. It was then that I realized just how alone we were in the hallway, no guards in sight, all the other goddess-touched girls gone. The smile that formed on her lips said that she knew that too. Kinsley knew that, if she wanted to, she could kill me now.

Kinsley tightened her grip on my wrist, digging her long fingernails into the skin so hard I was certain she would draw blood. She was still inches from my face, waiting, daring me to say anything in return.

I didn't.

I just snapped my fingers.

Kinsley screamed and released my wrist. The fire I'd started was contained to my fingertips, so I knew I hadn't burned her. Instead, she'd been startled.

The sudden heat near her hand was enough to make her spring back, shocked and clearly afraid. That wasn't at all what she'd expected me to do.

She looked at my hand, where the fire still twitched and breathed. I drew it back in slowly, letting her get a good look at it before I extinguished it.

I met her eyes and smiled. "Don't worry, Kinsley, I won't leave your body for the birds. I'll be sure to burn it."

As soon as she was gone, I collapsed against the nearest wall. The air hit my lungs in large gasps, burning my throat with each inhale. My hands were shaking, my palms sticky with sweat. All the confidence I'd had seconds earlier had dissipated and now I was just worried I'd made a mistake. Maybe I shouldn't have shown her my ability.

Juno had said that we would leave here saying things about the other girls—well, I'd given Kinsley plenty to tell her trainers. I'd also drawn a pretty large target on my back. Not to mention, I'd broken Culling rules by using my ability.

Just as I was about to abandon my wait for Uri and go back to my room, Dellacov rounded the corner and saw me.

"You okay?" he asked.

I nodded and pushed away from the wall.

He gestured to the dining room. "I'm just here to get Cohen. I heard there was . . ." He cleared his throat. "I heard dinner was eventful."

"A girl died."

"Yeah . . ." He rubbed at the back of his neck. "I'm sorry."

"What happens to us, once we're dead?" I hated the way I phrased it, the inevitability that laced my tone. I hated that I already knew the answer.

He shifted uncomfortably. "Burned. They'll burn the bodies on an altar. It's what the temple requires. They view it as a—"

"A sacrifice."

He met my eyes. "I know this isn't easy for you. But so many people see this as an honor. You've been chosen—"

"I'm really not in the mood for a lecture." I started to move past him, but he caught my shoulder, holding me in place.

"I'm not lecturing you. I'm just— You could be queen, Monroe. You are as likely to sit on that throne as any of them. And you're here now. The time for running, for wishing it were otherwise, is over. This is when girls either die or become monarchs. I'm not saying it's fair and I wouldn't wish the task on anyone, truly. But it's fallen to you. The goddess gave that mark to you. I'm not the most pious or the first to speak on the temple, but I don't believe the goddess would put any of you at a complete disadvantage. You're equals in power—even if your abilities aren't the exact same. Don't count yourself out. Focus on winning, not on what happens if you lose."

With that, he turned toward the dining room. He'd just reached the door when Uri came out. When she spoke, her voice lacked its regular bravado. "Oh, Dellacov. I hadn't expected you to be . . ." she shook her head, brushing away the thought. "Cohen wants to be alone. He's fine. Upset and angry, but fine. You can go."

"Oh. Okay." Dellacov put his hands in his pockets, opened his mouth, closed it, and swallowed. "Y-you look beautiful tonight." He nodded to the dress she was wearing.

It was short by comparison, the hem falling a few inches above her ankles to showcase her shoes, which were the same crisp gold as the fringe dripping from the tiers of the bodice and skirt. It hung loose, in an older style, but still glamorous.

While Kinsley's bloodred dress had been trying to make a statement, Uri was a statement all on her own. She didn't have to try; it was inborn. And even though Dellacov had probably seen her dressed this way for a million different events, he was staring at her like this was the first time.

She swallowed and folded her hands. Even though she didn't say a word, her face said a lot of things.

Unlike Cohen, Uri wasn't very good at disguising what she was feeling. It sort of spilled out of her, like an overflowing bucket. Although she turned her face away to try to hide her smile, the flush of her cheeks was enough to show how pleased she was at his compliment.

Dellacov held out his arm to her. "Can I walk you to your room?" I didn't miss the slight shake in his fingers, the way his smile wavered as he waited for her response.

Her eyes darted to me, as if remembering I was there. A flash of disappointment crossed her face as she looked back to Dellacov. Uri swallowed hard and straightened, lifting her chin, as if she'd only just realized who she was—or perhaps who she wasn't.

"No." The words sounded empty, diplomatic. "I'm perfectly capable of walking myself back to my room, thank you."

His hand fell back to his side. "Sure. Of course." He chewed his bottom lip before he said, "I didn't mean to insinuate that you couldn't go by yourself. I just . . ." He cupped the back of his neck with his hand and sighed.

She looked over at me. "Monroe, I got your court invitation. Thank you for considering me. I'd be honored to join."

"Thank you."

"It'll be my pleasure."

Dellacov spoke again, "Uriel, I—"

"It's fine, Dellacov."

It wasn't fine. The look on his face said none of it was fine, but Uri clearly didn't want to talk about it and, at the end of the day, she was a princess.

She forced a smile. "I'll see you tomorrow, Monroe." She started to walk away but stopped and turned to look at Dellacov one last time. Her voice was gentler when she said, "Dellacov, thank you for the offer. Perhaps some other night. I could use some . . . quiet. It's been a rough evening."

Dellacov didn't say anything as she turned and walked away from us. His eyes followed her. He waited until we couldn't hear her footsteps anymore and then he left too, heading in the same direction. I knew that I was supposed to always have an escort, but I wasn't about to remind him of that.

Abandoned, I leaned against the wall again and exhaled. I'd only just collected myself enough to walk back to my room when I heard footsteps. I turned to see Cohen step out into the hall.

"Why are you still here?" His voice wasn't slurred necessarily, but it was looser, more relaxed. He sounded less like a prince and more like a young man.

I didn't mind that at all.

"I just needed a second."

Cohen nodded and shoved his hands in his pockets. "I need like five million seconds." He laughed at his own joke and then sobered. "Tonight didn't exactly go as planned, did it?"

"I guess that would depend on what you'd had planned."

"Well, I can tell you what I *didn't* have planned." He stepped closer to me. "I didn't plan for anyone to die today. I hate all of this—all the frills and damn anxiety. Everyone looks at me like I'm a trophy."

"Try being the one who'll end up dead."

I'd meant it as a joke, but as soon as it left my mouth, I knew that I didn't want him to find it funny. Speaking it aloud, leaving little room for any confidence that I was going to survive, made my stomach churn.

Suddenly, the hall felt cramped and that swelling panic I kept pushing down, down, down was at the forefront of my mind.

He froze when he saw my expression. "Oh, goddess, I've upset you again. I'm always saying the wrong thing." He stepped forward, his arm outstretched.

I moved back before he could touch me. "I should go to my room, it's late."

"No." He shook his head. "No, don't leave. Not yet. Not when you're crying."

And I was crying.

I wiped at my face, trying to get the overwhelmed tears to stop. "I'm okay. Like you said, tonight was just really . . . It was scary."

He nodded and let his hand drop back to his side. "Let me at least walk you back upstairs."

"I can find my way," I said.

"Maybe." He moved forward slowly, closing the gap between us, and this time I didn't dodge him. Cohen didn't touch me, just gestured for me to lead the way. "But I'd feel better if you didn't go alone."

I walked past him, heading in the direction of my room. Cohen followed, hands in his pockets and steps unhurried. I was nearly down the first hall when I suddenly remembered what Dellacov had told me while we were still on the train. I stopped walking so abruptly that Cohen bumped into me.

"What is it? What's wrong?" he said, alarmed.

"You're supposed to walk in front of me. Those are the rules."

"You didn't seem concerned with it yesterday."

"I didn't remember it yesterday."

He laughed. "I don't care about rules like that, Monroe."

Goddess, I like how he says my name. And I hated it, hated how my heart seemed to shudder in my chest when he looked at me. It was strange and foreign and . . . not at all terrible. But he was a prince and I was a goddess-touched girl. Our story, however short, could only ever end in disaster.

He was still watching me. I cast that thought away. "But Dellacov said—"

"Hugo likes bossing other people around. Just do what everyone else in my family does and ignore him."

He started walking again and I went with him, this time side by side. We were silent for a long moment and although he didn't speak, I could feel Cohen's eyes on me. I tried not to fidget although I desperately wanted to.

Finally, he said, "So, your brothers have been drafted."

"How . . . ?"

"I went through all of your files." When I just blinked at him, he said, "What? Did you think I was going to just marry one of you without knowing anything first?" His smile grew. "Uri is my spy. She makes it her business to know where everyone is at all times. So, it was easy enough to sneak into Hugo's office and take a peek. Plus, you made a scene trying to run away. The whole country knows about you and your brother. It was national news."

"The whole country?"

He nodded, his expression turning solemn as he said, "I heard about the videra finding you, and that you were drugged. I'm sorry that happened to you."

Everyone was always so sorry, but no one was helping me. No one was trying to fix things. No one was coming to save me.

Dellacov's words echoed back to me—*The time for running, for wishing it were otherwise, is over. This is when girls either die or become monarchs.* I was going to have to save myself. I *would* save myself. Somehow.

I swallowed and muttered, "I just didn't want to die."

"When I looked at your file, I saw that your birth certificate says you're a boy. There was also a draft demand issued in your name. Kind of weird. Was that—?"

"My mother lied. She wanted to try to keep me from having to do this."

"Ah, I see." He chewed his lip, the next question more sensitive. "And . . . And your hair?"

"I cut it myself," I admitted. "Also, it isn't fair that you can just read all about me. I don't know anything about you."

"That isn't true. I told you about my mother and about being poisoned. That's more than most people know." He shrugged. "Plus, I'd rather hear about you. You see what my life is like. Dinner parties and my parents acting dysfunctional at every opportunity. The most exciting thing I do is play cards and occasionally spar with Dellacov. It isn't newsworthy. Tell me about your family. Do you know where your brothers have been stationed?"

I shook my head. Maybe talking about me wasn't a bad thing. Cohen knew things that no one else did, and what he didn't know, he could find out. "Did my file say anything about my brother Ambrose? He was the one with me at the train station."

"No one told you?"

The breath left my lungs. "Told me what?"

"He was arrested and then shipped off to training. I read where they'd sent him, but I don't remember off the top of my head."

"But he's unharmed? They . . . They didn't hurt him because of me?"

"No. He's fine." It fell quiet, and Cohen said, "You know, I could find out where he is, if you want?"

I stopped walking. "Would you?"

Cohen stopped too. "Of course."

"Thank you."

"What about your other brother? Do you know where he is?"

I shook my head. "But Kace will work his way up the ranks as quickly as he can. He wants to be a royal guard one day."

"Really? That's ambitious."

"Kace has been obsessed with the position since he was a kid. My father was a city guard and might have been promoted to royal guard if it hadn't been for—"

"For the last war?"

"For me."

"Yeah, you sort of threw a wrench in their plans, didn't you?"

I nodded.

"It's pretty amazing to have been loved so much that your parents would move to Varos to save you. I don't know a lot of people who would travel so far. It isn't— That place doesn't have a great reputation."

"Have you ever been there?"

He hesitated and then nodded. "Yes, when I was much younger. I remember it being very dirty and the people there were— Most weren't kind to me. I had a lot of doors shut in my face."

Something in his tone grated at my nerves. "It isn't a bad place and the people there aren't bad either. We're all—Everyone in Varos is just trying to survive."

Cohen and I continued down the hall in step with one another. Both of us quiet, both of us lost in our own thoughts. After a second, he said, "I hope your brother is able to get his promotion. You should at least know where he is in the meantime. Same for Ambrose."

Once again, I was presented with his kindness, his openness, and I didn't know what to do with it. As much as I appreciated his offer, I kept waiting for the other shoe to drop. We didn't know each other, and there were nine— *now eight*—other girls to draw his attention. Why, out of all of them, was he looking at me?

"Why help me?"

He paused at the top of a set of stairs and tugged at his tie, loosening it. "Because I can. And it hurts nothing for you to know. To have some semblance of peace when it comes to your family's future. I'd want that, if I were in your shoes. I'd be worried if I didn't know where my sisters were."

I nodded. "Well, thank—"

"Hey, do you want something to eat?" He pointed at the stairs. "The kitchen's that way."

A startled laugh escaped me at the absurdity of the question.

"You know, I can make a mean omelet." He just kept talking, his blue eyes wide and childlike.

Prince Cohen Warwick was staring at me like I was his friend and, despite all the things that stood against me, I wanted it—I wanted his friendship. Not only that, I wanted that smile, as crooked and boyish as it was. It made me feel present. Alive.

But I didn't feel deserving of those things, not when there were other girls here too. Certainly, not when those other girls would have to die for me to truly have him. But in that moment, I wanted to feel normal. I wanted his friendship—and anything else he might offer me.

Slowly, Cohen backed toward the stairs. When he looked at me again, his face was flushed and he was grinning from ear to ear, unencumbered by any crown or responsibility.

"You hungry?"

Good goddess, he is handsome when he smiles.

"And I've got these," he reached into his trouser pocket and produced Uri's deck of cards. "Best three out of five?"

I wondered how many people in this huge palace had seen him look like this, hair askew, tie loose, smelling of red wine, and smiling like he was feeling it. My chest felt warm, filled to the brim with something I couldn't name—something I wanted to suppress.

"Cohen, I don't think it's a good idea for us to . . ." I swallowed. "I'm not supposed to be . . ."

He shook his head, that impetuous smile growing even more crooked. "Please, don't say no."

I stared at him for a long moment, warring with my common sense and my desire to have experiences beyond what I'd known so far. I'd never had a young man look at me the way Cohen did. I'd never had the chance to and I craved it.

He was bread crumbs and I was a starved bird—willing to take any stray piece, any small ounce of humanity. With him looking at me, I didn't feel so terribly alone. But this felt . . . fast. And yet, so did everything else. I guess time had no real meaning once it started to visibly tick down the seconds of your life.

"Well?" he said.

Goddess, this was a mistake. I could feel it. And yet, I found myself nodding. "Yes."

18

The Palace Kitchens
The night before Sanctus Halletta

We sat facing each other on wooden stools, a large butcher-block counter between us. As soon as we'd arrived, the kitchen staff had become scarce. Now I was entirely alone with a prince.

To his credit, Cohen *could* make a decent omelet; but he struggled with bacon. He almost started a grease fire three times. I stayed near the stove, invisibly soothing the flames without his notice. It was good practice and, had I been planning to ever tell them about this, Juno and Tallis would have been proud.

For a long time, Cohen talked and I just listened. He told me about growing up in the palace. It was strange to hear him tell stories about holidays, banquets, and visiting dignitaries. These things were casually blended with stories of epic games of hide-and-go-seek and rooftop escapades.

He spoke so casually, explaining how he'd been raised. Britta and Uri were constant characters in his stories, while Larkin was always on the fringes—often never mentioned. The way he spoke about her made her sound similar to Viera. The distrust in his voice said that the similarity was enough to keep him at a distance.

He and Uri had spent their childhoods throwing fruit from balconies during state occasions, trying to make it into the circle of their mother's crown as she passed them in the procession below. Cohen had amused me with information about Uri—like the fact that, if she didn't get her way, she used to hold her breath until she passed out.

I'd laughed, but I hadn't been at all surprised.

Britta was the disciplinarian in his stories. She was the oldest, the levelheaded one, the one who took the blame when things went too far. She was always standing in her mother's way, challenging the queen even though it wasn't necessarily her place to do so.

"I owe her an apology for the way I behaved tonight," Cohen said. "I shouldn't have gotten so upset. Britta was just trying to keep the queen from becoming angry. And, if I'm being honest, I do need her to mother me. I feel like I'm a mess most of the time." His lips quirked up at that admission. "Especially of late."

I shuffled the deck of cards in my hands, preparing to deal them. "She seems like a good sister."

"Britta has always looked out for Uri and me. Our mother—she's a queen and she's . . . well, she isn't the most affectionate. Our parents have just never been there, not really. Not the way I think parents are supposed to be. There were no bedtime stories or hugs. If we woke up with nightmares, we were either left alone or comforted by a nanny. Britta is older than me by seven years, nine years older than Uri. The older we got, the more she sort of took on the role of a mother—even when she needed one herself. I can't blame her for wanting to protect me, even now."

"That must have been difficult," I whispered.

"Which part?"

"All of it."

He only sighed in response. "Deal me in."

We played best two out of three, and then—at Cohen's insistence—pushed it to three out of five. I emerged triumphant each time, but the losing never seemed to bother him. We talked some as we played.

As the night turned to early morning, I felt myself unfurling. It was strange, to feel so comfortable with someone I'd known for only a few days. Somehow there was safety with Cohen, and an ease between the two of us that I didn't feel with anyone else in the palace.

Maybe it's a sign. Or maybe it's goddess-driven. Maybe I'm supposed to feel this way about him—he's the prince in my Culling, after all. He's supposed to be the prize. Was it possible that the goddess made all of us to feel this way about him?

I wasn't sure, but I hoped that he felt that way about only me. And . . . And it seemed like that. We were friends—something I'd never had before. As we played game after game, it was like we were the only two people in the world. And it was a good world. One without Cullings and crowns. One without expectations and dangers. One where I was just a girl, and he was just a boy.

It was the alcohol.

That was why his gaze was so intense. Why he smiled when I commented on something he'd said earlier—it had nothing to do with me. He was just feeling the drinks. That's all. That was why he was telling me all of this. He was drunk. Buzzed. The way his fingers brushed mine as he stole a card was clumsy, not sensual.

As it grew later and our game of cards grew lazier, the topic of our conversation shifted back to me.

Are you more like your mother or your father? Did you like attending school? Which solstice is your favorite? Who taught you to play Cages and Crowns? Do you like cake? Have you ever listened to any of the popular radio dramas? What sort of books do you read?

With every question, I gave him another piece of me, another small shred of information that no one else had. But he'd given pieces too, and I clung to each shred of information. I let the honesty and normalcy of it ground me in the safety of the present. *Tonight, I am alive.* Tomorrow—Tomorrow I might not be. Why shouldn't I lean in? I didn't plan to lie down and die, but that didn't mean that death wasn't still just days or weeks away. So why should I deny myself the experiences that other girls took for granted? I wanted to be wanted, to be something more than the mark on my skin.

Somewhere along the way, Cohen found another bottle of wine.

He'd been laughing all night, a sharp ringing sound that made me smile even when I tried not to. It scared me, how easy it was to talk to him. How easily he unfolded himself in front of me, vulnerable.

He should stop. I should stop.

"What did you want to be when you grew up?"

I stacked the abandoned cards from our last game and sighed. "I've never thought that much about it."

"Think about it now. If you weren't marked, what would you want to be?"

For some reason, that question made me tired. It filled me with a weariness I'd been denying and was unprepared to face. I grabbed the empty plates and walked to the sink. I could feel his eyes on me as I went.

His openness was in part due to how much he'd had to drink. But even without taking a sip of wine myself, I'd told him everything he'd wanted to know. Cohen was a distraction. A handsome, smiling, boyish distraction that kept me from dwelling on the fact that someone had died tonight. A lack of appetite had been the only thing standing between me and possible death.

My throat tightened at the thought.

Nine girls. Now there were only nine girls left. Eight between me and the crown.

I wanted to believe that I was safe with Cohen; after all, he'd been nothing but kind to me. But a girl had been poisoned at dinner. Killed by his mother. How could a woman like that have a son like him?

"So?" Cohen asked.

I couldn't even remember the question anymore.

I turned the tap on, thrilled, as I always was, to find clean, hot water. Like a security blanket, I grabbed the frying pan Cohen had used and started washing it. Warm water, soap, and the back-and-forth motion of scrubbing something—all of it was familiar to me. What wasn't familiar was the boy now standing behind me.

Go back to your seat.

Stay right where you are.

"You're going to get that dress wet," he said, his voice so quiet.

I ignored him and reached for one of the dirty plates.

"Monroe?" His hand caught my wrist, held it still underneath the faucet. "Have . . . Have I done something wrong?"

Goddess, no. You're doing everything too right. And that feels wrong.

For a second his eyes settled on my mark. At the sight of it, Cohen's face shifted and grew serious. There were so many things he could be thinking, and I wondered exactly where his mind had landed. Whatever he was thinking, it wasn't good.

I swallowed and met his eyes. "Cohen—" But I couldn't finish, couldn't even find what I wanted to say. I pulled my hand away and turned the water off. The flames of the lanterns nearby were nothing compared to the roiling heat trapped inside my chest. It made each breath too tight, too short, nearly painful.

And Cohen was right there, looking at me. Waiting as if I held the answer to all of life's questions. There had to be some way to make him see that this—whatever this was—couldn't happen. We couldn't be friends.

That dark place where I'd been shoving all thoughts of the prince seemed to swell to an impossible size until I couldn't contain it.

He was going to marry whoever won the Culling and there was a good chance that it wouldn't be me. My life was already on the line—did I really want my heart there too?

You can die unloved and sheltered—or you can lean into whatever this is and live for as long as you can. I swallowed and closed my eyes, trying to steady myself. Sweat coated my palms. When I looked again, Cohen's eyes were like a stormy sea. *Oh, goddess. This is going to hurt like hell.*

But I wanted—I wanted so much more than had been offered to me. There were lifetimes of unseen things, unfelt emotions, unfulfilled fantasies. But here I was. Wearing a beautiful dress, standing in a palace, being looked at by a prince. Maybe there was a way to live a lifetime in a matter of weeks.

Cohen's gaze drifted from mine down to my mouth, then back. I couldn't breathe. Couldn't move. My hand was pressing against his chest and I couldn't remember when I'd done that—I didn't know if I was holding him there or pushing him away.

Then he was kissing me.

My eyes fluttered closed and the whole world stilled. It was gentle and tentative, neither of us certain. I didn't know what I was supposed to do with my hands. Do I touch him? But Cohen knew what to do.

His hands found my face; rough thumbs ran circles along my jawline, my cheeks, encircled my waist. What was once a nervous kiss deepened when I didn't pull away, when I kissed him back.

He tasted sweet, like the red wine, and I was drunk on him. Nothing else mattered. Not the Culling or the other girls or his mother. Or the fact that I could be dead in a week.

This. He mattered. Him touching me, kissing me, those things mattered. What I wanted mattered.

Cohen pulled away just enough to smile at me. He exhaled, a breathy sound, a nervous sort of laugh. My heart was racing, blood rushing in my ears so loudly I could only focus on the feel of his lips as they brushed mine again, on his hand as it threaded through mine.

Just when I thought he was going to kiss me again, we stopped, both of us breathing heavily, our foreheads pressed to one another like we were using each other as a crutch. I'd never seen eyes as deep as his. I thought I might drown in them.

Cohen's voice was trembling. "Monroe?"

I nodded, my only answer. I didn't know what he was asking or what I was agreeing to, but at that moment the answer was yes. Yes, to all of it.

Yes.

But that moment died too quickly, our breathing calmed, and reality snuck in like a pickpocket to steal away the joy I'd coiled tightly around my heart. Suddenly I was faced with what having this boy would cost. Looking at those blue eyes, I found myself at a loss.

Oh no. Deep, dark dread stabbed a knife directly into my chest. I couldn't have him. Not without becoming a monster. And if I didn't become a monster I'd die.

Cohen's face caved, his brow furrowing as I gently pushed him away. I was starting to shake, my entire body reacting to the realization that I'd just kissed him.

I'd never been kissed before, much less by a prince—a prince I couldn't have. A prince I shouldn't even be alone with. A prince who was looking at me so earnestly, his blue eyes wide, his lips swollen.

But if I died, he would kiss someone else. He would marry someone else. This would never mean as much to him as it did to me.

Cohen called my name as I left the kitchen, but I didn't turn back. I forced myself to keep going. One foot in front of the other until I was back in the safety of my bedroom.

Palace Bedroom

Sanctus Halletta

Sleep didn't come; it ran from me and I was too overwhelmed to chase it. As the sun rose, I sat on the floor next to the bedside table and practiced lighting a candle, making the flame in my hand and pulling it onto the wick. I built the mental bridge between myself and the object and then eased the flame across.

Tallis had given me the candle at training the day before. She'd wanted me to practice working with fire without using my hands—and I knew I could do that. I could shape flames from across the room; I just struggled to move them through empty space.

Spark the fire, throw it to the candle, pull it back to my hand, and put it out. I repeated the actions over and over again, until I could do it quickly. It was mindless.

If I was focused on that, I didn't have to think about Cohen.

Or kissing him.

I was dressed for training. The candle had burned down to a pool of wax on the table and the golden light of dawn crept across the intricate carpet of my bedroom. When there'd been nothing left of the candle to burn, I waited for my trainers to arrive.

Tallis hadn't even had time to knock before I was pulling the door open. Her eyes widened when she saw me. "I didn't expect to find you up already, it's early."

"They announce the first trial tonight, don't they?"

"The first pairing of it, yes."

I bounced on the balls of my feet, anxious to get moving. "Can we go?" I asked.

"Sure." She was about to pull my bedroom door shut when she saw the candle on my nightstand. "Goddess, what happened to it?"

"I've been practicing. Like you wanted."

"But you were busy last night with the dinner. How did you have time to—"

"I made time."

Tallis frowned, but only nodded and pulled the door shut behind me. "How were things last night? Did you speak to any of the other girls?"

As we walked, I told her about Aviana's death and about Kinsley getting in my face. Tallis didn't scold me for using my ability; she just warned me against doing it again.

Juno was waiting for us as the door to the lift slid open onto the training corridor. He crossed his arms over his chest as he took me in. "So, how was it?"

"There are eight girls between me and the crown," I announced. "Aviana is dead."

His eyes widened. "Dead?"

"The queen poisoned her at dinner last night."

He swallowed and rubbed at the shadow of stubble on his jaw. "Damn. That's . . ." He shook his head, at a loss for words. "The guards came and took her trainers from the barracks last night, but no one told us anything. I didn't think she was dead."

Tallis walked over to him and touched his arm. Her fingers grazed the material of his gray shirt, sliding down it until the backs of their hands just barely touched. It was quick, but definitely more than friendly.

"Monroe's been practicing with the candle. It was melted down to a stub." She beamed at me. "I can't wait to see you in practice today."

"Me too," Juno agreed.

I followed Tallis and Juno toward the room we'd be using. Juno had just gotten the door unlocked when another one of the training rooms opened and Cohen stepped into the hall. He was covered in sweat, his white cotton shirt stuck to the plains of his torso in a way that was a little more than distracting.

All I could think about was that kiss—and how he'd smiled at me. My heart sped up and I couldn't breathe. Juno and Tallis hadn't noticed the prince and were already gone, the door to our room left open for me. I didn't look at Cohen as I hurried past him.

I'd almost reached the doorway when he spoke up, his voice hoarse. "Monroe?"

I paused, my hand on the door frame. I kept my back to him, unable to even look in his direction as I said, "Yes?"

"I just wanted to say good luck tonight."

I hated this. I hated everything about it.

He continued, "Uri told me at breakfast that she's accepting your invitation. She'll be on your court. I didn't know you were asking her, but I'm glad you did."

I heard him step forward and I turned to look. Those blue eyes were wide, pleading.

"Please say something."

Goddess, where do I start? All I'd been able to think about since I'd left him last night was what it had felt like to have him touch me. All my life I'd wanted to be seen. I'd wanted to exist. And . . . looking at him now, seeing the concern written on his face, all the unanswered questions—I had no words. I'd never felt this way before, so at odds with my head and my heart.

My throat burned. "I'm sorry for running away, I just—"

Tallis called my name from the training room.

Cohen took another step toward me. "Don't go yet."

"I have to practice." I hated myself as the words left my mouth. "Thank you for the well wishes. But I should go."

His brow furrowed and he stepped back. In that moment, Cohen looked so much like a regular boy—so normal, so flustered. I wanted to let myself forget who he was.

He rubbed at the back of his neck. "Listen, about last night— What happened with us— I shouldn't have—"

"Monroe?" Tallis was at the door now. She glanced between Cohen and me. "Everything okay?"

"Yes, we're fine." Cohen straightened, and suddenly he was the crown prince again, and I was a marked girl. He nodded curtly to me, then to Tallis, before he turned on his heel and walked away.

"What was that about?" Tallis asked as we watched him go.

I sighed and walked past her into the training room. "I have no idea."

19

The Training Rooms

Sanctus Halletta

Tallis and I sat facing each other in the middle of the floor, a candle between us. I watched as she struck a match and held it up at eye level.

"Light the candle," she said.

I reached forward and touched the wick with my hand. It caught fire.

"No." Tallis shook out the match before it could burn her fingers and sighed. Before I could say anything, she blew out the candle and grabbed another match. "Try again, cheater."

"I did what you said."

"You did it wrong," Tallis said. "Why would you use your hand when I'm already holding a match?"

"Because," I said, snapping my fingers to make them spark. "I can create fire. I don't need the match."

"But you *do* need the match," she argued. "Using the match is unexpected. Using your hand," she pushed mine back onto the floor, "is obvious and being obvious in the Culling will get you killed. You have to use your ability to your advantage and if you can do it in an unexpected way, all the better. I don't know all the ins and outs of your ability. But I would imagine you aren't limited to creating flame with just your hands. Practicing with the candle will hopefully spark, pun intended, some new understanding about how your ability functions. At the very least, it isn't a bad idea for you to test yourself and learn new ways of using what you've been given. In an ideal world—an ideal fight—you'll be able to conjure fire from your hands, but—"

"But the arena isn't going to be ideal," I said.

"Exactly. The first thing you need to do when you get in the arena is set shit on fire. The ground, your opponent, your clothes. Whatever will catch and hold. The other goddess-touched girl will come for *you*. They'll want to disarm you, and the most obvious way to do that is by disabling the use your hands. Think ahead. Think differently. If you can set a large, strong fire to pull from, you could fight without your hands. You just need to learn to move that flame and wield it. If you do, you'll be unstoppable. You'll be queen." She lit another match and held it at eye level between us. "Now, light the candle."

Moving my fire, the flames that I could create, was easy. It felt like an extension of myself. But a lit match was foreign. I could tug at it, expand the strands of it, pull it apart until it dissipated—but to move it . . .

The fire on the match didn't belong to me. Still, I felt it. I always knew what was happening with a nearby fire. I didn't have to look to know if the fire in the stove was dying. I could sense it, almost like something within me was fading—as if that spiderweb tether between the existing flame and me was fraying.

Tallis cursed and shook out the match just as the flame reached her fingers. "Hurry it up, Monroe. We don't have all day and I'm running out of matches."

I straightened. "Light another one."

She did as I asked and held it up.

I focused on the flame, concentrating on the connection between it and me. I pushed it to the wick of the candle. The flame on the match flickered and tilted, as if hit by a gust of wind, then went out.

"Damn," Tallis breathed, disappointed.

I shook my head, but didn't say anything. I could still feel the flame, the slight warmth of it licking at the air. It wasn't gone, just *in between*.

I willed it to grow, pushed it forward, out from me and into something else. I wanted to snap my fingers and release the building pressure inside my chest. But I didn't want to create another fire, just move the one I still held. Seconds passed, dragging out like hours in my mind.

The heat grew until it hurt. Until my eyes were watering with the pain of it. I felt suffocated, like a weight was pressed to my chest, as if my lungs were being split open from the inside. Each breath was an effort.

I didn't know what to do and Tallis was just watching me, her eyebrows lifted in expectation. But I had no idea how to dispel the flame now that I'd pulled it to myself. I'd made it grow, but I didn't know how to release it. White-hot panic surged and I looked at Tallis, as if she could tell me what to do.

Her expression grew worried. "You okay?"

Unsure what else to do, I pictured the wick of the candle and snapped my fingers.

It was like fresh air pushing through my lungs—like a deep breath on the coldest day of winter. I'd done it. I knew I had before Tallis made a sound, before I even looked at the candle.

The flame flickered there, bright and warm—right where I'd sent it.

Tallis clapped her hands together. "You did it. That's so good. Juno!" She turned to look at him. "Juno, she did it. Did you see?"

He sat up in his chair in the corner and rested his elbows on his knees. "Very good, Monroe."

I smiled, triumphant and exhausted in equal measures.

Tallis nodded to the candle. "Now try to put it out."

I eased the flame away, pulling at the invisible tether until it snapped. The fire sizzled out. Tallis grinned and gathered the candle and matches into her hand.

"You'll keep these in your room. I want you to practice moving the fire around, just like you did with the other candle, but this time use the matches. Let's see how fast you can do it."

"And once you've got the hang of it," Juno added, "move the candle farther away. I want you to get comfortable working with fires that are farther away from you."

I nodded.

All during the previous night, I'd thought about how the bonds between the fire and the candle worked. All I'd done was pull the flame from one place and then send it mentally to another. While using a match felt different than moving my own fire, the process was the same.

Juno eyed me as I walked to the water cooler and poured myself a cup. "You look like you have something on your mind."

I downed the entire glass. "I'd like to practice with the dummy again."

Juno nodded and stood up. "All right. Let's practice then."

I set the cup down and led the way over to the target. Earlier, I'd managed to burn small patches in the mannequin's torso, but each time I'd lost control of the flame too soon. I hadn't let it go, not like I had with the match and the candle. I'd held on to it, tried to keep it attached to me. After practicing with both methods of moving flame, I felt like that was wrong. I needed to let it go and then reattach to it.

Tallis walked over to where I stood and I turned to her. "Can I have one of the matches?"

She looked confused, but she nodded anyway and handed me the matchbox. I took one out and scraped it across the striking surface. It hissed and sprang to life, a flickering bit of fire.

As soon as it was lit, that invisible tether snapped into place and my body felt what my eyes saw. I reached into that dark space between the match and myself. I took hold of that tether and I pulled, yanking the fire away and into me. The match hissed and fire tilted, flickered, and went out.

Just like before, warmth encircled my bones, wrapping around my heart like a vise. Before I could think too much about what I was doing, I slid that invisible thread forward and away, toward the target. I let the fire fly from me, untethered, and then, just as it slid from my grasp, I caught hold of it again and made it catch.

For a split second, I thought I'd failed. Then the dummy exploded into flames, an onslaught so hot and dense that the foam melted on impact. I sprang back, surprised. Tallis cursed as pieces of the target dripped to the floor, hissing.

But Juno only slapped a hand to my shoulder. "Now, *that* we can work with!"

Palace Bedroom
Sanctus Halletta

Monroe, I wanted to thank you for asking me to join your Culling court. I hope you like the dress and don't mind that I changed the seamstress's plans. I thought this might suit you better.

— Uriel

I read Uri's card while I waited for the bath to fill. It had been delivered alongside my lunch. The note, written on heavy expensive paper complete with a personalized header and royal crest, had been folded atop a large white box.

I hadn't had the guts to look at the dress yet; I was trying to take this one step at a time. The thought of having to attend a ball and be paraded around in front of random people was enough to make me sick. Doing that in a dress gifted to me by a princess—I couldn't even think about it.

I'd trained with Juno and Tallis for over five hours. We pushed hard, alternating between running laps, core exercises, the basics of hand-to-hand combat, and target practice. Juno had been thrilled with how quickly I'd learned the first few fighting maneuvers and was already planning out the following week's training schedule. No one mentioned that the first trial was approaching and, if I was chosen and lost, there would be no need to train.

They were so optimistic. So hopeful.

During the walk back to my room, Tallis told Juno about what I'd done to Kinsley after the dinner. I'd expected a lecture about following the rules, but Juno had only shrugged. "I'm glad you put her in her place. Did you burn her?"

"No. Just scared her, I think."

"You should have scorched her, the little entitled brat. *That* would have put her in her place."

Tallis nodded. "If she thinks she is going to just waltz in and get the crown, she's in for a surprise. Our girl's got a fair shot."

"More than a fair shot," Juno said. "Head-to-head, you might pull out a win."

They were talking like this was just a simple bet—like the word *might* didn't contain my death. None of us could talk with any certainty about how I would do in the trials.

While I'd been working hard and had noticed a lot of improvement in just three days, I had the sinking suspicion that Tallis and Juno were overly confident regarding my abilities. Still, I let their encouragement wash over me, let it strengthen me and bolster me until I believed them—or until I could pretend to believe them.

My hair was still damp from my bath as I sat in the middle of the bed and scanned Uri's card again. Despite Tallis and Juno's reservations, I was thankful to have her on my side. In a place with so many enemies, I needed friends.

Whatever she'd given me, no matter how uncomfortable I might be with it, I'd wear it for her. With that resolution in mind, I took a deep breath and flipped the lid open, exposing the thin silver paper inside.

I pushed it away to reveal the bodice of a gown unlike any of the ones the seamstress had filled my closet with. This was exquisite dark-purple silk that shone blue in some lights and black in others.

I removed the gown from the box and draped it over the end of the bed. The top of the dress was fitted, meant to hug the curves of my torso. It dipped into an elegant heart shape with a black organza overlay that covered the bodice of the dress as well as the shoulders and back. It was coated in tiny little crystals that glittered like stars against a purple-black sky. It was, hands down, the most beautiful thing I'd ever seen.

There was nothing in my closet that could even compare to this dress. Sure, those gowns were pretty and feminine, most of them flowy chiffons in various pastels, but this wasn't like that. This was queenly. It had weight to it.

I unbuttoned each small black shining button until I could see the inner lining. It was tailored, stitched, and pulled in certain places. It had been hemmed too, more than a few inches folded under so it would fall right on a thin, short girl—so it would fit me.

It was clear, that this dress had once upon a time been fitted for someone else, a different girl. I smiled. This wasn't just a dress Uri had commissioned for me. She must have had one of her own gowns tailored.

This was the dress of a princess. I bit my lip and looked back at the open door to my closet. *Good goddess, I was going to have to wear heels.*

20

The Ballroom

Sanctus Halletta: The Commencement Ball

We went in turns entering the packed ballroom and announcing our Culling courts. I was third, after Nadia and Tessa. I don't remember most of what I said, only that Uri agreed to stand with me.

After my announcement, I was free to wander around and just watch everyone else. Cohen stayed as far away from me as possible, and I didn't seek him out.

Music played, causing the people milling about to sway with the tempo. Wine and champagne flowed; glasses filled as soon as they were drained. The queen sat in her throne just staring out at it all, her gaze heavy and dangerous.

She'd spent the beginning of the evening watching Cohen. He was relaxed and smiling, but it wasn't the smile that he'd shown me—this was trained, tucked in, and buttoned-up.

The suit he wore was pristine, a black tuxedo with tails, white vest, and white bow tie. He had a purple-tinged rose pinned to his lapel, a silver watch chain dangling from his coat pocket, and cuff links. Not a hair out of place.

He looked how I imagined his mother wanted him to.

Before last night I would have found it charming, but I didn't anymore. This was just another clever mask. I couldn't look at him without seeing his flushed face, the way his eyes had shone after he'd kissed me, how nervous he'd sounded earlier outside the training rooms.

That was the real Cohen, not this.

"Monroe!"

Uri hurried over to where I'd been hiding behind a large pillar. I'd been standing there for the last half hour. From this vantage point, I could see everything in the ballroom, but I was out of Viera's line of sight, which was how I wanted to keep things.

Tallis and Juno had disappeared almost as soon as I'd finished my announcement. Tonight, they were guests. They could eat, drink, and dance just like everyone else. But something in the way Juno had been looking at Tallis made me think they were interested in finding a hiding place too.

Uri said, "I circled the ballroom twice looking for you."

She was wearing a turquoise gown similar to the one she'd worn last night. The color made her dark eyes glitter like jewels. She grabbed my hands in her gloved ones. "You look amazing. Like a queen. I wanted to tell you before you announced your court, but I felt like it wasn't the right time. What do you think of your gown, too much?"

I shook my head and lifted the hem, just enough to get the purple fabric to shift to almost black. "I love it. Thank you for sending it."

"You're welcome. I can't have my future sister-in-law looking anything less than stunning."

"You should be enjoying yourself," I said. "Don't you have someone you should be dancing with? Like Dellac—"

"No!" Uri swallowed and looked out at the open ballroom. "No," she repeated, her voice growing soft.

The king and queen were on the dance floor, waltzing to the first real song of the night. Their eyes were on anything but each other. At the sight of them, Uri frowned.

"We're just friends," she said, still not looking at me. "Hugo and I— We can't be anything but friends. My mother would kill him if . . ." Her brown eyes found mine, searched my face. "Cohen and Britta tease, but they're careful to keep it far from my mother's ears. Can I trust you to do the same?"

I nodded. "You can trust me. I'm sorry I said anything."

"Don't be. It's fine." She touched my shoulder. "Thank you." Her expression changed to open excitement as she caught sight of her brother from across the ballroom. "Cohen!"

I hissed through my teeth as she stood up on her toes and waved to him above the heads of the gathered crowd. The prince turned in our direction and, once he saw his younger sister, started weaving his way toward us.

Before Cohen could even get to where we were, she gathered her skirts in one hand, shot me a mischievous grin, and said, "Anyway, I'll see you around, Monroe. Please enjoy the dance and the evening. Tell my brother I said hello and not to get too terribly drunk."

"Uri—!"

She disappeared into the crowd just as Cohen reached me. The corner of his mouth twitched as he watched her disappear through a large set of glass doors and into the dimly lit garden beyond. "What is she up to?" he asked.

"Trouble," I said.

"Always."

We stood there in awkward silence for a long moment, both of us pretending to be overly interested in the music and the chandeliers and the dozens of footmen walking around with trays of finger foods and tall flutes of champagne.

The orchestra changed over to a slower song, pulling my gaze to the middle of the ballroom. The king and queen stepped apart, diplomatic in their touches. As Viera turned and surveyed the ballroom, I stepped deeper into my corner, out of her sight. I watched the queen walk back to her throne and sit down.

As if that was permission to proceed, Cohen turned to look at me. "Shall we?"

I blinked at him. "Shall we what?"

He grinned. "Dance. That's what this is, after all."

I shook my head. "I don't dance."

"You do tonight. I have to dance with all of you at least once. I'd like to hope you'll be a little more obliging than that though, otherwise I'll be stuck dancing with the wife, daughter, sister, or great-aunt of every Synod member here."

"What a curse," I said.

He offered me his arm. "Trust me, you have no idea."

I glanced toward the small dais where Viera sat on her throne. Kinsley and Larkin stood nearby, and Synoder Raveena had taken up a spot next to the queen. No one else was on the dance floor and once Cohen walked into the middle of that room, no one would take their eyes off him. All hells. "I'll make a fool of myself," I said. "Why not start with Kinsley or Tessa or . . . or— I don't know. Anyone else."

"I won't let you make a fool of yourself."

"I can barely walk in these heels. There's no way I can dance in them."

The corner of his mouth twitched. "Then take them off."

I gaped at him.

He shrugged. "The skirt is long. No one will notice if you're barefoot. Everyone will be too busy looking at the gown anyway—and the beautiful girl wearing it." He lifted his arm slightly. "Dance with me."

The beautiful girl wearing it. My heart gave a traitorous little twinge at his words.

Before I could think too much about what I was doing, I turned around and started walking toward a bench over by the garden doors. Cohen followed.

"Monroe?" He caught hold of my wrist and tugged me to a stop. "Are you really going to make me find someone else?"

Those ocean-blue eyes were so wide, so unused to rejection, that I almost lied to him. *Yes*, I almost said. *Yes, you can find someone else to dance with.*

But instead, I said, "I'm trying to sit down so I can take off these damn heels."

He rewarded me with a radiant smile, the sort of smile that he never seemed to show anyone else. That same feeling of looming danger swelled in my chest, colliding sharply with the memory of what it had been like to kiss that mouth. To have him hold me and thread his fingers through my hair . . .

Goddess above, it is hot in this ballroom.

I turned and walked to the bench. Cohen stood, all princely in his posture, and watched as I unbuckled the pretty black heels I'd put on that evening. The pumps weren't incredibly tall, but they were more than I was used to. Even after practicing pacing my room over and over again, I'd still felt a little like a newborn deer when I'd climbed down the grand staircase into the ballroom. My fingers had been white-knuckled the whole time. I'd been terrified I'd trip and embarrass the hell out of myself.

As Cohen led me toward the center of the dance floor, I felt that same bone-chilling panic. People turned to watch us pass; cameras flashed as reporters crowded the balconies above our heads, each of them vying for the first glimpse of the prince and one of the remaining goddess-touched girls. The flutter of gossip and compliments seemed to grow to a crescendo as everyone focused their attention on the two of us. The orchestra eased to a stop and began playing something new—something slow and rhythmic.

The white marble slabs of the floor were surprisingly cold against my bare feet as Cohen eased us to a stop and turned me toward a photographer standing to one side of the room. The prince's hand on my waist was heavy as we both smiled—just like we'd done a few days ago during our engagement.

A few of the other goddess-touched girls stood nearby, sipping glasses of wine and whispering to one another. Tessa wore a beautiful sage-green dress that brought out the porcelain of her skin and the deep red of her hair. I didn't miss the way her eyes narrowed as Cohen stepped deeper onto the dance floor, easing me along with him.

The balconies above us were filled with an audience of Erydians, some staring and pointing. The royal family had sold tickets to the event, allowing the common people of our nation to witness what only the elite were good enough to engage in. There were children, little girls wearing paper crowns. The air caught in my throat as I noticed the intricate ink-drawn marks on their faces, arms, hands.

Cohen saw me looking and leaned closer to me, so his voice would carry over the music. "They're pretending to be one of you."

"But why?" I turned to look at him as one of his hands found my waist, while the other took hold of mine. "At the end of all of this, nine girls end up dead."

Cohen's brow furrowed, and I knew that I was shattering the illusion for him. I was ruining this magical moment with the reality of my situation, but I couldn't help it. All those little girls up in that balcony would return to their warm, safe houses tonight. They would be tucked in by parents who loved them. Someone would wipe away the marks on their skin—none of them would ever scrub themselves raw trying to make it disappear.

The prince sighed. "I think it's the hope in it. Everyone imagines themselves as being the one who makes it. The one who survives. The one who gets the crown and the happily ever after. And there's something lovely about that. Every generation a new girl comes from obscurity to become queen. It sounds like a fairy tale."

"Maybe it would be a fairy tale if it was based in love."

"Who says it can't be?"

The music seemed to swell, and Cohen began to lead me around the dance floor. I'd practiced with Juno in the training room earlier that day, but it was different with Cohen. The dance was slow and steady. The rest of the room seemed to fade away until it was just his hand on my waist, his blue eyes watching me.

"Who says this Culling can't be based in love?"

"The arena," I said. "The temple. Every sacred text. The hundreds of years of past Cullings. The war that we fought with Vayelle almost two decades ago, and the war we are about to fight. The documents I signed when I got here. There is not one thing in the Culling that has anything to do with love. It's all based in blood."

"Maybe, but shouldn't I have a relationship with the one I marry? Shouldn't I at least know she's a good person? Shouldn't I at least know that she is nothing like my mother?"

"Is that what this is about? Was last night about finding out if I was anything like your mother? I don't want to be a test, Cohen. I don't want you to pretend to be in love with me so you can decide if I would make a good queen. I certainly don't want you to do that if you're going to do the same thing with all the other marked girls."

I tried to move away from him, but he was quick. Before I could even get a full step away, I was spun in a circle again and then pulled back to him, his hand pulling me closer, his fingers running along the buttons at the base of my back. Cohen leaned in. "I'm not doing the same thing with all the other marked girls. I'm— Goddess, Monroe. I'm trying to court you."

It was only his hands that kept me from tripping on my own two feet. "Court me?"

He nodded, his expression serious. "You're all Uri has talked about since she met you on the train. She came straight to find me as soon as she got back to the palace and she told me, right then and there, that she'd found the girl for me. And I thought . . . I thought she was full of it. Because Uri is a little crazy sometimes and she is always up to something, but then I saw you and I just— I like you. I like you and I want to court you. Properly, if you'll let me. And if you won't, I at least hope you'll let me be your friend. For as long as we have."

"You did all of this because of Uri?"

"No. Goddess, no. I have my own reasons. But she played a part too. And she's still playing a part, the little shit." He nodded to the purple flower pinned to his lapel. "Notice how we match?"

I hadn't. My throat felt impossibly tight. "And the kiss last night?"

"What about it?"

"Is that something we're doing now?" I hated myself as soon as the question left my mouth. I shook my head, wishing I could inhale the words. "I just— What I meant to say was— Are we— This changes nothing. I'm still in the Culling. I'll still have to fight and die and—"

"Or win and be queen."

"Maybe. But courting comes with some sort of promise. Some sort of intention."

He lifted my hand and pressed a kiss to the engagement ring on my left hand. "We have those things."

He was infuriating.

"Why not someone else?"

He shrugged. "Why not you?"

"Has anyone ever told you that you're incorrigible?"

"No, but I don't mind the sound of it."

"What about the Culling rules? What happens if we're caught? Your mother would kill me."

"We won't get caught."

"There's only risk for me."

"I think there's plenty to be gained."

"For you."

"For both of us." He spun me again and then drew me back to him. "My parents were strangers when they were crowned. Same for my grandparents and great-grandparents. Same for every king and queen in our country's history. Wouldn't it be better—stronger—if there was some choice in it?"

"This is the Culling we're talking about. There are no choices. Not for me anyway."

"I believe you can win it."

"You haven't even seen my ability."

"Your ability is fire, Monroe. Which of the girls has a stronger chance than you?"

"That's the key word: *chance*. I have a chance."

"Fine, let's be pessimistic for a moment."

"It's not pessimistic, it's realistic."

"Semantics." He shrugged. "Let's pretend you lose. You lose, but we've spent the last few weeks getting to know each other. We're friends. Maybe more, I don't know. Either way, win or lose, we will have spent the last few weeks—possibly the last few weeks of your life—having fun. And if you win, that works in our favor too. We will have had an interim of true courting before our marriage and things will be easier for us because of it, I just know they would be."

"Why me?"

He sighed. "You always get caught up on that."

The music started to slow. "Because you never answer me. If you're wanting to form a relationship with the girl you think will win, why not Kinsley?"

"Because I . . . Because I know her already, and I'm not interested."

"Then why not another girl?"

"Because I want you. I think you're beautiful. And you aren't caught up in the politics of this. You haven't tried to impress me or force yourself on me. You've been honest about how you feel about all of this and . . . and I appreciate it. It's refreshing, honestly. All of this. All of you. It's . . . nice. I mean, good goddess above, you're dancing barefoot in the middle of a ballroom, Monroe. And you're someone I think I could be friends with, and that's what I want in a marriage. It's what I want in my queen. It's that simple. I just want you."

The air rushed from my lungs in a startled sigh. "Oh."

The music eased to a stop and our dance ended with it. "I can't save you from this, so let me try to make it better—less miserable and lonely and horrible for you. Let me do what I can. What can it hurt?" he asked, his voice rising slightly so he could be heard over the applause. "You said it was better to draw from the pile early on and take the risk when it was at its lowest. That's now. If we draw now, we'll have an arsenal when we're crowned."

When we're crowned.

"But this isn't a game of cards."

He opened his mouth to reply, but we were interrupted as another goddess-touched girl approached, ready for her dance. Reluctantly, Cohen stepped away and turned to Joslyn. The sun-kissed sheen of her skin contrasted beautifully with the soft periwinkle of her gown, and her hair had been pulled up into a sleek roll at the base of her neck. Her smile, which was wide and nervous, seemed to falter a little when I didn't step away from Cohen at her approach.

"I hope I'm not interrupting anything," she said.

Cohen shook his head. "No, we were just finishing up." He offered her his hand and she took it, her light-brown eyes darting uncertainly to me as she did. An emotion, slick and oily, seemed to slither in my gut as he bent down and kissed the engagement ring on her hand. I took that as my cue to leave.

I found the bench where I'd stashed my heels and went to work putting them back on. With the layers and layers of organza and silk, it proved to be more difficult than I'd imagined it would be. I'd leaned back to take a breather, a shoe half on one foot, when Dellacov approached me. "Do you need assistance, Miss Benson?"

I sighed. "No. I got it."

"Do I want to know why you're barefoot?"

"Half barefoot."

He smiled and conceded. "Half barefoot."

"If you must know, it was your prince's idea. I didn't think I could dance in the heels, and he told me to get rid of them."

"Sounds like an idea Cohen would have." He came to a stop directly in front of me and knelt down. "Here." He reached for one of my feet.

I pulled away from him. "This is improper."

"Think about how you got into this situation, and then ask yourself if you really care about propriety."

I didn't.

Dellacov made quick work of fastening the buckles. He was finishing with the last one as I worked up the courage to ask, "Has Cohen said anything to you about me?"

His eyes darted up to mine. "What makes you think he would?"

"You're friends, aren't you?"

"I guess you could say that." He stood up and moved to sit on the bench next to me. "I think, since he's my friend, that it would be a breach of confidence to tell you anything that Cohen's said to me about you."

"So, he *has* talked about me then."

He laughed. "He might have mentioned you in passing."

"Well, did he tell you he kissed me?" The sound of my hand hitting my mouth as I tried to catch the words seemed to echo between us. "That was— I didn't mean to— That isn't any of your—"

Dellacov's smile took up half of his face as he said, "He may have mentioned something about that."

My face was a hundred degrees. "I didn't mean to say that."

"Why are you asking all of this?"

I shrugged, trying to act nonchalant. "No reason."

"I'll let you in on a little secret: Cohen is a romantic. When he isn't immersed in his required studies, he's got his head in a book. He likes adventure and grand gestures. He wants to see the good in people. And he can be a little— He can look past things to see what he wants sometimes."

"I can't look past the Culling."

"You shouldn't look past it. It should be your only focus."

"Cohen disagrees."

"Cohen is a prince. His part in this is less . . ." Dellacov sighed. "I think he fancies you as being a damsel that needs rescuing from a dragon."

"I'm a damsel that has to fight a dragon all alone in the middle of an arena. And, if I win . . ." That dark roiling power in my gut seemed to open an eye at the idea. "If I win, there's a possibility that I might become a dragon myself."

"It's my job to encourage you to remain focused. Cohen is my friend, but his desires in this are of little importance. If you play your cards right, you are weeks away from being crowned queen. Then the kingdom is yours. The Synod is yours. You will have the ability to make changes, and I think you're the sort of person who would make good changes."

"Everyone speaks so highly of me. None of you even know me. I've been here for less than a week."

"Uriel speaks highly of you. She talks you up to anyone she can."

"But Uri doesn't know me either."

"Maybe not, but she's a part of your court now. And you asking her to be an advisor . . ." He trailed off and I knew he was trying to choose his words in a way that would put distance between himself and the princess. "It meant a lot to her. She doesn't get chosen for things very often."

"She seems sweet."

"She is." He cleared his throat. "And she's a good judge of character. Uriel is let into rooms that no one else is allowed inside. She witnesses things and hears things because she is overlooked and ignored. No one thinks she can do anything, so they expect nothing of her. But she knows what to look for in a person, and she saw something in you that stood out. And you proved her right when you invited her to be a part of your court. You've endeared yourself to her and, subsequently, to the people closest to her. That includes Cohen and Britta."

Cohen was preparing to dance with Kinsley now. Her gown was black velvet, strappy, and fitted around her hips. She'd worn her hair up in a braided coronet that made her facial features more severe and showed off her mark. Her makeup was dark, her lips colored blood red, a stark contrast to her warm brown skin.

She was poised in a way that could only come from practice. I didn't think for one moment that this was her first time on the ballroom floor. It couldn't have been her first time dancing with the prince. She anticipated each move too well.

Dellacov and I watched through a gap between bodies as she posed for the cameras and showed off her gown. All the while, her gaze kept darting to her father, who still stood by the throne. He smiled with pride as she turned to look at the prince.

"She was bred for this," Dellacov said. "She was four when her mark appeared. Her mother had just died, and her father was named Speaker. As soon as they moved into the palace permanently, she began training. She took lessons on etiquette and history right alongside the princesses. We were all sort of raised here together. As friends."

"Are you still friends?" I asked as the music started and the two began to dance.

He was quiet for a long moment. "She and Cohen had a little bit of a falling-out a few years ago. She started spending more time with Larkin and the other daughters of Synod members and less time with us. But we're all still friendly with each other."

"She doesn't like me."

"She probably doesn't like you because Uriel likes you. Which means Larkin won't, since Larkin hates anything that Uriel likes. She's terrible like that. And Kinsley and Larkin are thick as thieves. When one does something, the other is close to follow. It also doesn't help that Cohen seems . . . attached to you."

"You sure do know a lot about the royal children."

"It's my job. I've been apprentice to the Captain of the Royal Guard since I was seven."

"Now here you are, taking the lead."

"Yeah . . ."

I nodded toward the garden doors next to us. "Uri went that way. Maybe since you're the Captain of the Guard, you should go and check on her. Goddess forbid something happen to her while she's out there all by herself . . . alone . . . in a dimly lit garden."

The corner of his mouth twitched. "Goddess, you're as meddlesome as she is."

I feigned innocence. "I'd just hate for her to be in any sort of danger."

"Fine then." He stood up and straightened the fall of his jacket, muttering a quiet, "Meddlesome ladies," as he turned and took off toward the propped-open doors to the garden. The breeze sweeping into the ballroom was cool and smelled of summer's end.

Couples milled about the ballroom, laughing and talking, all of them eager to join the dance. I hadn't been keeping track, but I thought Kinsley might be one of the last goddess-touched girls. Soon the floor would open to every couple.

Maybe Cohen would seek me out again. Then we could talk more and maybe . . .

The idea seemed to fizzle out, leaving me feeling cold and uncertain as I watched Kinsley dance with the prince. The first song had just ended, but they hadn't stopped dancing. In fact, they continued to smile and dance for another two songs.

They were comfortable together, all too friendly. I didn't like the way she put her hand on his chest; the way she straightened his tie, ran a fingertip across the top of the flower on his coat; the way she leaned her head against his shoulder as the music slowed, as their dancing slowed—as she leaned up, so close to him . . . and they kissed.

The world seemed to narrow. To grow quiet and then monstrously loud all at once. Around me, people cheered and yelled out their approval. Their dance ended to massive applause.

The queen was smiling, Kinsley's father beaming. Cameras flashed and by the time they exited the dance floor, the crowd around them was so thick I could no longer see them from where I sat.

My heart hurt in a strange sort of way—it wasn't broken necessarily, but it was bruised. Drained. My throat burned with days of unshed tears, but I refused to cry now, not here, not over something so silly. Let Cohen kiss who he wanted. Let him have Kinsley. Dellacov was right; I needed to focus on the Culling. The first trial was in two weeks, and I might be in it. I might die.

But goddess, my chest ached with every breath. What did it mean? What had our kiss meant? What did this kiss with Kinsley mean? Dellacov had said they'd been close once, but . . . but they seemed . . . I wasn't sure what they seemed like. In love? Definitely more than friends.

And it shouldn't have bothered me so much, but I'd wanted what Cohen was offering. I'd wanted to walk into the Culling believing that if I died, I would have spent my last few days or weeks living. Last night had felt old. And young. Like it was a lifeline to something far larger than me, larger than anything else I'd ever experienced.

Kinsley was everything a queen was meant to be. And the crowd standing around me was right—they did look lovely together. The image of the two of them seated side by side on matching thrones would be striking.

But she isn't queen yet, that dark power in my blood seemed to sing.

PART TWO

—

A Game of Cages

Late Summer
Gazda County, Erydia

Nine Goddess-touched Girls Remain

21

Kinsley would fight Joslyn at dawn on Sanctus Alida. Their trial was announced at the ball, after I'd already left. Viera had drawn two names at random. I'm sure everyone was very pleased with the picks—after her stunt with Cohen, Kinsley was a crowd favorite.

If Tallis and Juno had noticed I'd left the ball early, they didn't mention it. I suspected they hadn't stayed very long themselves. Tallis had been late to get me for training the next morning and when she'd shown up, her hair had been wet from a bath and she'd been wearing one of Juno's shirts.

The crisp white envelope in her hand had held the names of the two contestants and their abilities. Water and foliage. According to Juno, during the trial I was going to be seated in a viewing room along with the remaining goddess-touched girls. We would arrive early and stay until the body of the fallen girl had been burned and blessed by the attending priestess. Even though I wasn't fighting, I was supposed to wear training clothes.

The next two weeks were filled with preparation for my own impending trial. It took up all my time, and I wanted it to. Each day, Juno was focused, working me until I collapsed and forcing me to get up and keep going. I got better with every session.

He ran me until sleep was impossible to dodge. Until unconsciousness encircled me before my head even hit the pillow. I welcomed the distraction and the burning in my muscles.

I didn't see the prince, and I did everything in my power not to think of him. To not remember how it had felt to stand so close, to have him hold me. To be kissed by him.

I refused to think about it. Instead, I ran, and I hit, and I kicked, and I dodged, and I spun, and I crawled, and I aimed, and I burned.

And burned.

And burned.

"You'll see during the trial," Juno would say, "that the girl who can move the fastest will win. You can't sit still, not ever."

So, I practiced running and using my ability, which was harder than anything else I'd ever done. When I managed that skill, we moved on to hand-to-hand combat. Tallis was slight and willowy, her build more aligned to that of the other goddess-touched girls. Because of this, Juno used her as an example, having her fight me over and over again. I left with bruises and sore ribs, but I learned quickly.

We'd roll all over the training room, bang against walls, topple over chairs, shove each other against the metal cabinet. Anything I could get my hands on became a weapon. If I could detach the arm of one of the target dummies, I was going to hit Tallis with it. If she could get her hands on one of the chairs, she was coming after me.

It was a game every time to see who could be the most creative. My ability was off-limits when practicing with them, so I'd learned to be resourceful. I'd learned to think outside my initial instincts. I would need to pay attention to the arena when I saw it and look for things I could use when it was my turn.

This was what I thought of as I woke and dressed on Sanctus Alida.

The palace was still asleep, the world outside black. The twinkling city lights that made up the skyline of Gazda were gone, doused in slumber. I dressed in that darkness, letting it wrap around me and hold me.

I imagined, just for an instant, that I was the one fighting today—that I was Joslyn, set to face Kinsley. Kinsley's ability was listed only as—*foliage*. Plants. She had the ability of plants. I had no idea what that could even mean.

It didn't sound as intimidating as I'd assumed her ability would be, but it did align with the shape of her mark.

With all that in mind, I couldn't decide which girl I thought would win. It was water against plants. Of the two, I worried less about fighting plants.

Water scared me. The moment I saw it listed on the form I knew that Joslyn was one I'd need to watch out for—but perhaps Kinsley would take care of her for me. It seemed wrong to hope for that.

I sat on the edge of the bed and pulled on my boots. I was sore and bruised. New muscles screamed at me with every movement. I didn't look any different and no one would even notice, but I felt more prepared, which I thought was important.

If I were going against one of the girls today, I knew that I was more combat-ready than I had been two weeks ago. And I was more determined. I'd started to lean into the dark voice, let it whisper a little louder. Sometimes it said things that scared me. But most of the time, it pushed me to work harder. It reached greedy, grubby hands toward something it believed was rightfully ours.

Royal Transport

En Route to the Arena

Deca Market, Gazda

Sanctus Alida

We sat facing each other on two benches in the back of a black van. Joslyn sat on one side, Kinsley on the other. Outside, the world was still dark and once the doors were shut, we were left squinting through the gloom at one another, our faces lit only by the soft glow of a yellow light above our heads.

For the first time, we were alone with each other.

It was silent.

Beneath us, the engine started up and the vehicle shook as the guards loaded into the front cab. Kinsley leaned against the side of the van. The hood of her tunic was pulled over her head and I couldn't see her eyes, but I knew she was staring at Joslyn.

We rocked as the van hit a bump in the road, all of us lurching forward and then sliding back on the benches. Autumn had come earlier than usual in Gazda, leaving the air cold with morning's chill. Our breath came out in puffs.

Heidi spoke up. "I was told the longest trial lasted about fifteen minutes."

Nadia rolled her shoulders and pulled a knee up to her chest. "My advisor said you can tell who will win within the first sixty seconds."

It fell silent again as everyone thought about that. Fifteen minutes after sunrise, one of these girls would be dead.

"Is it true that you can create fire from your hands?" Elodie was looking at me, intently.

She had tiny features, a small nose, small pursed lips, and straight bangs that made her look younger than I thought she probably was. She seemed to look at everything, everyone, all at once. She could read minds. Tallis had known about Elodie, but she'd said the ability required touch to work.

I pulled my knees in, putting distance between my legs and hers.

The corner of Elodie's mouth pulled up in a hesitant smile. "Don't worry, I don't much care what you're thinking about right now."

"Well? Can you?" Joslyn prompted.

It was the first time she'd spoken that morning, the first time she'd lifted her head and even looked at any of us since she'd been put in the van. Her eyes were glassy and bloodshot. I wondered if she'd slept at all the night before.

The other girls were looking at me, too, waiting for me to say something.

I sighed. "Yes."

Heidi turned in her seat, trying to look out the window. When she couldn't see anything outside, she turned back and gazed down at her hand. She wiggled her fingers. "That must be cool." Although the words were a compliment, her tone was bored.

"What about you?" Nadia said, eyeing her. "Aren't you like a walking nightmare or something?"

Heidi grinned. "Just don't let me become *your* nightmare."

I think she might have meant it as a joke, but no one laughed.

Her gift was another one that I didn't understand. All I'd ever been told was that she had the ability of terror incitement. As if that was a good enough descriptor. I opened my mouth to ask about her ability but stopped when the van shuddered to a halt.

Seconds later, the doors opened inside a large concrete garage, the belly of the arena. Above us, it roared like a waking beast, angry and impatient. The cheers of thousands of people echoed through the concrete halls, so loud I couldn't hear anything else. They were screaming for blood, screaming for a new queen. Today a sacrifice would be made to the goddess and a girl would emerge, one step closer to the crown.

We walked single file, two guards at our backs and three leading us, to a small room on the edge of the arena floor. A massive window faced out into the open field beyond, at floor level and perfectly placed. Two rows of benches faced toward the glass. This was where we would stay during the fight.

We were assured that the glass separating us from the arena was shatterproof and one-way. While we could look out, no one from outside could look in. We would be alone with each other, but we were forbidden to fight, and anyone who broke that rule would be brought before the queen.

Kinsley stood next to the window looking out onto the arena floor. It was red dirt and grass, flat like a table. Thick stone walls stretching fifty feet into the air towered over us, too tall to climb and too thick to break through. There was only one way in and one way out: the metal gate across from our room.

I stepped up to the glass but kept my distance from Kinsley, unwilling to do anything to upset her. Her arms, which were wrapped around her torso, tightened when she saw me.

I held my breath, waiting for her to say something. The last time I'd seen her was when she and Cohen had kissed on the dance floor. The memory of it was enough to set my teeth on edge.

Kinsley watched me out of the corner of her eye, a soft smile on her face. Her voice was soft, a breathy acknowledgment. "Monroe."

I ignored her and stepped closer to the glass, pressing my hand against it. A quick sweep of the field told me there wasn't any fire naturally inside the arena. The nearest flames were coming from torches on either side of the tunneled entrance across from us. I doubted I would be able to use those in a fight.

Kinsley spoke again. "You know, I'm coming for you next."

I pushed away from the glass and turned to look at her. "You don't get to decide who you fight. There are rules we have to follow."

"Sure." Kinsley laughed as she tugged at the hem of her black tunic. "Tell that to poor Aviana."

While I may have been worried about going up against someone with water abilities, I wanted Kinsley to lose to Joslyn. Even if it meant I might have to fight the ability of water.

On a bench farthest from the window sat Joslyn. She was curled in on herself with her head on her knees. It was hard to ignore the way she shook, her entire torso rocking with the movement. Nadia sat next to her, but she didn't reach out or say anything.

No one was going to comfort her.

We couldn't. Not here.

Bile rose in my throat and I had to look away.

Kinsley looked at Joslyn too. "At least it will be easy."

When I didn't respond, she turned back to the window. It was dark outside still, and the arena floor was lit by huge stadium lights. I'd never seen anything shine so brightly in my life; it looked like six separate suns all blazing down on us.

But the sky was changing, fading from black to gray, the edges burning purple, yellow, red, and pink. Dawn was moments away, beautiful and terrifying.

In the corners of the arena, technicians were manning large cameras equipped to film parts of the trial. They'd stitch it all together later and charge people in the poor counties a few coins to watch it.

Any minute, the guards would return to fetch the two contestants, and this would start. The first trial of the Culling. When we left the viewing room, the Culling pool would be down to eight.

Seven corpses between you and the crown, that voice hissed.

"Can we get this over with?" Kinsley said. "I'm getting tired of standing here."

I turned to look at her. "I wouldn't be in a rush if I were you."

"Yes, well, if I were *you*, I'd be worried too. You'll die in there. You're an outlier in all of this. No one wants a queen from Varos. What do you know about leading a country? Your family are dirt-poor farmers. They're good for nothing but hard labor and filling the queen's coffers. My father says you'll be dead by the end of the month. If it isn't me who kills you, it'll be someone else."

"Don't be so full of yourself. You haven't even started fighting yet. You have no idea what you're up against."

"If it were up to me, and it will be soon, I'd hand Varos over to Vayelle. Let them do what they want with it. Everyone knows it's goddess-forsaken land anyway. Why not let the pagans in Vayelle do what they will? No one wants the people there to be moved to higher ground. The Synod has been blocking those requests for years. At least if Vayelle had the land it wouldn't be Erydia's problem anymore."

Blocking the requests? Ambrose had been signing petitions and sending letters to our magistrates for years. The floodlands had been growing, each season bringing with it more mudslides and taking more of our coastline. Without aid, most of Varos would be underwater within the next few years.

"I don't know what will happen to me," I admitted. "But I hope and pray to the goddess that you *never* wear that crown, Kinsley."

Without warning, she grabbed the front of my shirt and shoved me against the glass. The other girls yelled and got to their feet. Someone called for guards, for help.

The words came through gritted teeth. "I'm so tired of your damn mouth. He pities you. That's why he showed you any attention at all. The dirty, starved little girl from Varos. He saw you and he felt bad. I told him it was unhealthy for you. That you would let it go to your head."

I couldn't move, couldn't breathe. My eyes were locked on Kinsley, waiting for her to make good on her promise to kill me. We held each other's gaze, neither of us daring to look away. She was quivering with pent-up energy.

I took hold of her wrist, trying to get out of her grasp. Despite the way my legs shook, my voice was surprisingly steady as I said, "Let me go."

She only stepped closer, pushing me harder against the glass. The hand that wasn't wrapped in my shirt grabbed my right hand, shoving my arm to the side and away from her. Pinning me in place. She was careful to keep her hold on me as far from my mark as possible.

She was still afraid of being burned—*Good*.

"You listen to me." She leaned in, her face centimeters from mine. "I'm going to slaughter you, tear you limb from limb. When I'm done, no one will even recognize who the hell you are. Do you understand me?"

While I would fight Kinsley and I would win, today wasn't the day for it. Better, I thought, to let her believe that I was afraid of her. People who were afraid could do terrible things.

And to save myself, *I* would do terrible things.

I nodded and slid down the glass, cowering before her. Her eyes seemed to spark with malice, and her mouth turned up into a pleased smile. Her grip on me loosened.

"Varos trash." Without warning, she spat in my face.

My knee collided with her rib cage so abruptly that there was no opportunity to avoid it. She buckled at the waist, nearly staggering backward. Before she could recover, I elbowed her in the face and shoved my boot into her stomach, shoving her away from me—just like I'd practiced.

Kinsley cried out and only managed to stay standing because she caught hold of one of the benches. With her distracted, I moved toward the door, making sure to keep her in my line of sight as I went.

By the time I'd escaped her range, Kinsley had straightened. She pressed a hand to her face as blood trickled from a split lip. "You little—"

A guard opened the door to the viewing room. "We heard yelling! Everything okay in here?"

I spoke before anyone else could. "We're fine."

He looked around. The other goddess-touched girls were on their feet, all of them facing the window where Kinsley stood looking at me. Blood had dripped down onto her shirt and the decorative leather breastplate she wore.

She looked absolutely murderous.

Oh, yes, if this girl were going to kill anyone outside of a trial it would be me.

The guard cleared his throat, uncomfortable. "It's time."

Kinsley wiped her bloody hand on her pants. "Perfect." She brushed shoulders with me as she walked by and muttered a quiet "Varos bitch."

"Hey, Kinsley?" I turned to watch as she headed for the door. "I want you to think about the floodlands in Varos today. About what it must be like to watch the tides rise with no hope of escape. I hope it's all you can think about as Joslyn drowns you."

At the mention of her, Joslyn's head lifted, and she looked to me—her skin was a greenish sort of color. She was the only person who hadn't moved during my struggle with Kinsley, and she hadn't moved to go with the guard either.

He moved forward as if he was prepared to drag her into the arena, but Nadia held up a hand to stop him. Hesitantly, like reaching for a wild animal, she leaned over and touched Joslyn's shoulder. The girl flinched at the contact. Nadia's voice was gentle as she said, "Joslyn, it's time. You have to go now."

The girl turned to Nadia. The whites of her eyes were veined and red, watering, the pupils dilated—and she looked like she might be sick at any moment.

"Joslyn?" Nadia said again.

Her voice was a hoarse rasp as she whispered, "Please, I don't want to die."

22

We sat looking out onto the arena as the sun inched higher, spreading crimson across the sky like watery blood. The stadium was filled to capacity. People were sharing seats and pushing closer to the railing, closer to the arena floor.

The royal family sat in their own box looking down on the field below, a tribunal of priestesses around them. Today they were the eyes of the goddess herself.

There were so many people, all of them cheering and clapping, fathers lifting toddlers onto their shoulders to see. Vendors walked the aisles, passing out golden paper crowns and silver, blue, and black flags. Little girls were having vines drawn on their faces.

Like a whisper in the dead of night, the chanting started—*Queen Kinsley. Queen Kinsley.*

Viera stood, approached the railing of the viewing box, and raised a fist high into the air. Silence fell. Cohen rose and followed his mother, moving to stand at her side.

He didn't look at the crowd or down at the field; instead he looked up toward the sky and the upper edges of the stadium. The sun was breaking over the rim of the arena now, casting beams of light through the clouds and dousing the entire world in a soft pink glow.

The crowd cheered again when they saw the prince. A few of the goddess-touched girls clapped too. Someone behind me, Tessa maybe, commented on how handsome he looked.

She was right. Cohen was handsome. He wore that princely mask, poised and self-assured. But this smile wasn't the one he'd given me.

Had he really spent time with me out of pity?

One of the girls said, "We all know which girl he wants to win."

"Her father is the Speaker of the Synod," Nadia said. "My trainers say Kinsley and Cohen have been paired together for years. It's practically an arranged marriage."

Heidi huffed. "Cohen doesn't seem to mind. Did you see the way he kissed her at the ball?"

"Inappropriate," Tessa agreed.

Vivian nodded. "And with all of us standing there watching too."

"He shouldn't have favorites," someone else said.

I stayed silent, just listening and watching the projected image of Cohen on the broadcast screens. He hadn't mentioned Kinsley in his childhood stories, but then why would he? He knew she was my competition. It would have been strange for him to talk about her with me.

I wondered what the marked girls would say if they'd known that he'd also kissed me . . . in private . . . while he was drunk.

Grier sighed. "It was embarrassing."

Someone else shrugged. "He's going to end up marrying her, no matter what we do."

Heidi turned in her seat. "What makes you so sure he will?"

"Viera likes Kinsley," Elodie said. "She'll win because the queen wants her to."

"Damn the queen." Heidi stood up and turned to look at us. "And damn all of you if you plan to die without a fight."

Cohen had stepped up to the microphone. Up close, he looked ragged, like he hadn't slept the night before. The trial hadn't even begun and Cohen already looked like he wanted to leave. Behind me, the girls were still bickering.

I spoke up. "It's starting."

Outside, the crowd fell silent too, everyone waiting, breathless, for the Culling to officially start.

Cohen's voice echoed through the quiet stadium, bouncing off the concrete walls, turning into its own soft chant. "Today we begin the Culling. The goddess has blessed our nation with these worthy candidates—all of them as gifted and as capable as the next. The Culling pool has already dropped to nine, leaving us one step closer to finding out who our next queen will be. Today you will witness the first of the Culling trials. It is these trials that will decide not only the fate of each of the goddess-touched girls, but also the fate of Erydia."

Cohen scanned the crowd and, for a second, his rehearsed smile slipped from his face to reveal the exhaustion beneath. He swallowed and looked to his mother. With a nod of her head, Cohen stepped away from the microphone and she stepped forward.

Viera clapped her hands together. "Let us begin."

With that, the metal door across from us creaked open. The tunnel beyond was dark and empty, lit with flickering torches. Everything stilled as the crowd leaned in, collectively inhaling, enthralled as Kinsley and Joslyn walked side by side into the middle of the stadium.

They paused, only for a second, and then separated, walking thirty paces from one another—ten for the goddess-touched girls, ten for Erydia, and ten for the queen.

Joslyn walked toward the glass, facing us, while Kinsley faced away. For a long moment, there was only silence. Then a buzzer sounded.

Kinsley turned first and pulled her hands up as if lifting an invisible weight. Her arms flexed; her hands shook.

The floor shook.

Joslyn stood with her back still to Kinsley, her eyes closed, her hands open at her sides. It was as if she were giving herself to the goddess—surrendering. She swayed, slightly off-kilter.

Behind me, Heidi cursed.

With a deafening roar, the earth cracked, split, and opened as vines spiraled up from the ground. Kinsley's face broke into a grin so vicious it was nauseating to watch.

She clenched her fists, then threw her palms forward. In a fluid motion, vines surged, like a wave of writhing snakes. Joslyn's eyes flew open just as the first vine caught her around the neck and yanked her back.

She spun, hitting the ground on all fours. The vines encircled her, catching her flailing arms and legs. Joslyn kicked and bent, but their hold on her only tightened.

Kinsley circled her prey, slowly rotating her fingers, controlling the vines to combat each of Joslyn's erratic movements.

Above our heads, the crowd was yelling, screaming for blood, screaming for a fight. But this wasn't a fight; it was a slaughter. Slow and lazy.

Joslyn roared, but her scream was drowned out by the cheering crowd. A hand broke free from the vines. The green tendrils tightening around Joslyn's neck, browned and cracked, flaking to pieces on the dirt floor of the arena. With another shout of fury, she pushed out with both hands and the vines slithered away from her.

A cheer went through the crowd as Joslyn stumbled to her feet, her arms outstretched toward Kinsley. In response, Kinsley sent more vines, this time stronger, larger. A wall of water met them halfway.

The two struggled for a moment, Kinsley fighting to make her vines push through Joslyn's barricade. Finally, Kinsley gave up and knit the vines together, creating a fortress of vines to shield herself from Joslyn's wave.

The girls circled.

Joslyn changed tactics. She started pulling water from Kinsley's vines. They cracked and pulled away as they had before. Within seconds they were wilted, turned to blackened flakes on the arena floor. A cry came from Kinsley, indignant, frustrated.

This was supposed to be easy for her.

Water split the remaining vines down the middle and shoved them against the far sides of the arena. Joslyn stepped forward, through a tunnel of water and wilted plants, an avenging goddess herself.

Kinsley moved forward too, pulling her vines back to her, causing new ones to snake from the earth. They slithered through the cracks in the red clay, shifting the earth, pulling it apart.

With a guttural scream, Joslyn ran at Kinsley, water flowing from her hands. Before Kinsley could deflect, it merged and became a large ball of water. A sphere that locked around Kinsley's bare neck. In the blink of an eye, the water was over her jaw, her cheeks. It covered her nose, her mouth.

Kinsley clawed at the water, her nails only marring her own flesh as the liquid pushed through her fingers. It didn't so much as react to her touch. Her face turned a sickly shade of blue.

Joslyn stood a few yards away, her arms outstretched, using her hands to hold the ball of water in place.

I got to my feet, standing without even realizing I was doing it. This was it. She was going to kill Kinsley.

The other girls were on their feet too, all of us moving in a sort of trance to the glass. Beyond it, Kinsley writhed against Joslyn's hold. She dropped to her knees in the dirt.

The crowd was standing. Shrieking. Cheering.

Joslyn smiled, tightened her fists, and stepped toward Kinsley—ready to end it. The girl was almost dead—her face bright red, dark-brown eyes open and silently screaming. Pleading.

Then, in a moment so quick it was almost imperceptible, everything seemed to shift.

The crowd was deafening. The buzz of a million bees. The cacophony of a thousand scraping violins. The world inhaling and exhaling all at once.

Joslyn stood with her back to the glass.

Bubbles were starting to trickle from Kinsley's mouth.

"Oh no," Tessa breathed.

A shiver, almost imperceptible, went through Joslyn's body and she twitched, pitched forward at the waist and threw up.

One of the girls in the viewing room cursed as Joslyn lost control of her ability. The water fell away, splashing down around Kinsley's torso. She coughed, sputtered.

It was only a second, an instant of weakness. Joslyn swayed on her feet, but she lifted a hand, tried to straighten and pull the water back into place.

But it was too late.

Vines snaked from behind Joslyn and caught her around the throat. Her nails dug into red mud as she tried and failed to escape. There wasn't even time to scream as she was pulled back and thrown against the glass of the viewing room.

We all sprang away in surprise. There was a chorus of loud curses and a few muttered prayers. But the goddess wasn't going to save Joslyn now. She wasn't going to save any of us.

Joslyn's hands clutched at the vines as they twisted and tightened around her neck. Slowly, Kinsley rose to her feet, never taking her eyes off Joslyn's writhing body. She approached, using her hand to push the vines tighter and tighter around Joslyn's neck.

Joslyn's mouth was open, trying to scream, trying to beg for help.

Blood filled her eyes. Her face flushed red, then purple. She stopped moving. Stopped fighting.

It fell silent, everyone in the arena leaning in, watching. Kinsley walked a slow circle around Joslyn's body. The vine slithered and twitched, wrapping around Joslyn until her entire face was covered.

They crushed her neck with an audible crack.

At the sound, the crowd came alive again, applause and cheers—chanting for Kinsley once more. She didn't notice. Her eyes were still locked on Joslyn's unmoving body, her fingers tracing and weaving the vines ever tighter. Crushing her further.

The queen announced Kinsley as the winner of the first trial.

Kinsley didn't even seem to notice. Carefully, as if unwrapping a present, she eased vine after bloody vine from around Joslyn's neck, until she could get a good look at the girl.

Joslyn was broken and bent. Her hands were still frozen, gripping at a vine that had worked its way into her mouth. Like a bandage being removed from a cut, each vine allowed more blood to gush forward.

As the last vine was pulled away, Joslyn's head flopped forward onto her chest. Blood oozed from her ears, eyes, nose, and mouth. Large red welts snaked around her body, a map of the damage the plants had done.

It was not something I would easily forget.

The queen called for Kinsley to take a bow. Told her she could leave the stadium. She congratulated her on her win and thanked those in attendance for coming.

The crowd was wild, cheering for Kinsley. Erydia was one goddess-touched girl closer to knowing who the next queen would be. The people's choice had triumphed.

When Kinsley didn't move, didn't acknowledge the crowd, someone came and escorted her from the arena. Even as she was pulled away, she turned and looked over her shoulder at Joslyn's lifeless body.

And smiled.

23

We were forced to wait in the viewing room until the priestesses had burned Joslyn's body. Kinsley had not returned to the viewing room and for that I was grateful. I had no desire to see her, not after what I'd just witnessed. No one said anything, but the room seemed heavy with thought. We all knew what the trial had looked like. Joslyn had been about to win and then . . . then she'd gotten sick.

"Poison," Grier said as we'd walked back toward the van that would return us to the palace. "That's what it looked like, right?"

I thought so too, but I hadn't said so. No one had. And there had been little discussion about it since. Once we were back at the palace, we were taken to our rooms and told to wait for our trainers to contact us. We would have two more weeks to train and then we'd receive the next Culling pair. After that, there would be another two weeks until the trial. So I had at least a month before I'd have to go back to the arena—either as a spectator or as a competitor.

I'd already showered and changed into a new set of training clothes— more than ready to get out of the ones I'd worn to the arena—when breakfast arrived. The first thing I noticed was the note from Cohen. His handwriting was sloppy and boyish, nothing like Uri's swirling cursive. The small yellow paper was folded neatly and wedged beneath the plate.

I sat cross-legged in the middle of my bed and ate my breakfast slowly, hoping it would settle my stomach. I scanned the letter between bites:

Good morning.

As promised—Ambrose Benson is training in Nolajan. He will eventually be sent to Vayelle to do reconnaissance work. I've also inquired about Kace. He's training in a camp in Varos. I've asked Dellacov to look at him as an option for a palace guard. With the trials in full swing, we're in need of a few more. We'll see what happens. Maybe your brother will get that dream promotion sooner than he thought.

I'd love to see you, if you can make the time. No pressure though. I'll leave it up to you. The extra stationary is so you can write to your brother. I've told the maids that anything marked with black wax should come to me and I'll see that it makes its way to him. Just pass it to one of the staff and they'll give it to me. And if you wanted to maybe address a letter to me, that would be okay too.

Enjoy your breakfast.

Cohen

I blinked my eyes against the sudden onslaught of emotion. He'd remembered to ask about my brothers. I'd forgotten about that, too busy focusing on our kiss and everything that had happened since. But he'd remembered. And he'd asked to see me.

Just as he'd said, Cohen had included a piece of thick parchment, a plain brown envelope, and a block of black wax. I could write to Ambrose and let him know I was okay.

Despite how confused I was at Cohen's behavior and my feelings for him, my heart warmed. For a split second, I just sat there like a lovesick girl, holding his letter against my chest.

But the reality of it all came crashing back in a wave of Kinsley's words—*He pities you. That's why he showed you any attention at all. The dirty, starved little girl from Varos. He saw you and he felt bad.*

No. With everything at stake, I needed to focus on surviving. I wouldn't write to him and I wouldn't let him see me. My only chance at survival was to win and I needed to focus every ounce of energy on that task. And if Viera was influencing trials and killing girls on a whim, I couldn't afford to draw a bigger target on my back. Not if I intended to win.

Oredison Palace, Gazda
Two weeks later

I rarely saw the other girls. Every once in a while, I'd pass one of them in the hallway or hear them practicing with their trainers. I knew they were training as hard as I was, all of us focused on what the next trial might bring. We wouldn't know until Fidelium—the day of secrets. A temple-designated time for confession and forgiveness.

Cohen and I danced around each other. He knew my practice schedule and always managed to be in the training area at the same time as I was. Tallis thought he lingered in the hall to speak to me, and she'd sometimes ask about it, but I always brushed her off. There was nothing between us. We'd shared one kiss and a few rounds of cards.

Every time we saw each other, he'd mutter a quiet greeting, ask how I was, and I would never do anything more than nod in response. My acknowledgment was born of obligation. He was a prince and it felt inappropriate to ignore him. But no more inappropriate than it was for him to watch me so closely. To ask to see me; to try to speak to me.

And it wasn't just him seeking me out; he was asking Uri about me too. On more than one occasion she'd come to my room to ask if I wanted to play cards with the two of them. "Cages and Crowns is more fun with more players," she'd say. But any pretense of it being a casual invitation would disappear as she explained, "Cohen wants to see you" or "Cohen wanted me to see if you'd play."

No matter how many times I said no or avoided her questions, Cohen always found a way to be where I was. Some small part of me wanted to be worn down by his persistence. It would be nice, easy even, to forget what had happened with Kinsley at the ball and the things she'd said to me before the trial. Maybe there was a way to look past the fact that his mother had probably poisoned Joslyn to give Kinsley the edge she'd needed to win.

Goddess, it would be nice to stop fighting the pull I felt toward him. That swirling power that dwelled in me seemed to reach for him just as much as it reached for the crown. Maybe my ability saw Cohen and the throne as being one and the same, but my heart saw it differently.

No matter how hard I tried, I could never quite forget the fact that he'd followed through on his promise and had let me write to my brother. There was no way he could know how much that meant to me. My lack of any real appreciation toward him certainly didn't convey that.

I wondered if it had disappointed Cohen when I'd slipped the letter under Dellacov's door two weeks ago. That would have been one more rejection in a line of smaller ones. And yet he still waited for me, asked about me, wished me luck. His kindness was its own sort of oppression.

Four days before Fidelium, I was sent a summons to attend an etiquette lesson. According to Tallis, there had been some public criticism of the goddess-touched girls after the Commencement Ball. A few girls had overindulged in the wine and champagne, and while the crowd inside the ballroom had been enamored with Kinsley and Cohen's kiss, the population outside of Oredison Palace, who had seen it displayed in the black-and-white headlines and crackling film of local cinemas, were less charmed. Tallis had spent the better half of the previous night telling me all about how the reporters had caught it on film.

"It's early for a prince to be doing things like that. People like the sport of the Culling, but they like it played fair. Between the ball and Kinsley's stunt in the arena, it's obvious that rules are being broken."

So the people in Gazda weren't upset that we were being made to fight and die in the Culling; they were angry that we weren't doing it strictly by the rule book. Lovely.

All I could think as she talked was about the kiss between Cohen and

Kinsley and about my mother. Had she seen the headlines? Was she relieved to see that my name wasn't one of the ones pulled for a trial? There were no cinemas in Varos and the newspapers were often days, if not weeks, behind. The only television set would be in the pub, and she wouldn't darken that door.

Likely, she had no idea. Maybe that ignorance was a blessing.

"Behave," Tallis had said before she left last night. "Stay out of trouble. The queen doesn't care about the people's opinions, but she won't let outright childishness go unpunished. The girls behaved badly at the ball and the Synod is playing damage control. Just, for the love of the goddess, please don't draw attention to yourself. The last thing we need is Viera looking at us."

I'd only nodded, certain that my behavior would have very little to do with whether Viera looked my way and everything to do with what her son did. She'd care about me if he did. She'd care to hurt me if she thought it would hurt him.

As if she'd caught whiff of the news, Uri had arrived at my bedroom the morning of the lesson with a warm tray of breakfast and a new dress. Both were equally welcome.

Like Cohen, Uri had made a habit of being around. Even when I rejected her invitations to play cards in her suite, she would make the time to come and see me. She would bring stacks of novels with her—books with unbroken spines and paper that smelled of freshly pressed ink, not mothballs. She loved steamy romances and daring heroines.

I was willing to read anything that took me out of my present situation. I wanted to leave my body and live in someone else's head, if only for a moment. Those stories always had happy endings. The pieces of the plot always layered together perfectly, leaving nothing amiss.

They were nothing like real life, and I was thankful for the distraction.

Uri was another form of distraction.

She would ask me on walks, and I would listen as she recounted all the most riveting gossip. Which maid was dating which guard; what dignitary was visiting from where.

And Cohen was right; Uri was a spy. She always knew what was happening. She was both seen and entirely unseen within the palace. And she always had some bit of news, something to say.

But today she was unusually quiet.

When she finally did speak, she asked, "Did something happen between you and my brother?"

I nearly spilled orange juice all over my bed. "What?"

Uri set her plate down on the tray between us. "Has anything happened with you and Cohen? You're avoiding him. He says you are. He's . . . He's my brother so I sometimes find him to be incredibly annoying, but most girls don't. All the other goddess-touched girls are fawning all over him every chance they get. But I invite you to sit in my dimly lit parlor and play cards—semi-alone with him—and you reject me every single time. I'm beginning to take it personally."

I'd never had a friend like her before and I didn't want to lie. However, I also wasn't sure I wanted to tell her that I'd kissed her brother.

"I've spoken to him a few times."

Uri nodded slowly. "That's it? Nothing more interesting than a conversation?" Her brows rose. "So, you didn't kiss him then?"

"Who . . ." I paused and closed my eyes. "Dellacov."

When I opened my eyes again, she was smiling to herself. "He may be Captain of the Royal Guard, but he's truly terrible at keeping secrets. It's a fatal flaw, I think."

"I don't want to talk about it. And I'm not interested in seeing Cohen. Not right now."

I slid off the bed and went to the mirror. The etiquette lesson would be starting soon and I was nervous. It would be held in a large music room in the northern wing of the palace. For the occasion, Uri had chosen a green dress made of flowy crepe with cream roses embroidered along the folded collar and waistband.

When I'd reached for a pair of brown flats, the princess had shaken her head and pointed me toward a pair of cream-and-tan heels. Wearing the dress and the shoes, I felt like a young woman rather than a teenage girl.

I fiddled with my hair. It had grown out a little and the curls were beginning to lie more naturally. I forced a smile, adjusted the fall of the dress, and turned to show Uri the final results. When she barely glanced my way, I went back and sat on the edge of the bed.

"You seem distracted," I said.

"I'm fine." She reached forward and buttoned the cap sleeve of my dress. I stayed quiet, waiting. She didn't meet my eyes as the silence grew and became uncomfortable. Still, I waited. Finally, just when I thought I was going to have to speak, Uri broke the silence.

"Do . . . Do you think Kinsley won on her own?"

I hesitated, surprised at the question.

After the trial, the other girls had discussed what had happened. Most agreed that someone must have done something to keep Joslyn from drowning Kinsley. Out of shock and self-preservation, I hadn't said a word.

Regardless of whether Kinsley had won the fight on her own, she'd still managed to kill Joslyn. She was still the one we were going to have to contend with. The last thing I needed was to make my already-rocky relationship with her worse.

Uri was looking at me, her expression earnest. Once again, I was reminded of the countless casualties in the Culling. Yes, nine people would die to solidify a new queen's rule, but so many more people would suffer depending on who that new queen was.

Uri would suffer.

A nagging thought pushed to the forefront of my mind, saying what I'd been trying to ignore for weeks now—*Would Viera ever really step down? She had entered the Culling for herself. She'd killed multiple girls. Why would she give her crown away and go into retirement? That didn't seem like something she would do, even if it was what was expected of her.* My mouth was dry as I tried to ignore the way my chest ached at the very thought.

"Do you?" Uri asked again, her golden eyes wide with worry.

"No, I don't think she did," I answered. "Someone had to have helped her."

"I think so too," she whispered. "And I'm scared of what that might mean."

I had to remind myself that while Uri and I were friends, she was still a princess. It was easy to forget that the queen was her mother. Nothing about this was simple for her either.

I tried to keep my voice light as I asked, "Do you think it was your mother?"

"I— That's what everyone else thinks." Uri shook her head. "But I don't think so. I thought that initially, but I know my mother would have claimed the kill if it was hers, even if that meant shaming Kinsley."

"Why does she like Kinsley so much?"

Uri shrugged. "The devil you know is better than the devil you don't. I mean, Kinsley was raised here with us. She was our friend before she was marked. And she's . . . she's easy to manipulate. Her father has a lot of sway over her. She cares greatly for his opinion and had always put his desires above everything else. If she is queen, it means he is essentially king. She'll follow his lead. My mother knows that. She also knows that she has the same level of control over Synoder Raveena."

I chewed the inside of my cheek. "And what about her and Cohen?"

"What about them?"

"They kissed at the ball, and all the other girls think they have a history."

"They do," Uri said. "I think, growing up, they both liked the idea of each other. If they fell in love then maybe the Culling and being forced to marry each other wouldn't be so bad. But there isn't anything there anymore. Kinsley wants the crown and her father's approval more than she wants Cohen. Love is a transaction to her."

"So it's possible that Viera would help Kinsley?"

"If my mother must step down, she'd do so for Kinsley. With her being queen, she'd have some control still. Kinsley is blustering and has her moments of being brave, but she listens to Mother more than any of her true daughters do."

"Interesting."

She took a deep breath. "Yes. Britta thinks Mother must have poisoned the girl the morning of the trial, or maybe even the night before. Cohen, being stupid, said something about it at dinner last night and everything sort of exploded."

Uri met my eyes and searched my face as if trying to decide if I could be trusted. Suddenly, she looked on the verge of tears.

White-hot fear filled my chest. "What happened?"

"The same thing that always happens when Cohen oversteps. He's been sick with a fever for hours. Throwing up too, according to Britta. She's been with him." She brushed crumbs from the skirt of her dress as she said, "He'll pull through. He always does. But my mother will make sure he suffers a bit first."

"She poisoned him?"

I couldn't seem to get my mind to wrap around it. I'd watched Aviana die at her hands. It shouldn't have come as a surprise to me that she would harm her own children; Cohen had told me as much himself. Still, I couldn't imagine what could cause a mother to hate her son that much.

Uri shrugged. "Everyone is calling it food poisoning, but the timing of it is just too . . . perfect. We all know she hurts him, and she was *angry* with him last night. It's nothing new. I can't begin to tell you the number of times Cohen has gotten sick. He tends to speak his mind, which I'd say is his best characteristic, but it gets him hurt. Luckily, he's tough. And Britta is a good little nurse. Trust me. They both have plenty of experience with this."

I blinked at her. "But she's his mother. *Your* mother."

"I know." She pressed her lips together. "I love my mother, because she's my mother, not because she's earned my affection. Because of that love, I don't want to see her hurt. But I also don't want to see her remain queen."

Uri watched me, waiting to see what I was going to say. Maybe she thought I would have some political agenda of my own. Certainly, everyone else around her did.

As a goddess-touched girl, I felt like a pawn, but I couldn't imagine what it was like to be Uri. I may have wanted freedom from my mother's control, but that control had always come out of love for me.

I said, "I'm sorry that Cohen is sick. In a few months there will be a new queen, and hopefully things will improve."

"I hope so." Uri turned away, trying to shield her face from me. Still, I saw the way her bottom lip trembled. For an instant, it looked like she might cry . . . but then the mask was back.

24

The Music Room

Four days before Fidelium

As fate would have it, we arrived in the music room just as Kinsley did.

Kinsley smiled when she saw me and made a beeline in my direction. She was trying to come up with something demeaning to say to me. I could see it in the curve of her lips.

She landed on, "You shouldn't wear heels if you can't walk in them."

I sighed, already exhausted by her. "Thank you for pointing it out. Now, if you have nothing interesting to say to me, I'll just be going."

I'd never wished for pockets more in my life. What did people do with their hands when they wore a dress? Do I cross my arms? I wasn't supposed to cross my legs—I knew the rule on that—but no one had said anything about my arms.

I forced a smile. "How does your lip feel? All better?"

It had been two weeks since I'd seen her. After everything with the trial, we hadn't been around each other. She was still beat up from her trial, the evidence of what Joslyn had done to her a yellowed mess of bruises and tiny cuts around her neck from where she'd tried to get the water away from her face. But I could still see the healing split in her bottom lip from where I'd hit her. And I'd be lying if I said that I didn't find some sick satisfaction in knowing that I'd left a mark.

Her chin quivered, just the barest shadow of weakness. Then Kinsley straightened. "It's fine. I had forgotten about it, actually."

I hummed in response and muttered, "I'll be sure to hit harder next time."

Her smile turned feline. "Aren't you going to congratulate me, Monroe?"

"Congratulate you for what?"

The corner of her mouth twitched. "On my win against Joslyn."

A waiter walked by with a tray of drinks and I took the opportunity to snatch one. Perfect, finally something to do with my damn hands. I downed a good bit of it, thinking it was water, and stupidly started coughing when it turned out to be white wine.

Kinsley smiled, once again feeling superior to me.

I cleared my throat, still wincing from the drink. "*Did* you win? I mean, I saw the fight, but I seem to recall you needing a bit of help toward the end. Really seemed like Joslyn was going to drown you. It's lucky she got sick the way she did. That was great timing for you."

Kinsley stepped toward me, so close I could feel the heat of her breath against my face. "What are you trying to say?"

It was at that moment Nadia walked over. "Kinsley, Larkin's just arrived, I think she's looking for you."

Kinsley pressed her perfectly painted lips together and ran her eyes across my body like there were a million spiders running down my spine, but I didn't step away from her. I didn't move. "Run along, you shouldn't keep the princess waiting."

"Kinsley?" Nadia prompted.

Kinsley's mark wrinkled as she narrowed her eyes. For a second, I had to decide what I would do if she attacked me. There were three candles nearby. I could feel the heat of the flames, tiny pinpricks of white-hot fire. If she lunged toward me, I would toss the wine in her face and then I would throw fire.

I rallied myself, drawing to my full height. If we were going to fight, I'd strike first. The flames from the candles flickered and a few of the nearby girls turned to look, confused.

Kinsley didn't seem to notice as she exhaled and said, "Enjoy yourself, Monroe." Before I could say or do anything else, she walked away, leaving Nadia and me standing alone.

Nadia's voice was little more than a whisper as she said, "She scares the shit out of me."

I set my glass on a nearby table and nodded.

"I didn't know if you needed rescuing. I mean, you . . . you seemed like you were handling things okay on your own. I just didn't want her to, you know, kill you or something. And after what happened before the trial, I thought she might." She tried to smile but it came out looking uncomfortable.

Nadia was trying so hard to be friendly, but we weren't here to make friends. I didn't want to know or like any of them. I couldn't, not if I might have to face them in the arena. But she was looking at me, that nervous smile on her face, and despite all of my bravado, I wasn't Kinsley.

I touched her shoulder. "I'm sorry. Thank you for coming to help."

At the touch, warmth shot up my fingertips, the sensation turning hot as it spread up my arm and across my chest. I stepped back from her and looked down at my hand. My skin was tingling, like a million tiny pinpricks of electricity running through my veins.

I took another step back and looked at her. "Wh-what was that?"

Nadia's dark, doe-like eyes were huge. "Nothing." She chewed absentmindedly at a hangnail as she muttered a quick, "Just ignore it."

"It wasn't 'nothing.'" My chest still felt warm like I was standing too close to a fire. It didn't hurt, just took my breath away. "What did you do?"

She lowered her hand from her mouth and said, "I didn't mean to do it, I'm sorry. It can be a bit invasive."

"What—" The knowledge of her ability struck me, and I nearly choked. "You *healed* me?"

She glanced around, her eyes darting to the goddess-touched girls nearest us. "Keep your voice down. I don't want to get in trouble. I didn't— It was an accident, okay?"

"What do you mean? You healed me. Healed me from what?"

Nadia shrugged. "I'm kind of new to using it. I only got my ability a couple of months ago and sometimes when I'm nervous I just . . ." She bit the nail of her index finger and frowned at me. "It's so embarrassing. Please don't tell anyone. Especially not Kinsley; she'd eat me alive if she knew I didn't have good control over it."

"But why is it embarrassing?"

She lowered her hand and held it out to me, so I could see the black marks that covered each fingerprint on her left hand. It looked as if Nadia had pressed her fingertips against an ink pad.

"It isn't cool or anything," she said. "I can just sense when people are hurting and I can fix it."

"But that's amazing," I countered. "And useful. You can really heal people just by touching them?"

She nodded.

"That's awesome."

"Not in a fight to the death, it isn't," Nadia whispered. "What am I supposed to do, heal you to death?"

Toward the front of the room, near a large piano, Mrs. Arden, the governess and royal housekeeper, was beginning to herd goddess-touched girls toward a small group of tables set for tea. I caught sight of Kinsley, who was talking to Grier by one of the large bay windows. Nadia followed my gaze. I was about to say something else about her ability when a thought occurred to me.

"You touched Joslyn right before she went into the arena."

Nadia started biting her nails again. She nodded, and her gaze slid sideways to Kinsley. She didn't want to make an enemy of her any more than I did. Still . . .

"You said that you could tell when people are sick." I kept my voice low, my head angled so only Nadia could see my face. "What did you sense when you touched Joslyn?"

Nadia opened her mouth to answer me, but her words were cut off as the elderly woman approached us. "Ladies, now isn't the time for gossip." She gestured toward a table at the back of the room.

We were barely in our seats before Mrs. Arden was introducing herself to the girls she hadn't met yet. She read out a list of names, reacquainting herself with each of us and our abilities. Judging by the way Uri's nose wrinkled as she lounged in her seat next to mine, Mrs. Arden wasn't a favorite when it came to the rotating carousel of governesses she'd had growing up.

Mrs. Arden explained the table setting, discussed the different spoons, the materials used to make the china set, the quality of the imported tea. Then she demonstrated how to serve a table, explained when and where that was appropriate for us to do. Once she was done, we practiced, taking turns going around our small table. Nadia, Grier, and I each poured a cup and served the person next to us, careful to follow the rules.

When it was Uri's turn to serve me, she intentionally missed the cup, filling the saucer instead. It spilled over, staining the lace tablecloth. I had to press my lips together to hide a smile as Uri exaggeratedly said, "Oopsies!"

"Uriel!" Mrs. Arden chided, catching sight of the stain as she paced the music room.

Uri pursed her lips, her eyes turning innocent as she said, "I apologize, Mrs. Arden. How very clumsy of me."

The old woman bowed her head. "You're a princess, Uriel. You must learn to be more careful."

Britta was watching from a nearby table, her fingers pressed to her lips to keep from smiling.

Uri caught her sister's gaze and muttered a quick apology to the tutor. "Yes, ma'am. I'm so sorry. It won't happen again." She waited until Mrs. Arden had turned away from us before she stuck her tongue out.

When it came time for us to practice sitting and standing with grace, Uri went out of her way to break every rule. Mrs. Arden said to sit with our knees together—Uri crossed her legs. Mrs. Arden said to make sure our dresses were pulled down—Uri hitched her skirt up. Mrs. Arden said to never slouch or cross our arms—Uri made sure she looked like an angry humpbacked crone.

By the end of the lesson, Uri had everyone around us smiling, even Britta, who'd done her best to remain unamused by her sister's dramatics. Mrs. Arden was at her wit's end, and her white hair was a mess from the many times she'd anxiously pulled at it in an effort to keep her composure.

Her voice was tight with anxiety as she congratulated us on how well we'd done. "We should have had one of these lessons earlier but your Culling training was deemed 'more important.'" She cleared her throat and tugged at the bodice of her dress. "*Clearly* priorities were out of order. A mistake that I doubt will be made again. I digress. Should you have any further questions about how you ought to behave in any given situation, I am more than willing to assist. That being said, you are dismissed."

Once she strode from the room, we dispersed, all of us heading toward our respective rooms. Even though she was heading away from where I was staying, I followed Nadia. She flinched slightly as I fell into step next to her.

"So," I said, keeping my voice down, "you were just about to tell me what you sensed when you touched Joslyn."

Nadia sighed and shot me an incredulous look. Her gaze found Kinsley, who was walking a few yards ahead of us. "I don't think we should talk about it. I, uh— The last thing I need is to put a target on my back, you know?"

"We already have targets on our backs."

She chewed her bottom lip. "Still, I don't want her coming after me."

"You're gonna let some plants scare you?"

"It isn't the plants, and you know it." Nadia wrapped her arms around herself, her voice no more than a breathy whisper as she asked, "She doesn't scare you? Honestly?"

I hesitated. "I think, in the game we're playing, fear is a gift we give to other people. I don't want to give my fear to Kinsley. She doesn't deserve it. She's just a bully."

She chewed on a nail as she muttered, "Well, so was the queen and look where it got her."

"But no one wants another queen like her, do they? Eventually other people will see just how similar they are."

Nadia laughed, a quiet, hopeless sound. "We'll all be ashes before anyone else realizes the kind of person she is." She sighed. "And by then, I think it will be far too late."

25

Palace Bedroom

Fidelium

I was so anxious that I barely slept the eve of Fidelium. I was already awake and pacing when my breakfast arrived. Dread scraped away at my composure and made sitting still impossible.

If it was my name on that announcement, it would be fine. I would be fine.

I'd *have* to be fine.

The maid carrying the tray smiled broadly as she entered the room, her steps unhurried. She wished me good health and abundant forgiveness, her smile faltering slightly as, in my impatience, I nearly forgot the traditional Fidelium response.

I forced a smile and returned, "And the same to you and your household."

The girl set the tray on the dresser by the door and curtsied. "May the goddess will it."

I nodded, every muscle in my body tensing as I resisted the urge to push past her and grab the crisp white envelope perched against the glass of orange juice. Her footsteps were still echoing down the hall as I tore open the heavy paper and unfolded the card.

Heidi Larson and Grier Jennis will fight—

I couldn't even finish reading it before I was weeping. It wasn't me. I had more time. My knees gave way and I had to clutch the dresser to remain upright. Orange juice sloshed onto the envelopes of two more letters.

Heidi and Grier. Sanctus Eszter.

Two weeks from now.

Thank the goddess.

I grabbed the other letter from the tray and sat on the edge of the bed.

My knees still shook as I flipped the envelope to examine the seal—the navy blue of the royal crest. Cohen's letter was written in hasty, boyish scrawl:

So, I've been thinking a lot about you recently. I know you're mad. And I understand why. I'm not trying to say you shouldn't stay mad. But please just let me explain myself. In person. And without a million other people around. Have dinner with me tonight in the kitchens, just like last time? Seven o'clock. Best three out of five.

Don't say no.

– Cohen

Nope. Hell no.

I put the letter down. Picked it back up. Read it again.

No. I wouldn't go to the kitchens with him. I was stupid to have done that to begin with, and I wasn't going to get pulled back in a second time. I didn't want to even think about it.

I *couldn't* think about it.

Just like before, he'd included stationary and a block of simple black wax. It was an offer to respond. But what could I even say? I wasn't sure a friendship with Cohen—or anything more—was in my best interest. I needed to focus on the Culling. Just because I wasn't fighting in the next trial didn't mean I wouldn't be called upon to fight in the one after that. I needed to be ready.

I tucked his stationary and the wax in the drawer of my dresser and dressed for the day. It was a holiday, so I wasn't required to train. Juno had asked for the day off, but Tallis had sent a note to me the night before telling me that she'd come by just after breakfast to see if I wanted to practice.

I'd just finished lacing my boots when her knock came at my door. I headed into the bathing room in search of pins to tie back my hair as I called, "Enter!"

"Morning and blessed Fidelium," Tallis said as she shut my bedroom door behind her. "May you have good health and abundant forgiveness—and all that shit."

My laugh echoed off the tiles of the bathing room. "Same to you. It's Heidi and Grier, did you see?"

"I did. I got the notice about half an hour ago. I think I'll consider it a Fidelium miracle. Juno said not to let the news turn you lazy. That means we've got at least another two weeks to train and he expects you to work your ass off for every second of it."

"I won't let it make me lazy."

She stopped in the doorway and leaned her shoulder against the frame. "Good to hear. You ready to train?"

"Almost." I slipped one more pin into my hair and then followed her out into my bedroom. She paused by the dresser and picked up the letter Cohen had sent with breakfast. She frowned as she scanned its contents.

"It's— We're just friends."

Her attention snapped to me. "Defensive, Benson?" She let the letter fall back onto the tray.

I ignored her. "You ready?"

Her teeth scraped over her bottom lip. "Actually, there's something I wanted to discuss with you before we go." She nodded to my unmade bed. "You ought to sit."

Tension coiled tight in my gut at her words. "What is it?" I asked, easing onto the bed. "What's happened?"

"Nothing has happened. Everything's fine. I just . . ." She lowered her voice. "I need you to listen to everything I'm about to say." She glanced at the closed bedroom door and then back to me, her brow furrowing. "Do you understand?"

No, I didn't. But I nodded anyway.

"I have a message for you. Ambrose Benson is your oldest brother." She swallowed, her hands flexing at her sides. "He's from Varos. Blacksmith's apprentice. He's engaged to Ellora Hoffman—the miller's daughter. He was at Demarti Station with you trying to get through the Suri Gap. He got the fake papers from a Culled smuggler in Linomi. He sold three handcrafted blades, a new saddle, and a necklace for them." She reached into her pocket and pulled something out—a thin chain of silver hung from her fist. She swallowed and said, "He traded *this* necklace."

Panic set in, cold as ice in the pit of my stomach. "Where is he?"

Tallis shook her head. "It doesn't matter. What does matter is—"

I snapped my fingers, calling fire to flesh. Sparks danced against my skin. "It *does* matter. Where is my brother?" Had they discovered that he was working with the rebels to get me out of Erydia? That necklace—it was Ellora's and as precious to my brother as any item could be. The fact that Tallis held it now was bad. Very, very bad.

Tallis crouched down so we were nearly eye level. "Listen to me, Monroe. Ambrose is safe. I . . ." She held the necklace out to me. "Here. He told me to give you this."

My fire fizzled out. *He told me to give you this.*

I blinked at her, my entire body tense with fear. "He . . . He isn't dead?"

"Goddess, no."

Tentatively, I reached out and took the necklace from her outstretched hand. I'd never seen the small chain and pendant before, but I knew exactly what it was. My eyes darted from the rough-etched rabbit-head charm to where Tallis still crouched. "He gave you this? *Ambrose* gave you this?"

"In a way. He asked that it make its way to you." She nodded to the chain pooled in the palm of my hand. "When the smuggler realized what your brother had sold it for—that it was meant to get a goddess-touched girl out of Erydia . . . Well, everyone sort of agreed that you were too valuable to be lost in the Culling. Not when you're here. Not when you have access to what we need."

"Access?"

"Ambrose wants you out. A deal was made and— Some of the higher-ups thought the necklace might send a message to you. We didn't want there to be any question of whether we were being honest. Treason isn't the sort of shit you play around with. We needed to get our point across and Ambrose agreed that you'd know the necklace. Know that it had come from him."

My fist tightened around the necklace as I connected the dots that I'd been too blind to notice before. I'd thought the choice of a rabbit charm was a personal touch for Ellora—a way to signify how much she loved animals. I remembered my brother talking about the delicate piece of jewelry, how pretty he thought it was—even with its darkened metal and rough-hewn edges. Ambrose had obsessed over the necklace for weeks after he'd first seen it displayed in a merchant's storefront window. He'd thought it would be a sweet gesture to solidify their promise to marry.

Now I understood the deeper meaning behind it.

After all, he'd told me that Ellora's father had helped get him the tickets and the papers to help us escape. Mr. Hoffman, who was working with the Culled.

It was clever, really, to choose that charm. The hare was a symbol of the rebellion, but it was also a part of the royal crest. Rabbits were often used in temple imagery and were frequently mixed into the myths and fables of our nation. It signified purity and sacrifice. A bountiful harvest and a good hunt.

It wasn't uncommon for Erydian children to have stuffed rabbit toys—I'd had a handmade rabbit doll when I was small and I'd slept with it until I was into my midteens. Yes, it was now a symbol of the rebellion, but it was as insignificant as it was significant. Giving Ellora a necklace like this wouldn't have been odd at all. And now . . . now I had it.

Ambrose's words from the train station filtered back to me.

I'll find a way to save you.

I met Tallis's wide eyes, trying to slow the racing of my heart as I whispered, "What was the message?"

Her voice was soft enough that I had to lean forward to hear her. "Ambrose said that if you want to get out of the Culling alive, the Culled is the way. We . . . We're going to execute the royal family and dismantle the

Culling from the inside. We'll stop the competition and let the remaining goddess-touched girls go."

Too simple. It sounded too simple. And why tell me at all?

Too valuable, she'd said. *Not when you have access to what we need.*

The sharp edges of the rabbit's ears dug into my palm as I asked, "What does this have to do with me?"

"You're close to the prince." She held up a hand to stop me from objecting. "You can deny it all you like, but we both know he's interested in you. So is the princess. Use that to your advantage. Get him to talk to you. Get information. Get yourself into rooms that the rest of us can't get into. Then tell us what you learn."

"And if I won't do it? What happens if I say no?"

She licked her lips and shook her head, her eyes digging holes into me as she said, "*Don't say no.*"

"This is treason."

"This is your chance to make it out of here with your hands clean."

But that wasn't true, was it? Maybe I would be able to escape the Culling trials, but Tallis was asking me to trade those deaths for the deaths of others. "What happens after the Warwicks are dead?"

"Vayelle is helping us to overthrow the Warwicks and the Synod. We've got their forces backing ours. It isn't like we're fighting alone."

"You're exchanging one problem for another. How would being ruled by a foreign country be any better than keeping the government we have?"

"They aren't going to rule over us. It's just like the last war. For them, it's a fight against archaic religion and temple-enforced poverty. They want the temples and the worship of the goddess ended. They are supporting the people's demand for change. No more human sacrifices, no more Culling-won queens. They are prepared to help us set up a rule of our own. It'll be better than now. We will vote in people to speak for us. The voiceless won't have to stay that way. They want what we want."

"And Cohen and Uri, what will be done to them?"

She was silent.

I shook my head. "I'm not helping you kill them. They've done nothing wrong."

"Don't throw away a chance at survival to save a boy who would just as easily see you dead in the arena. Same goes for Uriel. She may be sweet to you and send you pretty dresses, but she hasn't lifted a finger to stop you from being forced into this competition. Don't let them fool you, Monroe. Your death, and the death of countless other teenage girls, is what will keep them in power. It's what's kept the Warwicks in power for centuries. Cohen doesn't care about you. He'll marry whoever wins the Culling. This isn't some romantic children's story where everyone lives happily ever after. People are dying and more people will die unless we do something to stop it. It's his life or yours."

I looked down at the necklace in my hand. "You tell the Culled that I'll help them, but only if I have their word that Cohen, Uri, and Britta won't be killed. If . . . If they mean what they say about having a better government, then they can start it by not killing people based on simple-minded hatred and a whim. Cohen can stand trial for any crimes he's committed. Same thing for the princess. They're . . . They're my friends. And they've always been kind to me. The least I can do is give them a chance to speak in defense of themselves."

"The king and queen are—"

"—are the problem. So is the Synod and the temple and the magistrates and anyone else who would support laws that let innocent children starve. I don't believe for one second that Cohen would be in favor of those things—not even to stay in power. He's— Maybe he'll prove me wrong, but I don't think he's a villain."

"So, it all hinges on that then?" Tallis asked. "You'll work with us but only if we spare your prince?"

"Yes."

And that was that. My step first into treason was complete.

Tallis left with that as my only answer. She told me I should wear the necklace—the few rebel spies in the palace knew to be on the lookout for a goddess-touched girl wearing it.

"We look after our own," she assured me. "Once you're with us, we'll do whatever we can to keep you safe. We'll have eyes and ears on you. And when the time for the attack comes, the necklace will act as a marker of whose side you're on. That way we can make sure you get out."

"I'll wear it once I've gotten my promise," I told her.

I hid the necklace in the drawer of my vanity and told myself I wouldn't think of it until the Culled had given me their word regarding Uri, Britta, and Cohen's safety. Maybe their blood could be easily washed off someone else's hands, but I knew it would cling to me and I couldn't bear the thought.

I awoke that night to a knock at my door. Watery moonlight streamed in through the tall bay windows and the timepiece on my bedside table read half an hour until midnight. There was another knock.

For a moment, I thought it might be Tallis. Maybe she'd gotten a response from the rebels. It would have been fast, but I didn't know how long it took to pass messages in and out of the palace. Though Tallis had said that their chain of messengers worked quickly, it had been only a matter of hours since I'd spoken to her.

"Monroe?"

I recognized the voice immediately.

Cohen.

He knocked again. "Monroe?"

I threw off the covers, slid to the edge of my bed, and froze.

"I just want to see you." The door creaked, like he was leaning against it. "Let me try to explain things."

The hall outside was bright enough that I could just make out the shadow of his boots beneath the door. I watched that shadow, half terrified that he would leave and half terrified he might stay.

If I opened the door, what would he say?

What would he do?

The floor was freezing against my bare feet as I stood up. I wished there was time to look at myself in the mirror. I'd slept in tomorrow's training clothes, save for an undershirt, and I knew I must be a wrinkled mess.

I shouldn't care. But I couldn't help but comb my fingers through my hair as I walked to the door. I didn't open it, I just stood there trying to decide what to do about this boy.

This prince.

I could feel Cohen leaning against the door, waiting. "Monroe, please."

Anxiety danced a twirling waltz in the pit of my stomach. My words were breathy, no more than a groggy whisper as I said, "Okay, I'm listening."

Cohen exhaled. "I was stupid—"

I laughed. Well, that was one way to start this conversation. At the sound, Cohen stopped talking, waiting to see if I would speak. I pressed my lips together and leaned my forehead against the door.

"Go on."

He cleared his throat. "I just— What I said to you at the Commencement Ball, I meant it. I meant all of it. And I know . . . I know how things looked with Kinsley and that damn kiss, but it— I . . ." He stopped, inhaled a rattling breath. "Monroe, this would be easier if I could see you."

The air caught in my lungs. "Keep going."

"What happened with Kinsley was a mistake. I didn't mean for it to happen. We were dancing and then she kissed me and I . . . I didn't know what to do. But you should know that it isn't the same as what happened with you and me. I kissed you because I *wanted* to kiss you. I think I've wanted to kiss you since I saw you sitting on that stage. Maybe it's stupid, but I like you. You're genuine—at least, I believe you are. And you are far too good to be participating in something like the Culling. But you're here and . . ." There was another pause, so long I wondered if he was about to leave, to walk away and just never finish. Then he said, softer, "You're here and I just want to spend time with you. When I don't see you, I wonder where you are. I think about you and that kiss all the time. I can't help it. Believe me, I've tried."

My chest ached. "But you don't know me."

"I feel like I do," he said. "I don't know why, I guess it doesn't make sense. Maybe it's the goddess or fate or . . . wishful thinking." He laughed and tapped a nervous rhythm against the door. "I can't control what happens in the Culling. It's in your hands. All of this is in other people's hands. But I can protect you, at least for a while. I can sway the trial picks. I have. I will. My mother is dying to see you up against Kinsley, but—"

"You kissed her too." I hated the hurt in my voice, I hated how fast my heart was beating.

"That was . . ." He trailed off. "She did that for attention. Her father, he's— She did it to please him. I was as surprised as anyone. I left after the last girl danced. My mother was furious. Didn't you see?"

"No."

"Well, I left, and I've stayed away from Kinsley since."

"She said that you only gave me attention because you pity me."

"She's a liar. And if her trial is any indication, she's also probably a cheater."

Something else he said gnawed at the back of my mind. "Wait . . . have you been keeping me out of the trial picks?"

Silence.

"Cohen?"

"Uri has."

I nearly choked. "Uri?"

"Dellacov sets up the drawings. She's got access to his office; he keeps it unlocked for her. She hangs out in there sometimes when he isn't there, so it was easy for her to pull your name out. I mean, Uri's on your court, so it isn't like she's opposed to giving you extra time to prepare."

Well, that explained Uri's questions. Even if Cohen hadn't been the one to tell her about our kiss, asking her to sway the drawings was hint enough that something was going on between us.

I stepped back from the door. "Joslyn is dead. So, you're saying that she's dead and my name wasn't even in that drawing? Cohen, that could have easily been me. Maybe . . . Maybe it should have been—"

"Please don't be mad." When I didn't say anything, he cursed under his breath. "I've made things worse, haven't I?"

I pulled the door open so fast that Cohen almost lost his balance and toppled into my room. He caught himself on the door frame and stepped back, putting a foot or so between us.

I was breathing heavily, my mind reeling with the image of Joslyn's face, purple and bleeding—those bulging bloodshot eyes. I felt the sharp tug of the fire as it burned her corpse.

"I just . . ." I closed my eyes against the memory. "Cohen, that could have been me."

"But it wasn't you. And thank the goddess for it."

"It isn't fair. You're cheating and you're making me cheat. And now Joslyn is dead. How does that make me any better than Kinsley using your mother to win?"

Maybe it was stupid to feel this way, but I'd thought maybe the goddess was on my side. As names were drawn and my training continued, I'd let myself believe that the goddess was giving me time. And while I knew that Cohen had been trying to help me, I felt like he'd stolen something oddly sacred from me.

He shook his head and the expression on his face told me that he wouldn't budge on this. What he'd done to help me, it meant something to him. For whatever reason, he'd crossed a line for me and he wasn't going to take it back.

I ran a hand through my hair. "They need to choose again for the next trial. It should be fair."

The muscles in his jaw tightened and, for a second, I considered what his mother would do if she realized he'd tampered with the trials. What she might do to Uri for helping. He'd risked being tortured by his mother for me. He'd risked Uri's torture for me.

Cohen voice was quiet as he asked, "And what good would that do?"

My hands were shaking. "If I win, I will have done it on my own, fairly. I don't want other people to die for me."

"Welcome to the party."

I shook my head. "Don't try to pretend we're the same. We aren't. No matter what happens here, you get to keep your life and your crown."

"Monroe—"

"I don't want your help."

Cohen leaned forward, a hand braced on either side of the door frame. "I didn't realize you were so proud."

"You don't know me at all. You don't know a damn thing about me or my pride." My voice broke, and I had to look away from him.

Cohen took a small step forward, his hand just brushing my shoulder before he pulled it away. He swallowed. "I—"

"Why are you being so nice to me? Why do you even care? There are other girls here. Do you go to their rooms in the middle of the night? Do you kiss them?"

All of his bravado melted away and suddenly it was just Cohen standing there. He was sweating, his blond hair matted to his forehead, his face flushed red, almost feverish. He looked so exhausted and I was reminded that, just a few days ago, he'd been fighting poison.

Poison that his mother had given him. Poison that might still be in his system.

"Why?" I breathed. "You said at the ball that you had your own reasons. Why me?"

His voice shook as he said, "Do you remember a soldier from three years ago?"

A soldier from three years ago.

A memory, dim like a fading ember, bloomed in my mind. "A soldier—?" I stopped, took a step back. I looked at him. Really looked at him. "Cohen?" I breathed.

He opened his mouth to respond but the words died on his lips as the sound of footsteps echoed down the hall. They were faint and headed in our direction.

At the sound, Cohen stepped back from my door. He shouldn't be here. He'd broken so many rules with me—for me.

The sound grew and my panic grew with it. Before I could overthink what I was doing, I reached forward and grabbed him by the shirt, pulling him into my bedroom. The sound of my door slamming echoed into the silence of the night.

We both froze, breathing heavily, like two kids playing hide-and-go-seek. I'd turned, pressing my back to the door. Cohen stood over me, his mouth near my ear, our bodies terribly close, my fingers still clinging to the dark-blue fabric of his shirt as we waited in the darkness.

The footsteps grew louder, then the door shook against my back as someone knocked. My heart was in my ears.

They knocked again.

I forced my voice to be calm, to sound tired, as I called, "Yes? Who is it?"

"Dellacov," he said from the other side of the door. His voice was so loud it was like he was in the room with us. "I thought I heard something. I was just checking to make sure you were okay."

"I'm fine. Thanks. I just . . ." I faltered.

Cohen smiled and shook his head, amused.

"I tripped on my way out of the bathing room." I hated myself as soon as I said it.

I tripped? Seriously?

Dellacov didn't buy it either, but he was clearly not willing to push the matter as he said, "Okay? Sure. Have a good night, Monroe."

"You too."

His footsteps retreated back down the hall, and I waited until he was out of earshot before I slammed my fist against Cohen's shoulder.

"Ouch! What the hell?" He tried to step away, but I still had his shirt in a death grip.

"That was *you*? You were the soldier. *You* got separated from your unit?"

"No."

I'd almost forgotten that feeling, the recognition I'd felt when I'd seen him for the first time at my announcement. It had been vague and strange—just a flicker of remembering. I'd assumed that he just reminded me of Uri, that they shared a family resemblance, but no. No, I knew him. I'd met him before.

Three years ago, in the pouring rain.

He'd been much younger. Skinnier, less man and far more boy. And, goddess, he'd been coated in mud. He'd been soaked through, his hair appearing darker, his face paler. But the blue of his eyes—that young soldier had had bright blue eyes too.

Cohen swallowed. "I wasn't a soldier, I was just dressed as one. And I didn't get separated from my unit, Monroe; I ran away. It was the last time I was allowed to leave the palace. I was far enough from home and I took my chance. After that . . . After that there wasn't another opportunity to leave. My parents made sure of it."

I pressed my lips together. "You saw me."

I thought back to that day, the way the soldier had been shaking. I'd pulled him through the rain and mud into the house. Even now, I didn't know how I'd managed it.

I remember needing a fire, needing to warm him. I'd been stupid and too trusting and—and I hadn't ever had the guts to tell Ambrose the truth of what I'd done, what I'd shown that stranger. Ambrose would have shot him. He'd have killed him if it had meant keeping me safe.

I swallowed hard. "You saw me light a fire with my hands. You saw my mark. Why didn't you say anything? Why didn't you tell your mother about it as soon as you got home?" My fingers trembled as I pressed them to my mouth. "She— I could have been—"

Cohen reached out and carefully pulled my fingers from his shirt. He held my hand in his. "Who do you think I was running from?"

"I was so sure you'd tell someone. I spent forever worrying that soldiers would come and take me away."

"I never said a word. I never even mentioned a girl. As far as anyone else knows, there were only ever three boys in that house. I wouldn't have given your secret to her."

He was so different than I'd ever expected a prince to be. And there seemed to be no explaining it. I couldn't put into words how strange it was to find myself standing there with him, surrounded by the impossibility that was our friendship.

The Culled couldn't understand it.

I barely did.

I fought against the urge to smack him again. Goddess, he was so handsome and so damn sweet. "Honestly, Cohen. You don't even know me. Do you treat every stranger this way?"

"Not every stranger. Only the pretty ones."

My mouth fell open at that.

"I'm only kind of teasing," he admitted. "You saved my life. With or without an ability, you could have easily run away and left me to die." He scratched at the back of his neck and sighed. "I don't know. You didn't have to do what you did. No one has ever just been kind to me, apart from my sisters and Hugo, not without knowing I was a prince, and definitely not without expecting something from me. There is almost always an ulterior motive. But you . . ." He trailed off, running a fingertip along my palm, over the mark that was there, shrouded in darkness. "I hate the way my parents are. I hate how they treat people. All I wanted was to be the opposite of the sort of people they were. And you . . . you helped me when you didn't have to. You were a light in a dark moment in my life, and I've found it hard to forget about you. Especially once I realized you were marked, and I'd eventually see you again."

"I couldn't let you die."

"But you could have," he said. "You could've let me freeze to death in that stupid chicken coop. It would've been entirely my own fault. That was the third house I'd been to. I asked two other families for help and they turned me away, too afraid of my uniform to risk it. But you didn't turn me away. You didn't even think twice. And I haven't forgotten. I won't *ever* forget. I don't have a lot of good role models, but I've always set the bar with you. I knew I'd see you again, and I wanted . . . I wanted to be deserving of the kindness you showed me. I've tried to echo it whenever I can."

"Why were you in Varos? You were too young to be properly enlisted and there's no way in hell your parents would let you serve—"

"I told you my mother was hateful and terrible to me when I was a child.

I was sick all the time because of her. My father feared she'd kill me eventually, especially as I grew older and the Culling drew closer. I spent a few weeks in Varos shadowing our military. My father wanted me to see how things were run and he's always thought that experience was the best teacher. And it was a miserable enough job that my mother didn't argue with him when he decided to send me away. I think he just wanted to put distance between the two of us—she was . . . Well, you know how she is."

"If you ran—"

"It was a dumb decision. I just wanted out. I wanted out from under her hatred and away from my father's expectations. And I was a kid." He shrugged. "I rarely had the chance to behave as one, not really. So I guess it's understandable that I'd be an absolute idiot the moment I was left to my own devices. When I was told that my time shadowing was done and my father would be coming to get me and take me back to the palace I . . . I couldn't go back. The night before he was supposed to arrive, I ran. I made a childish decision and ran away from camp, hoping for— Truthfully, I don't know what I was hoping for. All I know is that I ended up on your farm. I was dressed like a solider because I stole fatigues before I left. I thought they would be better than the shirts and trousers I'd been sent with. The uniform kept everyone at bay. It might have been what killed me if it hadn't been for you."

My mind was spinning, trying to knit together every interaction I'd had with Cohen since I'd arrived in Gazda. "Why didn't you just tell me to begin with? You could have said something."

"I thought maybe you would recognize me. Then, when you didn't seem to remember me at your announcement, I worried maybe I'd confused you with a different girl. Or maybe it was some fever dream. But it *was* you." He shrugged.

"Why not tell me when you were sure?"

"It never seemed like a good time."

"Not a good time?" I gestured around my darkened bedroom. "But now is?"

"It's Fidelium. And by the customs of Fidelium, you have to keep my secret or take my guilt and shame upon your own soul."

"I don't think you have any shame."

The corner of his mouth twitched. "Yes, well, it's probably best for you to keep the secret and not risk it. Just in case."

We were silent for a second, both of us lost in our own thoughts.

Cohen said, "I understand if you're still angry, but I like you, Monroe. I really, really like you. And I get that maybe I shouldn't. You're right, I don't know you." His voice quieted. "But I've thought about you for years. As soon as the Culling was announced and girls started to show up, I waited for you. I knew . . . I knew that I wanted to repay your kindness and I wanted to know more about who you were. It's crazy, I know, but I've imagined being your friend for years—and while that doesn't sound like a lot, I don't have a lot of actual friends. So, the thought of knowing you— It's important to me." His face heated. "Goddess, that's embarrassing to say."

I understood. I'd created imaginary friendships with tons of the people my brothers had told me about. I'd wished to be Ellora's friend for so many months now that I felt like I knew her. But pretending to know someone and actually knowing them were two different things. And while Cohen might have held on to the thought of me for a long time, I'd only just come to know him in real life.

Cohen broke through my thoughts. "I know what you risked by helping me that day. I understand it now even more than I did before. And I just want to get to know you. I'd like to be your friend . . . or maybe a little more than your friend, if I'm being honest. But I also understand if you don't feel . . ." He cleared his throat and exhaled a shaky breath. "I understand if you don't necessarily feel the same way."

He was watching me, those blue eyes searching, waiting for me to respond. He looked so young, so unsure. His mother would kill him if she knew he was here, if she had any idea what he'd been doing . . . what he and *Uri* had been doing to help me.

Before I could overthink it, I rose up onto my toes and pressed a kiss to his cheek. Just as I was pulling away, he cupped my face and pulled me back to him, kissing me for real. It was gentle and tentative. And I kissed him back, giving myself entirely over to it, if only for a moment.

I let him hold me. Let myself melt into his arms, lean into him. He tasted of honey and chamomile tea.

When we finally pulled away from each other, we were both breathing heavily.

His smile was nervous as he whispered, "What was that for?"

"For not telling your mother about me," I said. "And because I wanted to kiss you when I knew you were sober."

"Were you worried that I wasn't sober the first time?"

I shrugged. "A little."

He bit his lip, uncertain, and then leaned forward, kissing me once more. This one was light, just a brush of lips. "That's for saving my life," he said against my mouth.

My heart was beating so loudly I couldn't seem to think straight. I didn't know what to say. How could I possibly explain what I was feeling when I didn't understand it myself?

I leaned my head into his shoulder and whispered, "You're going to end up with whoever wins the Culling and—and I can't promise that'll be me."

"So, I'm supposed to just not have a choice in it?"

I looked up at him, offering him a sad smile as I said, "That's the game, Cohen. Neither of us gets a choice."

"But can I at least have a chance?"

Hours ago, I'd been asked to betray him. Tallis had told me that I should take advantage of his kindness and use it to get information. And while I could tell myself that it was for the Culled and my freedom that I wanted to say yes to him, I knew the truth. I knew that I was desperate for affection, and he was there—prepared to be kind and sweet.

Cohen Warwick made me feel alive and it had been a long time since I'd felt that way.

"There are dignitaries visiting from Pellarmus," he said. "They'll be here in the next few days. Prince Darragh—he's a friend of mine—he'll be with them. We usually socialize after dinner. You know, after the adults have retired. Would you want to join us tomorrow? Uri will be there. Hugo too. It's casual, just a group of friends."

It got quiet.

"You know," I said, "you're not very good at pretending to be unbiased. Everyone in your family is going to know something is going on if you keep having my name taken out of the pick and trying to get me invited to family functions—" I stopped talking abruptly as his hands found either side of my face.

I tried to focus on what I'd been saying, but I couldn't think past just how close we now were. His exhale ruffled the waves of my hair. "I don't care who knows. I'm incredibly biased."

I swallowed down my own insecurities and asked, "What about Kinsley?"

"I don't care about her. I promise."

"But you have a history."

He nodded. "Maybe, but we don't have a future. I swear. Any feelings I had for Kinsley died years ago. She's just trying to please her father."

I reached behind him and pulled the door open. The hallway outside momentarily blinded me as it flooded my bedroom with bright-yellow light.

He didn't step away, just stayed where he was, his hands still cupping my cheeks. I forced myself to say, "It's late and I have training at dawn."

Slowly, he lowered his hands.

The prince chewed his bottom lip. I watched that mouth for a long time. Waited, in the spot between breaths, to see if he would lean in. Would he kiss me again?

But he didn't, he just looked at me.

After a long moment, I gestured toward the hallway. "I'll see you tomorrow night, Cohen."

"Yes. Tomorrow." I didn't miss the smile on his face as he shoved his hands in his pockets and strolled out of the room.

26

Oredison Palace, Gazda

Two weeks until Sanctus Eszter

The next morning the formal invitation to a state dinner arrived. That day, I trained with Tallis and Juno until I was thoroughly exhausted—even summoning a spark took effort. During all of it, Tallis didn't say anything to me about the Culled. Judging by the way she kept our conversation directed toward the Culling, I could tell that Juno probably wasn't in on her treasonous plot.

I waited around the training room to see if she'd try to talk to me privately, but she didn't. When it was time for me to return to my room, she opted to let Juno walk me back. I ate my lunch alone and then took to my bed, where I slept until it was time to get ready for dinner.

The sun was just beginning to set over the city as I bathed and dressed, putting on one of the soft pastel dresses from my closet. It fit tighter in my waist, my shoulders, my chest, my hips—evidence that I'd gained muscle and much-needed fat. Turns out that when I wasn't starving, I *did* have curves.

I left my room early and took my time walking to the dining room. Despite all of my reservations, I was excited to see Cohen. Last night, the way he looked at me . . . I hadn't minded it. In fact, I wished he would look at me like that again.

I let the memory of last night, those kisses, warm me as I walked down flights of stairs, down glittering corridors, and past large gilded mirrors. Even though I'd never been to this room in the palace, no one had come to escort me. I'd simply been told to head toward the ballroom.

So, I did.

I made it to the bottom of the grand staircase before I ran into Nadia. She wore a maroon gown with lace three-quarter sleeves and a full skirt that made her look like she was floating. She caught my gaze from across the room and paused long enough for me to catch her.

"Do you have any idea where we're supposed to go?" I asked.

She fiddled with a curl that had fallen loose from its updo. "I asked a guard a few halls back and he told me that the dining room is a little way down from the ballroom." She nodded toward the large oak doors we'd gone through for the Commencement.

We started walking in that direction.

"You . . ." She chewed her bottom lip. "Monroe, have you heard from your family?"

For an instant, I thought she'd somehow found out about my letters to Ambrose, but then I registered the worry in her tone. "Heard from them about what?"

Nadia lowered her voice. "About the attack in Varos. That's where you're from, isn't it?"

I stopped so abruptly, Nadia nearly tripped over the skirt of my dress. "Attack?"

She stopped walking too. "Yes. The attack." Her eyes widened. "Your trainers didn't tell you?"

I pressed a hand to the wall to steady myself.

She stepped forward. "Apparently, a group of rebels attacked a temple—Illodo, I think."

My mind whirled. Illodo Temple was on the southern edge of Varos, almost into Fajvurrow. It wasn't near my family's homestead, but it was close enough that I struggled to keep my voice calm as I asked, "What happened?"

Nadia's face crumpled as she realized that I truly didn't know. "It's just— Well, my trainers said that a group of rebels attacked the temple. Ransacked it. They killed over a dozen acolytes. A few priestesses too." She sucked on a knuckle as she said, "The queen's already retaliating.

It's common knowledge that the Culled recruits in the outer cities and towns. Vayelle supports them. And Varos is the closest to the Suri Gap. It's notorious for having—"

I gripped Nadia's arm. "What is she planning to do?"

A wave of warmth spread from my fingertips and across my chest, soothing my aching muscles. Nadia stepped away from my touch. "They found an entire safe house of Culled rebels in Varos. And they discovered letters and plans. Evidence of sympathizers. I was told that the people they found—they were spies and soldiers. Some of them Vaylish. Others . . . Others were Erydian. And there were tons of letters and things outlining other safe houses and groups in other cities. Our soldiers killed the people they found."

Our soldiers.

"What— Nadia, what is she planning to do?"

She winced. "The draft age is being lowered to thirteen in Varos, as a punishment."

I nearly choked. "Thirteen? But . . . But they're children—"

"I wouldn't have mentioned it, only I thought you probably already knew and . . . I wanted to check on you. On your family. It's terrible. I'm so sorry. I shouldn't have said anything at all. It was stupid of me." She wrapped her arms around herself. "I wouldn't have said anything if I'd thought you didn't know."

"Lowering the draft won't help anything. She's punishing innocent people."

"I'm not sure she cares."

I felt like I might pass out.

"Lowering the draft won't help," I said again. "Especially not in Varos. It'll only make things worse. If . . . If people are joining the Culled it's because they feel like they have no other choice."

She shushed me lightly. "Don't say things like that. Not where people can hear you." The unnatural soothing warmth of her touch was a shock to my system. "Monroe," she said, her grip on my arm turning tight, "I think maybe we should find somewhere for you to sit down. You aren't feeling well."

I stepped back from her. "I—"

"Monroe?" Cohen stood at the top of the stairs dressed in a navy blue suit, the waves of his blond hair combed back from his face to reveal concerned blue eyes. "What's wrong?"

Nadia spun to look at him. "I-I told her about the Varos draft. I didn't know that she hadn't been told."

Cohen hurried down the stairs. As he reached us, his hand moved to cup my elbow, the fingers of his other hand snaking around my waist until I was leaning on him. My throat burned.

"She's going to kill thousands of children," I whispered.

He opened his mouth and then closed it as Kinsley turned the corner in front of us. She paused, her head tilting to one side as she took us in.

Cohen spoke quietly to me. "The Crown is feeling pressure from the priestesses and the Synod. This is the second attack on a temple in less than two months."

"That doesn't make it right. This isn't going to help anything."

"I know. I know that, I just— The draft age won't change if the Culled surrender."

"Goddess, Cohen. The Culled isn't just one person, they're—"

Kinsley's footsteps echoed against the marble tiles of the hallway as she came to a stop in front of us. Nadia took a step back, her wide brown eyes still trained on me. Her fingers twitched, and I knew she wanted to help, wanted to soothe the anxiety weighing against my chest. I wondered if she could.

Kinsley spoke to the prince. "The queen's looking for you."

Cohen nodded. "I'll be right there." When she didn't turn to leave, he said to her, "You're dismissed."

Cohen didn't turn to look at her again. He just pulled me farther away. "Monroe, I understand that this is upsetting—"

I cut him off. "The winter stretch is coming. Varos is going to freeze. Listen to me, Cohen. Thousands will starve."

"If they surrender—"

"It's against temple laws for women to hunt. Most respectable businesses won't even hire us. If she takes all the men over the age of thirteen, it'll destroy

Varos. Slavers will take their pick of whatever women and children are left. The city will be defenseless. People will die. Thousands will die and it will be all the queen's fault."

"Enough. We'll talk about this later."

Tears stung at my eyes. "My mother could die."

"There's nothing I can do about it right now. I'll talk to my mother. I'll talk to both my parents. But . . . But you're visibly upset and I can't— You can't be seen like— You're . . ." He swallowed and lowered his voice. "You're talking treason."

Nadia spoke up. "I can walk her back to her room?"

I shook my head. "I'm fine. I just— It isn't right, what she's doing."

Cohen met my eyes. "I know that. I do."

"I'm fine." I pulled away from his touch and wiped at my eyes. *"I'm fine,"* I said again.

He chewed his bottom lip and turned toward the far end of the corridor where a few guards lingered, their expressions tense with concern. Cohen said, "Miss Benson isn't feeling well. Please escort her back to her room." They stepped forward and he turned back to me, his voice turning soft. "Rest. I'll have food brought up to you."

I shook my head and took hold of his wrist. "I can go to dinner."

Cohen offered me a smile. "No, I insist." He gestured for Nadia to go on ahead. "I'll come check on you after this is over."

Nadia sent me a backward glance as she moved in the direction of the state dining room. I could see words pressing against her lips, could feel the worry in her stare. Kinsley still stood nearby; her gaze locked on Cohen's fingers as they threaded through mine.

He leaned down so his words could only be heard by me, our faces so close that if I stood up on my toes, our lips would brush. He said, "I'll take care of it."

And I wanted to believe him.

I waited until the guards had disappeared down the hall and then I left my bedroom. I had no clue where the Culling trainers stayed or how to get in touch with Tallis, but I needed to find her.

I'd been told that the Culled within the palace would keep an eye out for a girl with a rabbit-head necklace. That was how they would know who I was, and that I was on their side.

When Tallis had given me the necklace I hadn't known if I'd ever be able to wear it. Now, with the queen lowering the draft and my mother's life on the line, I found that clasping the chain around my neck was easy.

Maids and footmen turned to look as I walked past them, still dressed in the gown I'd planned to wear to dinner. I passed a few guards, but most were too preoccupied with their assigned duties to pay much attention to me.

I resisted the urge to fiddle with the necklace as I walked and instead opted to leave it where it was, clearly displayed against the hollow of my throat. I walked until I hit a corridor I'd never been on before. I'd heard Tallis and Juno talk about staying in a barracks of sorts and that told me that wherever they stayed, it wasn't inside the palace proper.

I'd only just made it to what I thought might be the main doors to the palace when Dellacov caught sight of me. "Miss Benson?" I stopped in my tracks, my hand on the doorknob, and turned to face him. His head tilted to one side. "Cohen said you'd gone to your room."

I swallowed and backed away from the door. "I'm not feeling well."

Dellacov nodded slowly, as if he didn't quite believe me. "Yeah . . . Cohen said that too."

"Do you know where my trainers stay?"

"That depends; what do you need them for?"

I floundered. "It's my monthly cycle. I just— Tallis said she had a tonic I could try to help with the pain. I was going to ask her for it. I didn't think . . . I didn't think I'd be able to sleep otherwise."

Dellacov's face turned red enough to match his hair. "Oh. Wow. Yeah, I can . . . Uh, why don't I go get the tonic for you and—"

"No. I'd . . . I'd really prefer to talk to her. I'm just . . ." I fiddled with the skirt of my dress, doing my best to feign unease as I said, "It's personal. Please, can't I just go see her?"

He chewed his bottom lip. "You aren't allowed to leave the palace and you definitely aren't allowed into the trainer barracks. It's against Culling rules."

"You're Captain of the Guard," I said. "I'm not breaking the rules if I'm with you. It's really important." I pressed a hand to my lower abdomen and winced for effect, praying that Dellacov would be uncomfortable enough to humor me.

"Why don't I fetch Tallis and bring her and the tonic to you?"

Thank the goddess above. "That would be great. Thank you, Dellacov."

He nodded in the direction of my room. "You head back upstairs, and I'll come to you."

I did as he said, praying the entire walk back to my bedroom that Tallis would play along. I burned time as best I could, pacing and waiting and worrying. If Tallis didn't come to see me, I wasn't sure what I would do. All I did know what that I was angry and hurt. And I wanted to do something.

I heard the sound of Tallis and Dellacov's muttered conversation just before she bid him good night and opened my bedroom door. She was still feigning a smile as she shut my door behind herself and leaned her entire weight against it. As soon as the door clicked shut, the smile fell away.

"Goddess, Monroe," she hissed. "You just scared the shit out of me."

"I'm sorry."

"You're sorry?" Tallis demanded. "The Captain of the Royal Guard just came strolling into the barracks and asked for me—*by name*. I thought I was dead. Absolutely dead. And then he proceeds to tell me that you're having your monthly cycle, and you need some tonic. Are you kidding me?"

I pushed away from where I'd been sitting on my bed. "I didn't know what else to say. I needed to see you."

She ran a hand through her hair. "You should have seen me scrambling to come up with a stupid tonic. I had nothing. Absolutely nothing to even pretend to give you. Thankfully one of the other trainers took pity on your lying ass and sent me with this . . ." She dug into her trouser pocket and pulled out a small blue bottle. "I hope you aren't actually having your monthlies, because I definitely wouldn't trust anything Kinsley's trainers offer you."

My eyes widened. "Kinsley's trainers sent that?"

"Yes, and you aren't allowed to even breathe near it." She slipped it back into her pocket. "Now what is all of this about?"

My voice was barely a whisper as I asked, "Have the Culled sent a response for me?"

She crossed her arms over her chest. "They don't want to agree to anything like that, Monroe. You're asking them to make a promise they may not be able to keep."

"But what did they say?"

"They said that they would do what they could to keep the prince and princess alive. It isn't a promise anyone can one hundred percent keep. But I've been instructed to do what I can to get Cohen, Britta, and Uriel out of the palace before the attack. What happens to them afterward is out of both of our hands."

"Then I'll help. I'll do whatever you need me to do."

She nodded slowly. "What made you change your mind?"

"Did you know about the attack in Varos?"

She nodded. "I only just heard, but yes."

"Why would the Culled do that? Why attack the temples?"

"I told you, the future is a place without the goddess. The temples have always been a place of judgment and oppression. You know that."

"You're spewing ideals at me, not information. I want a concrete reason. I want to know what they accomplished by killing priestesses in Illodo. Because Viera is retaliating. She's lowering the draft in Varos because of it."

"It's war we're fighting, Monroe. There are going to be casualties. The sooner we can overthrow the Warwicks and their Synod council, the better. If they're removed from power, the temples can be disbanded without violence."

"Then what do I need to do to help get Viera off the throne?"

Guilt turned my resolve sour as Tallis straightened. "You sure?"

"As sure as I can be without exactly knowing what you want from me."

"We need a good map of the palace and a concrete guard schedule. We have two different spies in the royal guard currently, and they can't get their hands on the full schedule. It's locked up somewhere and it's always changing. Since our assassination attempt on Cohen failed, they've been smarter about who they let see the full guard placement."

"So that was the Culled then?"

Her brows rose. "Don't sound so disapproving, Monroe. Things would have been better for you if he were dead, and we both know it. Without him, a massive part of the Culling disappears. He's the only male heir. We kill him and the line of Warwick kings and goddess-touched queens dies with him."

I couldn't deny that I'd wanted that. Back before I knew Cohen, I'd been disappointed to find out that the gunman had missed. I'd wanted him dead. After all, Tallis was right—without Cohen, the temples and their system of a goddess-chosen queen began to disintegrate.

"How can I help you get any of that information?"

"We think it's in the prince's bedchamber. He approves the schedules. The guard rotations and placements reset every week. We're under the belief that the new one goes up on Mondays."

I blinked at her. "And?"

"And I think you can find a way into his bedroom."

My knees gave out and I slumped back onto the mattress once more. "Oh, Tallis. I can't— I'm not trying to—"

"I'm not saying you have to bed him, Monroe. Just . . . Just find a way into his room. You're a smart girl."

I was an inexperienced girl. And she was asking me to get into Cohen's bedroom without appearing suspicious. There were a million ways that could go badly for me.

"So, what, you want me to steal the schedule and give it to you?"

"I want you to copy it down. Don't take the original; that's too obvious. Take a piece of paper and a pen with you and jot down what you see."

"I think you overestimate the amount of time I'll have alone in his bedroom."

Her brow rose. "Not if you play your cards right."

Palace Bedroom

One week before Sanctus Eszter

Cohen didn't come that night, or the rest of that week. I spent my mornings training with Tallis and Juno, using it as an excuse not to think about what might be happening in Varos. Every day or so Tallis would find an excuse for us to be alone and she'd interrogate me on what I was doing to help her get her hands on the guard schedule. As far as she was concerned, I wasn't doing nearly enough.

But what did she expect me to do? I couldn't seek him out. I was expected to be training and preparing for my own Culling trial—and that was what I was doing. Tallis had made it clear time and time again that if the Culled couldn't get the guard rotation and a good map of the palace, then they couldn't attack.

"It's the only thing we're waiting on," she'd told me. "We've got the forces ready. There are safe houses in the city. But we can't make a move until we're sure about the timing of it."

That meant that my trial could happen long before the Culled was able to attack. I used training as a way to avoid thinking too much about that as well. Every passing day brought me closer to the moment when my name really would be called. Eventually, I'd end up in the arena and I needed to survive it.

Uri still came by my room every morning and shared breakfast with me. She became my source of information, and I told myself that I wasn't being a bad person by passing along whatever stray information she threw my way. The youngest princess was my only friend and the more she spoke to me, the more evident it became that I was her only real friend too. I hated the tight, oily feeling in my gut each time I relayed her words to Tallis.

Necessary.

It was necessary.

Friday afternoon, a week before Grier and Heidi's trial, Uri was pacing a dent into my bedroom carpet. "They've been arguing," she told me. "The queen is sending Britta to the border. Did I tell you that?"

She hadn't.

"Britta leaves in a few weeks. They're hoping she can help with morale. And, in their defense, royal visits, especially from princesses, do usually raise spirits. But things are bad right now. Cohen was saying that there are entire units that have deserted."

I raised a brow at that. "Entire units?"

"Hundreds of soldiers," she explained. "They're siding with the rebels or with Vayelle. Honestly, I think they're one and the same." Uri tugged anxiously at her braid. "And Britta is heading into that. So, naturally, we're worried. It's dangerous for her to go, and Cohen's trying to sway her—but Britta is stubborn and thinks she can actually help." Uri turned to look at where I was perched on the edge of my bed. "More than likely, the queen isn't giving her a choice."

"Your mother is putting children on her front lines. I doubt there's anything Britta can say that will soften that blow."

Uri nodded. "It's ridiculous. And Father is saying nothing, as always. She's lost her mind, and he's too drunk to notice."

"What—" I chewed my bottom lip, dreading the answer. "What is Cohen saying?"

"He's trying to get her to raise the draft back to eighteen. He's trying to slow things down, keep our forces on our side. Of course, it doesn't help that Vayelle is pushing back. We've already had larger skirmishes in the Suri Gap, with our soldiers taking a beating. The Vaylish armies are stronger and larger—even with our draft in place. And Erydians are aiding their forces. This new lowered draft has only spurred the doubters to become full-on deviants. When the queen and the Synod gave the orders about lowering the Varos draft, I think they were hoping to corner the rebels, force them to surrender, but obviously that didn't work. They've only made things worse. Now the queen's solution is to offer rewards for any information on the rebels."

I thought about my brother and Ellora Hoffman and the countless others who had joined the Culled in an effort to make some sort of positive change.

In a place like Varos, where poverty and starvation were more common than not, neighbors would turn on each other. Entire families could suffer at the hands of the rumor mill.

"And what's being done to the rebels?" I asked.

"They're stringing people up. The temple has started looking for Culled sympathizers. I think Britta just wants to go so she can try to appease the priestesses." Uri settled onto the bed next to me. "But it hardly matters. I'm not sure this can be stopped."

I bit back a snide remark and instead said, "I'm sorry that she's having to go."

Uri sighed. "No, I should be sorry. You're preparing for the Culling and here I am venting about my stupid family. I should be asking about you. How are things? You never told me why you didn't come to dinner the other night. Darragh is a charmer and he was disappointed to have only seven goddess-touched girls to swoon over him."

I hesitated. "I got upset when I found out about the attack and the lowered draft. I was afraid for my family. And Cohen didn't think it would be a good idea for me to go to dinner."

She chewed her lip. "Oh. He was right to keep you from having to sit through dinner. It was miserable. Most of it was spent with Darragh and my mother arguing. Pellarmus has a strong military, but they're a peaceful people and reserve their forces for unavoidable fights. He was upset about her choice, to say the least."

I sighed. "It's definitely upsetting."

"I'm so sorry, Monroe. I can't imagine how you must feel knowing that your family is so close to such violence. Is . . . Is there anything I could do?"

"No, but thank you."

She opened her mouth to say something else but was interrupted by a knock at the door. Uri stood up at the sound, her posture stiffening and turning undeniably royal.

I stood too, far less elegantly, and called, "Come in."

The door creaked as Cohen opened it and stepped inside. He glanced between the two of us, his smile turning wide and boyish. "Oh, no. Am I interrupting something?"

Uri slumped slightly and plopped down onto my bed again. "I was just about to tell Monroe about how you used to play with my dolls."

His ears flushed as he said, "Liar. I used to kidnap your dolls and hide them."

She shrugged. "Last time I checked, that's playing with dolls."

I smiled.

Cohen's gaze darted to me, and he sobered. "How are you?"

I lifted a shoulder in response.

He stepped farther into the room and shut the door behind himself. "I, uh, I meant to send a note to explain why I didn't come to check on you the other night. I'm sorry. The evening— It turned into an argument and then Darragh stayed longer than expected and I got busy—"

"It's fine," I said.

His eyes moved to his sister, who had crossed her legs and was now gazing at him, her elbow propped on her knee, her chin in her hand. "Uriel, don't you have important princess things to be doing?"

She wrinkled her nose. "I'm Monroe's advisor. Anything you have to say to her you can say to me."

He sighed heavily. "You know, the queen is in meetings until after dinner and poor Hugo is in his office. All alone . . . and in need of someone to rearrange the perfectly placed items on his desk."

Uri pressed her lips together to hide a smile. "But Father—"

"—is on a hunting trip until tomorrow evening."

She glanced sideways at me.

I nodded toward the door. "Go on."

She got to her feet. "You . . . You won't tell anyone?"

"Tell them what?" I asked simply.

"Thank you." Uri grinned. "Thank you both."

It was silent for a long time after she left.

Cohen stayed by the door, his expression earnest. He was dressed simply, tan pants and a white button-up shirt with sleeves rolled to the elbows, showing muscled forearms. His fingers ran through his hair, mussing the waves and knocking longer strands into his eyes.

His words were quiet. "Do you want to go for a walk?"

"Where to?"

He shrugged and held out a hand to me. "Let's go on an adventure."

The palace ballroom was dark and empty as we stepped inside, letting the large oak door fall shut behind us. Cohen nodded to a row of candelabra by the door. "Can you—?"

Before he could even finish the sentence, flames were dancing on the wicks. He grinned from ear to ear. Without another word, he took hold of my hand and pulled me to the center of the room. He pulled me into his arms and we danced a little waltz, the room silent aside from our laughter and the echo of our shoes.

The two silver thrones stood before us, constant reminders of why I was here—of the things at stake.

Weeks ago, we'd stood in this room. We'd twirled around and around. Cameras had flashed. People had cheered.

It felt like that was eons ago. Another lifetime.

At the end of our silent dance, the prince pulled away from me and walked to a pianoforte shoved in a far corner. Cohen fiddled with the keys, the reverberations of each note long and crisp.

I walked to where he sat and he made room on the bench for me. "Do you know how to play?" I asked.

He smiled to himself. "Only a few things," he admitted.

As if to prove his point, he played a quick, slightly off-key version of the Erydian national anthem. When he missed the last note, missed it a second time, and then a third, he laughed and pulled his hands away.

"My tutors were determined that I would be a musician. They said it was a good skill for a king to have." He straightened his shoulders. "'Now, Prince

Cohen, you never know when you might need to entertain guests,'" he said, doing a fair impression of a patronizing old man. Those blue eyes danced along the planes of my face. "I guess they were right."

I reached out and touched a cream-colored key. I'd never seen an instrument like this, much less played one.

My father had grown up as a performer in the music district of Hadrian Square. When he'd met my mother, he'd been playing the violin in the street, surrounded by silk banners, booths selling flutes, and vendors peddling hand-carved drums. Lorraine Cinridge had taken one look at Philip Benson and had known he was the man for her. She had always made it sound like some fanciful story.

Cohen began to play another song, this one slower, the tinkle of keys like frost creeping on a window. As he played, he asked me questions. Nothing about Varos or the Culling, just random questions: What was my favorite toy as a kid; did I have any pets; what was my favorite meal; did I like hot or cold weather; did I enjoy dancing; did I have a favorite holiday; would I rather eat snacks that were salty or sweet; do I like dressing up; was I a morning person or a night person; do I like to draw; would I rather—

And question by question he unraveled me. One song turned into the next, a blend of melodies and clumsy fingers. As he played, I remembered the way my mother always described meeting my father for the first time.

"It wasn't love at first sight," she always said. "It was just knowing. Just plain and simple knowing. Like I'd turned a corner in my life, laid eyes on that boy with musician's hands and thought: *Ah, yes. There he is.* And even though I'd never looked for him, there he was—found."

And sitting there next to Cohen, our shoulders brushing, our smiles painfully wide, I understood that feeling. That knowing. I felt it deep in my chest.

He said, "Tell me the one thing you miss from home."

I watched his hands dance along the keys. His head was tilted down and blond hair fell into his face. I wanted to run my fingers through it.

I considered. "My oldest brother, Ambrose, always picks white aster flowers on his way home. He would leave for days at a time, going off to hunt with my other brother, Kace. Or sometimes he'd be gone to trade in Linomi or one of the other markets. But when he came back, he almost always had aster flowers for me. Our house always smelled like them. And I could almost keep time with them, tracking the passing days by when they began to wilt and when he'd leave and return with a new batch." I fell quiet.

Cohen continued to play. "And that's what you miss, the flowers?"

"I miss home. I miss the predictability of the days. And the feeling of going to sleep without worrying about being in an arena."

"Did you not worry about it as a child?"

I shrugged. "Yes. But it seemed like a distant thing. Less real. And I sort of always hoped I'd escape it."

"So, you really never planned to come here?"

I looked down at the mark on my hand. "Being here has nothing to do with planning. I think . . . I think the goddess has been writing my story for a long time. I've tried to run from it. My mother tried to run from it. But maybe what's meant to be will be no matter what I do."

Cohen sighed. "I'm sorry."

"It isn't your fault."

"Maybe, but I feel partly responsible. I wish the Culling were a choice—for me and for you."

"And what would you choose if it were?"

His voice grew quiet. "I would choose you."

The breath caught in my throat. "Oh."

His fingers slowed against the keys, and he glanced over at me. When he saw my expression, he stilled, the notes trickling away until the ballroom was silent.

"Me?" I whispered.

He nodded, just once.

A chill went up my spine, a white-hot thrill of unbridled joy. I leaned forward on the pianoforte bench and kissed Cohen. It was quick, afraid. Unsure. When he didn't move, I started to pull away. Maybe . . . Maybe it had been a mistake. Maybe we weren't at the point where we could just—

But then his hands were off the keys and tangling in my hair, and he was kissing me again. Deeper, slower, better. I slid forward on the bench, moving ever closer to him as his teeth nipped at my bottom lip and I opened to him. Just like with the dance, I let him take the lead. I was content to follow, to let him guide me. For a moment, being here with him actually felt like my choice.

Cohen held my hand as we left the ballroom and wandered the halls of the palace. We paused in the doorway of a massive library, and he told me about all the histories and priceless documents kept inside.

"It probably isn't the best place for someone like me to be," I joked. "I'm prone to lighting things on fire, priceless or not."

He laughed and pressed a kiss to my forehead before he tugged me along after him once more. "The best books aren't there. Those are all dusty dictionaries and things. The best books are the novels. Uri and I have shelves stocked full in our rooms."

I knew that already. Uri had been bringing books to my room for weeks. Telling him that his sister had already shown me the wonders of the palace books felt a little like robbing him of his joy, so I said nothing. I wanted him to show me too.

Cohen's hand tightened on mine as he asked, "Do you like reading?"

"Yes. My mother had these dusty encyclopedias and an old atlas. I used to sit and read through all the information over and over again. It was like a window to the world. An outdated window to the world, since the books had belonged to my great-grandparents, but still."

"What about stories?"

"I like those too. I've read most of the classics. And some newer things too," I added, thinking of the books Uri had loaned me. "My brothers would bring me all their required reading for school. By the time Kace was finishing up, I was reading the books and just telling him what they were about."

Cohen feigned shock. "Cheater."

"Kace would probably be embarrassed if he knew I'd told you that. He's never been the best student, but he's supersmart in other ways."

"I've heard."

I turned to him. "Really?"

"Yeah. I told you that Dellacov was looking into getting a few more palace guards. He's got your brother in his sights. He's very dedicated and, from what I've been told, he works incredibly hard. He's outshining a lot of his peers."

"That sounds like Kace."

"Would it make you nervous for him to be here?"

"I don't know. I don't think so."

The idea of seeing either of my brothers was more exciting than anything else. This was the longest I'd ever gone without seeing my family. Most days my fear of an impending Culling trial was enough to keep any homesickness at bay, but just then . . .

"Would the other goddess-touched girls see it as an advantage? I feel like me having family here would be breaking some sort of rule."

Cohen's hand was warm around mine as we came to a stop at a fork in the hallway. The stairs up ahead would take me back to my bedroom; the right hallway would take him toward the royal bedchambers. "At this point, you and I have already broken so many Culling rules, I don't think it matters anymore."

I was still looking down the hall where I knew his bedroom must be as I muttered, "I guess that's true."

Tallis wanted me to get into that room and find the guard schedule. With another trial only a week away and another pairing soon to be announced, time was not on my side. I needed to get out of the palace before my name was called.

Cohen sighed and turned his attention to the staircase. "I should return you to your room. If we're not careful, we'll be caught. This section of the palace is usually empty around now, but it won't stay that way. And I need to get ready for a meeting with the Synod."

He started to pull his hand from mine but I tightened my grip. "No. Not yet. It's— It's been nice to spend time with you. I'm not ready to go back to my room."

Cohen pulled his timepiece from his pocket. "I've got an hour to bathe and dress before this meeting. I'll be late if we spend much more time together."

"Can I . . ." I trailed off, suddenly unsure what to say. "I'm lonely. All the time. I just— Can't I just be with you as you're getting ready?"

He hesitated, prepared to deny me, but I rose up on my toes. The kiss was quick, but the way my fingers tightened in the front of his shirt promised more. "It's been magical, being with you today. I'm not ready for it to end. Give me just a little more time. Please."

Before I could say anything else, he was kissing me again. Reckless. We were out in the open; anyone could walk past and see. But then again, Cohen said he was almost always watched. Certainly, the queen's spies were already well aware of what we were doing. And I needed to do this.

Cohen kissed me until I was breathless, until the world had narrowed down and it was only the warm press of his mouth and the taste of him— sweet and fresh and somehow always unexpected. My fingers dug into his hair, mussing the curls.

I felt like I was falling off the edge of a cliff and there was no bottom, nothing to stop this endless plunge. I struggled to remind myself of why I was there. *I'm in the Culling. I'm going to die in the arena. My mother is in danger of starving. The Culled needs information and this boy*—goddess, this prince— *could take me right to what I need.*

As Cohen's hands moved to encircle my waist, I wished I was pretending. I wished the shiver that went through me was fake.

My voice trembled slightly, the words treasonous and uncertain as I whispered, "Please. Please, Cohen. Don't make me go."

He kissed me one last time and then pulled back. "Only because you said please."

We'd only just made it to the second-floor corridor when we heard the screaming. For a moment, neither Cohen nor I moved. We just stood there staring back at the empty hallway behind us. Sound in the palace was a strange thing. The ceilings were high, the floors polished slabs of marble or warm wood. Things echoed and bounced and pinpointing the source of a particular sound was difficult—but Cohen didn't seem to struggle in the same way I did, not as he took off running toward the northern side of the palace, back toward where my bedroom was.

I kept pace with him as we skipped the electric lifts and took the stairs, two at a time, until we'd reached a corridor similar to the one that I lived on. For a split second, I thought it might even be the same hall, but then I saw the art and realized that the view of Gazda from the window was a different, lower angle. We took two left turns and then we found them.

Dellacov stood out in the hall speaking to a maid. The girl looked no older than fourteen, her thin body trembling as she cradled her head in her hands. Guards drifted in and out of an open doorway, their conversation muffled. Cohen left me standing by one of the windows as he approached Dellacov.

"What's happened?"

The Captain of the Royal Guard said nothing, only nodded to where I stood. "Monroe should go to her own room. I've sent guards to secure the other girls."

I took a step back, already preparing for the order to come, but Cohen didn't even acknowledge what his friend had said. "What's happened, Hugo?"

The maid slumped against the wall moaned through her fingers in response and shook her head. Dellacov motioned to a footman standing nearby. "Take Miss Carter to my office and get her a cup of tea. Don't let her speak to anyone and, for the love of the goddess, don't leave her alone. I'll deal with her shortly."

The footman touched the girl's arm, guiding her away from the wall and ushering her silently down the hall and into a servant's stairwell. Cohen watched them go, his jaw tight with annoyance. "Hugo, I will not ask you again—"

Dellacov whirled on him, his voice a sharp hiss. "One of the girls—Vivian—is dead."

Cohen took a step back, startled. "What?"

"The maid just came to deliver clean clothes, and she found the girl dead. Sprawled out on the floor of the bathing room."

Dellacov pointed to one of the guards who had just walked out the open bedroom door. "Please escort Miss Benson back to her rooms and make sure she stays there." He looked to me. "I don't know what's happened or if anyone else is in danger. For now, all goddess-touched girls are to remain inside their own quarters until this can be investigated."

Cohen spoke as the guard approached me. "What do you think has happened? Who would kill Vivian?"

"I'm sure any number of people in the palace would. Starting with every single goddess-touched girl and ending with—" Dellacov cut himself off, but we all knew what he was going to say. *Ending with the queen.*

Cohen ran a hand through his hair. "What's the cause of death? What happened to her?"

The guard's hand found my shoulder. "Miss Benson?" he prodded, shifting me toward the lift at the end of the hallway.

As I turned away, I heard Dellacov say, "I only just got here a few moments before you did. But . . ." He sighed. "She looks the way the other one did. The one from dinner."

Aviana.

Which meant—

Cohen turned on his heel and called to the guard walking with me. "She's to have an escort from now on. They all are. All of the girls. I want guards outside their doors and guards walking them to and from the training rooms."

The guard and I stopped, waiting to see what Dellacov would say in response to that order.

After a second, he nodded. "Agreed. I'll assign extra guards to those halls as soon as I've finished taking Miss Carter's statement."

27

The Training Rooms
Oredison Palace, Gazda
One day before Sanctus Eszter

It was poison. That much I knew, even if the palace publicized Vivian's death as being a suicide. They said that she must have gotten her hands on some sort of medication and taken too much. During one of our guarded training sessions almost a week later, Tallis told me that the medics who examined Vivian's body claimed that it was clearly a poisoning.

"That's three," I said as we walked back to my bedroom. "Three girls that have died that way."

"Only two that we know for certain," Tallis said. "And that . . ." She eyed the guards walking a few yards behind us and lowered her voice. "And that's if we count Joslyn. And we don't know for a fact. We definitely don't know that what happened to Vivian was any more sinister than a desperate, frightened girl trying to escape her circumstances."

"Yes, we do." I dug my fingernails into my palm, trying to steady my breathing. "There were no other marks on her. Nothing else to blame. And . . . And her trainers swore that she hadn't had access to any medicines and wasn't planning to end her own life."

Tallis and Juno knew all of this. They'd been the ones to give me that information. Next to me, Juno sighed heavily. "Just keep your head down and don't say anything that would have *anyone* looking in your direction."

"There are only seven of us left now." I held up my hand and counted them off on my fingers. "It's me, Kinsley, Nadia, Grier, Heidi, Tessa, and Elodie."

Juno nodded. "Tomorrow it'll drop to six."

The air caught in my lungs. "It's been over a month since I got here, and it still feels strange."

"I'm not sure it will ever stop being strange." Tallis nudged my shoulder with her own. "Soon there will only be five people standing between you and the throne."

We stopped outside my bedroom door. "I never really thought I'd make it this far."

Juno smiled at me. "I knew you would. You're going to win it. Queen Monroe."

Tallis nodded, but I could tell her thoughts were elsewhere. I knew she didn't believe in a future with Erydian queens. If the Culling ended before the rebels could attack, and I somehow won it, would I become her enemy or would their plans change?

Juno didn't seem to notice my change in mood. "Get some sleep tonight. I want you wide awake and paying attention to tomorrow's trials. You could be next."

The Arena Viewing Room
Deca Market, Gazda
Sanctus Eszter: Second Trial

We crowded into the small viewing room as we waited for Grier and Heidi's trial to begin. Guards lined the walls of the room—a new fixture. We said nothing about Vivian's death. The topic had quickly become taboo. No one wanted to speculate too much about it for fear of being the next one targeted.

Even Cohen hadn't spoken to me about what had happened beyond telling me that he believed it was poison. Seated on the bench farthest from the door and closest to the window, I could see him up in the royal box. While the other girls commented on how handsome he looked in his navy suit and light-gray tie, I stayed silent.

We'd spent nearly every day of the last week together. I spent my evenings with him and my mornings with Tallis and Juno, or cringing through etiquette lessons alongside the other girls.

Each night, Cohen and I would go on a walk. The guards didn't follow us the way they trailed me during the daytime. We were almost always alone as he showed me the palace, room by room.

And even though I knew I should pull away from him—even though I knew I was risking my heart by falling for him—it was easy to forget our reality when I was with him. When he was kissing me.

But looking at Cohen just then, I couldn't see the person who had walked with me yesterday. This wasn't the same person who had taught me how to climb from the trellis at the second-story window. It wasn't the same boy who'd promised me that he wouldn't let me get hurt in the process. It wasn't the same boy who had kissed me when I'd made it to the bottom unscathed.

Something was wrong.

Uri sat to his left, her dark hair pulled into a braided crown atop her head. She was watching Dellacov, who paced at the gate of the arena. The queen saw her looking, smirked, and said something to Cohen, pointing to Dellacov as she did. The prince blanched and touched Uri's arm to pull her attention away from his friend.

Someone came into the room to collect Heidi and Grier.

I'd struggled to sleep since the last trial. My dreams were full of bloody battlefields, snaking vines, and thrones that crumbled when I tried to sit on them. I didn't want to watch another trial or witness yet another version of how I might eventually die.

"Hi." Nadia's soft voice startled me from my thoughts, and I almost toppled from the bench in surprise. As she reached out to steady me, that familiar warmth spread across my torso. She snatched her hand away and blushed.

"Sorry. I didn't mean to scare you."

"You didn't scare me," I lied. "I just— It's fine."

When she didn't move away, I patted the empty seat next to me. Nadia looked around. All the other girls had spread out, leaving wide gaps of awkward space between them. Meanwhile, I was inviting her to sit directly next to me.

She chewed the inside of her cheek. "You sure?"

I nodded.

She frowned, but slowly sank onto the bench. "How are you feeling?"

"Can't you sense it?"

Her brown skin flushed and she ducked her head. "Oh, um, yes. But it's weird to assume, or . . . I like to ask still."

"I feel better, thanks. How about you?"

She shrugged. "I'm still here, so that's something."

It grew quiet, all of us looking out onto the arena. Nadia strummed her chewed fingernails against the seat of the bench and turned to look at me out of the corner of her eye.

She lowered her voice and said, "If Kinsley could kill with her eyes, you'd be dead."

I had to resist the urge to turn around and look. She was sitting on the bench behind mine, closer to the only exit. The smile on my face was more confident than I felt as I said, "Thank the goddess that she wasn't blessed with that ability."

Nadia nodded. "She's terrible. It's too bad Joslyn didn't kill her when she had the chance . . . " She winced at her own words. "Goddess, that was a terrible thing to say. I didn't used to be this way, I swear."

"The Culling kind of does that to you," I muttered.

She crossed her ankles out in front of her and tugged at the fabric of her green shirt. "I don't want anyone to die." She paused her fidgeting and turned to look at me, her brow furrowed.

I nudged her with my shoulder. "Me either."

She smiled and leaned closer to me. "Before, you asked me if I'd sensed anything with Joslyn. Yes, I did. But I don't know what it was. At the time . . ." She started chewing at her bottom lip. "At the time, I thought it was just like an illness from nerves."

"I feel like it had to be more than that."

"Elodie said that she read Kinsley's mind. But she didn't see anything. Apparently she said something to Kinsley about it—called her a cheater or something, I don't really know. Anyway, Kinsley beat the crap out of her for it." Nadia glanced over at Elodie. "And . . . And of course, no one said a word about it."

Elodie sat as far from Kinsley as possible. There were large gashes on her face. They were deep and, even with the stitches and evident healing, looked like they would probably scar.

I'd heard about the fight, but I hadn't seen it. It had taken place right after one of our etiquette lessons, after I'd already gone—in a hurry to meet with Cohen and tour the library.

"I offered to heal her," Nadia said. "She refused my help, told me to keep my hands off her. I feel bad. If she would've let me do it instead of the medic, she might not have any scarring. But she didn't trust me, which . . . I kind of understand."

"I trust you."

I don't know why I said it, but as soon as the words were spoken, I knew that they were true. I did trust Nadia.

She was quirky and quiet, but there was something about her that called to me. Even though I knew I shouldn't, I wanted her friendship. I'd never had sisters or attended school so I had little experience with other girls my age. But there was solidarity in female friendship, a sort of camaraderie that I saw in the way that Uri and Britta looked at each other, in the way that Tallis looked at me.

It was a respect and an understanding that was foreign but no less craved.

"Well, thank you for that," Nadia whispered. "Really."

I nodded. "Don't mention it."

"It sort of sucks that we have to kill the only other people who understand what it's like to be like this." She held up her hand, flashing her mark. "It's isolating, you know?"

I did know.

I'd been standing at a mental crossroads for some time, just trying to decide if I could actually do it. Could I kill someone else? Could I kill Nadia?

"What about . . ." I swallowed and lowered my voice even further, careful of the nearby guards. "What about Vivian?"

"I didn't sense anything with her. But . . ." Nadia sighed. "That doesn't mean anything. When Aviana was poisoned at dinner, I sensed it as it was happening, not before. And it isn't like we see each other that often outside of trials and our lessons."

"I guess that's true."

"They're at the gate," Tessa said, breaking my train of thought.

Across the arena from us, Heidi and Grier stood side by side in the tunnel, their gazes straight ahead. I knew that Grier could control people with her voice and Heidi—well, I didn't understand what Heidi's ability was. Nadia had called her a walking nightmare. But Heidi didn't look like a nightmare at that moment; she looked nervous.

Cohen was at the microphone again. He showed his teeth, but the smile was false—his mask. "Welcome."

The crowd cheered, screamed his name. There were no chants this time, no one screaming Heidi or Grier's name. I tried to imagine what it must be like to stand at the gates of the arena and wait for your fate to be decided—I never wanted to face it and yet I just wanted to get it over with.

Cohen repeated the same spiel from the previous trial. It was detached and clinical. He listed off the three dead Culling girls—Aviana, Joslyn, and Vivian—and reminded us all of the importance of sacrifice.

I hated every word he spoke. I wished he weren't the person saying it. But at that moment, he was a prince, not the smiling young man I'd grown to know.

Cohen's words, "May the goddess be honored," seemed to echo around the arena for forever. The crowd chanted it back to him, but no one in the viewing room repeated it—not even the guards.

Which of us wanted the goddess to be honored by our blood? I didn't want to die, not for a blessing and not for a crown. Being devout wasn't going to save any of us from dying in that arena.

Cohen was just about to step back from the microphone when he noticed that his mother had not joined him at the railing. She still sat in her chair, one of her guards kneeling next to her.

The guard was saying something to the queen—something that made Cohen's smile falter. He paled. Uri was turned in her seat, her eyes darting between the queen and her brother.

Cohen turned back to the microphone, his expression resolute. Dread, raw and aching, rose in my gut as he addressed the whispering crowd.

"My fellow Erydians, as many of you know, we have been working to solidify our relationship with Vayelle. After numerous border breeches and rebel uprisings, we were forced to issue a draft and begin the process of strengthening our military. We have been pushed to declare war against our neighbors. There have been attacks in Varos and Fajvurrow, all of them carried out by a rebel group known as 'the Culled.' Hundreds of homes and settlements have been ransacked. Innocent people have been killed."

He swallowed and glanced backward at his mother. The queen was on her feet now, her sharp gaze drilling into her son's back. This wasn't news she'd wanted shared. But Cohen didn't care; he turned back to the microphone.

"A weapons facility in Pallae has been compromised. Four days ago, rebel forces bombed a factory, killing everyone inside—nearly five hundred people dead. We have just received news that the people responsible have been seen in neighboring cities, rallying forces to attack Gazda." He hesitated, let his words sink in, let them boil throughout the thousands of people gathered. "Because of this most recent event and its proximity to Deca Market, we are canceling today's trial."

There were cries of outrage, cries of horror at the news; but more than that, were the cries for blood. Demands for the Culling to continue.

At Cohen's announcement, the royal family was swept from the arena, escorted by two dozen heavily armed guards. Around them, people booed and hissed. They cursed Cohen as a coward and screamed for the fight to go on. Behind me, goddess-touched girls were whispering.

Dellacov arrived at the viewing room moments later and quickly herded us, like confused cattle, down the long concrete hallway and into the cavernous parking deck. Heidi and Grier were already there, standing next to the transport with Cohen and Uri. The king, queen, and Larkin were already waiting in a long black car.

Before we could ask any questions, Cohen said, "We'll discuss everything when we get back to the palace."

He was using his court tone, stiff and practiced. And yet, there was the small hint of anxiety in his voice, a sort of tightness that wasn't princely.

Cohen cleared his throat, as if that could erase the way his eyes kept darting to the car, to his waiting mother. I didn't know what had been said in the royal box, but it was clear Cohen had made this decision without his mother's blessing.

That would cost him.

He remained at the doors of the van as we all filtered inside.

He looked so worried and, for an instant, I was tempted to go to him, to reach out and take his hand. But I didn't. I couldn't. I just forced my gaze away and tried not to show how truly afraid I was.

The Throne Room
Oredison Palace, Gazda

"How dare you speak for the Crown."

The sound of the queen's voice carried, echoing down the polished hallways of the palace. Her shrill screams grew louder as we walked toward the throne room. *That was good*, I thought. *If she was screaming then maybe she wasn't poisoning.*

I'd never been in this wing of the palace. It was showier than the rest, intentionally opulent and strategically confusing, with hallways that ended in dead ends and multiple staircases that led to the same floor. The air smelled of fresh-cut roses and the citrus tang of newly scrubbed floors.

The other girls gawked at the intricate wallpaper and lovely pastoral paintings. All the while, the queen kept yelling at Cohen, and my eyes kept moving farther ahead, toward where I knew he was.

"It was not your place to announce sensitive information," she was saying.

"What did you want me to do? Allow the trial to go on, even with the rebels within striking distance?"

It was the first time I'd heard him speak since the shouting had started. His voice was soft, but not weak—merely compliant. He was trying not to stir an already bubbling pot. I supposed that this was what a prince did until he was king.

"You gave them what they wanted," Larkin said, her voice soft and even. "These rebels want the Culling ended. They want the goddess and all her temples burned to the ground. Would you allow them to do that as well?"

Cohen's voice was sharp as he said, "They could have bombed the arena, killed everyone. The entire royal line and all the girls in one fatal swoop. Then what?"

Larkin didn't hesitate in her response. "You showed these radicals that bad behavior gets rewarded. They got exactly what they wanted. You stalled the Culling. A stronger ruler would have—"

He cut her off. "You have no idea what a ruler would and wouldn't do. You have no idea what you're even talking about." We arrived at the door to the throne room just in time to see Cohen glare at Larkin.

She tilted her head to one side. "Little brother, don't pick fights you can't afford to lose."

Viera saw us first, her lips quirking up into a sly smile. She was seated upon a large onyx throne embedded with swirls of white gold and diamond. The king stood to her right, but he wasn't focused on his children.

He was rocking on his heels, back and forth, like the pendulum of a clock. Boredom and stubble bloomed across his face in equal measure. Red cheeks and a purplish stain on the front of his pants said enough about how he'd spent his morning. I could no more understand how this man was Cohen's father than I could how Viera was his mother.

"Welcome, ladies." My attention snapped to the queen. She gestured for us to come farther into the room. "Who was meant to fight today?"

Slowly, Heidi and Grier stepped forward, separating themselves from the group. Viera looked to her son, then back at us.

From the corner of my eye, I watched Uri step forward from the shadows. Cohen tensed too.

Viera didn't look at any of her children; she just settled her blue eyes on the two girls before her. "My darling son overstepped when he announced the suspension of your trial. As queen, it is my decision what happens in a Culling, not his. I apologize for his impertinence." She leaned forward on her throne, thin hands braced on the onyx arms of the chair as she looked between Heidi and Grier. "Remind me, ladies, what are your abilities?"

They both hesitated and exchanged a glance.

Viera laughed and tapped a long fingernail against the stone. "Come now, no need to keep secrets. We're all friends here."

"I can torture people." Heidi's quiet voice echoed across the marble tiles.

"Torture people," Viera repeated.

"I can access fear and manipulate it. I can make people think the worst has happened." Heidi bit her lip. "It's hard to explain."

"And you?" The queen's gaze moved to Grier. "Something to do with your voice, I think."

"I can control people with my voice."

"Oh?" Viera smiled a large catlike grin, as if she'd just landed upon what she was looking for. "How interesting."

Larkin looked at Cohen and then to us, her dark eyes sliding across the row of girls as if we were inanimate objects to be played with. She said, "One of them should be dead. The total should be down to six."

Viera nodded slowly, her expression thoughtful. "It's a fight I would have liked to see."

"We'll reschedule the trial," Cohen said. "A few days won't make a difference."

His mother held up a hand. "Let's play a game."

The whole room fell silent.

The queen leaned back on her throne and eyed the row of goddess-touched girls. She pointed to the front of the group, to where Elodie stood, her head bowed. "That one," she said, as if the girl were a jeweled necklace. "State your name and ability."

Elodie blanched. "Oh. Um—"

Viera snapped her fingers. "I don't have all day."

The girl said, "Elodie Ketar. I . . . I can read minds, but only . . . only if I'm touching the person. It's weird—"

"Splendid." Viera turned away and pointed to Grier, who stiffened at the attention. She asked, "Your name?"

"Grier Jennis."

"Very good," the queen crooned. "Grier, tell Elodie to stop breathing."

Grier's mouth fell open in surprise. Elodie stepped back, her eyes turning wild as she tried to find somewhere to go, somewhere to hide. Guards moved to block her path, herding her toward the middle of the throne room.

Cohen stepped forward. "Mother, it's my fault. I made the decision—"

She held up a thin hand, her gaze still locked on Grier. "I said, tell her to stop—"

Grier's voice was high-pitched, breathless as she turned toward Elodie and gasped, "Stop breathing!"

The girl froze, every muscle in her body going rigid as she looked, wide-eyed, at Grier. Elodie's mouth was open in what looked like a silent scream. Her hands kept tightening against her sides, clawing at the fabric of her shirt.

But she did not breathe.

The stitched gashes on her cheeks began to turn silver as her face flushed, turned purple. Her eyes watered.

Grier's brown skin was pallid as she turned to look at the queen, her eyes beseeching. "I— Can I make it stop? Please, can I make it stop?"

Viera didn't even look at her; she only watched as Elodie's body began to shake. Her knees cracked against the marble floor as they gave way.

Grier was in tears, her bottom lip trembling as she begged, "Please. I don't want to kill her. Please, Your Highness—"

But it was too late.

Elodie's body slumped forward, twitched, and then went still. In the silence that followed, I watched the three black bands encircling her upper arm fade to nothingness.

Grier's hand did nothing to muffle the gut-wrenching sob that broke from her chest. She stepped forward, like she might go to Elodie, but Viera gestured Dellacov forward.

He took Grier by the shoulders and turned her toward the throne. Heidi still stood to one side, her mouth a thin line as she took in Elodie's lifeless body. I knew what she was thinking; it was what we were all thinking—

That could have been me.

Viera said, "I have never allowed my children's shortcomings to go unreprimanded. I am raising monarchs, not idle farmers. Mistakes, especially ones that affect our nation, cannot go without punishment."

The queen beckoned for Grier and Heidi to step forward. When neither girl moved, Viera smiled and nodded to Dellacov.

If they would not approach her throne willingly, she would have them brought by force. From the corner of my eye, I saw Uri take another step forward. For the smallest of seconds, Dellacov's gaze met hers. There was a slight plea there—*please don't get involved.*

He touched Grier's arm and nudged her toward the raised dais where the queen sat waiting. She took a few slow steps forward, Heidi shuffling at her heels. Once they were moving, Dellacov moved to stand with us again. His head turned just slightly, and I knew that he was looking at Uri again. She only shook her head, the smallest of movements, and he looked to the throne again.

The queen held out her hand as the girls reached the bottom of the steps. She offered them her ring to kiss. Grier's shoulders shook, tears streaming uncontrollably down her cheeks as she bent and carefully pressed her lips to the dark stone.

Viera smiled and then shooed Grier away. Heidi kissed the ring quickly, like a frightened animal grabbing food and darting back into its hole. She almost tripped in her hurry to get away from the throne.

When it was done, Viera looked down at her ring and smiled, as if their mouths had left a mark. Her blue eyes darted to Larkin, then to Cohen. At her mother's attention, Larkin's face split into a wide smile, as if she'd just won something.

And maybe she had.

This was the girl, I told myself, who hadn't been invited to any of Uri's brunches. She was the one who never spoke, who sat at her mother's heels and behaved. This was the sister who darted in and out of Cohen's childhood stories like a ghost, a phantom who was barely there—and now I wondered why. I wondered why she chose now to speak, now to smile, now to turn her cold black gaze on us.

Viera's gaze leveled on the two girls standing just in front of me, only inches away. And I knew. I knew before anything had even happened, before anyone moved.

I'd seen that look before.

A sound came from Cohen, a desperate cry, which he stifled behind tightly closed lips. Uri was not so well trained—she screamed, a sharp frightened sound that was both lament and warning. It echoed around the room, bouncing off the high ceilings and raising the hair on my arms.

Behind me, Dellacov pushed forward, trying to get to her, trying to interfere. But he wasn't going to Uri, I realized. He was darting toward the front of our group. But he was too late.

Grier was dead before anyone else even realized what was happening.

28

Palace Bedroom

Sanctus Eszter

Tallis brought me dinner that night. Juno was attending a meeting of the remaining goddess-touched trainers. "They're limiting our training sessions for the next few days," she told me. "The attack on Pallae and then what happened in the throne room . . . it's got everyone on edge. Juno said to tell you to keep practicing with the candles and to do core exercises."

We sat on the edge of my bathtub, allowing the water to run and obscure our whispers as we spoke. "Kinsley and Heidi have technically already had their first trial. That means I'm either against Nadia or Tessa, right?"

"Not necessarily. It's possible that Kinsley and Heidi could get called up a second time for your trial or before you even fight. Everyone's name is in the cup for each drawing, so there's really no guarantee. You should be prepared to fight any of the four of them."

I fiddled with the water spigot, turning the water from hot to cold and then back. "What . . . What actually happened in Pallae?"

"The Culled didn't kill anyone in that factory. We have rebels working there. The people gave those weapons to us of their own free will. The explosions happened after. I wasn't there, but my contacts tell me that it was Erydian soldiers who set the fires and killed all those workers. Some of our people were killed too. The royals are telling the story that suits their purpose, not the truth."

I nodded, still unsure.

"Your brother was there."

My head shot up. "Ambrose?"

"Yeah. He helped load the trucks. He's been working with Alexi Hoffman—do you know him?"

"No."

"He's Ellora Hoffman's younger brother, I think." Tallis shrugged. "I've never met her, but I know Alexi and his father. They've both been working with the rebellion for a while."

"Is . . . Is Ambrose okay?"

She nodded. "Yes. I think he was already on his way back to one of the safe houses by the time the explosions happened and the soldiers arrived."

Silence fell between us. I fiddled with the rabbit-head necklace, rolling it beneath the fabric of my shirt. I didn't wear it often and never when I was with Cohen. The charm usually stayed hidden in my vanity drawer or tucked under my shirt and out of sight. Tallis had suggested I wear it more frequently now, especially as things with the Culled grew progressively more tense.

"We're bringing in new spies and soldiers all the time," she'd told me. "I let them know about you when I can, but it isn't always possible. Everyone in the Culled will recognize the hare symbol though. They know we have a spy in the palace with a necklace like that. *We* know what it means, but most everyone else here wouldn't think twice about it. Don't flaunt it, of course, but you're probably fine letting it be seen. It's just a necklace, after all. There's nothing to tie you to us."

Even with those assurances, I'd been careful about it with Cohen. I could come up with an explanation easily enough, but I didn't want to have to lie to him. So far, nothing treasonous had happened between us. I'd tried more than once to get into his bedroom and had been derailed each time. After what had just happened with Grier and Elodie . . .

"What Viera did today was scary," I said. "She isn't even pretending to play by the rules. She's actively participating in the Culling. I don't . . . I don't think she'll step down. Even for Kinsley."

"That's why we're doing all of this. Are you having any luck getting the documents I asked for?"

I shook my head. "I've hinted around with Cohen, and I've come close to going to his room a few times, but even if I were to get inside, I wouldn't be alone. It wouldn't be like I could search."

Tallis nodded. "One of the maids we have working with us searched a few days ago while she was straightening his room. She didn't see the schedules in there. I think they're probably in Captain Dellacov's office."

"With the increase in guards, I'd think that they would probably be changing how they do things. Maybe Cohen isn't signing off on the patrol schedule anymore?"

"It's possible. We still need to try to get our hands on those papers though. There's been talk of trying to attack without them, but we'd have to move in more of our forces than we have readily available. A lot of the Culled is based on the other side of the Demarti Mountains. We've got a series of camps in Vayelle where refugees are going. It would take months to get as many people as we'd need."

"What's the plan now?"

"Right now, we want to cut the head off the snake. If the queen, the king, and the head of the Synod can be killed or imprisoned during this initial attack, things would go smoother moving forward. I don't have all of the details, but I think the goal is to weaken the Warwicks' hold on the throne and disrupt the Culling. From there, we'll stage a full coup."

Palace Bedroom

One week before Sanctus Valencia

A week passed in near isolation. I wasn't allowed to train, and Tallis and Juno were kept away from me. With things strained both inside and outside of the palace, Dellacov was on high alert. I'd been locked in my room with guards posted outside for days. Only maids came and went.

Each time one entered my room, they commented on how quickly I went through candles. I'd done what Juno had asked of me; I did whatever exercises

I could inside my bedroom and spent my evening playing with the fire in the hearth. I pulled it from the fireplace to the candle on my nightstand and back, over and over again.

Each morning a maid would bring my breakfast and a small stack of beeswax candles wrapped in linen. After the first day or so, the palace staff started to bring candles with each meal, already anticipating my need for more.

When the knock came at my door around dinnertime on Monday, I assumed it would be more candles and hopefully a warm meal. I'd had a plate of fruit and cheese for lunch and, following an afternoon spent jogging in place and doing core exercises, I was starving.

I was surprised to open the door and find Cohen standing there. He was dressed in a simple pair of cotton sleep pants and a loose shirt. His hair was still wet from a bath. This Cohen was different, less of a prince and more of a friend. I hadn't realized just how much I'd missed him until he was there, standing in front of me.

He said nothing as he handed me a small folded card embossed with the royal seal. It was heavy paper, the weight of it familiar in my hands. I'd seen it before, two other times.

I took it from him but didn't open it.

The look on his face spelled out my name in crisp, bloodred ink. We both just stood there for a long moment, me looking at the unopened card, him looking down at his shoes.

Finally, I mustered up enough courage to ask, "Against who?"

Cohen's throat bobbed as he swallowed. "Tessa. She controls air."

I set the note down on the table next to the door and stepped aside, allowing him to walk in before I shut the door—leaving us alone together.

"Next Monday at dawn?"

He nodded. "Sanctus Valencia."

Something inside my chest burned so harshly it brought tears to my eyes. Cohen reached out, his fingertips just barely grazing the skin of my cheek before I brushed away his hand. These were frightened, angry tears.

I hadn't truly trained in a week. I hadn't heard from Tallis or the rebels in days. I'd had no opportunity to try to get the information they needed to attack the palace. And we were so close. The Culling could be disbanded but, if I lost to Tessa, I wouldn't live to see it. I could die before I had the chance to be saved.

"I should have had two weeks' notice. Two weeks to know and train."

"You're right. I'm sorry. I— My mother didn't pull the names and there was a lot of political unrest. I asked them to push the fight back a week to give you the normal amount of time, but the Synod and my mother voted to keep things on schedule."

A frightened sob hiccuped from my chest and I covered my mouth with my hand to stop myself from losing it. *Oh goddess. A week. One week. Seven days.*

"Monroe." Cohen reached out and this time I didn't move away. He pulled me against his chest and held me there.

This was wrong—letting him hold me when I was plotting his destruction. And yet my muscles relaxed as I leaned into him. I'd never realized just how nicely my head fit underneath his chin or just how good his arms felt wrapped around my waist.

I never wanted to forget it. Faced with possible death in a week's time, everything seemed fragile and terribly precious. I wanted to etch the feel of Cohen's embrace onto my skin, smudge it into the blackness of my mark and hide it there, for only me to see.

My time was running out. If I was going to escape the palace, I needed to go now. If I didn't, I would be dead. I would be ash. My mother would weep. Kinsley would get the crown, and the prince, and her life.

Or Viera might refuse to relinquish the throne.

All of this was enough to make me step away. This—Cohen—*I couldn't have him.* I wasn't like the girls in Uri's books. I didn't get a happy ending. I wasn't the girl who ended up with the prince.

I was the girl who burned it all down or died trying. I had to be. The alternative was to fight and win the Culling. And I wouldn't be myself if I did that. I'd have to kill at least another person, probably more than that.

And so, I couldn't have Cohen. The mental image of our future was elusive and, in that image, I was always a different person. I understood that to be his, *truly his*, would mean that I would have to stop being me.

Cohen frowned as I sat down on my bed, wedging my hands under my thighs to hide their shaking. He stayed by the door, his hands stuffed in his pockets. He was watching me with his mother's blue eyes: sharp, analyzing.

He'd run away before.

Maybe Cohen would understand, maybe he would help me—help the Culled—if I asked. But I couldn't get the words past my teeth. I couldn't tell him.

I met that heavy gaze as I asked, "Do you *want* to be king?"

The question came from a place of want. I knew his answer, but I still asked it because I wanted him to say no. I wanted him to tell me that the crown didn't matter to him. That he just wanted to leave, to get away from all of this and—

"Yes."

It took a lot to keep my expression disinterested, unfazed. Cohen being king wasn't part of Ambrose's plan—or the plan of this organization he now worked with. The Culled didn't want a Warwick on the throne.

He looked up at me, watching my face as he said, "My father is a weak king. A drunkard. His weakness has allowed my mother to take full control of the kingdom and abuse his children. She has unbridled power over everything, everyone. But it won't always be that way. I intend to have an equal ruling with my queen."

"You'd make a good king."

I said it because it was true. Cohen would be a good king, a compassionate king—if kings were something Erydia was going to continue to have. I didn't understand how anyone who knew Cohen, saw him the way I did, could want him dead. He wasn't his mother.

"Thank you. I hope so." He bowed his head, and his ears flushed at my words. "We're lifting the confinement tomorrow morning, so things should go back to the way they were before."

"I wish I had more time to train."

He nodded to the door. "We could go now."

"There are guards—"

"Not right now there aren't. We could go down to the training rooms and no one would even notice. And I'll be a gentleman. I'll get you back in time for you to get a good night's sleep before your trainers show up in the morning."

When I didn't say anything in response, he said, "Or you can stay here and sulk."

"I'm not sulking."

"You're worrying. I can see it written all over your face. Let me distract you."

Despite everything, I still wanted to say yes. I wanted to pretend that I was normal. I wanted to kiss him and let him hold me. Let him take me on adventures.

I wanted to stay his friend—be more than his friend.

Cohen still watched me, his face trained into the neutral expression of someone who expected to be rejected. And I didn't want to push him away. I wanted to smile at him. I wanted to stay his friend. But Cohen might one day regret wanting me.

I could ruin him.

"One hour."

One thing was certain: Cohen Warwick had damn good aim. Despite his cajoling, I'd opted to sit out this training session. Instead, I sat in the chair Juno usually occupied and watched as Cohen threw knife after knife into the chest of one of the practice dummies.

"Where did you learn to do that?" I asked.

He fiddled with the harness of knives he wore. I'd be lying if I said that I didn't find the contraption of leather and steel to be somewhat sexy. It crossed over his chest and seemed to emphasize the length of his torso and the width of his shoulders. And his arms. Goddess, in that short-sleeved shirt, he looked so strong.

He hid it well underneath suits and jackets, but Cohen was fit. I'd suspected as much when I kept seeing him hanging out around the training rooms, but I hadn't ever thought to ask exactly what sort of things he did. Knife-throwing and guns seemed to be his weapons of choice.

"My father used to be good at it. He's got arthritis in his hands now so he isn't as steady as he once was. He taught Hugo and me how to do it when we were about ten. It's been something I've been working on perfecting for years."

"You seem pretty close to perfect."

"Yeah, but the target is standing still. I don't get a ton of practice working with something that's moving. I don't know if it would be useful at all in a fight. But it's fun to show off at parties."

I laughed. "What sort of parties?"

His ears flushed and he shook his head. "The knife-wielding kind, I guess."

I opened my palm and examined the golden pocket watch he'd handed me when we'd first arrived. Cohen had insisted that the hour together didn't start until we reached our destination. We'd arrived around forty-five minutes ago, so our time was waning.

"Don't do that," he said.

"Do what?"

"Watch the clock."

That was hard to do when I might be dead in a matter of days. I swallowed and said, "It's getting late."

"Is there something else you'd rather be doing, Monroe?" he said as he took aim at the target once more. "Am I boring you?"

Emboldened by the teasing tone in his voice, I said, "I'd like all of this a little better if you'd kiss me."

He smiled and threw his remaining knife. It landed a few centimeters short of the X marking the heart. Not his best shot. He cursed under his breath and turned to look at me. "You'd rather be kissing?"

The blood felt hotter in my veins. "I was promised a distraction."

"Very well then." Cohen undid the harness and hung it on a hook in one of the weapon cabinets. "Let me distract you."

I told myself that I was with Cohen for the Culled. For my brother. For all the people that were being overlooked and used. But as he led me into the dark library and into the moonlit sunroom beyond it, I knew that this was for me. Every kiss, every touch was uncertain and yet determined. And I drank it in, let myself relax, and just reacted to him.

I didn't know if he was more experienced than I was, but his movements were far more confident as he initiated each caress and guiding touch. I wasn't his first and that didn't bother me. What did was the nagging question of whether I would be his last, his forever. That pushed insistently at the back of my mind—a thrum that seemed to echo the curling heat in my gut.

Goddess, he was something.

And it wasn't love—at least I didn't think it was. It didn't need to be. Not just then. This was exactly what I'd been promised. It was purely carnal and purely a distraction—and I wanted it. I wanted him.

At some point, the kisses turned more desperate, and then he was pulling me closer to him until I was straddling his lap on one of the couches. My shirt went first, and I was oddly amused at how his fingers shook against the strap of my undershirt. Then I was tugging his shirt free of his waistband, prepared to make us a little more even.

We were drawing cards and the risk was only growing.

"Monroe?" Cohen asked, his voice a hoarse whisper against the skin of my neck. His fingers ran along the band of my trousers as he trailed soft kisses along my jaw.

I nodded, but some small part of me seemed to hesitate as I realized the seriousness of our actions. This wasn't a game. It wasn't simple and this—having sex with Cohen—was just a way to temporarily escape from my problems. And it was something once given, I wouldn't be able to take back.

I wanted to live and experience life, but I didn't want my first time to be a distraction. Not for me and not for the person I shared it with. The hand that had been tangled in Cohen's hair moved to press against the hard lines of his chest. He was already done unbuttoning my trousers as I gently, but firmly, pushed him away.

As soon as he felt my resistance, he stopped and pulled away from me—putting distance between us. "You okay?"

I nodded. "I . . . I think I'd like to go back to my room."

"Did I do anything to hurt you? I didn't mean to—"

"No." The word came out quick and sharper than I'd intended. "No," I said again, softer, "I'm okay. I just— I'm tired and I don't think now is a good time." I eased off his lap. For a moment we just sat on opposite ends of the couch, both of us half undressed, both of us breathing heavily.

"I'm sorry," he said.

The anxiety that had been building in my chest from the moment he'd handed me the trial announcement was near bursting. The wall I'd built to separate the panic from myself was filled with holes and I was almost drowning in it. Goddess, I was going to die. I had days. Days until—

I forced myself to say, "I'm okay. Just . . ." My throat felt like it was going to close. It hurt to breathe or to try to speak.

His hair looked silver in the moonlight, and I wondered for a moment if I should have let him continue. Maybe if I'd just kissed him back, the terror of my situation wouldn't have come crashing down so soon. There could have been a few more minutes of bliss and intentional ignorance, there might have been hours of stolen time left. Now that his hands were gone, I was faced with the reality of the arena and . . .

I was going to be sick.

"You're crying."

I opened my mouth to say something, but the words died on my lips as the lights of the sunroom flipped on, and we both turned to see Britta standing in the doorway. My hands instinctively moved to cover myself and Cohen shifted so his body partially blocked mine.

His sister didn't look at him as she said, "Cohen, go to your room. Now."

"Britta, I can explain—" He reached down and grabbed my shirt from where it had been discarded on the floor.

"It wasn't a request." The words were angry and sharp. "Put on your shirt and go to your room. *Now*."

Cohen turned to look at me, and I nodded. "Go on."

He handed me my shirt before he got up from the couch and grabbed his own from where I'd tossed it onto a nearby chair. He was still tugging it into place as he came to a stop in front of his older sister. "We didn't do anything wrong."

Her jaw was tight with restrained anger as she responded, "Maybe not, but you would have."

"Monroe isn't—"

"Monroe and I will discuss what she is. *You* will return to your room, and you will stay there until morning."

For a moment, it looked like Cohen might argue with her, but he didn't. He just shot me an apologetic look before he left the sunroom, closing the large set of double doors behind him. Britta waited until we heard the outer doors to the library shut and then she started talking.

"I'm only going to say this once, so it would in your best interest to listen to me. My sister is playing a matchmaking game. Uriel is a child. She is a romantic and a dreamer—but you cannot afford to be; you are goddess-touched. This behavior is dangerous, both for you and for my brother. As you have seen, displeasing my mother can have disastrous, often irreversible, consequences. And no one displeases her the way Cohen does. You cannot run around blatantly breaking rules and flaunting your affection. It is stupid and reckless. What if someone else had caught you here? What if it were Kinsley's father? You are one of her biggest threats. He wouldn't hesitate to get rid of you to earn more of my mother's favor."

My hands shook as I clutched my shirt to my chest. "I'm sorry."

"You may think you are in love with my brother—but love is a privilege you haven't yet earned. When you wear the crown, then you can have him. I will congratulate you and wish the two of you well. But until then, he is not yours, and you are not his. You will keep your hands to yourself, and you will keep your distance from him. If you cannot manage that, then I will do what

I need to do to keep him safe so he can sit on the throne. Have I made myself clear, Miss Benson?"

"Yes, Your Highness."

She nodded to me. "Get dressed and then go straight to your room. Do not seek Cohen out again."

She left me sitting there, still holding my wrinkled shirt to my chest. I managed to keep the tears at bay long enough to straighten my clothes and get back to my room. But once inside, I wept. I wept large, hiccupping sobs until there was only exhaustion and the pure, blissful oblivion of sleep.

29

Training with Tallis and Juno had become more intense since my trial had been announced almost a week earlier. Now we knew who I was fighting against and could begin to prepare. Obviously, with Tessa using air, I needed to be careful. She could not only take the oxygen from my flames, but she could suffocate me.

Juno always made it sound so simple when he talked about it.

"You strike first—make it count. A few good burns should hurt her enough to throw her off her game. If you need to, snap her neck. Do it quick though—you don't want to be close to her for too long. You're better off with long-range shots."

Snap her neck.

He'd spent three hours teaching me exactly how to do that. Tallis was a few inches taller than Tessa, but they had the same general build, so he'd made me practice it with her. The positioning of my hands, exactly how much pressure it would take to do it.

I wanted to impress him; I wanted Juno to believe I would win. I thought if he believed in me, then maybe I'd believe in myself. But pretending to kill someone and actually doing it were two different things.

Juno came to get me from my room after breakfast on our last day of training. We had a matter of hours to prepare me for the trial. *Hours.*

I could have hours left in my life.

I hadn't eaten dinner and I'd barely touched the omelet Cohen had sent that morning. We'd barely seen each other since Britta had caught us in the sunroom, but he'd still sent food for me every morning. And while the gesture was sweet, I almost never ate it. The fear of Viera interfering in my trial was too great.

Juno barely spoke on the walk to the training room. I wasn't sure he knew what to say to me. He'd worked hard to teach me and I had learned so much from him, but at the end of the day, I was the one in the arena.

And all the training in the world couldn't predict how I would actually do when the time came.

Tallis was smiling as I walked to the water fountain after my first few sets of exercises. "Ready to kick ass tomorrow?"

"As ready as I'll ever be, I think."

"You'll do great," Tallis said. "I know you will. You've already shown so much improvement. And you're stronger than she is—I know it. You just have to believe it yourself."

"No jewelry tomorrow," Juno said, nodding at the rabbit-head necklace that had slipped from under my shirt during one of the exercises. At his words, I unclasped the chain and slipped it into my pocket.

"And pin your hair back as much as you can," Tallis added. "You don't want it getting in the way."

"Sure. No jewelry and hair pinned. Anything else?"

Tallis pulled a small pile of clothes out of the bag. She handed them to me. "These are for tomorrow."

I unfolded the top item. It was a short-sleeved tunic, made of a very thin, tightly woven black chain mail. The clothes folded underneath looked normal, just black tight-fitted training pants and a thin red short-sleeve undershirt.

"What do you think?" Juno asked.

I looked up at him. "It's great. Thank you."

"The chain mail is specially made to fit you and your particular needs.

And the pants and shirt have been treated with a chemical that should keep them mostly intact," Tallis said. "It was fun to try to explain you to a tailor."

Juno nodded in agreement. "I think it'll look nice tomorrow. And it'll help keep your clothes intact."

Tallis leaned into his shoulder. "Yeah; the last thing we want is our future queen fighting naked."

I'd just bathed and changed into a nightgown when a knock came at my bedroom door. The maids had already long since come and gone, leaving me with my bundle of fresh candles and a tray of chamomile tea to help me sleep.

The knock came again, loud and insistent—not that of a maid.

"Who is it?" I called.

The only response I got was another firm knock. I sighed and grabbed a cardigan from where I'd left it at the foot of my bed. I'd only just tugged it on when the knocking sounded again, this time louder.

"I'm coming, give me a damn minute—" The words died on my lips as I opened the door and saw my brother standing there. I'd barely even registered that it was Kace before he had hauled me to his chest and was hugging me. He was dressed in the uniform of a palace guard, his hair trimmed short, and his face cleanly shaved—but he smelled like home.

His words were muffled against my dripping wet hair as he said, "I only just finished orientation training. I never thought it would end. I was so excited to come find you."

My eyes burned with tears as I stepped back, hauling him into my bedroom after me. The guards standing watch eyed us with apprehension, but Kace waved them off. "It's my sister."

I didn't wait for their approval before I shut the door, leaving us alone together. The words flowed from my lips, one hurried question after another. "How are you? Have you seen Mama or spoken to Ambrose? Did you hear about the lowered draft? And—"

"Slow down, Monroe. You're gonna make yourself sick." Kace laughed and ran a hand over the top of his head, flustered. "I'm fine. Excited to be here. This is— I never thought I'd get to really be a royal guard. It's incredible. And yes, I've spoken to Mama. She's doing okay, better now that she's getting your goddess-touched stipend. She's also getting money from me. I got paid just last week, and I sent all that I had to Varos."

"And Ambrose?"

Kace opened and closed his mouth.

A lump formed in my throat. "What is it? Is he . . . Is he all right?"

"He's deserted his post. No one has seen him in a few weeks. I wasn't sure if you already knew."

I'd thought the very idea of betraying Cohen had been difficult, but it was nothing compared to outright lying to Kace. "I didn't know. Last I heard, he was training. The prince told me about that when he told me about you."

Kace nodded and straightened one of the silver clasps on his uniform. "They've got a price on his head. Mama— I've told Mama not to speak to him and not to offer him aid. I doubt he'd be stupid enough to return home, but . . ." My brother shrugged. "I don't want her to get caught up in his bad decisions."

"A price on his head?" I walked to my bed and sat down on the edge of it. Kace remained standing where he was by the door. "Won't they just return him to his unit once he's found?"

"He's working with the rebels, Monroe."

I flinched at the venom in his voice. I'd expected him to be annoyed with Ambrose for not wanting to serve the Crown, but this . . . The look on Kace's face held more than just disapproval. I chose my next words very carefully. "Just because he's deserted doesn't mean he's working with the Culled. He never wanted to be in the army, you know that. It's possible that he's just—"

"He was seen during the slaughter in Pallae. That was one of the reasons I was brought here as quickly as I was. Captain Dellacov wanted me to look at the security footage that was captured and see if I could identify any of the people. They had reason to believe that a few of the men in Pallae were deserters from Varos. And they were right. Ambrose was there. So were Alexi

Hoffman, Orion McNealy, and one of the Stuart boys. I went to school with all three of them."

The surprise on my face was genuine. I couldn't believe what I was hearing.

"You . . . You told Dellacov that Ambrose was there, in Pallae?"

Kace interpreted my shock as being aimed at our brother's treason. "Yes. I did. It wasn't— I didn't want to, but Ambrose put me in an uncomfortable position. What he's doing is dangerous. And not just to himself. He's putting Mama at risk. They're executing entire families when members of the Culled are captured. If I weren't able to advocate for Mama . . ." He sighed. "Dellacov is going to do what he can to grant her amnesty. He realizes that she's a special case. I mean, with you fighting in the Culling, she could easily be the mother of the next queen. That alone should hold some weight."

"My trial is tomorrow."

"I heard. How do you feel? You look well."

I didn't feel well. I felt like I might throw up.

Kace had identified Ambrose as a rebel. He could have easily lied. He could have looked at the footage and told Dellacov that he didn't recognize any of the young men on the tape—but instead he'd given their names away. He'd put those families in danger, and he'd known what might happen if he did so.

"Monroe?" he prompted.

I cleared my throat. "I'm sorry, I was— I just—"

"Hearing about Ambrose is surprising, I know. I'm sorry. I probably shouldn't have even said anything about it, not with your trial happening tomorrow. You should be thinking about yourself."

"I'm fine. I've been training for weeks. My trainers think I'm ready."

"I'm proud of you for being here. I realize the Culling wasn't your choice to begin with, but you're here now and you're doing it. You're in the final five. That's amazing."

But I could die tomorrow.

The silence between us turned uncomfortable. "I'm glad you're here," I said after a long moment. "Will . . . Will you watch tomorrow?"

"Yes. All of the guards are going. The entire royal family and all of the goddess-touched girls will be there, so we're all allowed to attend. I think next time I'll probably be in the guard rotation. Thankfully I'm just watching tomorrow, so my attention will be all yours. I'm . . ." He swallowed, showing the first real sign of nerves. "I don't want you to think it's easy for me to watch you walk into that arena. It isn't. You're my little sister."

I wanted to believe him, truly. But Kace and I had always been pushing and shoving at each other. As the middle child, he was always wedged between Ambrose and me. Between the head of our household and a goddess-touched girl. We had always butted heads. He wanted the control Ambrose had and the attention I always seemed to attract.

He'd have taken my goddess-given mark if he could—and he'd have worn it with pride. And he had never, ever, been able to reconcile the fact that I could reject something he believed was so special. Even with death lingering just a sunrise away, I knew Kace wouldn't wish me out of this situation.

He didn't want me to die in the Culling, sure. But he did want me to fight in it.

"I think you could be queen," he said, his voice quiet. "I know you have it in you. I've always seen it in you. Now you just have to see it in yourself."

I forced a smile—forced myself not to delve any deeper into my own anxiety. "You'd hate it if I were queen."

"What makes you say that?"

I sighed. "Because then you'd have to do whatever I said."

PART THREE

—

A Game of Keys

Early Fall
Gazda County, Erydia

Five Goddess-touched Girls Remain

30

Don't forget to breathe. Don't lock your knees. Don't stop fighting. Don't let her keep you down. Don't turn your back on her. Don't get distracted. Don't let her out of your sight. Don't—

"Monroe, are you okay?"

I jumped and had to cover my mouth with my hand to keep from crying out in surprise.

"Shit. Sorry." Nadia chewed at a hangnail and nodded to the empty spot on the bench next to me. "May I?"

I gestured for her to sit but didn't say anything. I couldn't get my pulse to slow, couldn't get my heartbeat out of my ears. I'd barely slept and somewhere between lacing my boots and boarding the transport, I'd started shaking. It was an uncontrollable trembling that made my back hurt and my vision swim.

As soon as we'd arrived at the arena, I'd gone to my regular front-and-center bench. I needed to get myself under control—now. Before someone noticed. I breathed, slow and steady, in through my nose, out through my mouth.

Kinsley had positioned herself on the bench directly behind mine. And while neither of us had acknowledged the other, I could feel her gaze. I could feel Tessa's gaze too.

The sun was just breaking over the far side of the arena wall, sprays of yellow, pink, purple, and red spreading across the horizon. From my vantage point, I could still see the moon, a white half crescent, fighting the rising sun for center stage.

Tessa was pacing in a corner of the viewing room. She hadn't said a word to me, and I was glad of it. I worried if I opened my mouth I might vomit.

Somewhere out in that crowd sat my brother. I'd hoped I might see him before the trial started, but he didn't come back to my room, and he hadn't been one of the guards waiting with us. I told myself that it was good that he was here. That way, if I did die, someone would be able to tell Mama what had happened.

And Kace was the person to do that. He would sugarcoat it, so it didn't hurt her too badly. Last night, as he'd left my room, I'd resisted the urge to tell him that he needed to tell our mother that I loved her.

I'd wanted to say, *Tell her to light a candle for me. And to dry aster flowers for the hearth. If they give her any of my ashes, tell her to spread them somewhere warm and sunny. Not in Varos, if she can help it.*

But the words hadn't come.

Kace hadn't allowed any conversation about the Culling that wasn't positive. And I wanted to believe that his confidence in me was born of a desire to keep my spirits high. But I think, in truth, he just didn't want to consider that there was another alternative.

It was possible that he would watch my body burn today.

"Hey." Nadia slid closer to me and leaned in. "If you feel like you're being poisoned," she swallowed and shot a glance at Tessa, "just look over in this direction and I'll try to, uh, give you some juice."

"Juice?"

She glanced down at her ink-black fingertips. "I've been practicing doing it long-range."

I forced a smile. "And how's that going for you?"

"I think I'm pretty good, all things considered. I mean, there's like a fifty percent chance it'll work. So, don't bet on it or anything." She shrugged and went back to chewing on one of her nails.

"Those odds sound great."

She nudged me with her shoulder. "Hey, beggars can't be choosers."

"Thank you."

"Of course."

My throat was tight as I said, "If I don't win, I hope you do."

She sighed and touched my hand. "If one of us is winning this thing, it's you. Why do you think I'm trying so hard to impress you? Gotta stay in the queen's good graces, right?"

I didn't get a chance to answer her.

"Monroe and Tessa." A guard stood at the door.

For a second, neither of us moved. We both just turned and looked at him, the moment frozen. Then Kinsley spoke up, shattering everything. "Monroe, I'd appreciate it if you didn't die. I would like to have the honor of strangling you myself."

I stood up and adjusted my top, twisting the chain mail back into place. I hoped she couldn't see the way my hands were shaking. "I'll do my best, Kinsley. Nice to have you on my side."

"You know what they say, 'the enemy of your enemy is your friend.'"

"We won't ever be friends, Kinsley."

"Finally, something we can agree on."

The guard called my name again, annoyed and impatient. Tessa was already in the hall outside waiting. We were supposed to walk together into the arena. Like we were friends. Like one of us wasn't about to slaughter the other.

Juno's last advice for me this morning, right before I left to get on the van, had been for me to think of something that pissed me off. "If you look like you're ready to lose, you will. Kill them with your eyes first."

I thought of Kinsley kissing Cohen at the ball, the night after he'd kissed me. I thought about my mother, preparing to survive the winter stretch by herself. I imagined my brothers lying dead on a battlefield.

I imagined Cohen, throwing up and fighting a fever because his own mother had poisoned him. I imagined all the girls who had died before me—

the hundreds who would die after me. And I imagined all the things I hadn't done yet, all the places I hadn't seen and the experiences I'd missed out on.

While those thoughts didn't make me unafraid, they did remind me why I was fighting.

I stood at the mouth of the tunnel next to Tessa.

She was dressed in blue so dark it was almost black. It made her red hair seem brighter, like strands of orange fire pulled into a slick ponytail at the crown of her head. Her shirt was long-sleeved and rolled up to the elbows to reveal her mark—a row of three perfectly formed circles that ran from her wrist to her elbow.

I wanted to say something to her, but I couldn't quite find the words. I wondered if she had family or a lover back home.

Two guards took turns checking us for hidden weapons. I tried not to flinch away as strange hands ran up and down the insides of my legs, across my hips, over my chest, down my arms.

Farther down the dark tunnel, I could see the arena blooming into a new day, the white stadium lights being overtaken by the warm rays of the rising sun. It might be my last sunrise, and I couldn't even appreciate it.

The floor of the tunnel seemed to vibrate with the screams and cheers of the crowds above our heads. The guard who'd done my paperwork walked me midway down the tunnel and rotated my shoulders so I was looking out, directly into the arena. I knew that the goddess-touched viewing room was on the arena wall directly in front of me, but I couldn't even see the edges of the glass.

On either side of me, torches flickered. I could feel each flame, like an extension of myself.

Tessa stepped up next to me and, for an instant, her eyes darted to me and then to the row of flames next to her. She swallowed and dug her fingernails into her palms.

I waited, my hands shaking, for Cohen to speak. I hadn't seen him in days. Even with Britta's warning still ringing in my ears, I'd sort of expected him to try to see me last night, but he hadn't. I wondered if he was nervous too.

"Welcome," Larkin's voice clicked over the loudspeaker, even and smooth. "Thank you for your continued support of the Culling. Today is the third trial. The goddess has blessed our nation with ten worthy candidates, of which five remain standing. Today we will lower that number to four."

Applause broke out, but my heart sank.

Was Cohen not here?

My muscles tensed as the guards moved to stand on either side of the entrance. We were gestured forward. My legs shook as I moved toward the gate. The crowd was still cheering, but I could barely hear it over the sound of my heart racing. Larkin was still talking, repeating the same information that was given at every trial.

One of the guards addressed us: "Walk to the center of the arena and then separate. Thirty paces. You may begin when the buzzer sounds. As soon as the fight is over and the victor is announced, the winner returns to the tunnels. Understand?"

We both nodded.

Over the speaker, Viera's voice crackled to life: "Let us begin."

The Arena

It was sixty steps to the middle of the arena. Then another thirty steps away from each other—me walking toward the viewing room, Tessa walking toward the gate.

I'd spent all night thinking about the best way to fight her. I had the first three moves planned in my mind, stitched together and ready to be wielded, but it could all change in an instant.

We stopped, facing away from each other.

The crowd stilled. There was a ringing in my ears. I could feel my pulse in my hands, in my fingertips.

Goddess.

I dug my feet into the dirt and took a steadying breath. My muscles relaxed, no longer tensed from stress, but only flexed, ready.

One heartbeat. Two. Three. Four.

The buzzer sounded.

We turned at the same time, both of us racing to be the first to strike. Instinctually, I snapped my fingers and called fire to me. It flared to life, hot and quick. It grew, ate at my arms. Danced along the metal of the chain mail until it glowed red.

Dropping to my knees, I buried my hands in the dirt. The fire spread from me, feasting on the dry grass until there was a wall of fire between Tessa and me.

It hissed and popped, the largest fortress of flame I'd ever conjured.

This was the first step of my plan.

Tessa was quick too, but her ability wasn't visible like mine. She controlled air—and I felt her ability in motion more than I saw it. Fire ate at the ground around us, but it faltered, shrank back and quivered if it came too close to her.

Flames needed oxygen.

I needed oxygen.

I pulled the fire back, giving Tessa the illusion of winning. She darted toward me, but I shoved the fire forward and away, throwing it from my hands. My wall of flame crested and fell to the earth, missing Tessa by less than a foot.

She changed tactics. Thick black air shoved at my face, blinding me and overwhelming my lungs. I coughed, fighting against her heavy blanket of smoke and ash.

Unsure what else to do, I dropped to all fours and then to my stomach, using her hot air and my smoke as a shield. My eyes watered, immune to flame but not to the smoke caused by the burning ground. I blinked rapidly, trying to focus, trying to get my heart rate to slow. I felt like I was shaking with it.

Across the arena from me, Tessa stood silhouetted by bright stadium lights. She was covering her face with the hem of her shirt while she filtered the smoke with her hands, clearing away the congestion and leaving herself in a bubble of fresh, breathable air. After a moment, she dropped her shirt and spun in a slow circle, unsure where I was.

My fire was loose, eating away at the bordering grass and gnawing at the brick bases of the walls. I wondered what it would take to burn the entire place to the ground.

Tessa spun in my direction and began clearing a larger space of air. Still looking for me.

Using my feet and my elbows, I crawled sideways, sliding as quickly as I could toward her left side, back into the smoke. Tessa yelled something but I couldn't hear her over the roar of my fire, the crowd, the thundering in my ears.

I shoved the line of flames behind her forward.

Fire hissed as it feasted on the bubble of clean air she'd created. I let the fire reach her, but only to a point, only enough to startle her. She turned away from where I lay hidden and focused her ability on the inferno creeping toward her back.

I took one more second to breathe, and then I slid the flames on three sides of her forward, boxing her in, and leaving only one direction for her to go.

Toward me.

Tessa's ability caved as she started to panic, unsure where to turn. Adrenaline was making her foolish. Seeing only one clear path, she ran, bolting in my direction, running through pockets of flame, trying to drain them as she went.

But she couldn't take oxygen from the flames and clean the air at the same time. I'd left her no choice but to choose. Which was more important, being able to see or dousing the fire?

She did exactly what I'd hoped she'd do.

One hand grabbed her shirt hem and the other reached forward, drawing air from the flames as she ran from them, a frightened animal darting headlong into my trap.

She was two yards away.

One yard.

Two feet.

I lunged, my arms wrapping around her middle, as we both fell to the ground. Fire licked along my body, burning her in the places where our bodies met.

She screamed.

The sound was startling. It rang in my ears and chilled my blood. It was enough to make me stop, a knee-jerk reaction—a human reaction. That split second of pause was all Tessa needed.

Her hand found my throat as she looped one leg around mine, jerked me sideways, and flipped us. The maneuver pinned one of my hands beneath my body. I used the other to shove her head back, white-hot flame coming in contact with her flesh.

She screamed again, and tried to pull away, but I didn't let go. Tessa writhed, screamed, and kicked, but I held tight. I gripped her hair in my burning hand. The strands charred, broke, and tangled in my fingers. All the while, that same shrill scream of agony.

Me. I was doing that to her. I was causing that sound. I was myself and not myself all at once. And I wanted to stop—but that darkness in me, that roiling power, did not.

So, I did not relent.

I had her. I would win.

And then, she moved.

Her hands found my throat and crushed against my windpipe. I yanked at her fingers, tried to roll, tried to kick her off, but she didn't budge.

I took four breaths, gasped for air—and then there was only terror. Eyes watering, hands shaking, horror, unlike anything I'd ever experienced before.

There was no air.

The fire on my hands died as my oxygen supply did. Smoke swirled around us, heavy and black, blurring as I fought for air, for another breath.

Tessa let go of me. She removed her hands from my neck and shoved herself up onto her knees, straddling my waist. Even with her hands gone, I couldn't breathe.

There wasn't any air.

My chest heaved, but nothing happened.

Her fist collided with the side of my face, hard enough to snap my neck sideways. My vision, already blurry from tears, spotted. She drew back for another punch. In one last push of energy, I shoved up from the ground with one hand and grabbed her hair with the other. I rolled us sideways and back down to the ground, shoving her head as hard as I could against the hard clay floor of the arena.

She released her ability. I got one inhale before she gained control again. That was enough. It had to be enough.

Before she could react, I hit her, once, twice, three times. My fist ached and my knuckles bled. A fourth time. Then a fifth. Six, seven, eight. Her eyes rolled back, but I didn't stop.

I was shaking with adrenaline. My fingers found what remained of her hair and yanked her head up. I threw it down again. Smashing her face against the dirt and rocks. She made a sound, a groaning cry. The air around me surged into existence and I gasped, certain it would disappear again.

Fire lit on my fingertips, crawled over my hands, my arms. Still, she wasn't dead.

I knew because dead people didn't scream the way she did.

I hit her again, breaking her nose, cracking teeth from her skull. The fire ate through her red hair, licked at her skin. It scorched her clothes.

I didn't think—I only burned. This was instinctual. Weeks of practice, weeks of letting my ability breathe on its own, letting it stretch—and all for this.

This moment.

I didn't move until she stopped screaming, and even then, I didn't move. I stayed there. Crouched on top of her, one fist buried in her hair, the other pressing on her neck. I wanted to take her air the way she'd taken mine. It annoyed me that she wasn't even trying to breathe anymore.

I felt wild, out of control.

Fight back. Try to suffocate me again. I dare you.

But she didn't, and she never would again.

31

The Arena

They had to wait until the smoke had cleared to publicly burn the body, and by then there couldn't have been much left to burn.

I don't know when, but at some point, I stood up and walked toward the gate. Guards had rushed to meet me and I'd been ushered inside the tunnel, past Tessa's trainers and into Juno's waiting arms.

He hugged me so tightly to his chest I didn't think he'd ever let me go. If I closed my eyes, I could almost pretend he was one of my brothers.

Other people were there, saying things to me, asking me questions, telling me congratulations. The crowd still cheered, making the concrete shell around us shake.

"It's fine," Juno said.

But nothing was fine.

"That's enough." One voice broke through the haze—Uri's. I didn't see her, but I felt the crowd around Juno and me disperse as she said, "Give her some room to breathe."

Tallis touched my shoulder, drawing my eyes to her. She was red-faced and flushed, her eyes shining. "I knew you'd win."

A shrill laugh bubbled out of me. "Did I?" This didn't feel like winning.

I swallowed hard as a new emotion hit—relief, guilt, I wasn't sure. With it came hot tears. They swept dust, smoke, and dirt from my eyes.

Juno's grip on my shoulders tightened. "I'm so proud of you."

Uri came to a stop in front of us. I felt her eyes move up the length of my body. "We should get you back to the palace. You need to rest and see a medic."

Tallis said, "She can't go yet. She has to stay until the body has been fully burned."

I chewed my lip and turned to look at the gate. The smoke was still thick, obscuring Tessa's body. For a split second, I started to panic again.

Maybe I hadn't killed her. What if the smoke cleared and she was still there, waiting? What if she was waiting to take the air away again?

Uri frowned. "No. I think we've seen enough burning for today. Monroe will leave with me." She called a guard to prepare a transport.

After that, she hooked her arm through mine. For a second, Juno seemed unsure if he should let me go. There was an emotion on his face, something akin to fear. I knew that he saw how fragile I was, and he wanted to protect me. But he didn't try to stop Uri from pulling me down the hall with her.

I looked over my shoulder to make sure my trainers were following me, and they were, but they hung back, putting space between us. They were talking, their voices sharp and hushed. Juno held Tallis's hand in his, the grip white-knuckled as he looked at her.

Uri tugged on my arm to get my attention and I winced, hissing through my teeth in pain.

I was covered in blood, some of my own, yes, but mostly Tessa's. My jaw felt bruised. My hair was unpinned and the short curls clung to my skin with sweat. My throat hurt as I tried to swallow and my lungs ached with each breath.

But I was alive.

I'd won.

Tallis and Juno elected to wait and ride in the advisor transport, even though Uri insisted they could go with us in her vehicle. I hadn't wanted them to leave, but words were difficult.

Juno hugged me one more time. "We'll come to your room as soon as things are done here. Please clean up and try to rest. Princess Uriel knows where the palace medic is. If you—"

"I'll take very good care of her. I promise," Uri said, already sitting in the transport waiting for me.

Tallis ran a soothing hand over my hair. "You did it."

I nodded.

Juno squeezed my shoulder and released me. "Get some rest."

I nodded again as I slid into the car beside Uri. When my hands were shaking so badly that I couldn't buckle myself in, Tallis helped me.

I wanted to tell her to stay.

I wanted—

I wanted my mother.

The realization of it—the craving to be held by someone who loved me so unconditionally—made my throat tighten. It had been over two months since I'd seen my mama. I wondered what she would think of me now. Would she be proud of what I'd just done?

What did Kace think?

Juno shut the car door and Uri leaned forward, tapping on the glass partition between the driver and the backseat. The man at the wheel signaled for the metal door of the parking garage to be pulled up and then we were moving.

"You're trembling." Uri leaned forward and touched my hand. "Can I get you some water or . . . ?" She trailed off.

I let my forehead rest against the glass of the car window. It was cool and clear, giving me a view of the city unlike any I'd had so far.

Up close, Gazda was lovely cobblestone paths and tall, brightly colored buildings. Nothing like back home.

Uri was turned in her seat, watching me. Her concern, while well-meaning, was overwhelming. I wanted to get out of the car and run. It felt like there was more I needed to do.

"Was Cohen there? Did he see?" I surprised myself with the questions.

Uri blinked at me, opened her mouth, and then closed it. I saw the answer all over her face. She didn't have to say it. I knew he hadn't been there.

It shouldn't hurt nearly as much as it did. I exhaled, trying to keep myself from slipping off that steep edge. Tears burned at my eyes. My throat constricted.

I'd just killed someone.

Uri broke through my thoughts. "We don't know if Britta made it to the border. We've heard nothing from her and it's been days. Mother . . ." She swallowed and continued. "We think the queen has been lying to us. Cohen found out late last night that there's no record of Britta's transport ever arriving. He's been communicating with the war offices and our contacts in Varos to see if anyone knows where she is. Mother swears she knew nothing about it but . . ." Uri sighed.

Everything felt so fragile, myself especially, and I didn't know what to do. The world was spiraling out of control.

"But people don't just disappear," I whispered.

Tears flooded her voice. "No, but they do die."

There was silence.

Uri cleared her throat and straightened, folding her hands in her lap, like it was an official court dismissal of her feelings. She was better at that than I was.

Cohen had called Uri and Britta his best friends. He'd described Britta as a mother figure—and this was what Uri had been afraid of. She'd said it was a bad idea for her sister to go.

Dread ate at my frazzled nerves and I fought for something to say, a way to smooth this over, to make things better. But I was covered in someone else's blood.

I'd killed someone.

"Cohen is looking for her," Uri said quietly.

It wasn't good enough. Even if I understood that he cared for his sister—that he wanted to organize searches for her and make sure she was safe—I couldn't justify his decision not to come to the arena. It would have taken only a few minutes. The trials themselves weren't long. And it might have been my last time to see him.

But Uri *had* been there for me and she was with me now. And she was still waiting on an answer, so I said, "I hope he finds her."

She nodded and turned to look out the window, so we could both pretend I didn't see the tear that streaked down her face.

She swiped it away. "I hope so too."

I pulled my knees up to my chest and buried my face in them. I reeked of smoke and something else, something new and rancid—burned hair, burned flesh. I wanted to scrape it off with my fingernails.

I was a murderer.

A monster.

Uri's hand found my knee, a silent comfort. We sat that way the whole ride back to the palace, both of us lost in thought and neither of us having the ability to say anything else.

Oredison Palace, Gazda
Sanctus Valencia

It was silent inside the palace. Everything about it was too pretty, too perfect, too clean compared to what I was now.

Uri explained that a lot of the staff had trial mornings off so that they could watch the broadcasts with their families. She took it upon herself to see me to my room and offered to send a medic up to check on me, but I asked her not to.

Juno could fix me up when he got back. He'd bandaged all of my training cuts and scrapes. And I needed time alone. I needed to breathe. I needed to cry and scream without someone watching.

"Do . . . Do you know where my brother is?"

Her brow furrowed. "Is your brother here?"

"Yes. He's a guard. He was just transferred."

"Then he's probably still at the arena. Everyone else will stay until . . ."

Until the body is completely burned.

I nodded, not wanting to hear her say it. "Okay."

She paused outside my door and folded her hands behind her back. "I'm glad you won."

"If I died, you'd be out of a job."

Uri frowned. "I'd be losing a friend."

I pushed my bedroom door open and turned to look at her. "Do you mean that?"

"Yes." She moved forward just one step, her arms outstretched like she wanted to hug me, but she stopped short and buried her hands in the folds of her dress instead. I wondered how many times Uri had been hugged in her life.

She would hesitate, just a breath, before moving to touch anyone. It was the uncertainty of someone who was used to being sent away. She expected to be rejected.

But Uri wanted to reach out. She just wasn't used to people reaching back for her.

And so, I did—I reached out and hugged her. She made a sound, almost like a half cry, half laugh sort of choking noise, and wrapped her arms around my shoulders. When we stepped away, Uri was smiling, her eyes red from too little sleep and restrained tears.

She sniffled. "Please rest. It'll be an hour or so before your trainers get back, so if you need anything, don't hesitate to send someone for me or come find me yourself. I'll be in my room."

I nodded and stepped back into my bedroom, holding on to the doorknob as I watched her head down the hall. Her footsteps had almost faded away when I thought of something—an idea, just the shimmering edges of a plot.

I darted out into the hall.

"Hey, Uri?"

She stopped and turned back to face me. "What is it?"

"Is Dellacov here or is he at the arena with the other girls?"

"He's at the arena. Why, do you need him for something?"

"No." I spoke a bit too quickly and shrugged to try to hide it. "I was just going to ask him if he could send for my brother, but . . . it can wait."

"Okay. But please let me know if there's anything I can get you. You know your way to my rooms."

"Thank you." I offered her a smile and stepped back into my room.

I leaned against the closed door and waited until the sound of her footsteps was gone. She'd said I had about an hour before everyone else got back to the palace. If I hurried, I could get into Dellacov's office and get some of the information the Culled had asked for. Even if the newest guard schedules weren't there, I felt certain that Dellacov was the sort that would file the old ones away. If I could see a few of those, there was a chance that a pattern might emerge.

I didn't know when I'd have an opportunity like this again.

Having a goal, something I needed to do and do quickly, was soothing. If I was moving, working, I didn't have to think about what I'd done.

Ambrose needed me. And if I could get the information, then maybe I could get out of here—maybe I wouldn't have to go into the arena again.

With this thought at the forefront of my mind, I was able to push the guilt and shame away. Those were things I could handle later. I needed to do this. Now.

My hands shook as I grabbed my training clothes from yesterday off the floor so I could put them on. I was halfway through shaking out the pants when I saw myself in the mirror and stopped.

I looked terrible.

My clothes had stayed mostly intact with only a few places charred away on the pants. But the undershirt was a mess of rags, held together by threads and the chain mail on top of it.

There was a bruise forming on one side of my jaw and a blossoming red ring around my throat from where Tessa had choked me. And of course, there was blood. Tons of it. In my hair, on my clothes, smearing across my cheeks and my arms.

I looked down at the training pants in my hand, one pant leg correct and the other inside out. If I didn't change clothes, I could use the trial as an excuse. I could say that I was delirious or pretend I was in pain. If I was caught, I could say I was wandering around searching for the medic.

Yes. That's what I'd do.

I kept telling myself that I was alive. I'd survived. It wasn't my body they were burning in the arena today.

These things, the truth of what I'd done and why I'd done it, did little to help ease my growing anxiety. If I paused—stopped moving for too long—I would feel the air slipping away. I would feel her hands on my throat. I would see the look in her eyes when I'd set her hair on fire.

I'd hear the way she had screamed—

The hallways were empty as I walked toward Dellacov's office. I didn't remember him using a key when he'd let me in there on my first day. I knew he hadn't locked the door when we'd left. With any luck, that would mean it was open for me.

I had to believe it would be.

My legs shook as I approached the office door. I hadn't been to this wing of the palace since I'd arrived in Gazda, but thanks to my walks with Cohen, I'd learned my way around. And just like on that first day, the hallway was entirely empty of guards and servants. Cohen had said Dellacov kept the door unlocked for Uri, so she had a place she could go to hide away. There was a chance that had changed when he'd been promoted, but Dellacov seemed to be a creature of habit.

Even though Uri had told me that he was at the arena, I still paused, my ear pressed to the tall wooden door, and listened for any movement within. I was about to cross over the threshold between treasonous thought and treasonous action. Like the necklace, like the letter to my brother, this was something I couldn't take back.

I closed my eyes, blocking the image of Tessa's broken and charred body, and twisted the doorknob. It opened, free from any locks. Just to be safe, I knocked lightly and waited. When no one answered, I pushed the door open and stepped inside, quickly shutting it behind myself.

The room was dark, the only light coming from the early morning sun as it streamed in through the lone window. I locked the door behind me and then I felt along the wall for a light switch. I ran my finger along the cool silver encasement and then turned the knob, illuminating the room with soft gas lighting. Fire flickered in the white sconces on the wall, the reliable tug of the flames oddly comforting.

Dellacov's office was small, neat, and clinically clean. The morning sunlight cast shadows along the stacks of books and piles of papers. A large map of Erydia hung on the right wall. It was covered in brass pushpins, some larger than others. He'd labeled some of them as different military bases and troops. I didn't know enough about the war to know what was important and what wasn't, so I just started copying everything I saw onto the paper I'd brought with me.

My version of the Erydian map was crude in comparison to the printed one that Dellacov owned, but I did my best. I wasn't sure if any of this would be helpful to Ambrose or the Culled, but I figured that if I was here, I should get whatever information I could. When I'd copied the map to the best of my ability, I moved on to the desk.

While Dellacov may not have locked his office, he was incredibly careful about how he placed and organized his things. Every pencil was perfectly spaced out, every form in perfect order, lined up exactly how he liked it and stacked seamlessly. One pencil was left crooked, and he would know that someone had been here—it was his own alarm system.

I didn't even touch his chair; I just leaned over the desk and started carefully thumbing through the paperwork he had. Most of it was guards' time-off request forms.

I dismissed all of that and moved on to the desk drawers. The first was filled with more pencils, pens, and pushpins. I closed it and went to open the second drawer but froze.

There was movement outside the office—loud, heavy footsteps.

Shit.

If I hid and it was Dellacov, then I would have no way of defending my reasoning for being there, but if it wasn't Dellacov—

Whoever it was twisted the doorknob.

In a split-second decision, I slid his chair back far enough for me to fit snugly beneath the desk. The doorknob rattled again. Whoever it was, they were trying to unlock the door. My vision blurred, tinged white and red. I twisted, trying to lean far enough forward that I could see the door through a small slit in the boards of the desk.

What would I say? How could I explain?

The person knocked. "Hugo?"

Cohen.

For a second, I relaxed. Then I remembered that the last thing I needed was for the prince to find me hiding underneath the Captain of the Guard's desk, snooping for military information. I covered my mouth with my hand and closed my eyes—like a child playing hide-and-go-seek.

Outside the door, Cohen sighed. Then footsteps again, this time heading away. I waited, too terrified to move, as he retreated down the hall.

When I was sure he was gone, I eased out from under the desk and stood. I put the chair back and quickly sorted through the last two drawers of the desk, doing my best to put everything back exactly how Dellacov had left it.

I hadn't seen anything about the patrol schedules.

There were two boxes in the corner of the room. I riffled through one, but it was mostly old personnel files and records. I was just about to discard the other two boxes when the corner of a picture caught my eye.

I thumbed through the folders in the box until I could pull the page free. It was a map of the palace with what appeared to be guard posts marked. I didn't even bother trying to draw it. The pictures were too complex and too small, with detailed sketches of each floor on the front and back of the paper. I stuffed it into my pocket.

I didn't have a watch, so I didn't know how much longer I had before I'd risk being caught. Cohen might come back with a key. I did a quick scan of the room, straightening anything I thought I might have unaligned. When I felt like things were back to normal, I started to leave.

It was then that I saw Cohen had slid papers under the door. I crouched and shuffled through them. He'd scrawled a note on the top of the stack:

I'm sorry they're late. Let me know if you hear anything about Britta.

I thumbed through the small bundle. It was the next month's worth of guard schedules. Seven full pages of detailed shift switches and patrol placements, all of them signed by Cohen himself.

I brought them over to Dellacov's desk and started copying the assignments down. It wasn't neat, but with some focus it was legible.

When I was finished, I stacked the pile exactly how Cohen had, put the clip and his note back in their places, and then dropped it on the floor just inside the door. With one more look to make sure I'd left everything untouched, I turned off the lights.

Once inside the safety of my bedroom, I locked the door and hid the papers in the drawer of the vanity. I inhaled a shaky breath and looked around the room, trying to get my bearings.

I needed to act like I'd been here all along. I had to bathe and get in bed. I started the water running in the tub and went to work undressing. The chain mail clasped together on one side with small metal clamps and I couldn't get it off. My hands were shaking too much, my fingers far too clumsy to manage the precise action needed.

I wanted to scream, to scrape myself out of that damned metal contraption. But I couldn't—I couldn't get out. My body wasn't working right anymore. And I was mad. Suddenly so mad my vision was red with it.

I struggled with the laces of my boots and finally just kicked them off. They bounced across the room and hit the white floorboard on the far wall, leaving an ugly black smudge. I couldn't seem to care.

My socks and pants came off easily enough, and I went back to the chain mail but still couldn't get my hands to stop trembling long enough to unlatch even one clip. I was sweating and the room felt like it was spinning. I couldn't get out of the stupid armor.

Air came quick and fast into my lungs, never full breaths. My heart was in my ears. My stomach was in my throat. My blood was everywhere and nowhere all at once. My body shook, from fear, from chill—I was cold but it was a hundred degrees.

Someone must have knocked on my door but I didn't hear it. It didn't matter. None of it mattered. Tessa was dead and I was a monster, a traitor. Cohen was going to lose everything, every last thing, because of me.

I found the floor or perhaps the floor found me—I didn't know.

I didn't care.

The bathing room tiles were cold against my naked legs and the rim of the toilet was a lifeline I hadn't even realized I needed. Underneath me, the floor rocked, swayed, bowed, like it was dancing to the haphazard beat of my heart. Like it had given up being a floor and now wanted to be a ship instead.

Boots appeared in the doorway to the bathing room, first one set, then two. Someone called my name.

I looked up to see Juno staring at me, his eyes wide, afraid—except I didn't think Juno was supposed to be afraid of anything, especially not me.

I think I might have laughed. Or maybe that was just me crying. I didn't know anymore. Nothing made sense.

Tallis pushed past him and kneeled in front of me. She was speaking, they both were, but I couldn't make sense of the words. Juno bent at the waist, just low enough to grab me underneath my arms and pull me up.

I was dead weight, unable to move. I wanted to help him, but I couldn't. I didn't know how to control my body anymore. And plus, the floor was moving too much for anyone to stand anyway. I didn't understand how he was managing it.

I tried to apologize to him, for the moving floor, for the fact that I was wearing just underwear and stupid chain mail, for the fact that I threw up on him. But no words came out.

Tallis helped him get me standing.

I was soaking wet and I couldn't remember how that had happened.

He held me tight against his chest, like a hug—a brotherly hug. *Yes*. This, this made sense. This was right. Nothing else in that moment felt right to me, only Juno's arms.

Tallis turned off the water faucet. The bathtub was overflowing.

Then Tallis was yelling, her voice so shrill it cut through even the ringing in my ears. Over the top of Juno's shoulder, I watched her leave the bathing room.

I said something to him, about how he ought to go and help her. *She needs help doing something, I don't know what, but she's screaming so loud. Goddess,*

Juno, can't you tell her to shut up? If he'd help, maybe she'd quit screeching. My heart was going to explode if she didn't.

Good goddess, make it stop.

"It's okay." Warm air tickled my neck as Juno said, "We're getting help. You're going to be okay. I've got you."

The floor rippled and shone against the cool light of the sun as it broke in through the high windows of the bathing room. Beautiful. So stupidly beautiful, I thought I might cry. Maybe I already was.

The floor isn't the floor anymore . . . it's a lake. It's— How can it have so many choices . . .

"You're going to be okay," Juno said against my hair. "I promise. Just stay with me."

Where else would I go? Juno was here and I was safe. I was already okay. But it wasn't worth trying to explain to him. So, I smiled and leaned my cheek against his chest, breathed him in.

I closed my eyes, and finally, the room stopped spinning, Tallis stopped screaming, and everything, all of it, was gone.

32

I woke up sweating and breathing heavily. It was dark and for a second, I couldn't remember when or where I was. I tried to sit up but a hand on my shoulder stopped me.

I turned and found Nadia curled up on the bed next to me. I blinked rapidly, sure I was imagining her—but no, she was really there.

I rolled to face her. "What the hell—?"

She pressed a finger to her lips to quiet me. "Don't try to sit up. Not yet."

I squinted through the darkness. I was in my bedroom, but things didn't look quite normal. There were new chairs scattered around. It was unnerving, seeing the silhouettes of figures but not being able to make out their features.

Slowly, like recalling a long-forgotten nightmare, I remembered the trial. Pieces of it, flashes of consciousness, as clarifying as they were disorienting, danced along the edges of my memory. There were other things too—a darkened office, a filling bathtub, blood on my hands.

So much blood and so little of it mine.

Nadia was watching me, her big brown eyes glowing in a shaft of moonlight. She was searching my face, and I wondered what she saw. I wondered if I looked as different as I felt. Could she feel the weight of my guilt as precisely as I did?

Her hand was still on my arm, but her usual healing warmth was gone as she asked, "How do you feel?"

Words were hard. They were a maze of articulation that I just wasn't capable of. I stuttered and fought with my own tongue, trying to get my speech and my mind under control.

I'd killed someone.

I inhaled, exhaled. "What happened?"

"Well, I'm not a doctor, but from what I can tell a lot of things happened all at once." Her hand on my arm tightened its hold. "Have you been eating?"

I bit my lip. "Not . . . Not in the last few days."

Nadia opened her mouth to scold. I could see it written all over her features—the frustrated way her mouth pulled down on one side and the way her head tilted. But I cut her off before she could start.

"The food could have been poisoned."

She shushed me. "Keep your voice down or you'll wake everyone up."

"Everyone?"

She pointed to the foot of my bed where two new chairs sat. People slept in them, their bodies positioned in uncomfortable-looking positions. "Your advisors are there and," she leaned up and pointed to a spot behind me, "Cohen is there."

"Cohen?" I blurted.

Nadia hissed and I covered my mouth, as if that would bring the word back. I rolled over and there he was, drooping in his own chair, fast asleep. Blond hair stuck up at odd angles.

He looked like a child when he slept. Unconsciousness softened his features and turned him young and innocent. He was less of a prince just then, more like the boy he was when he looked at me. Something in my heart gave a contented squeeze at the sight of him, but I didn't dwell on it.

"Why is he here?" I was almost too afraid to ask it.

"Cohen met us at the palace entry after the trial. I think he thought you would be there too. Dellacov had just told him that you'd won when Tallis came running in yelling about needing a medic." She sighed. "Everyone started freaking out, and Cohen took off after her. They came here, and I just sort of followed them."

"Why? Did they ask you to come?"

Nadia shook her head. "I just went with them. I'm not exactly a medic, but I figured I could help." She smiled. "And friends don't let other friends die half naked in their bathing room."

"Thanks for that."

"Happy to help. And to answer your question, I think it was the perfect storm. You were malnourished, you had breathed in a lot of smoke, and you were in shock. All of those things kind of worsened the effects of each other."

"But I felt fine during the fight and even afterward."

She shrugged. "Adrenaline, maybe? I'm just a healer. I don't diagnose; I just fix a problem when I feel one."

I had to force my tone to stay neutral, unafraid, as I said, "But it wasn't poison?"

Nadia bit her lip. "I don't know. Whatever it was, it's gone now."

"Because you fixed me."

It wasn't a question as much as it was a reminder. I was here, alive—and Tessa was dead. I'd done that.

Nadia broke through my thoughts. "You'll probably be sore and some of the bruises are going to come through still, but internally I think you're good to go. Do you not remember any of this?"

I shook my head.

That was the scariest part. I couldn't remember. I knew I'd won the trial. I knew I'd come back here. I knew, just vaguely, that I'd gone to Dellacov's office.

Memories started to fizzle out at that point. Had I made it back to my room? Had Dellacov caught me?

"You were conscious initially, but delirious and rambling. I healed you and you ate some food, then you slept. Everyone just kind of decided to stay in case you woke up and needed anything."

"How long was I out?"

"Hours. From about eight or so yesterday morning until now. So maybe fifteen or sixteen hours. You woke up a couple times in between. Then I would try to heal you a bit more and that usually knocked you back out. It drains you . . . I think. It's like your body did a week's worth of healing in a matter of hours. You crashed afterward."

"Has my brother been here?"

She nodded. "I met him earlier. His name is Kace, right?"

"That's him."

"He's been checking on you every once in a while. I think Captain Dellacov has all the guards working overtime."

"That sounds like Dellacov."

"I'm sure he'll check on you again whenever he gets a chance. He was really worried, but I told him that I thought you'd be okay."

"Thank you. For everything you did."

She lowered her hand and shrugged. "Don't mention it. I'm glad I could come to your rescue. It's nice to feel like my ability is useful."

"It is useful."

She was quiet for a long time, and when she spoke again, her voice was so soft I almost couldn't hear it. "As soon as I'm chosen, I'm dead. I won't last ten seconds in the arena."

"Nadia—"

"Not against any of the people who are left. Heidi tortures people with her mind, Kinsley kills people with plants, and you . . ." She pressed her lips together and shook her head. "I'm an easy target."

"I would never kill you."

And I meant it.

She swallowed and rubbed at her eyes, trying to hide the way they watered. "But you will. And if you don't then one of the other girls will. We aren't here to make friends."

"Do you want to be queen?"

She shook her head.

"Me either."

"But, Monroe," she said, seriously, "you can't let Kinsley become queen. We can't have another thirty years of Viera or anyone like her. And her father is terrible. It'd be like having him as king. We need a queen who can fix things and make them better."

"It isn't up to me."

She sighed and wrapped her arms around herself. "I've thought a lot about this. I'll probably go against Heidi. She'll kill me easily—"

"Don't do that. Don't sell yourself short."

"I'm selling myself for exactly what I'm worth—and that's *nothing*. I can't protect myself with my ability, and my hand-to-hand combat isn't good enough to keep me in the game. My trainers barely even work with me anymore. They've just resigned themselves to it."

"It doesn't mean you have to."

"Easy for you to say." She looked around the room, at my friends sleeping just feet away. "They know you have a shot at being queen. Cohen knows it too, otherwise he wouldn't be here."

"I won't kill you, Nadia."

"Someone will. I'll die, and you'll live and be queen."

Silence reigned; a sovereign made of shadows on a cold stone throne. Together we waited, listened. The only sound was our ragged breathing and the distant patter of footsteps in the hallway.

I met Nadia's eyes. "Agree to disagree."

Her brows furrowed. "Agree to disagree. Now, get some sleep."

I peered through the gloom at Cohen's sleeping form. I'd seen this before, once three years ago. I'd been afraid of that soldier for so long. I'd believed he was a threat to me.

Now here he was, sleeping next to my sickbed like a lost puppy. If only he'd just been a soldier, and I'd just been a regular unmarked girl.

Behind me, Nadia's breathing evened as she drifted into what I hoped was a peaceful sleep. She deserved as much. The room grew quiet, filled with only the breathing and soft snores of the people closest to me—the only friends I'd ever had.

This was a moment I wanted to hold on to, to grip in my fists and press against my heart, letting it warm me for days. These people were here for me, to love and support a killer. A murderer. Their friendship was more than I could have ever asked for and far more than I felt I deserved.

Cohen, Juno, and Nadia were all gone when I woke up. Only Tallis remained, still asleep in her chair at the foot of my bed. And while I didn't want to wake her, I was tired of lying still. I shifted in bed, using my elbows to slowly prop myself up. For a second, the room swayed and my head swam.

Tallis stirred in her seat, but didn't wake as I inched past her chair and went into the bathing room, shutting the door behind me to muffle any noise. The room was a mess of wet towels. They spread across the tiles, soaking up the water from where I'd overfilled the tub.

I was dressed in one of the nightgowns from the closet. It was light-blue pastel with white ribbon designs and a hem that fell a good deal above my knees. I started to pull it off slowly, easing it along the skin of my thighs, taking in the varying shades of blood red and rich purple that covered my flesh like paint splatters.

The colors bled together in places, creating a blue so dark it appeared black. I had new marks now, different from the one on my hand. I'd earned these. Tessa had earned these.

My stomach was clear from visible marks, proving that the chain mail had done its job. Even so, my abdominal muscles groaned with every slight movement. My left side hurt if I breathed too deeply and upon prodding, I decided that it was probably a rib, tender from being hit.

Up the nightgown slid, over my chest, to my collarbone covered in fingernail scratches, healed by Nadia to faint pink lines. The bruises on my jaw and my cheek were faded yellow from her touch, while my neck was a circle of black-blue marks. Those bruises were in the shape of someone's hands.

Tessa's hands.

My stomach churned and I dropped the nightgown back into place.

"You okay in there?" Tallis called.

I cracked the door, but she pushed it open the rest of the way and threw her arms around my shoulders, holding me in a tight embrace. I hugged her back even though the feel of her arms around me was stifling.

"You scared the shit out of me last night." She held me at arm's length. "Don't you ever, *ever*, do anything like that again, you hear me? You could have hit your head or drowned yourself in this stupid bathing room. You should've screamed for help."

I wanted to tell her that I didn't remember what had happened. I hadn't known I was going to pass out or that I was spiraling toward any sort of collapse. But there wasn't any real reason to argue with her, so I just said, "I'm sorry I scared you."

She pursed her lips. "How do you feel now?"

"Tired."

"You should go back to bed."

I shook my head. "I've already slept for hours."

"And your body could use a few more."

I ignored her and walked out of the bathing room. "I have something to give to you."

"Oh?"

I opened the vanity drawer. While I could remember bits and pieces of being in Dellacov's office, a small part of me worried that I'd imagined it all. Everything felt like a dream. Hazy and too bright. Too colorful to be real.

Every muscle in my body relaxed as my hand found the folded papers. I took them out and shuffled through them. It was all still there.

I handed it over to Tallis.

She carefully unfolded the first paper, my drawing of the map and the plotted bases. Her mouth fell open as she realized what it was. "How did you get this?"

"I went to Dellacov's office yesterday while everyone was still at the arena. I copied the map and swiped the palace diagram from a box in his office. I've also got the next month's worth of guard assignments."

Her mouth fell open. "The next month's worth?"

I nodded.

"You could have been seen. Hell, Monroe. What if you'd passed out in his office?"

"I wasn't seen, and I didn't pass out," I said. "It was the perfect time to get in without anyone noticing. The Culled wanted me to get the information and I did. Now . . . Now I need you to get it to them so they act. I don't want anyone else to die in the Culling."

Her focus was on the diagram of the palace. "Will he notice this is missing?"

"I don't think so. At least not right away. It was packed away in a box with a lot of other things."

She spread the picture out on the vanity and ran her finger over the intricate details of each floor. At the top left of the page, there was a sort of key written out listing the main rooms and giving them symbols.

"It says there are emergency exits under the palace, near the training rooms . . ." She whistled. "Wow. They must be well hidden; I've been looking for weeks." She smiled up at me. "Well done, Monroe. That might be our in. I was expecting a guard schedule or something. But this . . . this is great. Truly." Tallis folded the page and tucked it into the front of her shirt.

"When will you tell the rebels?"

She gathered the other pages and a set of blank stationary from my vanity. I could already see her calculating things in her mind as she was stuffing them into her pockets. "I'll write to them tonight, as soon as I know for certain about the tunnels. If they don't work, we'll need another plan." She was distracted, already planning her next move. I followed her to the door.

"Tallis?" She didn't turn around. "Tallis?" I said again, this time catching her arm in my hand. She stopped and faced me. "How long until they strike?"

"Messages travel fast. And we have troops hidden within the city as we speak. Our first objective will be to kill the queen. I don't think we'll try to gain full control of Gazda this soon, we just want to stop the Culling and get Viera off the throne."

"But when?"

Her expression grew serious. "I would be ready to move out in the next week. If we have an in, we won't hesitate. Our forces are ready and so are the people of Erydia." She smirked. "May the goddess be honored."

33

Palace Bedroom

Two days after Sanctus Valencia

Cohen brought dinner to my room Wednesday evening. It was the first time I'd seen him since I'd woken up to find him asleep at my bedside. It was also the first time I'd seen him since I'd officially become a traitor—and a murderer.

His smile was hesitant as he said, "I thought maybe we could talk?"

I forced a smile and stepped back to let him inside.

He set the tray on my unmade bed. "I brought soup and sandwiches. Nothing too creative. But I made it myself, if that counts for anything."

I eased onto the edge of the bed, trying not to slosh the soup. "I thought you only made omelets."

He grinned. "You thought wrong."

I patted the empty spot on the other side of the mattress and Cohen sat. For a long moment, we were both quiet. He looked at me, those blue eyes so intense they sent a shiver down my spine. This was a different look than Cohen usually gave me. It was questioning, worried.

I chewed my lip. "What is it? What's wrong?"

"I thought you were dead. And then when I found out you weren't, I thought you were going to die. No one knew what was wrong with you."

I forced a smile. "But I'm fine now."

"We have Nadia to thank for that."

I nodded.

"I didn't realize that the two of you were friends, but she stayed all of

Monday night with you. And by the time the palace medics arrived, she'd pretty much settled you down."

"I don't remember it—any of it."

"It was scary. You were out of it."

"Nadia said that it was smoke inhalation and malnutrition."

He nodded. "I spoke to her about it yesterday. She said you hadn't been eating."

"I was afraid there would be poison in the food."

"There *is* poison in the food. I can almost guarantee it."

"And you aren't afraid of that?"

Cohen sighed. "I'm used to the fear of it. But the fear of losing you, twice in one day . . . that was new."

I turned back to the food, suddenly uneasy with the intensity in his gaze. "Uri's been like a jailer, coming by and sitting with me while I eat." I smiled. "She's determined to make sure I'm actually eating. Did she tell you that she's thinking of cutting her hair short? She says it'd be in solidarity with me and in celebration of my win—which are goddess-awful reasons to cut your hair but you know how she can b—"

"When I went to meet the transports, Dellacov told me that you should already be in your room. But I stopped here first, before I even went down there, and you weren't here."

The urge to move was all-encompassing. I wanted to touch my hair, rotate my wrists, look away from him. But I forced myself to shrug as I said, "Maybe I was in the bathing room and didn't hear you knock."

He was quiet for a second. "Maybe."

I grabbed one of the bowls of soup and stirred it, watching the golden broth swirl around the edges of the glass bowl.

Those blue eyes were still examining me, scanning the fading bruises on my body, the tiny cuts on my knuckles, the way my hair still dripped from my bath.

I lifted my chin, determined not to let his presence rattle me. "I was surprised when Larkin started the trial and not you."

"I'm sorry about that."

I set the bowl of soup back down. "Uri told me that Britta's missing. Have you been able to learn anything?"

"No, she's just—she's just disappeared."

He looked so tired, weary from pressures I couldn't begin to grasp. Somehow, I'd managed to add myself to his list of worries. He'd slept in my room in case I woke up and needed anything. Him—a prince—taking care of me—a traitor.

He cut through my thoughts. "But I'm sorry. I'd planned to be there. I watched the broadcast of it, but there was a lot of smoke, and the technology isn't very good in the best of conditions. Even at the end the announcers weren't sure who'd won. Initially, they declared Tessa the victor. Then . . . then they said it was you. That you'd won. I've never been more relieved to see someone else dead."

"She took all the air away." I paused, trying to remind myself that I could breathe, that there was oxygen in my lungs and that I wasn't back in the arena. It was hard to look at Cohen as I said, "It wasn't just that she was strangling me with her hands; there wasn't any air at all. Nothing."

"But you won. You survived."

"I won," I whispered.

Cohen reached for his bowl of soup and for a few minutes we ate in relative silence. It was never uncomfortable with him. Relationships like this were probably rare for Cohen; he was expected to have something intelligent to say at all times. But not with me. I expected nothing—wanted nothing.

At least nothing that he or his crown could give me.

A question was nagging at the back of my mind, something that had been bugging me for over two weeks. "Hey, Cohen?"

He hummed in response.

"The ring that your mother wears. She always makes you kiss it. And Grier and Heidi kissed it too, then Grier died. Is— Does the ring—"

"It's infused with poison," Cohen explained. "It's one of my mother's favorite games."

"Then why do you kiss it? Why give her the opportunity to hurt you—"

"She doesn't need a stupid ring to hurt me. It's just a symbol. The danger is everywhere else." He gestured around us. "The wallpaper in the dining room is made with arsenic. The plants in the garden are all toxic. And like I said, our food is almost always laced with something. That stupid ring is just one more way for her to publicly put me in my place."

"Cohen, what . . . what if she doesn't step down? What if she refuses to give up the crown? She could let the Culling play out and then kill the last girl standing."

"By law, she has to—"

"She doesn't play by the rules and you know it. You've said it yourself." My voice was sharp, raised, but not quite yelling. I had to take a second and calm down, remind myself that even though Cohen was my friend, he was still a prince. And I was speaking treason—loud enough for the guards outside to hear. "I'm sorry."

He pursed his lips and turned away from me, his eyes heavy with an emotion I couldn't name. Regret ate at my bones and I forced myself to stay silent, even though I wanted to continue to push him. I wanted him to understand, even if I couldn't explain it to him, that I was justified. When the ashes cleared and my treason was revealed, I needed him to understand why I'd done it all.

I wanted him to be on my side.

Cohen whispered, "What is it you want me to do, Monroe?"

I bit my lip, annoyed to find myself lingering on the edge of tears. "I don't know. I don't know what I want."

He sighed and smiled, a crooked, half-hearted smile. "We're so close. Another month or so and this'll be over. Then I'll be king. I've got to wait it out."

I nodded, not because I agreed with him, but because I didn't know what else to do. Cohen wouldn't be king. He wouldn't get the opportunity to try to make the changes he wanted to make. The Culled was going to kill his mother and take his crown.

I just didn't want him to get harmed in the process.

I saw him gauge the distance between us on the bed. Over a week had passed since our last kiss and so much had changed—I'd changed. I'd killed someone. I'd agreed to be a rebel. I'd begun to give up on the dream of him.

I shifted, folding my legs and turning sideways, adding to the distance between the prince and me. I slid forward toward the tray like I was grabbing a sandwich. I just needed to break the moment, before we did something we might later regret.

Before Cohen did something he would later regret.

He frowned and turned away from me. His ears flushed a deep shade of red, proof that I hadn't been as sly as I'd hoped. He knew that was a rejection.

I'm doing it for him, I told myself. *I'm trying to protect him*. I didn't want to break his heart any more than I already had. We were friends, yes, but it would be worse if I let him think we were anything more than that—if I let myself believe that we were anything more than that.

We finished eating in silence.

My mind was a web of tangled desires.

It would be so easy to tell Cohen what I was planning. Maybe he would understand. Was it possible that Cohen could hate his mother enough to want her dead? I didn't know. Certainly, he had enough reason to want that.

He'd run away once. Maybe he would run away again. But how could I even bring up that possibility without incriminating myself?

Cohen turned to look out one of the windows, over the Gazda skyline. This was his homeland, where he'd been raised. It was bright and colorful, with comfortable temperatures and days that were sunny more often than not. His world wasn't like mine. As much as I wanted him to understand how I felt, I knew that even with his mother poisoning him, he couldn't understand. We weren't the same.

After a long second, he turned to look at me. Sometimes, his eyes could be so intense they were unnerving. In moments like that, I could see fragments of his mother in him.

Just then, Cohen looked like her.

It was the ocean-blue eyes, the slight tilt of his chin. I didn't know what Cohen was trying to see in me, or if he ever did see it, but I hated how easily I saw Viera in him. But then he smiled, the gesture wide and unnervingly honest. It banished that flash of the queen and replaced it with the boy I lov—

With Cohen.

I stood up and walked to the door, setting the tray down on the dresser. I couldn't look at him, couldn't think past the hammering of my heart. Wicked. I shouldn't care for him. What was worse, I was letting him care about me.

Cohen pushed up from the bed and crossed to where I stood. Each movement was careful, prepared for me to tell him to stop. His fingers brushed up my arms, from my wrist to the crease in my elbow and back.

I swallowed and caught his hands in mine. Cohen's fingers and palms were callused, rough from training and exercise. They were different hands than I'd expected a prince to have, and I was always surprised by them.

He looked down at our interlocked fingers. This was so easy, so natural. And even though I shouldn't have, I wanted it. I wanted him. But it wasn't fair to want a prince while trying to ruin his kingdom.

I was wicked.

A wicked and terrible liar.

Cohen's breathing was shallow, every movement so careful, so slow. To him, I was a skittish animal, easily frightened away. He was testing my boundaries, afraid I would turn him away. And I should.

But I wanted to feel like the girl I'd been before I'd killed Tessa.

One of us moved, maybe it was me or maybe it was him—it didn't matter. The next thing I knew, I was kissing him. It was tentative, and unlike our other kisses it remained that way. Each breath, each brush of our lips so painfully fragile.

It ended too soon, neither of us willing to push the other into doing more, giving more. I buried my face in his chest, and he rested his chin against the top of my head.

Cohen sighed.

I waited for one of us to speak, for the moment to shatter the way moments like this always did, but it didn't break. It just remained, simmered. Constant.

He pulled back slightly, shifting so he could see me there, curled into him. His lips brushed my forehead, so soft and unassuming. A question.

But I didn't have the answer.

34

The Training Rooms

Three days after Sanctus Valencia

Tallis wasn't at training Wednesday or Thursday. Juno said she wasn't feeling well, and that he hadn't really seen her either. The male and female trainers stayed in separate wings of the barracks, so he was working from what someone else had told him.

"I asked one of the guards if they'd check on her, and I was told that she was resting." He reached forward and adjusted my starting stance for hand-to-hand combat, moving one of my arms up a little higher.

His expression flickered into concern for just the briefest of moments before he struck out, swinging a fist in my direction. I ducked, despite the fact that I hadn't realized we were starting. I dropped low, blocked his second hit with my forearm, and then shifted to the left sharply, catching him in the gut with my knee.

"Good," he muttered. "That was a good reaction time."

We were both sweating after a two-hour practice and I was beginning to lose focus. "How much longer?"

"Getting lazy?"

"Just getting tired," I said. "You made me run three miles before we got started on anything else. I'm exhausted."

Liar. I was such a damn liar. And Juno knew it too.

The truth was that I was emotionally tired. Drained. I'd struggled to focus on his words as he'd gone over what had happened in my trial. While I think he was trying to be helpful, what I'd done to Tessa was difficult for me to think about, even harder to talk about.

I wasn't eager to relive the arena, although I had imagined it numerous times over the last few days. I dreamed of it constantly. Found that I couldn't dip my head underwater during baths anymore. I couldn't handle any sensation that made me feel like I couldn't breathe.

But Juno hadn't understood that. Tallis was usually the one who picked up on my emotional cues; without her there, it was like we were on opposite continents.

He talked about what had happened to me with such ease. To him, my trial had gone well, and I'd shown everyone that I was capable and well trained—something he was very proud to have a hand in.

But I hadn't slept soundly in days. To tell Juno how weak I was, how fragile I felt, was embarrassing. I didn't want to disappoint him, so I'd just kept quiet about how broken I felt. And I did feel broken.

In whatever words I could muster, I'd explained what I'd done in the arena. We'd practiced a few maneuvers, going over different ways I could handle similar situations.

I'd wanted to tell him that no maneuver in the world would get me out of that hold—not what Tessa had been doing to me. That was different. It had nothing to do with the placement of her hands. But I couldn't even get the words to form. I couldn't make myself talk about it.

The memory of a dead girl's hands on my throat, her fingers leeching my body of oxygen, was driving me crazy. I might have won, but I didn't feel triumphant. It didn't matter how many laps I ran, how many push-ups I did or targets I burned—I couldn't escape this.

Juno offered to walk me back to my room after training but I declined. I'd started tearing up toward the end of our session and that had set off some of his brotherly instincts. He ordered me to drink a glass of water and bathe, then bed. We wouldn't train tomorrow; instead he wanted me to spend the day resting as much as I could.

I told him that I would and let him give me an awkward hug before he sent me off toward my rooms. I could feel the weight of his stare as I walked to the lift. The look wasn't just pitying; it was also nervous.

Everyone was watching me. They were all so afraid I would freak out again. But I wasn't going to. I was fine. And treating me like I was fragile had never been Juno's way of doing things, so I didn't appreciate him starting now.

I wanted him to push me. I wanted him to tell me to suck it up and fight back.

I needed someone to tell me that I was alive. That I'd survived. That I'd *won*.

I'd just stepped out of the lift and onto my hall when I saw Cohen standing at the opposite end. It seemed as if he'd been heading toward my door, but he paused when he saw me.

He was dressed in a navy suit, gray vest, and dark-black tie. His blond hair was combed back the way it had been the first day I'd met him. Looking at him then, the afternoon sunshine casting long shadows against his face, he was incredibly handsome—incredibly royal.

He looked like a grown man, different and yet familiar.

Just last night, he'd kissed me. His arms had felt like home, the closest thing to safety that I'd felt in weeks. My chest ached at the memory of it and I hurried toward him.

I smiled, expecting him to smile back, but he didn't.

That mask, the one he wore so well, changed. There was a look on his face I didn't recognize and it made me hesitate. His mouth was pressed together in a thin line and his eyes were hard, staring straight ahead, almost looking through me.

But it was his posture that was the most unnerving.

He'd relaxed into a stance I knew far too well; it was the same way his mother stood. Feet shoulder-width apart, shoulders back, hands clasped behind his back, chin up. Those blue eyes straight ahead. All he was missing was the crown.

This wasn't the Cohen I'd grown used to—this was Prince Cohen, and he might as well have been an entirely different person. Something was wrong.

I thought Cohen might meet me halfway, but he didn't. He stayed where he was. Tension pulled tight in my gut and I quickened my steps, stopping only a few feet from him.

His jaw was clenched so tight it trembled. He looked like he might cry, like maybe he'd already been crying. Good goddess, it was Britta.

I reached out to him. "Cohen, what is it? What's happened?"

"Please don't come any closer."

I stopped and let my hand fall back to my side. The tone of his voice matched his posture: stiff and commanding. I took a step back and looked behind me. I half expected to see his mother or another goddess-touched girl standing there. But no one was there to see him—to see us.

So why was he pretending like we weren't—

Around the corner from where Cohen stood, there was movement, the shuffle of feet. He held out a hand, a silent command for the person to stay put. My mouth tasted of metal and ash.

I barely heard myself ask, "Who's there?"

When no one answered me, I took another step away. Cohen didn't even glance in their direction. He was still looking at me, those dark cold eyes catching me by surprise.

I swallowed against the tightness in my throat. "Cohen, what's going on?"

Slowly, he reached into the pocket of his coat and pulled out a rectangular brown piece of paper. He held it between two fingers and twisted it, so I could see the black wax seal, broken, on the envelope.

For a split second, I didn't understand. And then the realization struck me. When Tallis had taken my stationary from the desk, she had also taken the black wax. The wax Cohen had given me so I could write letters.

I've told the maids that anything marked with black wax should come to me.

I hadn't even thought about that since he'd given it to me, and I definitely hadn't thought to stop Tallis from taking the stationary and using it.

His voice was soft, a threat, as he said, "Why don't you explain this to me."

I took a step forward. "I don't know what that letter says. I didn't . . ." I swallowed, searching for the exact right lie to tell. The black wax was incriminating only if the contents of the letter held treasonous things—but even then, I could just lie and say that the wax and paper went missing. Any maid who had come into my room might have taken and used it. Whatever this was, it didn't have to point to me.

"I didn't write any letters."

He nodded slowly. "Your advisor was taken into custody yesterday morning. She was suspected of communicating with the rebellion. Dellacov— We had reason to believe she was a spy."

"Tallis isn't a spy."

"Why are you lying to me?" His throat bobbed. "Why *have you* been lying to me?"

"Cohen—"

"You're mentioned in this." He twisted the envelope so I could see it. "I knew your brother was a traitor. I was told as much. But you— She says in this letter that the information you found has already been delivered. She said— Monroe, she called you 'their goddess-touched spy.'"

Frightened tears stung at my eyes but I fought past them. "There are other goddess-touched girls, why would I—?"

"Am I supposed to believe that your brother is a rebel, your advisor is a spy, and you . . . you had no knowledge of any of it?"

"I— Cohen— It isn't— I didn't—"

"You have done nothing but speak treason this whole time. And I-I trusted you. I told you things that I haven't said to anyone else. I thought you were— Goddess, Monroe. How long have you been sending information to the Culled? How long have you been using me as a way to gain information?"

"Cohen, I never meant to hurt—"

He cut me off, his voice so loud it made me jump. "Just answer the damn question, Monroe."

I said nothing. What could I possibly say?

"This whole time?"

I could hear all the unspoken questions, all the things he didn't ask: *Were you a traitor when I met you? When we kissed? When I told you about running away? When I told you I wanted you to be my queen?*

I shook my head. "No. Not the whole time."

"Was it all a lie then?" His voice was so soft, like he was afraid to ask the question, but needed to know. "Were you using me the whole time? Just for information? Was it all just a game to you?"

"You have never been a game to me, Cohen." My chest ached. "I care about you."

His throat bobbed and, for an instant, my Cohen was back. But with a shake of his head, he was a prince again. "No, you don't. You don't give a damn about me."

"But I do," I whispered. "That's the worst part."

"The *worst part* is that you lied to me." He closed his eyes, inhaled. "The *worst part* is that I believed you. I trusted you. For some stupid reason, I thought you were different, that you didn't have an agenda. And all this time—" His voice cracked and his eyes darted to the envelope. "All this time, you've been planning to use my trust to—" He didn't finish—he couldn't.

If he kept talking, he might not be able to continue acting as regal as he was. He might have to show emotion. And he was done giving me that—I was back to closed-off Cohen. I was back to glimpses of his feelings. And I'd earned it.

I bit my lip, trying to use the pain to keep myself from crying. "I'm so sorry."

His fist clenched around the envelope. "I thought . . ." He trailed off, shook his head. "It doesn't matter what I thought." He waved Dellacov and two guards forward from around the corner.

I stepped back from him. "Cohen—"

He held up a hand to silence me. "Monroe Benson, you are under arrest for high treason, a crime punishable by death. The queen will be made aware of your transgression and she will have the final say as to what becomes of you."

35

The Cells

Three days after Sanctus Valencia

In that moment, as the locks clicked and I was left alone in the cell, I went from being a person to being a caged animal. I could feel the eyes on me, even if I couldn't see them. The wall that held the door had a rectangular window with glass that was clear in the hall, but solid from inside my cell. I couldn't see out, but I could be seen. Before he'd left, Dellacov had removed the handcuffs. There wasn't anything for me to break or burn; the cell was cold stone and the only furniture in the room—a table and two chairs—was made of metal.

He'd left without saying anything to me. I didn't know when he would be back or how long it would take for Viera to decide to kill me. All I knew was that I had to do something, I had to get out.

Tallis had given me away. Maybe not intentionally, but she'd said enough to allow Cohen and Dellacov to fill in the rest. And I wanted to be mad at her for it, but I found that I couldn't be. I'd done this. I'd agreed to help the Culled. It had ultimately been my choice. When it came down to it, I'd sought Tallis out again that second time. I'd asked her how I could help.

And while I hated breaking Cohen's heart, I didn't regret doing the things I'd done. Somewhere along the way, my desire to survive had been surpassed by my desire to make a change. Helping the Culled wasn't just about trying to escape the Culling. I'd wanted to stop Viera's rampage; I'd wanted to see her dethroned. I wanted to be a part of the solution, because the more I looked the more problems I saw.

I curled into one of the corners of the room, just below the window and partially out of sight of anyone standing in the hall. The temptation to burst into tears was strong, but I found that the emotion behind that desire was born of anger more than fear. Viera was the one deciding my fate, and I had no doubt what she'd choose to do with me. It's what she wanted to do to all of us, her own son most of all.

The sound of a lock clicking broke the silence of the cell and I froze, my eyes darting for somewhere to hide. I hadn't expected my sentence to be carried out so soon. I thought of how quickly Aviana and Grier had died—there'd been no way to fight it. No real struggle.

I slid up the wall until I was standing and held up my hands, prepared to attack. I rocked on the balls of my feet, trying to ease my racing heart. If I could strike first and catch her off guard, maybe she wouldn't have time to poison me. I could—

The door opened and the prince stepped inside.

I expected guards, Dellacov at the very least, but he was alone. Cohen closed the door behind him and whoever was outside locked us both in the cell. Even though we were alone in the room, I wondered how big our audience was.

He didn't look in my direction right away. Instead, he just shoved his hands in his pockets and sighed. That slight hint at his real feelings was on display for just the briefest of moments, then that blue gaze darted sideways, to where I stood in the corner, waiting to defend myself.

He looked at me for what felt like eons. Just ran his eyes up and down my body, like he was searching for the evidence of my treason, for whatever clues he had missed over the last few weeks.

When I didn't speak, Cohen stepped forward and pulled one of the chairs out from the table. Without looking at me he said, "Sit."

I watched as he sank into the seat opposite the one that he'd pulled out for me. Rough fingertips grazed the tabletop. Those same fingers had grazed my face, my arms, my shoulders. My lips. They'd run through my hair last night.

"I won't ask again, Monroe. Sit down. If you can't manage it on your own, I'll have a guard come in and assist you."

I sat.

It felt like an eternity passed before he said, "Who else in the palace is helping you?"

"No one—"

"Tallis, clearly. But the two of you aren't doing this alone." He sounded tired, as if all of this had aged him.

"There isn't anyone else."

Cohen propped an elbow on the table and lowered his head into his hand, pinching the bridge of his nose as he said, "Her letter was meant for someone else in the palace. It was only delivered to me by accident. When she was apprehended yesterday, a guard searched her room. A maid saw the black wax and assumed the letter was for me. When I saw it on my desk a few hours ago I thought . . . I thought it had come from you. But . . . But I was wrong."

"There isn't anyone else," I repeated. "Just Tallis and me."

"And the Culled."

"Cohen—"

"Ambrose Benson is a deserter," he said. "But you already knew that, didn't you?"

"I don't know where Ambrose is."

"Kace identified him in Pallae. We had some grainy security footage, but it was good enough for what we needed. Kace didn't seem surprised at all to see him there, on film, helping to steal weapons from defenseless factory workers. When I met with your brother about it a few days ago, he told me that he was sorry. He told me that he was ashamed of his brother's behavior and couldn't condone his choices. Kace assured me that you and your mother were as loyal to the Crown as he is. Is he in on your betrayal?"

"Kace knows nothing about this."

Cohen sat back in his chair. "No. No, I didn't think that he did. Kace isn't a traitor. He proved that months ago."

The air left my lungs. "He— Months ago?"

"He should have let you run. Goddess, you're a curse. You're a curse and he should have let you go. I wish he would have let you go."

I felt something in my chest crack. No. *No.* What Cohen was implying, what he was saying, it wasn't true. It couldn't be true. There was no way that Kace would have done that. He may have disagreed with my choice to run from the Culling but he wouldn't have told someone that—

"*He*, at least, is loyal. Even if that loyalty to the Crown led to this. To you. Goddess, Monroe. Was that your plan all along? Did you plan to get caught? Did you plan to go across to Vayelle and join their rebellion? Were you already a part of it? When did this start?" Cohen leaned back in his chair and ran a hand through his hair. "When did you decide to use me? Was it before our engagement? Before I told you about my mother's Culling? Before our first kiss? Before we danced at the ball? When did it start and why . . . *why* did it have to end like this?"

My voice was weak, all the fight drained from me as I whispered, "Kace told the magistrate that I would be at the train station that day? He's . . . He's the reason the videra was there?" I knew the answer, and yet it just felt so wrong. So impossible. "He's the reason I was caught." I couldn't process anything else; my mind was too numb from the shock of that revelation. Too frozen on the memory of Ambrose screaming for me, of someone pressing a chemical-covered cloth to my mouth and nose.

That was all Kace's fault.

He'd betrayed us.

Cohen didn't respond to me. "I let you in. I let you close to me. I thought . . . I thought things were real and that we could have a future. I thought Erydia might see positive change through the two of us."

I swallowed. "I never wanted to hurt you."

"You've put countless people in danger. You've compromised our government, our very way of life."

"We've lived very different lives, Cohen."

His hand hit the table with enough force to make me jump. "The Culling was your opportunity to escape that!"

Raw anger filled my bones, the heat of my ability pushing at my skin, the feeling of it overtaking the shock. "And what about the others?" I demanded. "The thousands of people who are starving because food is too scarce, because taxes are too high, because we aren't allowed to trade for foreign goods, for medicine and technology. For the things that could help us."

He was silent.

"You said that you wanted a choice. You wanted to be able to choose who you end up with. I'm giving you that choice. You don't have to choose me," my voice broke, "but you do have a choice. I'm trying to give us *both* a choice."

He lifted his head and met my eyes. "You're trying to overthrow our government and terrorize my people."

"I'm trying to get out of here alive."

"It's too late for that, Monroe."

"Is it?" I felt light-headed. "It's only too late if you let it be. You're here. You can stop this. You could help me." I reached across the table, but he pulled away from me.

"Don't do that," he hissed. "Don't act like nothing has changed. Don't pretend like you ever cared about me."

"But I do care. I've never stopped caring about you, Cohen."

He reached into his jacket pocket and held something out between us. Something shining and silver.

The rabbit-head necklace.

A lump formed in my throat. "Where did you find that?"

"I went by your room Monday to see if you were back from the trial. It turns out you were, but you weren't in your room. This was on the floor next to some clothes." He picked up the necklace by its chain and let it dangle between us. "Where were you that day?"

"I told you, I was in the bathing—"

"You're still lying."

I flinched. "I was in Dellacov's office."

The necklace dropped to the table with a soft *clink*. "You can't even begin to understand what you've done."

"I did what I thought was right."

"What did you give them? Tallis said that the information you found had been sent already. What did you give them?"

"I'm not telling you."

"Dellacov is missing a map of the palace. And you weren't in your room when I stopped by there on my way to his office, so I'm guessing you were in there when I dropped off the guard schedule. So, let's just assume you handed that information over to them too. So, what else did you take?" I let my silence speak for me. "Have it your way, Monroe. My mother will get the information one way or another."

"You'll let her hurt me?"

"Don't do that," he said. "Don't put this on me. You handed over information that could allow Vayelle, our enemy, into my home—into *our* country." He swallowed and leaned back in his chair. "You have no idea who you're dealing with."

"And you'd rather your mother remain queen? She's tortured you for years, how can you possibly defend her? Shouldn't *you*, of all people, understand the lengths she's willing to go to remain in power?"

"She'll step down."

"No, she won't."

"You don't know that."

"She's already responsible for the deaths of at least four goddess-touched girls. Five if you count Joslyn." I bit my lip to ground myself, to keep the tears at bay. "I don't want to be poisoned, Cohen. I don't want to die like that."

His throat bobbed, and he looked away from me. "You will now."

"Fine. I earned that. But no matter what happens to me, something still has to be done. Things can't continue like this—"

"And you think Vayelle will be better?"

"They're giving us the opportunity to start over—without the goddess and without the Culling. We can elect real politicians. People from different cities who will fight for our people and make changes that will benefit everyone."

"Because you don't think I would?"

"Cohen, the old ways aren't working. The Culling is producing queens who aren't capable or knowledgeable enough to rule. I could never be queen. I could never make the decisions that have to be made. I wasn't raised to do this."

"That's why you would have a king. You would have had me."

"Your father has done nothing to keep your mother in line."

"That is different. *They* are different."

"It has been thirty years of abuse. Thirty years of reckless spending and creating enemies and killing people without a second thought. Viera has done nothing in her reign to help make the lives of her people better."

His voice was no more than a whisper as he said, "You will die for being an idealist."

"It's better than dying for a crown. At least I'll die for something I believe in. Something that could save other people. Save my mother and thousands of others from starving. At least I would be dying for something I want."

The silence stretched between us, like an impenetrable wall. This was not something we could overcome. He would cling to that crown, to that throne, forever—he would let me die.

I told myself that it didn't matter, that I didn't care.

Because of Viera, Varos was awash with runaways and criminals. People were enslaved. Thousands starved in work camps meant only to punish and demean. Under her rule, something as simple as a father stealing to feed his children was considered worthy of the death penalty.

And all the while, she fed her own children luxurious meals laced with poison.

Cohen looked down at the necklace and asked, "Did you even consider what this could mean for me, for my family? Uri is supposed to be your friend. You're supposed to care about her. Or was all of that a lie too?"

"None of it was a lie. I care about her. Cohen, I care about you. I asked for your safety. That was— It was— I would never want to hurt either of you."

"I wish you hadn't."

We held each other's gaze for a long moment.

There was more I wanted to say, words lost amongst the anger and fear. They kept getting caught on my teeth, on my tongue, on all the previous words and actions—on the lies I'd told, on the slight untruths, on all the things I'd omitted.

Seventeen years was a long time, but it was also so short and I'd had so few experiences. I knew so very little about life—less still about love. But if I had ever loved anyone in my life, I believed it was Cohen Warwick.

It was a certainty that didn't need vocalizing and yet I wanted to say it. I wanted to look him in the eyes and say so—but how could I? Somewhere in the midst of my betrayal, I'd lost the right to love him.

I asked, "What has your mother decided to do with me?"

"You know what she wants to do."

"When?"

"Please." His voice turned soft, truly afraid. "Who else in the palace is helping you?"

There was no answer I could give him. I didn't know. My only contact was Tallis and she was gone, imprisoned or dead, I wasn't sure. But still, I lifted my chin and said, "I'm never going to tell you, Cohen."

He made a pained sound in the back of his throat and leaned across the table toward me. His voice shook as he spoke. "I have to have someone else to blame. I'm trying to save you from yourself. Hugo was there when the maid delivered the letter. And I . . . I told Hugo about the necklace I'd found. I thought it had to be some odd coincidence. But then, with the letter and the news about your brother in Pallae and— I didn't think— I never actually thought you would be . . ." Cohen closed his eyes. "Monroe, you broke into his office. You clasped this pendant around your neck and you . . . you *lied* to me. You *used* me."

I had to bite my lip to keep from crying. "I know."

"I need to know who else helped you. Who else in the palace is responsible? You didn't do it alone. Tallis didn't do it alone."

He caught my gaze and, for the first time that day, all the masks were gone and I was looking at Cohen. Not the prince, just my friend. At that moment, he looked at me like he always had.

"Monroe, my mother will kill you. Please." He reached across the table and touched my hand. "Please, let me blame this on someone else."

"She'll kill me either way."

"I will protect you. Just— Let me blame this on someone else."

I believed in what the Culled was doing. I believed in anything that would make a change; anything that would help suffering families and put food on tables. I believed in ending the Culling. In stopping Viera. I believed that innocent girls like Nadia deserved bright futures, regardless of the marks on their skin.

I just regretted using Cohen. One more regret on my ever-growing list.

I wished that I'd pushed him away from the start. It was wrong of me not to do so and I'd known it the whole time. Now, sitting face-to-face with him, I'd give anything to take it back. To erase the kisses and the quiet moments, the private conversations and the smiles meant only for me.

I wished that I didn't think about kissing him every time I saw his lips. I wished that I didn't recognize the difference in the way he looked at me. I wished that I hadn't found him in that chicken coop. Having no relationship with Cohen would have been better than knowing I'd ruined what we had.

He was looking at me, his blue eyes shining as he waited for my response.

"I can't," I whispered. "I'm so sorry, but I can't. I don't regret giving the Culled the information they need. I just never should have fallen for you while I did it."

He inhaled sharply and nodded.

Without another word to me, Prince Cohen Warwick stood up, gathered the necklace, and left the room. I listened as the lock of my cell slid back into place and his footsteps faded away.

36

The Cells

"Monroe Benson."

I jumped at the voice and flinched away, prepared to strike out, but froze when I saw Larkin Warwick crouched before me.

I'd never spoken to Larkin, not once. She'd never even turned her gaze in my direction. Yet there she was, looking down at me like I was a pile of shit she'd accidentally stepped in.

I blinked a few times, trying to make sure I was seeing things correctly.

She stood. "Get up."

I didn't move.

Before I could react or block the blow, she kicked me in the ribs. "Up."

I pressed a hand to the sore spot as I eased to my feet. I couldn't fathom why she was here. Surely, she wasn't the person they'd sent to retrieve me for my execution. A job like that was beneath her.

I glanced to the door, which was shut. I hadn't heard her come in, hadn't heard the click of the locks or the sound of boots.

When I turned my gaze back to Larkin she was smiling, wide and catlike. My mind flitted back to a moment, weeks ago, when Larkin had looked at Grier that way. Back then, I had wondered why Cohen and Uri spoke so little about her, why she rarely appeared in their childhood stories.

"Did you sleep well?" Her voice grated on my nerves. It was too pretty, falsely sweet. She blinked at me, waiting for a response.

I wished for water. My throat was dry, still hoarse from smoke and a dead girl's hands. It felt like I had been screaming in my sleep and I wondered if I actually had.

My eyes flitted to the table where my empty water glass stood. Dellacov had brought dinner last night. Stale bread and a glass of water. That interaction had been the only sign that the day had turned to night. I wondered what time it was now.

Larkin cut through my thoughts. "When I ask you a question, you answer."

"I slept fine."

She moved toward the table in the center of the room, and beckoned for me to follow. Reluctantly, I eased out of my corner, every joint in my body crying out as I stepped toward the table.

I had no idea if anyone was at the window watching us. I found myself wishing that for this meeting, whatever this was, I had an audience. Where the hell was Dellacov?

"Can I get you anything? Food? Water?" Larkin pulled the nearest chair out and spun it so it was facing toward the door. "Why don't you sit? You look tired."

I stayed where I was, a few feet away. "I'm fine."

She made a sound, a sort of low humming at the back of her throat. Like I'd just said something she thought was cute. Her smile widened.

"You aren't a very good listener, are you?" She sighed and tapped the back of the chair with a long fingernail. "I said, *sit.*"

She spoke softly, sweetly, but it was venomous. Spoken through teeth clenched so hard I thought they might shatter in her mouth. It was the same way Viera spoke to Cohen—like he was an unruly child.

I sat. Obedient. Like the dog she thought I was.

Larkin placed her hands on my shoulders, her thumbs running across the collar of my thin training shirt. Her skin was cold and I flinched away. At my movement, nails dug into my bare shoulder. I hissed through my teeth but forced myself to remain still.

"You won your trial." Her voice was bored, like she was discussing the weather. "It was a good show."

There was a pause like she was expecting me to thank her, like it was a compliment. When I didn't say anything, her hold on my shoulders tightened further, her grip biting into my flesh like razor-sharp teeth. I bit my lip to keep from making a sound.

"I thought for sure you would lose to that other girl. Trisha, was it?"

"Tessa," I whispered. "Her name was Tessa."

"Oh, yes. I'm sorry. *Tessa*. I thought for certain that Tessa would kill you. In fact, I was betting on it. Lost a decent amount of coin when you managed to win." She tsked in disapproval. "I just hate it went things don't go as planned, don't y—"

"Why are you here?"

"Monroe, we're having a conversation. It's rude to interrupt. Didn't anyone ever teach you proper manners?" She moved her hands and dug her fingernails into new skin. "Play along, will you?"

I hissed through my teeth in pain and Larkin laughed, like this was all the answer she needed from me.

"Now, where were we?" She sighed and paused to think. "Oh, yes. The trials. Cohen called off the trial before yours. But of course, we must stick to our schedule. You were in the throne room that day. What were their names? The girls who were meant to fight?"

"Heidi and Grier."

"Heidi and Grier," she repeated. "And which of them died?"

"Grier."

"And the other? The one who suffocated?"

"Elodie."

"And what about the other one, the one that died in her bedroom?"

"Vivian."

"And the one to go against Kinsley?"

I closed my eyes. "Joslyn."

She laughed again, the sound soft and musical. "Yes, of course, I should remember. But I've never been very good with names. And there's just so many of you." She paused as if contemplating something. I flinched as she let go of my shoulders and stepped in front of me. "Did you like killing your goddess-touched girl?"

"I didn't want to have to kill anyone."

"Yes, yes. Of course. Very noble," she said dismissively. "But did you like it? Did you enjoy killing her?"

"No."

She crossed her arms over her chest and shrugged. "Well, I quite enjoyed killing mine."

I blinked at her.

She laughed so hard she bent at the waist. "Yes, silly, it was me!" She clapped her hands together. "I killed the girl. *Grier*. And Vivian too. I would claim Joslyn but then Kins would be sad, and I don't like making her cross." I opened my mouth to say something but she shushed me and pressed a finger to my lips. "You can't tell anyone. It's a massive secret, just between you and me."

I stared at her.

I'd watched both girls kiss the queen's ring. Larkin hadn't been anywhere near them, certainly not close enough to have killed Grier.

She was still grinning, waiting for me to respond to her confession. Maybe she was crazy. Maybe that was why none of her siblings ever talked about her.

I leaned back in my seat, trying to put some distance between us. "But . . . But Grier was poisoned. So was Vivian."

Larkin clapped her hands again like I'd just discovered a clue, a piece of a puzzle I hadn't realized I was supposed to be putting together. "Yes," she said, almost breathlessly. "Yes, you're right. They were."

She walked around the table, disappearing from my peripheral vision. I turned in my chair to look at her. She stood gazing down at the tray of food Dellacov had given me.

Larkin dipped a finger into the empty glass. At the bottom was the smallest amount of water. She collected it on her fingertip and glanced up to meet my eyes. "My mother can create poison from nothing. And I can't do that. But I can use what's already there. Just the smallest amount, that's all I need. I used to need more, but now . . ."

She lifted her finger and let the drop of water fall to the table. She looked down at it, smiled, and flicked her finger to the side. The drop of water rippled and drooped sideways. It was as if the table were slanted and the water was rolling down, down, down.

But the table wasn't slanted—it was Larkin. She was moving the water.

The poisoned water I had guzzled down hours earlier.

"But," I whispered, "there are only ten goddess-touched girls."

She shrugged. "Well, the goddess just didn't *touch me*, I guess."

"I don't understand—" I had to stop talking.

My mouth was watering like I was going to be sick and the room had begun to sway, rocking like a pendulum beneath me. I gripped the seat of the chair in white-knuckled hands, afraid I was going to fall off the edge of it.

Larkin didn't seem to notice. She just kept talking.

"I thought . . ." She circled the table and my chair so that she was standing directly in front of me again. "I thought that I could practice on you. Just for a little while. Until you die or I get bored. I doubt anyone will care if something happens to you." The corner of her mouth twitched. "I think that sounds fun, don't you?"

She lifted a hand, moving her fingers slowly. Stretching each joint.

I started to shake. A quiver that began in my spine and stretched throughout my entire body as the muscles in my torso tightened, straining. I tried to relax, tried to breathe through it, but my lungs wouldn't expand.

Frightened tears welled in my eyes and I made a sound, a scream—or what my body thought should be a scream but was little more than a whimper.

Larkin laughed and tightened her hand into a fist. Pain exploded in my abdomen and I pitched forward, fighting the nausea. I sputtered, nearly vomiting.

"Oh, no you don't." Larkin uncurled her fingers slowly and the pain receded.

My muscles relaxed and I exhaled heavily only to fill my lungs again, drinking in pure oxygen. My throat burned and I had to blink against the panicked tears in my eyes.

I needed to act, to do something—but I was so astonished, so shocked, that I couldn't get my mind and my body to cooperate. I reached for the fire in my blood, tried to conjure a flame, a spark, an ember, but I couldn't focus, make myself to do anything.

Larkin grabbed a handful of my hair and yanked my head back so hard I thought my neck might snap. I whimpered and tried to pull away from her. Instinct propelled me forward, weeks and weeks' worth of training telling me to fight back.

Now.

I called fire to my fingers and spun in the chair, grasping for her face, her arm, her clothes—anything. She sprang back and tightened her fist again. Pain bloomed through my torso, and I pitched forward.

I threw up this time, all over the tiled floor of the cell.

Larkin shoved me from the chair and I just barely managed to catch myself with my hands before she was kicking me. First in the gut and then again in the shoulder. My fire sputtered out, dissipating as I choked on my own vomit. A cry of pain and frustration escaped me as I lashed out, blocking the third blow with my forearm.

Sparks flew from my fingertips as I tried to rally my ability against hers. Larkin stepped away from me, pacing a small circle. "We don't have to keep playing," she said. "I could just kill you now."

I pushed myself up onto my hands and knees, my arms trembling as I fought against the urge to lie back down. Sweat dripped down my face and into my eyes, mixing with stunned tears. My vision was the night sky—a patchwork of stars and smeared reds and blues. Underneath my hands, the floor swayed, like a living, breathing thing.

It rolled and my stomach rolled with it.

Larkin continued to circle, slow and calm. I tried and failed to summon flame. My hands sparked but didn't catch. What flame I conjured was weak and quivering, unable to do anything more than simmer against my flesh as my body tried to fight off the poison she was manipulating.

She crouched next to me.

"Oh, come on." Her hand wound its way into my hair again. "I saw you fight. You can do better than that."

She was smiling, her eyes so dark they looked black. I watched as she rolled her wrist, cracking the joints—my muscles shuddered with each movement, pulling so tight they burned. I bit my lip to keep from making a sound. I didn't want to give her the satisfaction of knowing how much it hurt.

Larkin rolled her eyes and let go of my hair, shoving my head toward the floor as she stood up. She took the pain with her. The world around me slowed, my eyesight flickered and sputtered from darkened abyss to blazing, fire-tinged colors. The only sound was the steady beat of my heart—in my ears, in my throat, in my head, in my chest. The beat slowed, sped, slowed again.

I couldn't breathe.

I slumped forward onto the tiles, unable to even support the weight of my own head. I was just a heap of discarded bones. The pain that had been there seconds earlier was replaced by a dull throb and an uneasy quiver in my stomach. I waited for her to end it, but she didn't.

She just watched me.

Gradually, the feeling in my body returned, my heartbeat found its natural pace, and my vision cleared. Still, I waited for her to strike. When she didn't, I tried to push myself up, tried to stand. I managed to lift myself partially off the floor before her boot came down hard on the top of my head, shoving my face back to the tiles.

For a second, I was back in the arena, Tessa had her hands around my neck, and I was dying. Drowning in my own fear. I tried to force myself to move past the crippling terror, but I didn't know how—I didn't know what to do or how to free myself.

I was useless.

Larkin said, "You know, Cohen never fights back either. Sometimes, when no one will suspect, I practice with him. Of course, I'm always very careful. Wouldn't want the precious heir to die unintentionally." She sighed and pressed down harder with her boot. "Of course, when I kill my brother, I'll make sure everyone knows it was intentional."

I hissed through my teeth and tried to lift my head, but she was using all her weight to keep me down. The rubber sole of her boot dug into the side of my face, hard enough to leave a mark.

"He's a weak prince, and he'd make an even weaker king."

I would turn her to ash. I reached down deep within myself, to where that power lay coiled tight as a snake, prepared to strike. I coaxed that inner heat, pushed it from my bones.

There was a sound from behind me and Larkin tensed. I felt her attention shift, felt her begin to ease up. I took my chance.

Without warning, I lashed out, taking hold of her ankle with one hand as I spun sideways, yanking her boot from my face and knocking her down. She fell on top of me hard and I grunted in pain as I shifted again, pushing myself onto my elbows and then onto her.

Then it was my hands in her hair, my hands at her throat.

I had one second, one miniscule second, when the world seemed to freeze and I realized what I'd done. I saw the smile on Larkin's face, heard the click of the door behind me. Then I was being hauled up and away.

Dellacov slammed me against the far wall, his hands tight on my upper arms as he turned to look at Larkin. Two other guards flooded in after him, rushing for the princess. She didn't look at the men; she kept her attention on me. Her chest heaved as her gaze flickered between Dellacov and me.

He turned to look at me, his mouth open in horror. How much had he seen? Did he know who she was? What she could do?

Larkin's eyes welled with tears as she said, "She— I'm sorry, Dellacov, I just— It was a mistake—I came down here to talk to her, I thought maybe I could learn something but . . . but . . ." She whimpered and shoved a shaking finger in my direction. "She attacked me."

I shook my head. "Dellacov, I didn't—"

He shoved me against the wall. "Shut the hell up."

One of the guards helped Larkin to her feet and she clung to him, leaning on him for support as she was led from my cell. They said something about taking her to a medic.

I tried to pull out of Dellacov's grasp, wanting to go after them. I needed to tell Cohen, warn Cohen. When he held me back, I turned to face him. "Please— You have to listen to me. She's dangerous. She can—" He shoved me back, forcing my head against the wall with enough force to make my vision spark. My teeth collided with my tongue and I tasted blood.

He let me go and stepped back. "Good goddess, do you have a damn death wish? Attacking a princess—"

"I didn't attack her."

"I saw it with my own eyes." He turned away from me and I reached for his arm, catching a hold of the sleeve of his uniform.

"Dellacov, she can poison people. I saw it— She did it to me. And Grier—"

His eyes widened, and he yanked his arm away from me. "You're crazy."

"No, I'm not. She has an ability. You have to believe me."

He threw up his hands. "No. No, I don't have to do anything for you."

I followed him toward the door. "Tell Cohen he's in danger."

Dellacov spun on me. "If he's in danger, it's because of you."

I stepped back.

"They're all in danger because of you. Uri is in danger." His hands were in fists at his sides and I saw his fingers twitch, saw him think of reaching for his gun. I took another step back.

"Tell Cohen I have names for him. He wanted to know who was helping me, and I have names. Tell him to come here, come see me and I'll tell him. I'll tell him everything."

Dellacov turned and walked toward the door.

I went after him. "Tell him. Please! Please tell him I have names!"

Dellacov said nothing, didn't even look in my direction as he pulled my cell door shut, locking me inside. I was still yelling, still pleading, as the lights flickered off.

37

The Cells

I woke to the sound of a lock clicking open.

Time in the cell had always moved strangely, but with the lights turned off, the hours seemed to stretch on and on before me. Never beginning and never ending, just circling, like a hungry animal. But with the click of that lock, time paused, sat back on its haunches, and leveled its gaze on me.

Today was the day I might die. There had been so many times I'd thought that, but each time I'd been wrong. And now, today, might actually be it. I might finally have run out of chances.

I straightened as the door to my cell whined opened. I wanted it to be Cohen. If Cohen came back, it would mean that he hadn't given up on me, hadn't abandoned me. I'd be able to tell him about Larkin. Even if it didn't change anything between us, I still owed it to him to warn him about his sister. Cohen had never stopped being my friend. Maybe—just maybe—I could save him.

Save myself.

But as I squinted into the sudden bright-white light of my cell, it was Dellacov and not Cohen who stepped inside. And just like that, my hope died. The prince wasn't coming back for me.

I got to my feet slowly, fighting the way my legs shook. The room no longer swayed from Larkin's poison, but my head still screamed from dehydration and the force of her foot on my skull.

Dellacov watched me, his eyes hard with a dislike I knew I deserved. I wanted to plead with him, to beg for my life, but I wouldn't. I was done begging for things.

I remembered being a kid and listening to Ambrose talk about our father. He had said, "Do you know what happened the day after Mama found out Papa was dead?"

Kace and I had both shaken our heads, unsure.

"The day after Papa died, the sun came up. And chores still needed to be done. And there were still babies for Mama to deliver and bread to be made and . . ." He had shrugged. "The world just kept going, and all we could do was face it."

Tomorrow, whether I was here or not, the sun would still rise, just as it had today. Just as it had yesterday, and all the days before that—all I could do was face it. Face what I'd done, the choices I'd made, the things I'd believed in.

If I was going to die for believing in a better world, I would die with my head held high. I would die without regret or apology. Because at the end of it all, I had believed in a world without the Culling.

And I still did.

Dellacov swallowed. "Do I need the cuffs or do you think you can walk out of here without causing a scene?"

I met his eyes, dread already boiling in my gut as I asked, "Where are we going?"

"The bathing room, I've got to get you cleaned up. You don't want to die looking like that, do you?"

It took every ounce of pride I had to keep myself standing, to not fall to my knees and weep. But I had not cried when I'd walked into the arena, and I would not cry now.

I forced my voice to stay calm as I asked, "When?"

He didn't look at me as he said, "You have an audience with the queen in an hour."

I was on my own.

"So, will it be with or without the handcuffs, Miss Benson?"

I lifted my chin. "No handcuffs."

The hall utside my cell was empty.

I had so many questions, so many things I wanted to say. Had he told Cohen about Larkin? Had Dellacov told him that I wanted to see him? Had Cohen known and decided it wasn't worth coming—that I wasn't worth giving another chance?

When we reached the bathing room door, I was presented with a bundle of clean clothes. Dellacov said, "You have about fifteen minutes."

I nodded and watched as he unlocked the door and held it open so I could walk through. "What time is it?" I asked before stepping inside.

"Why?"

"I'm just hungry, that's all."

"You'll get your dinner when you're cleaned up."

Dinner.

So, it was evening then. I'd slept on and off for an entire day. An entire day.

I opened and closed my mouth, unsure about risking my next question. Just before the words left my mouth, I changed tactics. I lied. "Cohen said that Tallis had already been executed. When?"

I watched Dellacov's face, pleased when I saw the surprise flicker there. Either it was information he thought I shouldn't know, or he was surprised because he thought Cohen had lied to me.

"She was executed last night."

I kept my face blank, unmoved. Tallis had said in that letter that the information I'd stolen had already been given to the Culled. I felt certain that if she'd mentioned the planned attack on the palace, Cohen would have brought that up to me. Dellacov would have already had me interrogated about it. Of course, Dellacov wasn't stupid. He knew that if I'd stolen those documents, I'd done it with a purpose.

I was still formulating my next vague question when Dellacov said, "Juno Heist was executed as well."

I stumbled backward a step, bumping into the frame of the bathroom door.

"What?" Dellacov said. "Did you think he'd live through this?"

"He had nothing to do with—"

"Oh, believe me. He said as much as they were leading him to the firing squad. But it doesn't matter. He didn't need to be a part of the rebellion. You are. And you chose to turn away from your birthright. You chose his fate for him. Your choices are his choices. Your death is his death. You couldn't have damned him more if you'd burned his body yourself."

I'd expected Tallis to be dead. I hadn't wanted it, but I knew that it was as inevitable as my own execution. But Juno . . . I hadn't thought of him. When I'd gone to Tallis and offered to help the Culled, when I'd stolen those documents from Dellacov's office, I hadn't considered what it would mean for Juno.

I hadn't believed I would get caught.

"We're on a schedule," Dellacov said. "Go change."

I walked into the bathing room and turned, watching as Dellacov pulled the door shut behind me and locked it. He tried the doorknob twice to make sure I was secured inside. He wasn't taking any chances.

"Just leave your dirty clothes in there and I'll get rid of them," he called through the door.

I didn't say anything in response.

It was a very small room, with only a sink and toilet. The first thing I did was turn on the water and peel off my vomit-covered clothes. I wet my hair in the sink and I washed it as best I could using the lone bar of soap and my hands. I used the hem of my shirt to dry it and then went to work washing my body. I scrubbed until my skin flushed red from the force of it.

I was pale and shaking, my skin sticky with sweat.

I'd seen Cohen looking like this before, on the night of Fidelium. At the time, I'd thought for sure Viera was to blame. Now I questioned everything. Was it her poison or Larkin's that had tormented him for so long?

There was no way to know.

When I was finished, I dressed in what Dellacov had brought: a clean set of training clothes and underthings that looked like they'd been taken from my closet. I finished dressing and took three seconds to calm myself down.

Dellacov knocked on the door. "You okay in there?"

I'd turned the water off a few minutes earlier, a clear signal that I was done washing. "Yes," I said, "I'm just changing."

I looked at myself in the small mirror above the sink. The girl looking back at me was tired, beaten down, and bruised. This person was different. I didn't know her, didn't know what she was capable of.

I looked like a shadow of myself, too pale and too thin. But this girl, new and unfamiliar as she was, had survived a Culling trial. She'd killed someone to stay alive. She had betrayed her only friends and now faced the option of dying for that crime or continuing with it. It wasn't a choice.

I would not die here.

I would live to see the Culling ended and the world changed.

Dellacov knocked again. It was now or never. "Monroe?" He fiddled with the doorknob.

"Just another second." I turned the water on again. "Let me just wash my face."

I hastily ran my fingertips along the edge of the mirror, testing how securely it was hung on the wall. One firm tug and it was in my hands. The thing wasn't very large, but it was heavy, made of thick wood and sturdy glass. I weighed it, shifting it in my grasp until I had a firm hold.

The doorknob jiggled again and I stepped back.

The toilet was set to one side of the entryway, the sink on the other, both of them nestled toward the inner wall of the bathroom, closest to the door. I lowered the lid of the toilet and prayed to the goddess that it would hold my weight as I stepped onto it. The mirror shook in my hands as I leaned back, hoisted it above my head, and screamed bloody murder.

Dellacov did exactly what I'd predicted he'd do.

He came barreling into the small room.

There wasn't time for him to cry out as I brought the wooden back of the mirror down on his head. There was a sickening sort of cracking and the tinkling of glass as it shattered and bounced off the tiled floor around his feet.

Dellacov swayed slightly and his eyes grew wide as he saw me towering above him, holding my makeshift weapon. Then he was falling. I dropped what remained of the mirror as I dove forward, caught his arm, and tried to haul him back, away from the porcelain edge of the sink.

The weight of him pulled me from my perch and sent us both toppling to the floor. Shards of glass cut at my arms and I hissed through my teeth. But there just wasn't time to worry about it.

I quickly assessed the damage I'd done.

Two fingers to his neck told me he wasn't dead. I was more relieved than I probably should have been, but in spite of everything he was someone Uri cared about. I didn't want to hurt her any more than I already had. The small hope that I could escape, get out alive without killing someone else, was struggling to stay afloat.

I searched him, found a small ring of keys and a handgun strapped to his hip. I pocketed the keys. Dellacov was heavy, a dead weight on the floor, and it took all my strength to lift him enough to pull the belt and holster free.

I strapped it onto myself, using a thin shard of glass to poke a few new holes in the belt so it would fit snug, high up on my waist and hidden easily under my shirt.

When that was finished, I took off running.

I ran until I hit the first locked door.

I'd just found the right key and stepped through when I heard it, the sound of footsteps. The hallway was a black expanse of windowed cells similar to my own, all of them empty. A test of the nearest cell doorknob proved it was locked. I didn't have time to fiddle with the keys.

The footsteps grew closer, inching toward the bend in the hall ahead of me. My options were to retreat or push forward.

The choice was made for me when Uri rounded the corner holding a tray of food. She froze when she saw me, her expression tightening as she took me in. Her voice was raw as she asked, "Where is Hugo?"

I'd never heard her use his first name before, and hearing it now, with that worried question in her eyes, was enough to break my heart.

I moved toward her, my hand outstretched. "Uri—"

She stepped back. "Is he— Did you—"

"No."

"Then where is he?" She was breathless.

"The bathing room," I said. "Unconscious."

"Alive?"

"Yes."

She exhaled loudly. "My mother plans to execute you, the guards will be here any minute."

My throat tightened. "I know."

"Do you have a way out?"

I shook my head. "But I'll find one."

She nodded and straightened her shoulders, every ounce the princess. "Very well then." She inclined her head to the cell nearest her. "Lock me inside and leave."

I blinked at her. "What?"

"I can't let my mother know I've helped you. We have to make it look believable."

"Are you sure?"

She nodded. "The guards will let me out when they come looking for you. It'll be fine."

When I'd gotten the lock undone, I opened the door wide and stepped back, giving Uri room to walk inside. She made a show of dropping the tray in the hall, shattering the glass bowl of soup and the small cup of water in the process.

"I'll tell them you overpowered me." She stepped over the shards of broken dishes and into the cell. I found the light switch and turned it on, illuminating the entire block of rooms. "Be gone before they arrive."

I hesitated, my hand on the door handle. Uri offered me an encouraging smile and I nodded, just once, before I moved to shut the door.

"Monroe—" I stopped as Uri stepped forward. She wrapped her arms around my neck in a tight embrace. "Please be careful."

"Uri, I'm so sor—"

With a shake of her head, she pulled away and stepped back into the cell. "I forgive you. I forgive you for all of it."

It hurt to breathe. "Thank you."

I turned to shut the door but she reached out again and held it open. "I think he loved you."

Loved. Past tense.

My throat tightened. "I know. I think I could have loved him too."

Uri sighed. "I hope . . . I hope I never see you again. And I mean that in the best way possible."

Each thud of my boots against concrete was one step closer to escape. I was winded and shaking so badly it took a decent amount of focus to keep my legs from giving out, but I pushed through it. I was so close.

I only stopped moving long enough to find the key to the next lock, then the following two. I hurried up three different flights of stairs and down the last stretch of walkway, my throat burning as I sucked in lungfuls of cold air. The keys slipped against my palm.

The end of the last hall was marked with an intricately decorated wooden door—just like the ones used in the palace corridors—so different from the thick metal checkpoints I'd just run through. At the sight of it, I slowed my steps, giving myself time to gauge how I felt physically.

I snapped my fingers, testing the strength of my fire.

My ability pulsed underneath the skin of each finger. Heat pushed, hesitant and weak, around my mark. But even with my coaxing, the fire in my blood struggled to do anything more than spark. Annoyed, I pushed the fire from me, urging it from a glowing ember against my palm to a full flame and then to a blaze that ate across my wrist and lower arm.

That heat lasted only a few seconds and then it fizzled out. I tried to summon it again, but a wave of light-headedness had me rocking on my heels and gripping the nearest wall. This feeling was familiar to me, similar to what I'd felt just after my trial. I was working my way toward another crash and I couldn't afford to collapse now.

Not here.

I pressed my ear to the door and listened for any footsteps. No one would know I had escaped yet, and that alone gave me an edge. If I could make it to the training rooms unseen, then maybe I'd be able to find the hidden passageways Tallis had talked about. Maybe I could get out into the city and disappear, at least for a little while.

When I was certain that the hall outside was silent, I eased the door open and stepped into the brightly lit corridor beyond. For a moment, I just stood there listening. I had no idea where in the palace I was. What I could remember of how I'd gotten into the prison in the first place was hazy, masked by poison and hours of staring at fluorescent lighting.

I kept my head down and my eyes glued to the floor as I passed maids and footmen. No one spoke or called out to me. If they recognized me as a goddess-touched girl, or as a traitor, no one said anything.

I kept my pace even and unsuspecting, just a quick walk. I kept moving until the hallways were vaguely familiar. I glimpsed paintings I recognized, saw flashes of a garden path I knew from memory, smelled the rich aroma of the kitchens.

Time was running out. By now, people would probably be looking for me. Someone would find Uri locked in that cell and they would realize what had happened. Then, I would have an entire palace full of guards looking for me.

Up ahead, the corridor split into two, one direction leading toward the grand ballroom and the other leading toward private offices. Beyond that was the elevator. I took off running, hoping it was the same lift we used to get to and from the training rooms.

I headed for the lift.

I'd just rounded a corner when someone called my name from the opposite end of the hall. Something in my gut tightened at the sound, a natural reaction—a response born of intense homesickness and habit. I shouldn't have stopped. I should have kept running, but the voice was so familiar, so craved, it stopped me in my tracks.

"Monroe?"

I turned and looked at my brother, met Kace's eyes across the expanse of shining checkered tiles. My chest heaved with a sob I'd been holding in for days. Pain and fear and utter betrayal warred within me and for a moment, I just stood there.

What Cohen had said in the cells made my hands shake at my sides, but I thought this time he would choose me. I told myself that he would choose me. Sending me to the Culling was one thing. Sending me before the queen was another. Kace would choose me.

His eyes were wide, his expression earnest as took one step toward me and then stopped. I could see that he was afraid. Afraid for me.

"No one knows that I'm gone yet," I whispered across the expanse between us. "There's still time."

Kace crossed the distance between us and wrapped his arms around me, pulling me to his chest in a hug. I wrapped my fingers in the front of his uniform and said, "We have to hurry."

He nodded, holding on to me for a split second longer. When he spoke, his head still buried in my hair, his words were loud enough to make me flinch.

"She's here!" he said. "I've found her."

I've found her.

I tried to step back from him, but his hands caught my wrist and held me still. The look that had washed over his face wasn't what I had expected. It was disappointment, a sort of sour disdain.

Goddess, I was stupid. Stupid and naïve. I was wrong. I wasn't more important than a guard position or the queen's glory. Cohen had said as much but I hadn't wanted to believe it. I'd thought Cohen had to have had it wrong. Kace would never—

"She's over here!" he bellowed again, his grip on me only tightening as I tried to get away.

"Stop. Kace, please, stop!"

But this man wasn't my brother. This was Kace Benson, the Erydian soldier. He was no longer the silly kid I'd grown up with. And he was looking at me, as if I were . . . a stranger.

I tried to summon flame but only managed a surge of heat. It was enough to make Kace release me, my arms too hot for him to hold. Before he could reach for me again, I stumbled backward.

I could hear the thunder of boots heading in our direction. He had other guards with him. I was still staring at Kace as I backed away, moving toward the lift. He followed me with slow, even steps.

Oh, goddess.

I turned, but there was nowhere to run. I was trapped. The lift wouldn't open in time and there was no other way of escape.

Kace still walked toward me, his gait unhurried, his expression resigned. I didn't know this boy. Didn't know who he was anymore. Because, as the guards rounded the corner and pushed past him, moving to restrain me, Kace stopped being my big brother and became something else. A monster. A traitor.

Was this who Cohen had sent to capture me?

The guards yelled at me to stay where I was, telling me to lift my hands so they could see them. I took off running—arms pumping, knees shaking, lungs swelling—toward the lift at the other end. I'd almost reached it, my fingers just scraping the cool metal of the button, when strong hands hauled me back.

I screamed, clawed, kicked, and burned, as too many hands pinned me face-first against a wall. My arms were twisted roughly behind my back.

I elbowed a guard in the face as he tried to secure my wrists but another man just took his place. They were careful to steer clear of my fingers and the fire that licked its way up my skin. They secured the cuffs high on my forearms, yanking my shoulders back at an excruciating angle.

Defeat came before I was ready. Before I'd given up. But my body just couldn't do it anymore. I was fading and even adrenaline couldn't make my limbs move.

The fire hissed and fell back beneath my skin. I was exhausted and Kace was there, looking at me. Telling me that I'd done enough. That enough had happened. The fight was over.

"Don't embarrass yourself any further," he said.

But, of course, my brother couldn't be the one saying those things. He loved me. He hadn't wanted me to die here, in this palace, with these people. No. Kace had wanted me to become queen.

And here I was, ruining things.

Rough hands ran up and down my body. The gun was taken away. Dellacov's key ring was lost, dropped on the floor during the scuffle. I was left with nothing, no way of escape and no weapon aside from my broken ability.

I did not cry, did not even look at Kace as I said, "She is going to kill me."

He exhaled loudly. "You had the opportunity of a lifetime. A chance to help our family, to save Mama from starving—"

"I'm not the reason she's starving in the first place."

I spat in the face of the nearest guard, the one holding the gun I'd taken from Dellacov. The man lifted a hand to strike me but Kace stepped forward and caught his hand before it could collide with my jaw.

My brother leaned in close to me. "What Ambrose is doing is wrong. He's a radical. It can only end with him dangling from a noose. He should've never involved you."

"He was trying to save me."

"All he has done is damn you," Kace said, his voice close to my ear. "And where is he, Monroe? Where are these rebels now? Will they save you?"

"I shouldn't have to die in the Culling."

"All the two of you have done is gotten yourselves declared traitors, and our family, *our mother*, along with you. But I won't let her be killed for your mistakes. I had to make a deal. You left me with no choice. One of us has to keep her safe." His voice cracked as he said, "I thought once you were here—once they caught you and brought you here—you'd focus. You'd come to terms with it. I thought you'd both give up on trying to run. It's your birthright, Monroe."

Cohen's words came back to me in vivid clarity. *Kace isn't a traitor. He proved that months ago.*

My voice broke. "Why? Why, Kace? You could have let me go. You could have let me live."

Down the hall, there were people yelling. Announcing that the fugitive had been found. *Fugitive*—because that's what I was now.

More guards arrived. They congratulated their comrades like I was fresh meat, a hunt gone well. I stayed where I was, leaning my forehead against the cool surface of the wall. The world was spiraling around me.

A familiar voice said, "You found her, good."

My head shot up just in time to see Cohen stop a few feet away from me.

He was dressed for fighting. Black pants, dark leather boots, a tightly fitted gray undershirt, and a loose charcoal jacket. There was a bandolier of throwing knifes strapped to his chest.

He thanked the guards, his smile wide and unworried.

An outsider would have no idea that we'd ever meant anything to each other.

Kace still stood next to me, one shoulder leaning against the wall as he scanned my face. He acted as if he didn't recognize me, as if my treason was a physical trait—a mark just as visible as the one the goddess had given me.

I wanted to scream at him. I wanted to shake him.

"We should be going," Cohen said. "My mother is impatient. Do you . . ." He hesitated and looked at me fully for the first time since he'd arrived. "Do you have her under control?" His gaze faltered as he said it, darted to the floor, to the guards, anywhere but at me.

There were a few more muttered jeers and laughs from the guards. Cohen said nothing, just walked over to where Kace and I stood. I leaned farther into the wall, wishing nothing more than to blend in with it.

Those eyes were too much, too heavy to shoulder just then. My brother and Cohen spoke over my head, one on either side of me, like I wasn't even there.

The prince said, "Thank you for finding her."

I didn't have to look to know that my brother bowed. And I hated him for that. It broke something deep inside me to think of him respecting or honoring these people, these men who were going to put me before Viera.

But Kace didn't just respect them; he was one of them now. For once, Kace wasn't in Ambrose's shadow. He'd found something he was good at. They'd trained him, turned him into the soldier he'd always wanted to be. Maybe that dream was worth more than I was.

"It was the least I could do given the circumstances," Kace said. "I'm sorry for the trouble she's caused."

Cohen didn't respond. When I didn't turn my face toward him, he reached forward, grabbed my chin in his fingers, and made me look at him. It wasn't a rough action, just intentional—a power move.

Asshole.

His voice was quiet, so very quiet. Meant only for me, as he said, "You hurt Hugo, and he's pissed."

I tried to shrug my shoulders but the cuffs held them still. "Good."

The corner of his mouth twitched. "You don't mean that. If you did, he'd be dead."

I closed my eyes and turned back so I was facing the wall again. "Let's just get on with it."

I felt, more than saw, him step away.

"Walk with me." When I didn't move to go with him, he cleared his throat and said a bit louder, "Either you do as I ask, or I will have you forcibly taken before the queen."

I turned to look at him. "My arms hurt. Adjust the cuffs."

One demand to meet his.

If they thought for even a second that I would try to fight my way out of a group of a dozen armed guards, they were wrong. I was foolish, but not that foolish. Cohen knew that. He knew me well enough to know that I had already assessed my chances and realized I was stuck.

So, he got the key and moved the cuffs down to my wrists. He left them loosely secured behind my back, not so much that I could wiggle free, but enough that I could stand more comfortably.

When the job was done, we walked. Cohen and I at the front, the guards and Kace at least two steps behind. This had been the prince's request.

As we walked, I kept two steps behind him, something that was difficult to do since he kept trying to slow his pace, get in stride with me.

"Stop it." He kept his voice low so the guards wouldn't overhear. "Don't do that."

"We aren't equals anymore, *Your Highness*. I'm always supposed to be two steps behind you, remember?"

"Is that how you want to do this? Really?"

"And what *are* we doing? What is it you want, Cohen?" I demanded.

He stopped so swiftly that I bumped into him. With my arms behind my back, I stumbled, off-kilter. I teetered sideways, toward the wall, but he caught my shoulders and righted me before I could hurt myself.

Even once I was standing, Cohen didn't let go; he kept a loose hold on one arm. We were too close to each other for me to relax. He glanced sideways at the guards, who had taken a step closer to us. He nodded, a silent order for them to move back, before he pulled me forward.

We continued down the hall side by side.

"Did my reckless sister lock herself in that cell?"

"She had help," I conceded.

Cohen was quiet for a second. When he spoke again, his voice was so low I had to strain to hear him. "You could have been queen, you know? You were so close. And you would have been good. *We* would have been good."

I think he loved you.

It hurt to breathe. Every inhale was a fight to keep the next exhale from being a sob. My desire to be brave was overpowered by the reality of where we were going.

Viera was going to poison me in front of all the other goddess-touched girls. And this poisoning would not be as blessedly quick as Aviana or Grier's had been. It would be worse than what Larkin had done the night before.

"I never wanted to be queen."

A muscle in his jaw tightened and he nodded, just once.

"I only wanted to survive. That's all."

"I wish . . ." He trailed off and shook his head as he dismissed the thought. "Things should have been different, that's all. I thought they could be different with you. I thought you were on my court."

"I thought you were on mine," I whispered.

"I am." He shook his head again. "I was."

I think he loved you.

"It was low of you to send Kace after me."

"I knew you'd stop running for him."

"He betrayed me."

"And you betrayed me." Cohen's eyes were bright with malice and pain. "You should be grateful that Kace is here. He's the only thing standing between your mother and execution."

"My mother doesn't know anything about—"

"Whether she knows or not doesn't matter. You put Kace in this situation," Cohen said. "You made him choose between you and your mother. Between you and his queen. It's good that at least one of you is decent enough to do the right thing."

"The right thing? How is allowing countless people to starve and suffer *the right thing*?"

"I'll change things when I'm king. Kace is a royal guard now. He'll live to see that." He fiddled with the leather strap across his chest, adjusting the knives in their sleeves. "Being a royal guard is a prestigious position. It comes with a generous stipend and protection for your mother. Kace will be high in the ranks, away from the dangers of war."

"Is that supposed to make me feel better?"

"I just thought you might like to know they'll be looked after. Your mother will be well taken care of, I'll see to it myself."

"Kinsley will be your queen. She will never allow that. She'd kill my mother herself before she'd ever let you do something to help me. You will have no power with her on the throne next to you. Your dreams of a better kingdom will be overcome by her—her wickedness. And that's if you mother even steps down. And she probably won't."

His voice was sharp with distaste as he said, "I suppose it's good that you'll be dead then and won't have to witness it either way. It'll be my problem, not yours. But you're wrong all the same. I will be a good king. My mother will step down and whoever I marry will make the kingdom stronger. That person could have been you. *I wanted it to be you*."

For a second there was only the sound of our boots against tiles. "I wish . . . I wish that you'd chosen me," I said.

That hadn't been what he'd expected. Cohen was anticipating another angry jab. My soft words shook him enough to make his mask drop momentarily, so that I could see the hurt hidden underneath it.

To my surprise, he let it sit, let me see the fear in his eyes, as he said, "I can't. You know I can't. It would be a betrayal of everything I am. I have to do this. I have to fix things. Our people need strong leadership, now more than ever. I can be a good king."

"There are so many ways to fix things."

I could tell he had more he wanted to say, but he just nodded and turned his attention back to the hallway ahead of us. His hand on my arm tightened slightly. "I'll stand with you, until it's done. You won't die alone."

A part of me wanted to tell him to leave me alone, to let me face this by myself. I didn't need his kindness. It tasted of pity and regret. But the warmth of his palm against my arm brought more comfort than I wanted to admit.

The thought of standing before Viera sent my heart racing and made my hands shake.

"Do you promise?"

He nodded. "I swear it."

A fist of pure fear tightened around my heart. "Cohen, there's something else you should know. Earlier, Larkin came to my cell and she—"

"There you are." Viera stepped into the hall ahead of us. She smiled at me. "Our guest of honor has finally arrived. Splendid."

38

The Music Room
The day of execution

Viera moved toward us, and Cohen pulled me to a stop in front of her, his hand still tight on my arm. His palm was damp with sweat.

The group of guards behind us fanned out into a protective semicircle, trapping me further. As I'd walked with Cohen, I'd somehow forgotten just how vulnerable I was. My arms were secured behind my back. There were no weapons. I had no way to fight back. Even my ability was too weak to do anything. The prince was serving me on a platter for her. It was humiliating, especially knowing that she was aware of how he'd once felt about me.

As if she could read my thoughts, she said, "Have you said your goodbyes?"

Cohen's jaw was clenched so tightly that the muscles bounced beneath his skin. His fingertips dug into my arm. We didn't look at each other.

"Have the other girls arrived?" he asked.

The queen frowned when he didn't answer her question. "We're missing two."

"Are they on their way?"

"So many questions," Viera mused. Her tone softened. "Are you nervous, my love? You needn't stay if you think watching her die will give you nightmares."

Cohen stepped forward, pulling me alongside him. "Let's just get this over with."

I half expected her to say something else, to jab at him again, but she just stepped aside, allowing us to move past. Cohen pushed me ahead of him, roughly, putting himself between his mother and me. I turned back to look at my brother, just once.

Kace didn't meet my eyes. He was already speaking to the queen, his attention on her. He'd made his choice.

I swallowed and began again. "Cohen, Larkin came to my cell. She wants to—"

"Shut up."

I blinked at him, surprised. "It's important. Just listen to me for a second. Larkin—"

He met my eyes. "I said, shut up. Just— Stop talking. Please. *Please*, Monroe."

Cohen's hand drifted from my upper arm to my wrist and then to my cuffed hand. I couldn't breathe as his fingers laced with mine and he pressed a cool, small object into my palm. I started to ask what it was but one look from him kept me silent.

The touch withdrew, drifting back to my shoulder where his hand tightened against the fabric of my shirt and became harsher, a rough shove rather than a gentle guiding. I gripped the object in my fist. I was too afraid Viera would notice he'd given me something to even try to feel what it was.

We stopped in the doorway of a sumptuous music room, different from the one we used for etiquette classes. It was smaller, with only a scattering of three armchairs, a plush navy-and-cream throw rug, and two leather couches. On the far wall sat a stretch of floor-to-ceiling bay windows and, to one side, a rack of string instruments and a black grand piano.

In the center of the room sat a lone straight-backed wooden chair.

Larkin and Kinsley sat on the couches surrounding that lonely chair— two would-be queens prepared to cast judgment on me. Heidi and Nadia were nowhere to be seen, and for that I was grateful. If I was going to die here, I didn't want a massive audience.

The conceited look on Kinsley's face when she saw me was enough to scatter my fear. I regretted not being able to face her in the arena. On that playing field, I might have won.

Here, I was a prisoner, humbled and ashamed. More than anything, it annoyed me that she would be allowed to see me killed—slaughtered like an animal. They would have every advantage, and I would have none.

I turned my focus away from Kinsley and back to Cohen. His grip on my shirt tightened and he pulled me toward him, towering over me so much that I had to lean back against the door frame to see his face.

"*You*," he said. The word was angry and sharp; it matched the fire in his eyes.

I inhaled a tight breath, waiting for him to curse me. To damn me to hell or tell me he hated me.

He swallowed and glanced sideways at where Kinsley and Larkin were watching us. They were waiting to hear the prince put me in my place.

"*You*," he repeated, softer this time. His expression was open, honest, and almost afraid. He swallowed, cleared his throat, and said, "You deserve whatever the hell happens to you in there."

This was a lie.

His face said it was. I knew the truth of it. Even so, the tears welled in my eyes. I tried to blink them away, tried to wipe my face on my shoulder or my arm, but the cuffs kept me still. They let the tears fall.

Cohen stepped sideways, putting his back to the music room and shifting so I was out of Kinsley and Larkin's line of sight. One glance at his mother showed that she was still caught up with my brother and the other guards.

Quickly, and without a word, Cohen used the sleeve of his jacket to wipe the tears from my face. For a second, we just looked at each other. The moment stretched and solidified between us until it was a tangible thing, a memory I would take with me.

This would be cherished for however long I had left. The look in his eyes, the familiarity, the shadow of hurt, it all meant something to me. I would always be grateful that he'd let me see it to begin with.

For just a second, the mask was off.

He spoke so quietly I almost missed it. "Don't cry. Not in front of them. You're better than that."

Then he was pulling me forward, into the music room. No one spoke as I was directed to sit in the wooden chair. When I was seated, Cohen stepped back, taking up a place behind me. He put a hand on my shoulder.

To anyone else, it would look like he was holding me in my chair, but his promise still rang in my ears. *I'll stand with you, until it's done. You won't die alone.*

The people around me gawked and whispered amongst themselves. I couldn't be bothered to care. Not just then. Not when the seconds of my life were numbered.

I tried to make a plan, tried to decide what I would do once Viera came in and started torturing me. The fire within me was frail, a trembling thing that would require coaxing from a steady mind. And I was far from steady.

I felt too light, as if I were floating above it all. My head ached and it was only Cohen's hand on my shoulder, the stabilizing force of it, that kept me from trying to get up from the chair. I wanted to run. I wanted to be shot down. I wanted to fight. I wanted to do anything other than sit and die—once again a sacrifice.

Larkin sat on the couch nearest me, her legs crossed at the ankles. She was dressed simply, just a pair of gray trousers, a white button-up shirt, and black shoes. Not an inch of her was out of place, not a hair unsmoothed, not a wrinkle in her clothes.

Still, she looked half dead. There was no color in her cheeks and even as she leaned forward and smiled at me, there was no light in her eyes.

Larkin and Kinsley shared one couch, leaving the other empty. I leveled my gaze at the empty armchair in front of me. This, I realized, was where Viera would sit. Today, she was queen, judge, jury, and executioner.

I closed my eyes against their sudden burning. Something in me rose up as if it too wanted to strain, to fight, to rebel. And as that power reached out for me, I reached back. I stoked that inner fire, called on whatever force had given it to me.

Goddess, I don't want to die.

The words spread across the wild plains of my mind as I cast them away, in whatever direction one was supposed to send silent, frightened prayers. It was a strange thing to do, made stranger because this entity and I were more or less unacquainted—perhaps even enemies of sorts.

This was her doing. The goddess had branded me, marked me as her own. She had sent my fate running in this direction. I had tried—my mother had tried—so hard to keep from ending up here. I hadn't wanted a crown. I hadn't wanted to die in the arena.

Maybe that was the joke within the tragedy. I wouldn't die in the Culling; instead, I would be poisoned and put down like an animal.

I focused on that empty chair and on the windows beyond it. Outside, the sky was blossoming into a beautiful night, the moon just beginning the slow, swelling waltz of twilight.

I saw Larkin smile out of the corner of my eye. "How are you feeling this evening, Monroe?"

When I didn't turn to look at her, Larkin slid forward on the couch, moving into my line of sight and positioning herself closer to me.

"I asked you a question." She reached forward and tapped the top of my knee with a long, bony finger. "We've talked about this. When I ask you a question, you ans—"

"Don't touch me." I let each word fall from my mouth slowly, clearly. A threat, even if I had no way to deliver on it.

Larkin laughed and pulled her hand away. "Irritable, I see."

Cohen's hand tightened on my shoulder.

Larkin narrowed her eyes, her smile turning lazy as she said, "Clearly you need help remembering your manners." She turned to her brother. "You should never have let her grow so familiar with you, Cohen. It's bad for her. Now the poor thing has forgotten her place."

Viera's voice cut through the room. "Where are the other two goddess-touched girls?"

The guards and my brother filtered in after the queen. She circled the back of Larkin and Kinsley's sofa and came to a stop directly in front of the empty armchair across from me.

My eyes settled on her glinting onyx ring. I thought of Cohen kissing it. I thought of his lips on me.

It was then that I knew that I loved him—really knew it. His betrayal, his placing me here in this situation, did not dim my feelings for him. I knew it, because I didn't like the idea of him kissing anything—anyone—other than me.

"They should be here. There's no excuse for tardiness—not when your queen summons you," Viera said. "I'll deal with that later."

Larkin's mouth stretched into a satisfied smile as she said, "No sign of Uriel either. She must not want to see her champion die."

Cohen spoke up. "Where is Father?"

Viera's blue eyes were cold as ice. "He's *indisposed*. And I wouldn't sound so hopeful—if you think he'd stay my hand, you're mistaken."

When Cohen said nothing in response, she rolled her shoulders and said, "I see no reason to wait for the other girls—this one has wasted enough of my time as it is." Viera blinked at me, slowly, like a cat deciding the best way to eat a mouse.

I leaned back in the chair and fiddled with the item Cohen had pressed to my palm only moments ago. It took every ounce of willpower I had not to show the emotion on my face as I realized what I held.

A key.

It was warm and slippery from the sweat of my hand, but solid and usable. I closed my fist tight around it and focused my full attention on Viera. She was pacing now, walking the stretch of the bay windows.

"Cohen." She stopped and looked at him, took in his hand on my shoulder. Her brow furrowed, the only sign of annoyance as she said, "Have a seat."

He didn't move. Didn't even lift his hand from where it rested. It was a challenge of sorts.

A challenge that Viera dismissed when she said, "Very well then. Stay. It doesn't matter. She'll die either way."

Cohen stiffened.

The queen only folded her hands in front of herself. "I'd like to see the letter. I've already asked Dellacov to give it to me. I was . . ." She paused as if searching for the perfect word. "I was *amused* when I found out you were still holding on to it, like a lovesick puppy." Viera held out her hand.

Without a word, Cohen dug into his pocket and pulled out the treasonous letter. He stepped away just long enough to pass the wrinkled paper to his mother before he came back to stand behind me. She unfolded it and smiled as she began to read it aloud.

Every traitorous word.

The plea for Cohen, Uri, Juno, and Nadia.

My face heated and Cohen's fingers tightened against my skin, biting through the thin fabric of my shirt and pressing into already-bruised flesh. I wanted to sink into the carpet, to melt into nothingness.

When the queen finished the letter, she folded it again and held it up for me to see. "How foolish can you be? Did you learn nothing from what happened to the other girl?" She shook her head and threw the letter to the ground between us. "Did you learn nothing from the stupid child who dared to so much as touch my food before I gave her permission?"

I pressed my spine to the hard surface of the chair and twisted my wrist, trying to feel for the keyhole with my other hand. My movements were hidden by the wooden slats of the chair's back and Cohen's body. He stood close to me, staying just as he'd promised he would. Now I wondered what he'd meant by that. I didn't understand why Cohen had given me a key, but I wouldn't waste it. I would get free and then I would burn this entire place to the ground.

I would do it for Aviana and Grier and Elodie and Tessa and Joslyn and the hundreds of girls who had died playing this useless, senseless game—

Pain erupted, sharp and indignant, in my gut and I cried out. My body yielded, bending at the waist with the sheer intensity of it. Cohen's hand moved to my back.

I closed my eyes, tried to breathe through the pain. Every joint burned, stung, and quivered against her toxin. Fire swelled in my veins, rising up to meet it, but it was weak—as tremulous as I was.

Through it all, I focused on the edges of the key as it cut into my palm.

My stomach rolled and I dry heaved, spitting up bile and coughing on my own saliva, as my body tried to empty itself. I whimpered in pain and fear.

Then the pain was gone, pulled away, soothed by Viera or Larkin or the goddess herself, I didn't know. I didn't care. The room spun as I slowly sat up again. I had drool on my chin and shirt, but I couldn't wipe it away.

"Who leads the Culled?" Viera asked.

I shook my head and immediately regretted it as the world took off spinning again. My mouth watered with the onset of nausea, and I turned my face away from the queen, from Kinsley's too-pleased smile, from Larkin's amused smirk.

It was a mistake to look over my shoulder.

I caught sight of Kace's face.

To his credit, he wasn't smiling. He looked as pale as I felt. He'd hung back, his body pressed into one corner of the room, closer to the exit. I wonder if he'd wanted to stay or if that had been a part of his deal with Viera. Maybe he had to see me killed—proof that he was loyal to her.

The queen was still talking. "Who is in charge of their operation? I want names."

I didn't have names.

Like a knife slicing through the back of my skull, pain blossomed in my mind. It was strong and throbbing like a second pulse. Nerve endings lit, burned, and fried in a cacophony of agony that sent my neck flying back, had my head slamming against the back of the chair. Viera let the poison go, let it sizzle and die inside of me.

I was still shaking from the magnitude of it as she said, "I am your queen, and you will look at me when I am speaking to you." My vision swam, but I did as she said and turned my gaze to her. She was seething. "Who leads the Culled?"

Something wicked and vile rose up in me. I welcomed it, reveled in it. This was better than being afraid.

"I don't know—and even if I did, I sure as hell wouldn't tell you, you self-righteous bitch—"

Larkin's hand collided with the side of my face. A cry of pain and surprise tore from me. I tasted copper. Blood dripped from my nose, a slow trickle over my lips and down my chin. I turned away from her, lowering my head as I tried to summon fire, touch even the weakest spark.

Nothing.

Larkin said something, and I shook my head, trying to dispel the sudden haze in my vision. Before she could do anything else, I turned and spat a mouthful of blood onto her pristine white shirt. "Same goes for you, Larkin."

Then she was on her feet, her hand pulled back to strike me again. In an instant, Cohen's hand was off my shoulder and he was next to me, a wall of flesh and bone between us.

He and Larkin stood chest to chest, both of them breathing heavily. The room seemed to still; everyone tensed. He looked ready to strangle her.

Larkin just rolled her wrist, letting the joint pop as she eyed her brother. I knew she could sense every ounce of poison in his system, that she felt it just as surely as I could feel the heat of a nearby candle. It would be so easy, too easy, for her to stretch out and touch the toxin, let it grow.

The corner of Larkin's mouth quirked up in a patronizing smile as she let her dark eyes fall on me again. Cohen stepped sideways, just enough to block me from her view, and Larkin lifted her chin in challenge.

Dread pooled in the pit of my stomach, ice cold and nauseating. He had no idea what she could do—what she'd been doing to him.

When I kill my brother, I'll make sure everyone knows it was intentional.

Before I could stop myself, I said, "Cohen, leave her alone."

Larkin's smile was animalistic as she said, "Yes, Cohen, do as your little toy says."

The queen spoke, loud and commanding. "You will both stand down or you will remove yourselves from my presence. You are wasting my time as well as Miss Benson's. And she has so little left."

Cohen retreated to his spot behind me. He didn't touch me again, but I could feel his knuckles gripping the top of the chair. If I leaned back, just slightly, the tops of his fingers would brush the nape of my neck. As much as I wanted his touch, needed that ounce of moral support it offered, I forced myself to stay where I was.

"Now, Monroe," Viera said. I felt the creeping caress of poison. It ran soft fingertips along my spine as she continued. "Tell me about the Culled."

My mouth was dry, my throat tight.

She held up a hand. "Let me warn you, your answers will dictate how slowly or quickly I let you die. I can make it last days if I want—excruciating, agonizing days. So, choose your words with care."

I twisted the key in my hand, testing just how far I could rotate my wrist. Cohen had left the handcuffs loose, intentionally leaving me room to move around. My fingers ran along the band of the opposite cuff, searching for the small key insert.

I tried to keep my expression blank as I said, "They're just a rebel group—"

"Not good enough." The pain swelled again, burning at my stomach.

It was enough to make me bite my lip to keep from crying out. Tears welled, my hands shook, and I struggled to keep hold of the key. Through it all, I continued to feel for the small indentation of a keyhole.

"Let her speak!" Cohen's voice was sharp, nervous.

It didn't matter. I wasn't going to tell her anything. The edge I'd given the rebels, the exact maps and guard posts I had handed to Tallis, would remain my secret. I'd take it to the grave.

The pain receded again as Viera's head tilted to one side. "I'm waiting."

I spat blood onto the carpet and tried to level my breathing. I didn't know what to say, didn't know how to get out of this. The queen was watching me, her eyes narrowed in disgust.

I opened my mouth to say something, prepared to lie to her, if only to give myself more time, but I paused as my finger found the first keyhole. I swallowed, fighting for words.

I needed time. I needed something to say, something that would be believable, but have no truth to it. When I said nothing, only stared out at the bay windows, Cohen opened his mouth to speak, to lie or plead—I wasn't sure—but he was cut off by a knock at the music room door.

I used Viera's distraction to slide the key into the hole. I held it there, waiting. I didn't know when to use it. The room was filled with guards and I couldn't possibly fight them all, not before the queen or her daughter poisoned me.

"I'm sorry we're late," Nadia spoke from behind me, her voice hesitant.

I didn't turn around, just listened as the room shifted and adjusted to accommodate new people. More guards poured in and the first group surged forward, curving around the backs of the couches to make room. Nadia and Heidi quickly sat down, just far enough in my peripheral that I needed to turn to look at them fully.

I waited until things had stilled, fallen silent again, before I dared a glance at my friend. Nadia did not meet my eyes. Her mouth was a grave line, her eyes downcast. What must she think of all of this, of the things I'd done?

Shame clawed at my insides.

No one had believed in my ability more than Nadia. She had saved my life, even when doing so meant allowing me to continue in the Culling. I wondered if she hated me now. If she regretted the help that she'd given me and the glimpses of friendship we'd shared.

The doors to the music room were pulled shut again and everyone's attention moved back to the queen. I turned toward her too but Nadia made a sound, just the softest of coughs, and I hesitated. Our gazes met.

She looked to where Viera still stood but, as she turned her head, her hand, which had been closed in her lap, opened to reveal a tiny white-and-yellow aster flower.

My favorite. The ones Ambrose always brought with him when he came home.

The room stilled as I focused on that small flower.

Viera spoke, addressing me again, but I couldn't even hear her over the sound of the blood rushing in my ears. Nadia closed her fist around the bud, crushing it. Hiding it from sight. Still, my heart swelled.

Cohen's grip on my arm tightened in warning, but it was too late. Viera was already there.

She grabbed a fistful of my hair and yanked my head back so I was looking up at her. Her voice was deadly calm as she said, "Cohen, darling, you will take a step back. Now." She didn't look at him, didn't move her gaze from mine.

When he didn't listen, she yanked me up by the hair, pulling me until I was standing. The force of it made me lose my balance and I stumbled.

My hair pulled taut at the roots and my eyes watered in pain as the queen sent a jolt of poison through my veins. The key came loose from the cuff, slipped. I caught it just as Viera spun me, turning me to look at Cohen. She held me there, pressed to her, her nails digging trenches into the skin of my arm as she forced me to look at him.

"This girl," she growled, spittle and hot air hitting my cheek as she spoke to Cohen. "This insolent child would see you dead. She would kill you where you stand if you gave her the chance."

She sent another wave of white-hot agony, stronger than any I'd felt before, through my body. I screamed, a frustrated cry that tore through clenched teeth. My knees buckled and I shook involuntarily as my joints gave out and my muscles turned to jelly. I fell to my knees in front of the queen. She didn't release her hold on me, didn't stop her poison.

"She wants your birthright, *your throne*. She is willing to stab you in the back to get it and still you stand there like a lovesick idiot. She does not care for you."

Cohen swallowed and looked at me. "Let her go."

"Or what?" Viera seethed. "What on earth will you do?"

Beads of sweat gathered on Cohen's forehead, just a light sheen at first, then more. His skin turned pallid, the color of chalk. He swallowed but didn't make a sound. His eyes never left his mother; he knew, as well as I did, what was happening.

But Cohen was wrong about the source.

This wasn't Viera's doing.

Larkin sat looking up at her brother, her eyes wide, her mouth parted slightly as she watched her handiwork. A drop of blood oozed from Cohen's nose and his breathing turned ragged. I tried to move forward but Viera held me still.

The queen just watched, her eyes widening slightly in surprise as she realized what I already knew. Larkin was manipulating the poison. The girl leaned forward, elbows on her knees, and brought one hand to her lips.

Her fingers twitched, and he lurched with them.

She'd kill him right here.

Something grew within me, a sort of flutter—a restless beast awakening deep in my bones. I could feel Viera's poison stirring inside me, but it was weak, drowned out by something else, a low burning that soothed and calmed.

It was familiar, this feeling, and I had the sneaking suspicion that I had Nadia to thank for it. I also knew that my own fire was there, pressing up against the toxins, bolstered by the healing work my friend was doing. I looked to her and saw the focus etched on her face.

Those doe eyes were bouncing from Cohen to me over and over again. She was trying to heal us both, but Nadia could only do so much. Her ability was only so strong.

The way Cohen was standing had his back to most of the room so the guards didn't see what was being done to their prince. No one was going to step in.

Britta, his protector, was gone. His father was nowhere to be found. And Uri—Uri had chosen to save me. He was alone in this. Alone to face down two venomous snakes.

But I was there.

Viera's attention was on Larkin and Cohen, too distracted by this new development with her children to worry about me. My fingers trembled as I worked the key into the first lock. It stuck and I panicked, trying to twist it to no avail. I pulled it out and tried again, turning the same way once and then, when it still didn't work, I rotated the key the other way. The handcuff fell loose, dangling from the remaining wrist.

I didn't move an inch; I stayed just as I was, Viera's hand still in my hair, her nails still piercing my bare arm. Inside me, fire blazed to life, full and powerful, more than I'd felt in days. It pounded against my skin, a second pulse that echoed the first.

I started shaking again, but this time it was with my own restless energy. My ability, my fire, was a faceless monster waiting to be released. But not yet—I wasn't ready.

Cohen swayed on his feet. He opened his mouth, tried to say something, but no sound emerged. He was looking at his mother, despair and horror etched into his face. Those blue eyes glittered with disbelief. Surely, Viera would not actually kill her son—would not kill her heir.

But Larkin would. Perhaps Larkin had always planned to.

I saw the queen's brow furrow, watched as her eyes darted between her children. I wondered if she'd known about Larkin. Had she sanctioned every poisoning? Had she created this monster?

Cohen collapsed. A few guards moved forward, but a lifted hand from Viera made them stop where they were. Cohen remained on his knees, gasping for air. Something ancient and instinctual made my control slip, made my mark glow.

No.

I called it back, pulled it tight against me. Nadia must have seen something in me change because her focus moved to Cohen. I felt that shift, felt Nadia's healing energy disappear.

Larkin was taking her time, working slowly, letting the poison eat away at Cohen. His hands were fists against the carpet, his body bent before his mother. She did nothing, said nothing.

She just watched.

Nadia lurched sideways in surprise as she realized what was happening. A little cry of shock escaped her and she turned, scanning the room to see if anyone else had realized that Larkin was the poisoner. Cohen made a sound as her concentration broke and the brunt of Larkin's poison, what Nadia had been combatting, hit him.

Nadia turned toward the door. I looked for the first time too, taking in the new soldiers scattered about.

I saw him right away, my eyes finding him just as Kace saw him too. There, standing next to the door, dressed in a palace guard's uniform, was Ambrose. My mouth flew open but I made no sound.

Kace yelled something, a warning.

At the same time, Kinsley pushed up from the couch. "There . . . There are rebels—!"

"No—!" Nadia's cry was drowned out by another sound.

The sound of me setting Viera's dress on fire.

The queen screamed and tried to pull away from me, but I had my fingers wrapped in the fabric of her dress, creating a bridge for my fire as it licked at the pretty material. Before she could wrench away from me, I pushed up from the floor and elbowed her in the nose, hard enough to draw blood.

Around me, the room was a flurry of motion; people were screaming and yelling orders. Weapons were out. It was impossible to tell friend from foe.

The smoke from my fire was already starting to fill the room with a grayish haze, only adding to the chaos. Guards were yelling in confusion and pain as blades found their way between ribs and slid against throats.

Across the room, Ambrose was wading through the fighting, past flailing limbs and slashing knives. He narrowly missed being hit in the face as one of the guards tackled another man.

He was yelling my name, holding out his hand.

I let go of Viera's dress, gesturing the fire forward with one hand, while I stepped toward the center of the room. I could still hear Ambrose shouting at me, telling me to run. But I couldn't go, not now, not with Cohen hurt.

Nadia was on the floor with his head in her lap. He was shaking against her splayed palms, an involuntary twitching brought on by poison. Cohen gripped Nadia's arm, his eyes watering as he fought to speak.

I knelt down in front of them. "Cohen?"

He didn't seem to notice I was even there. His attention was on Nadia as she pressed her hands to his chest, her brown eyes focused, her jaw set, as she tried to heal him. Around us, the room was in chaos. The carpet was soaked in blood.

Nadia's face was grim as she glanced up at me. "I don't know what to do. I don't know how to help him."

I had to yell to be heard over the growing din. "We need to get him standing."

Cohen spoke, his voice gravely with pain. "Go. Now."

Nadia looked down at him and then looked to Larkin.

The princess was on her feet. She'd retreated behind the piano, far enough away to avoid the main mass of guards, but close enough that she could still poison Cohen.

He was her only focus, the only toy she cared to play with. And she was taking her time, letting the poison ease through his body. This was not the quick kill I knew she was capable of.

I stood up just in time to see Kace hit Ambrose from the side, ramming a shoulder into him with so much force it sent the two of them careening deeper into the fight. My curse was drowned out by a scream of fury as Kinsley unleashed herself on a nearby rebel.

One of the Culled had tried to grab her from behind. At the sudden touch, Kinsley's whirled hand splayed, tendrils of vines shooting from her fingertips like the claws of some monstrous beast. Now she had him pinned to the wall. I turned away as she tightened her fist.

The room was overflowing with too many people. Many of the Culled were dressed as Erydian palace guards, and it was impossible to tell which was which. I knelt next to Nadia and Cohen.

I had no idea what to do or where to go. Ambrose had once told me to shoot first and ask questions later—and that was exactly what I did.

Two palace guards came running over, reaching for the guns strapped to their hips. I didn't hesitate. Fire exploded from my fingertips, catching the first man in the face. He screamed and fell back against the solider behind him. I sent a second blast, this one larger than the first. It was enough to knock them both down.

They screamed in agony as my flames ate across their skin. Vomit rose in my throat as the smell of burned hair and skin filled the air, but I did not call the fire back to me. I let it loose, let it grow. It ate at the men, at the rug beneath their twitching bodies, at the armchair adjacent to them.

They screamed. Smoke filled the room.

I told myself I didn't care. Before this was done, I'd burn Viera's entire palace to the ground. Still, my hands shook slightly as they finally quieted.

Heidi scrambled over to us on her hands and knees. "It's Larkin! She's—"

"I know," Nadia and I said at the same time.

Heidi blinked at us. "Is she goddess-touched?"

I shook my head, still watching my fire as it crawled, like a snake, across the floor toward two more Erydian guards. I forced myself to look away, to not think of what I was doing—the people I was killing.

I shoved that fire forward with an invisible hand, commanding it to feast. Then I met Heidi's eyes. "I don't know. But she'll kill Cohen if she isn't stopped."

Nadia was trembling, her palms still pressed to Cohen's chest. She used the back of her hand to wipe sweat from her brow. "We have to do something. I'm trying but . . ." She looked to me. "I don't know what else to do."

I nodded and stood up. Heidi rose with me, both of us crouching low trying to hide amongst my smoke. We were prepared, eyes darting, bodies shaking with tension.

This was the stance we'd been taught, the only way we knew to be. But this wasn't the arena and these weren't goddess-touched girls. This was blood and sweat and close quarters.

I took in my surroundings. The only thing separating us from the majority of the fighting were the couches, which blocked off the center of the floor and left an empty pocket where Nadia and Cohen still sat.

I felt, more than saw, Viera put my fire out. At the dying of those flames, I spun to look at her. She now stood to one side of the room, her back to me as she turned that cool blue gaze on the nearest guard. She didn't bat an eye, didn't even look close enough to see whether he was a Culled rebel.

With a twitch of her fingers, he was on the floor. She moved slowly, limping as she walked down one side of the couch. The whole bottom edge of her dress was burned, the dark tights she wore showing patches of raw and bloody skin.

Still, what I'd done hadn't been enough. She'd managed to get the fire out and, with more flames blazing toward the door, I couldn't risk trying to start another. The smoke was already making me light-headed; anything more and I might not be able to make it out.

I slipped backward, trying to remain hidden by an overturned armchair as I watched Viera cross the room. I was no longer her focus. This was a slaughter, a culling of its own. Her fingers darted—slow, bored, no more than a flick of her wrist and a guard would fall.

She did it once, twice, three times.

It took a second for me to realize exactly what she was doing, exactly how this played to her advantage—not every guard she aimed at dropped dead. This would leave half a fighting pair standing, unaffected.

The Culled didn't live here, I realized. They didn't eat Viera's food or drink her poisoned wine. She couldn't manipulate something that wasn't there. She was weeding out the rebels. After each poisoning, a true Erydian guard would surge forward, taking their fallen comrade's place and killing the remaining rebel.

"Monroe!" Someone grabbed me from behind.

Instinctively I spun, nearly slapping them across the face with the handcuff still attached to my wrist.

Ambrose dodged it, catching my arm in his hand. He pulled me away from Cohen. "Leave him," he said. "Leave him, now. We have to go."

I turned away from him. Heidi and Nadia were getting Cohen on his feet and I tucked my arm under his, helping to bear his weight.

My brother tried to pull me toward the door again. "Monroe, we have to—"

"I can't," I said through gritted teeth, fighting against Cohen's dead weight. "I can't leave him. He'll die."

My words were drowned out by Heidi's scream. "Watch out—!"

From the corner of my eye, I watched an Erydian soldier throw a knife, aimed directly at Ambrose. He didn't see it in time and Heidi's warning came too late. It struck him in the shoulder and he stumbled forward, nearly knocking all of us over.

Anger tightened Heidi's expression. Without warning, she let go of Cohen, spun, and shoved both her hands toward the offending guard. For a split second, nothing happened. He didn't blink, didn't so much as stumble.

Then, from deep in his chest, came the most wicked, high-pitched, bloodcurdling scream. I'd never heard anything like it. Never wished to hear anything like it again.

Heidi growled, an animalistic snarl that sent a shiver down my spine. Under her gaze, the man scratched at his face, his arms, his eyes, clawing his skin so deeply it bled.

With the tilt of her head, the man's hands were around his own neck. His eyes bulged, the veins in his face rising up against ashen skin. I watched in horror as Heidi tortured the man without moving an inch.

Nadia moved sideways, toward my brother. Before he could stop her, she gripped the handle of the knife and yanked it from his shoulder. He yelped in pain and tried to shove her away but I grabbed him.

"Let her help," I yelled. "Just . . . please. Let her."

I didn't wait to see if he listened. Larkin's focus was gone from Cohen, turned on a rebel who had come too close. I bent down and Cohen gripped my arm. "You need to leave. Monroe, please. Please go. This is your chance. Take them and go."

Another guard came at Larkin from the other direction. She snarled at them through clenched teeth and made quick work of the first guard, one of her own men, dropping him dead with the same brutal efficiency as her mother. It took seconds.

With her back turned, she didn't see the second person dart forward. There was no time for Larkin to react before the rebel's knife was buried deep in her back. The princess screamed, feral and venomous.

"Monroe?" Cohen still gripped my arm, his eyes following his sister as she bent, panting against the top of the piano. "Monroe, look at me!"

I did. I met those blue eyes, the eyes that belonged to the queen that I hated and the boy that I loved.

"Please. Please, Monroe."

My name had never sounded so terrible, so broken. Cohen swallowed, wincing as Larkin's focus found him again. He exhaled, breathy and afraid.

"Please, just listen to me. You have to go. Take your brother and get out of here."

I hoped he could see the apology in my eyes.

There was no time to think, no time to reconsider what I'd already made up my mind to do. I reached forward, pressed a kiss to Prince Cohen Warwick's cheek, and pulled one of his throwing knives free from the bandolier across his chest.

Then I was gone.

39

The Music Room

The day of execution

Cohen didn't have time to stop me. I was running, crawling over the flipped armchair and sliding along the far edge of the wall. I heard Ambrose call my name, scream for me to come back, but I didn't listen. Months ago, my brother had promised to find a way to save me—but I would find a way to save myself.

Larkin was trying to pull the knife free from her back, but it was too high up, in too deep for her to dislodge without help. Realizing this, she turned her full attention back to Cohen, ready to finish what she'd started. I hurried my pace, slipping through gaps in the fighting.

As I reached the front of the room, I darted underneath the piano. She didn't see me hidden there and didn't seem to notice I was gone from where I'd been. I wasn't her target.

Cohen had made it to his feet, but as her poison found him again, he stumbled. Nadia moved away from Ambrose and grabbed a hold of Cohen's arm, helping to hold him up. Her eyes narrowed as she tried to heal as quickly as Larkin poisoned. Heidi moved to support his other side. My brother spun, searching for me.

I dropped to my stomach and inched farther underneath the piano, sliding toward Larkin. Cohen's throwing knife slipped against my damp palms, but I held it firm. It felt unnatural to hold a weapon.

For months, fire had been my only ally, but to add flame would be to add smoke and I needed to be able to see. The room was too small, too packed. Another distraction, even one of my own making, could prove fatal for my friends.

I paused as a shout went up—as the doors to the music room opened and more people flooded inside. They were screaming, jeering, and waving handguns and serrated hunting knives.

The air caught in my throat, terror holding my heart in an iron grip as I tried to decide what we could do against so many new weapons, so many new enemies. But then Ambrose turned and raised a fist in greeting. He whistled, long and shrill, the same sound I'd heard every evening as he'd come home from market. These were his people.

Our people.

Viera paused in her killing and yelled for the guards to rally. To attack.

Larkin's gaze moved from Cohen to the incoming rebels. I used her distraction to my advantage. Before anyone could notice or give her warning, I shoved forward from the ground with my hands, spun sideways, and caught her ankles in a solid kick.

She didn't see it coming. The pain of the blow was enough to make her cry out and stumble sideways. Before she could fall to the floor, Larkin managed to catch herself on the top of the instrument. It didn't matter. I was already up and moving.

I darted forward and shoved into her, using every ounce of strength I had to push her to the ground. The knife already in her back buried itself deeper as I crushed her against the carpet. She bellowed, in anger, in pain, in fury—I didn't care.

My elbow collided with her face before she could get her bearings enough to even think to poison me. I straddled her, pinning her to the floor with all of my weight. She rose up, trying to knock me off, but I held fast, one fist wrapped in the front of her shirt, the other still gripping Cohen's knife.

I brought the blade down, but she caught my wrist, pushing the knife away, trying to turn it toward me. I called fire to my hands and Larkin screamed as red-hot flame surrounded my fist, the handle of the knife, and her fingers. She pulled away, her palm already beginning to blister.

Larkin writhed under me, shaking with pain, fear, and anger. I started to lose my balance, but managed to right myself just as Larkin sent a sliver of poison coursing through my veins. It was weak, unfocused.

I could feel invisible fingers of power scraping, clumsily gathering what toxin was left. The dull pain was enough to make me tense, make me lose my concentration. Larkin backhanded me, the force of her slap enough to send me falling sideways.

In an effort to catch myself, I let the knife go. It missed the carpet and clattered against the hardwood floor. My flailing hands sent it sliding underneath the piano. I dove for it, reaching with shaking hands, but it was too far away.

Larkin gripped the toppled armchair in an effort to stand, but I reached out, catching hold of her pants in my flaming hand. I kept her on her knees as I sent ribbons of fire snaking up her body.

The scream that erupted from her was vicious, almost inhuman. She got to her feet, ripping from my grasp as she tried to put the fire out.

I stood too, resting one hand on the piano as I tried to get my bearings. Adrenaline had me shaking. The room was a mess of screaming people, dead or dying men and women. Blood splattered the wallpaper, flecked the pretty carpet. Smoke blurred everything.

I searched for my friends, for Kace or Ambrose.

I caught sight of the top of Cohen's head. He was standing by the door, trying to get Nadia out of the room. She was fighting against his hold, pointing in my direction, screaming something I couldn't hear over the fighting. Cohen looked too, over the bodies and people, to where I stood.

His eyes widened and he opened his mouth to yell—

But I didn't hear it.

My ears rang as pain exploded in my head, so sharp, so sudden, that I thought I would die of it. My vision tinged red and the room spun; it tilted sideways.

I screamed.

I'd thought the poisoners were using their full ability on me—on Cohen—but I was wrong. The pain before was merely a taste, a drop of water compared to the ocean that was this ravaging power.

Sweat-damp fingers gripped the piano as I tried to hold myself up, but my arms didn't work; my legs were useless. My body tried and failed to throw up. I gagged on oxygen and saliva, sputtered as my vision shattered into a million mosaic pieces.

This, I thought, *must be what burning feels like.* It was molten heat, in every fiber, every pulse of my heart. I tasted blood.

Through slitted lids, I saw Viera's lips pull back in a snarl. She was feet from me now, so close that she could touch me if she wanted to. But that wasn't necessary; my death wouldn't require her touch.

She could have done it quickly, the way she'd killed so many others—but I was a special case. I was important to Cohen. She knew that. So, she didn't make it quick.

A scream ripped through me, angry and frightened and uncontrollable. I only knew because of the dry burning in my throat. I felt each violent outburst from my lungs, my very being fighting against this inner shredding.

I was breaking.

Then I was silent. I leaned against the piano in an effort to remain standing. I couldn't breathe. In that moment, I was in the arena again with Tessa's hands around my throat. The oxygen was gone.

I heard my name bellowed on someone's lips—lips that had kissed me. Lips that had promised not to leave me.

The queen's smile grew.

Her hand lifted, moved forward. One finger shifted, bent only slightly. With that minuscule movement, I felt the poison rise, blister, and burn, scrape its taloned nails against my veins. Deep. Excruciating.

I think I screamed.

I think Cohen might have screamed too.

Then oblivion.

Nothing.

Everything stopped: the sounds, the screams, the pain. There was a moment of surreal stillness.

Three heartbeats.

Then Viera made a sound, a little gasp of surprise.

I didn't see him run toward her. I didn't see him push past the guards or jump over the back of the couch. But I saw the knife embed itself in her neck.

I saw it leave his fingers, twist slightly in midair, and land true, directly in the hollow of the queen's throat—just as with all those practices before.

And Cohen didn't stop moving. Before she could even try to keep him away, he pushed into her, one hand grasping her shoulder, the other plunging a second knife into her gut. He twisted it, once, twice, a third time. Then he held her gaze as he pulled it out and shoved it up through her ribs and into her heart.

She coughed blood into his face and still, he didn't move. Didn't step away. Cohen only watched as the light left her cold blue eyes.

They stayed there, in that odd embrace, for what felt like eternity. The prince held the queen upright, watching until her knees gave out and her eyes didn't blink anymore.

Then he let her drop.

The sound that ripped from Larkin's chest was savage, deadly.

Cohen stood holding the knife, his mother's blood coating his fingers and dripping onto the floor. The room, which had seemed to freeze as the knife had flown, as the prince had buried it deep in his mother's body, now sprang into motion once more. Around us, the Culled cheered.

But Cohen didn't move.

A boy, no more than thirteen or fourteen years old, appeared in the doorway. He was red-faced and panting. The eyes of the room darted in his direction as he grabbed the arm of the nearest rebel and tugged him toward the door. "They're coming! We gotta go!"

With that, the rebels scattered.

They grabbed lost weapons from the floor as they stumbled over dead and dying Erydians. Viera's poisoning had left her own forces outnumbered. Her remaining guards seemed stunned, too shocked by the death of the queen to move.

Off in the distance, something shattered, like a million windows breaking all at once. The entire palace seemed to shudder. An alarm began to wail. People were shouting, screaming.

This seemed to snap the Erydian guards out of their haze. They converged on Larkin, a protective shield of flesh and bone. Kinsley lay a few feet away, unconscious or dead—I wasn't sure which.

I turned and caught sight of Ambrose near the door. He was pushing against the flow of bodies, trying to reach me. He was screaming my name.

The Erydian forces tried to organize themselves. They yelled over each other, shouting orders. Larkin was still leaning against the overturned chair, holding her burned hand to her chest. She was pale as a sheet and shaking as she looked toward the slumped body at Cohen's feet.

Her poison brushed against my skin, running along my spine. A threat. I didn't know if it was her own weakness or the lack of poison left in my body, but the pain never swelled beyond a gentle, coaxing sort of ache.

Cohen didn't even glance in my direction as I approached him. When Viera had fallen, she'd done so in a way that left her propped up against the wall, head tilted back, glassy eyes looking up at nothing.

Looking up at her son.

I leaned down and grabbed the knife from her neck. Blood gushed out of the deep wound it left. I said nothing as I cleaned the blade on my pants and slid it back into his bandolier.

I took the second knife from his hand and cleaned it too. "We have to go," I said as I slipped the knife into the sheath. When he didn't look at me,

I pressed my palm, bloody from so many different people, against his arm. "Cohen?" The chandelier above our heads swung as another explosion shook the palace.

Finally, he turned to me.

He was ashen, his eyes wide. His mouth parted as he tried to form words, tried to say something, anything. I could feel him shaking beneath my hand.

His bottom lip trembled. "Monroe, I—"

"We're leaving or we're dead." Ambrose reached me, his hand gripping my upper arm as he said, "Get out of here." He pulled me away from Cohen and pushed me toward the door. "Run, now!"

Ambrose grabbed Cohen by the back of the shirt and shoved him after me. That seemed to snap something in him, made Cohen remember where we were and what was happening. He was at my heels as I entered the hallway.

Something deep in the bones of the palace was on fire; I could feel the pulse of it. Guards were running toward that growing blaze, disappearing from sight. At the other end of the hall, rebels were fleeing away like frightened animals.

"Monroe." Cohen caught my wrist in his hand and pulled me to a stop. "I need to—"

Ambrose came careening out of the music room and bumped into me. He shook his head, exasperated. "Less talking, more running." He tried to get me moving again, but I dug my boots into the tile.

"Where is Nadia?" I asked.

His eyebrows shot up. "Who—?"

"The girl who healed you."

He nodded toward the end of the hall. "I sent her and that blond girl ahead with some other rebels. I'm sure they're safe. Now, run."

Cohen turned to me again, his eyes wild with a new emotion. "My sister."

Ambrose tugged on my arm. "Run."

Cohen's grip on my wrist tightened. "I can't leave Uri. Larkin will—"

We jumped as another explosion sounded from behind us, this one larger than the last. It seemed the Culled had been busy. There was more screaming, Erydian soldiers were yelling for help. A rebel from down the hall shouted for Ambrose to hurry up.

My brother nodded toward the disappearing rebels. "Walk and talk."

We started moving again.

"Uri—" Cohen said again.

I fiddled with the remaining handcuff on my wrist as I asked, "Where is she?"

"With Hugo in the infirmary."

"And where is that?"

My brother interrupted before Cohen could answer. "We aren't going back for anyone. The transports will leave us." He pressed a hand to my back, forcing me to hurry my pace.

"I have to find her," Cohen said.

"More guards are on their way," Ambrose explained. "There've been some distractions, but they'll send people after us soon. They'll lock the exits, if they haven't already started."

We rounded a corner, following Ambrose back the way I'd come with Cohen earlier.

Before I could ask, Cohen said, "How the hell did you get in?"

"The emergency exit tunnels. There was a map . . ."

I felt Cohen's eyes on me. "And we're going back that way?" he asked.

Ambrose nodded.

Cohen glanced sideways at me. "The infirmary is near the training rooms. It would only take a minute to stop and—"

"Listen, *prince*," Ambrose snapped. "I don't give a damn what you do, but *my sister* is getting out of here. Now."

"Well, I'm not leaving without mine."

There was another explosion and Cohen turned to look. His steps were slowing, his energy dwindling, leaving him red-faced and trembling. I knew that feeling; I was teetering on a burnout myself. Adrenaline and shock made my muscles quiver with each step, but I pushed forward, forced myself to keep moving.

I said, "We'll get Uri and then we'll get out."

"And if she isn't there?" Ambrose demanded. "I won't let you get trapped here—"

Cohen didn't let him finish. "She'll be there."

We took the stairs. If the guards were smart, they would cut the power and that would freeze the lifts and lock any of the electric doors. Many of the Culled had come to a similar conclusion and the stairwell echoed with the thundering of heavy boots.

Even with his longer legs, Cohen stayed in step with me. It was hard to look at him, harder still to look at the bloodstains we left on the stair railing. This was who we were now—*what* we were.

I didn't know what it meant.

I had too many questions and too few answers.

I wanted to ask Ambrose about Kace. I'd looked for his body as I'd left the music room but I hadn't seen him. Despite everything, I thanked the goddess for that. If Kace had died, been killed by Ambrose or someone else, that would mean all of this—the way he'd spoken to me, the things he'd said—would be what I was left with.

And even if he'd betrayed me—he was still my brother. I needed more than that. The memory of the way he'd looked at me, how he'd stood there as Viera hurt me, left a bitter taste in my mouth.

That couldn't be my last memory of him.

But there wasn't time to worry about it now. Even if I wanted to. Even if it was all I could think about as we hurtled down flight after flight of stairs.

When we reached the bottom, we split off from where the rebels had gone and headed toward the training rooms. We reached another split in the hall and Cohen nodded to the left. "The infirmary is that way. Not very far. I'll go find Uri and circle back."

I threaded my hand in his. "I'm going with you."

"Hell no. Monroe is staying with me," Ambrose argued.

I didn't listen, just pulled Cohen in the direction he'd indicated. My brother cursed under his breath, but the sound of his footsteps proved that he was following us. Our pace quickened as we reached a set of metal doors. Cohen took the lead as we entered a hallway lined with a dozen or so small sickrooms.

He started yelling her name as we made our way toward a lit room at the end of the walkway. We'd almost reached it when Dellacov stepped through the doorway and into the hall.

My brother grabbed my shoulder and yanked me back, the force of it so jarring I nearly fell to the floor. Ambrose's hold kept me upright, but even once I was steady, he didn't let go of my arm. I froze and Cohen's grip on my hand tightened as he took in the gun his best friend now had aimed at my head.

Dellacov's voice was quiet as he said, "Miss Benson, you will step away."

Cohen lifted a hand. "Hugo—"

The gun shook in his hands. "I know you care about her." His voice was a frightened plea. "I understand that. But she's dangerous. You're smarter than this, Cohen. She'll kill you. She doesn't care about you or any of us. All she cares about is—"

"Put the gun down," Cohen said.

Ambrose tried to tug me backward. "We need to leave."

Cohen watched the gun with apprehension as he asked, "Is Uri here?"

"Miss Benson," Dellacov whispered, "I will not warn you again. Step away from the prince."

"Uri?" Cohen called.

Her head poked around the door frame. "I'm right here." She looked between Dellacov's gun and me. There was a slight tremble to her voice as she said, "Hugo, just let Monroe leave. Let her go and things can return to normal."

Cohen held out a hand to his sister. "We have to leave."

She stepped fully into the hall. "Leave?"

Ambrose spoke to Cohen through clenched teeth. "If you get my sister killed, I swear to the goddess, I'll . . ."

Uri placed a hand on Dellacov's arm. He didn't seem steady on his feet and certainly didn't seem like he should be holding a gun. His hair was matted in places with dried blood and there was a thick white bandage covering his forehead and one of his hands.

Cohen stepped forward, his open palm outstretched to his sister. "Please, just come with me."

"And where are we going?" Uri's eyes scanned Cohen, and then me, noting the blood covering us. Her face paled. "What . . . What is it? What's happened?"

"I—" Cohen's bottom lip trembled and he swallowed.

"The queen is dead," I said.

Uri's eyes widened and her grip on Dellacov's arm grew white-knuckled. "*Dead?*"

I nodded.

Her voice was little more than a whisper as she put the pieces together. As she took in the blood splattered on his face. "Cohen, please tell me you didn't—"

"We have to get out of here." I pointed behind us. "There are more guards coming, and if we don't get out of the palace we'll be executed."

"*You* should already be executed," Dellacov spat.

Cohen's voice shook as he said, "Uri, I can't stay. I . . . I have to leave."

For a second, she didn't move; she just looked at him. Finally, she nodded. "Okay then. Let's go." With that, she took off down the hall toward us.

Dellacov blinked in surprise. "I'm sorry, what?"

She took Cohen's outstretched hand and turned to look over her shoulder at Dellacov. "You heard him."

"But—"

"Your choices are to come with us or let us leave." Uri inhaled sharply and swallowed, trying to keep her shoulders back, somehow managing to still be a princess when her court was crumbling around her. "Please . . . *Please*, Hugo. Please come with me."

He shook his head, his eyes darting to me. "Did she kill Viera?"

"No," Cohen said.

And that was all. It was nothing more than the solidification of my innocence—but Dellacov understood. It was as if my innocence could only mean Cohen's guilt.

Dellacov kept the gun in his hand as we moved toward the tunnels. Cohen led the way, his fingers still wrapped securely around mine. No one spoke. No one asked any more questions.

The prince had murdered the queen—there was nothing more to be said. The choice had been made when Cohen had thrown that first knife. And I knew I was partially, if not entirely, to blame for this—for his personal undoing. A series of my choices had led him to do something he'd never wanted to do.

I wished I could take it back. I wished that it hadn't had to be him.

But I couldn't erase what had happened, so I just held tight to his hand. I clung to him as we hurried down hallway after hallway, through dark tunnels and down sets of rock-chiseled stairs.

While I couldn't begin to understand what he was feeling, I knew how it felt to be forced to kill someone. I knew that there was a mark on my soul that I couldn't remove. I wouldn't wish a weight like that on anyone.

"Let me go first," Ambrose said as we neared a doorway. Up ahead, the space opened into a low-ceilinged cave. "Just keep quiet and do whatever you're told."

The hushed voices of the remaining rebels echoed back to us, a low murmur of fear and anxiety. We stopped just out of sight and listened as they discussed the transports and what was going on in the palace above us.

Ambrose headed straight toward them and, for a moment, the group paused their conversation. Then they began talking about who had gotten out and who hadn't. They argued over whether or not they should send a group to try to rescue any of the wounded still left upstairs. I didn't listen to my brother's response.

Cohen was gripping my hand like he thought I might disappear, as if I were the only thing keeping him standing up.

I heard Ambrose ask if there was room on the transports for more people. Someone responded to him, but the whispers and echo of the cave made it hard to understand what was being said.

Uri clung to Dellacov, her fists tight in the fabric of his bloodstained uniform. She said something to him and he nodded in response before pressing a chaste kiss to her forehead. She only sighed in response and buried her face in his shoulder.

Ambrose came back to us. "There are two more transports out back and a third is on its way. Monroe will ride with the goddess-touched girls and the three of you will go on the other transport. I'll hang back and ride in the one coming."

I started to argue, but he shook his head. "It isn't up for debate."

There were only about twenty rebels left in the cave as we entered. The sound of footsteps could be heard coming from another stretch of passageways off to the right—the emergency exit. We were about to walk past them and into that second darkened stretch of tunnels when one of the rebels addressed Cohen.

"How much time do you think we've got before they send someone to check down here?"

Cohen seemed surprised, but then the royal mask was there, sliding effortlessly into place. "I doubt anyone will think about this exit, not with the chaos. Hugo—the Captain of the Guard—is in charge of those procedures and he's here." He nodded to Dellacov. "The king will—"

A girl, not much older than I was, spoke up. "Oh, we don't have to worry about the king anymore."

Uri inhaled a sharp breath. "Why?"

It was as if they all realized she was there at the same time. Or as if they'd just remembered that she was a princess, that this was her home, and that Cohen—queen-killer or not—was technically the future king of Erydia.

For a second, no one dared answer her.

Then, someone said, "Because the king is dead."

There was a long pause.

"Dead," she repeated. "How is he dead?"

Someone laughed. "A bullet in the brain did it well enough."

Around us, other rebels laughed too. Someone made a comment about the king being drunk, about how it had been an easy kill. One bullet had done the job. He hadn't seen it coming.

Cohen made a sound, something that might have been mistaken as a cleared throat if it weren't for the sudden shining in his eyes. I grabbed his hand and pulled him toward the cavern exit. Uri and Dellacov followed close at our heels.

It was dark out, dark enough to make it hard to see without my eyes first adjusting. We paused in the middle of a small gravel courtyard. It was little more than a small sheltered parking area camouflaged by tall trees.

I was afraid to look at Cohen, unsure what I would do if he cried. I couldn't see it, couldn't live with the fact that I'd done this—I'd forced him to this moment.

And yet, in the darkest part of myself, it felt right. I'd been forced from my home. Hunted. I'd given up a part of myself, my own freedom, because of Cohen's crown. And in some small, terrible way, it felt only fair that he might also have to lose something valuable too.

I hated that I felt that way. I hated that, somewhere mixed in with my own guilt was a sense of ease. This was what I'd wanted: Viera was dead. The king was dead. The Culled was making changes. I knew that the Culling would be ended because of what had happened tonight.

I jumped as Ambrose's hand found my shoulder. He pulled me away from Cohen and steered me toward the nearest transport. It was a simple black van, very similar to the one used to get to and from trials. The back doors of it were open and a bare light bulb shone dimly, illuminating the dozen or so people crammed inside.

It was already full, and I knew that I wouldn't be the last person to board it. Anxiety swelled at the idea of being pressed against so many unknown bodies. We would share oxygen. It would be hot, and dark. I didn't think—I didn't think I could—

I swallowed. "How far away is where we're going?"

"A few hours. They'll change vehicles a few times, but as long as you listen and do what the drivers say, you'll be fine. I promise." Ambrose gave my shoulder a light squeeze and then pulled me into a hug.

I relaxed into his arms, fighting against the sudden urge to sob. It had been such a long day—and it had been ages since I'd felt safe anywhere at all. I wondered if I would ever feel safe again.

His voice was rough as he whispered, "I promised I'd save you. I told you I would. But I think you did it on your own."

"I made a mess of things."

"Maybe," he said. "But I'm so damn proud of you."

I only held on to him tighter.

After a second, he stepped back and nodded to the van. "I'll feel better when you're gone from here."

I watched as four more people crammed onto my transport. Bile rose in my throat and I had to look away to get my breathing under control.

"You okay?" Ambrose asked.

"I'll be fine."

Behind him, the last of the rebels were piling onto the second transport. Dellacov was helping Uri inside—trying to get her a seat so she wouldn't have to sit on the floor.

On the path up ahead, the headlights of the third van bobbed faintly against the heavy darkness of the night. Someone called Ambrose's name, asking him a question.

"I'll see you there. I love you." With one last touch of my shoulder, he was gone.

I was about to climb into the van when Cohen spoke up from the shadows. "Wait." Cohen's hand found my wrist in the darkness as he stopped, toe to toe with me. He pulled at the remaining handcuff on my wrist.

There was so much that we still needed to say to one another. A million things had changed when he'd thrown that knife. And yet, so many things were the same.

"Here," he reached into his pocket and pulled out a key, small and identical to the one he'd given me earlier. I watched as he unlocked the cuff and let it drop to the ground beside us.

We were still and silent for a long moment.

I rubbed at my bare wrist. "Why did you give me the key?"

"I don't know. I thought . . . I thought I could do it and then . . ." He trailed off. "Even after I found out what you'd done, even when I was furious, I still wanted it to be you. I wanted to believe you were meant to be queen. I wanted to believe that the girl who'd saved me all those years ago was still . . ."

His touch drifted from my wrist to my hand. His fingers threaded through mine. I looked up at him, watching his heavy expression morph into a deep sorrow. This was a look he only showed me, the smallest glimpse through the mask.

He had lost so very much, so very quickly.

Because of me.

I reached up and brushed away a stray tear as it tracked its way down his face. "Don't cry," I said, quietly, so no one else could hear. "Not in front of them. You're better than that."

He let out a quiet, humorless laugh. "That was a stupid thing to say to you."

"No." I shook my head. "It was true."

He caught my hand in midair, pressing my palm to his face as he leaned in and kissed me—a real kiss. It was desperate, a push of raw emotion. This kiss sent the world spinning. It left me entirely sure and unsure all at once.

I was breathless as he pulled away.

Just before his fingers left mine, he pressed something small and delicate into my hand, wrapping my fingers securely around it.

Someone gave a last call for the transports.

"What is it?" I asked.

Cohen moved away from me, heading toward the van Uri and Dellacov had boarded. "Just something that belongs to you," he answered over his shoulder. "It'll fit better now than it ever did before."

I waited until he was gone and they'd pulled the doors of his transport shut before I unfurled my fingers. I stayed there for a long moment, just staring at the gift he'd given me.

My palm was slick against the object as I stepped into the transport. They made room for me, sliding down so I could cram onto the bench at the back, next to Nadia and across from Heidi.

No one spoke to me. No one asked who I was or where I'd come from.

For the first time in my life, it didn't matter that I was goddess-touched. Marked or unmarked, I was one of them now. I was a traitor, a rebel—one of the Culled.

So, as the doors shut and the van lurched into motion, I carefully clasped the rabbit-head pendant around my neck. I took a deep breath and wrapped my fist around the cool silver chain. Cohen was right—it did fit better than it ever had before.

ACKNOWLEDGMENTS

Okay, reader, deep breaths. We did it. I published the book and you finished reading it. It has been a dream come true for me, so I hope you enjoyed this first part of Monroe's story. If nothing else, I hope you were able to use these pages as an escape for a few hours. I hope it kept you up late into the night reading. I hope that if it *did* keep you up, that you're able to get a nap in tomorrow. Or at least snag a nice cup of coffee. You deserve it. Thank you for reading and for taking a moment to look at the acknowledgments.

There is no way I can adequately thank each person who has said a kind word to me, supported my dreams, encouraged me to keep going, shared my work with others, and just generally played a part in getting *Of Cages and Crowns* where it is today. I can't remember each Wattpad username, every comment, and every sweet direct message. But just know that I am grateful. If your name is not listed on these next few pages, it does not diminish your worth to me and it does not take away even an ounce of the gratitude I have. With that being said, I know I am already well over on my word count limit for this book (I always am), so we ought to get started:

My parents. There aren't words enough to describe how much I love you. I don't think this story would have ever been possible without the two of you constantly encouraging me, challenging me, and believing in me. You took my dream of writing seriously from the very beginning and never once wondered whether I could achieve my goal. In your eyes, I have always been a professional. Thank you for supporting my decision to study creative writing in college; not every student is as lucky as I have been. *Mama*, thank you for always feeding my imagination. Thank you for allowing little girl me to wear pretty dresses while playing in the mud. All that make-believe was preparing me for this moment. For this book. Thank you for understanding that I need to read and write, and for doing whatever it took to make sure I could have those creative outlets. *Daddy*, thank you for reading me the first Harry Potter book when I was eight years old. And for continuing to read the other six books to me, even after I was old enough to read them all on my own. You may think Jim Dale is the best book narrator for that series, but he's got nothing on you. Thank for being the first person I trusted to read my books. There is no one I trust more with the worst version of my stories. Thank you for being my soft place to land and for always believing that I would get published. I did it.

Joshua. You are the best brother in the world. So much of who you are and what you mean to me has found its way into characters in this book. Monroe is lucky to have a brother like Ambrose, but he is only a shell of the young man you are. I love you.

Kayleigh. I'm grateful to have you in my corner, always ready to fight alongside me (despite not always knowing what we were fighting for or against). I'm beyond blessed to have you as my best friend and adopted sister. Thank you for abandoning your baby and your husband to go get cookout with me the night I signed a book deal. We sat in a dark OfficeMax parking lot and laughed until we cried. You wanted it for me as badly as I did. It was a dream come true for both of us.

Marissa, Sydney, Sarah (Shaywood), and Keanna. You have no idea how much of you has wormed its way into this book. While writing *Of Cages and Crowns*, I didn't see it—but now, after rereading it about a million times, I catch myself constantly being reminded of "The Decker Girls" and the lifelong friendships we've crafted. You find your way into everything that I write; I hope it always stays that way. See you in the group chat.

Katie Pie. You are the coolest "dus" I know. I love you to the moon and back. Thanks for hanging out with your old lady cousin while you were a senior in college. I'm writing this letter in February 2022, but I can confidently say that we probably still need to finish that season of *Married at First Sight*. I love you, sassy pants.

Loridee De Villa. The publishing journey wouldn't have been the same without your friendship. I'm thankful to have had you to stress with, talk publishing with, and laugh with. We did it. The books are on the shelves. I'm proud of us.

Aunt Sheila. If you were here, you would have made this book a best seller on your purchases alone. Everyone would have gotten one for Christmas and you would have had boxes of them stashed in your spare bedrooms, your garage, and your car. You would have also probably used a coupon, so you would have been saving on each purchase, which would have inevitably translated into you buying even more books. I miss you every single day. I wish you could walk into the bookstore and see it for yourself. I wish I could walk into a bookstore with you and show you. I love you.

Papa Crump. I didn't quit. You were the best storyteller I've ever known. I miss your voice and your hands and the way you laughed. Thank you for believing in me and always asking me *when* I was going to publish a book—as if it were always a guarantee and I was just dragging my feet in making it happen. Thank you for loving me. I know you would have been so proud. You would have also told me to invest some money in the stock market—I'll see what I can do.

My English professors at Gardner-Webb University—Dr. Buckner, Dr. Davis, Dr. Duffus, Dr. Land, and Dr. Stuart (to name a few). Thank you for teaching me about the grace of first drafts and for giving me the space and time to write. Thank you for introducing me to the blessing and curse that is NaNoWriMo. Thank you for letting me take the unconventional path with my senior thesis—without that final project, I wouldn't be where I am today. Craig Hall will always be home.

Anna Grace Francis. Thank you for reading over my edits. I love being able to talk writing and vintage things with you. I hope our books are one day shelf buddies.

Kelly Peterson. Thank you for being a good literary agent to all authors— even those you don't represent.

Wattpad Books and Wattpad Team. This version of *Of Cages and Crowns* is a product of your patience, hard work, and belief. Thank you for investing in this story and in me. Thank you to Deanna and Fiona for reading and rereading (and then reading yet again) this book. Hopefully you aren't too tired of it. To Jen, for making me smile while looking through all of your careful copy edits—your commentary and insightful suggestions were golden. To Austin, for being a good friend and good advocate for me when I needed it most. You have been a shining light through the sometimes stormy sea that is publishing—there is no one else I'd rather have guiding me through this process. Thank you to everyone who has played a part in getting the book to where it is today. I appreciate your hard work and your passion for storytelling. The world needs to hear the stories and voices of young people; thank you for giving so many people a place to belong. I'm grateful to have been able to work alongside some of the people who help make Wattpad what it is. Also, thank you to whoever noticed *Senseless* on Wattpad back in September 2018 and decided to feature it. That book led readers to my Wattpad profile where they saw this book, and now here we are.

The readers on Wattpad. I may have written the book, but you brought it to life. You fought for the story. You begged for the physical copies. You shared it with friends. You saw yourself in Monroe and you advocated for her story being published. Thank you for waiting up until midnight (or whatever time it was for you) to read the chapters as I posted them. Thank you for the fan art, the sweet messages, the Goodreads reviews, and the support you've given me over the last few years. This book is for you. Every single one of you. I hope you always see some part of yourself in Monroe. You are pure magic. You are goddess-touched.

ABOUT THE AUTHOR

Brianna Joy Crump grew up on the outskirts of Raleigh, North Carolina. While attending Gardner-Webb University, she fell in love with small-town college life and telling stories. After a year of teaching middle school and being a barista in Raleigh, Brianna moved back to GWU to continue her education and work as a residence hall director (a job that she accidentally fell in love with). Brianna currently lives in Pembroke, North Carolina, where she works as a community director at the University of North Carolina at Pembroke. Brianna spends her days writing books, advocating for college students, and attending far too many Zoom meetings. She has her BA and MA in English, two cats named Jinx and Salem, and an obnoxious number of plants. *Of Cages and Crowns* is her debut novel.

Turn the page for a preview of

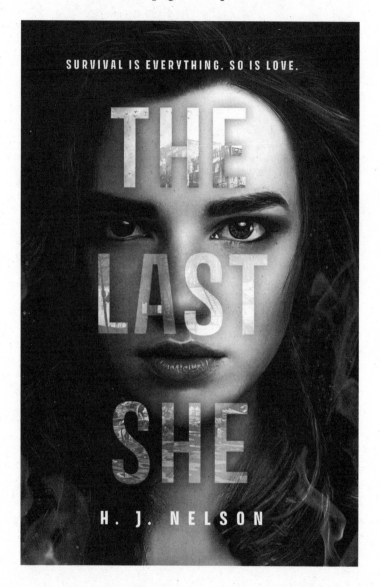

SURVIVAL IS EVERYTHING. SO IS LOVE.

THE LAST SHE

H. J. NELSON

Available now, wherever books are sold.

ONE—ARA

I crouched below the ruined bridge and scrubbed the blood off my fingers. River rocks tinged with gray, ochre, and green wavered beneath the current. Father would have reached for one, but I didn't. Instead, I rubbed my hands against each other, watching the swirls of red disappear into the flow.

Look, Ara, three skips. Think you can get four?

All around, the trees faded to colors of blood and pus, as if no time had passed. But no traffic roared across the bridge, and the center had given way, the two ends stretched out like doomed lovers' hands. My camouflage backpack rested between the eaves of the bridge, and below it, a squirrel lay spread-eagled on a river rock. His body was laid open, his face crushed. Without a bow or bullets for my pistol, I'd had to smash him with a rock. I couldn't risk lighting a fire and had eaten only the kidneys, liver, and heart. The salty taste and chewy texture only reminded me how long it had been since I'd eaten a real meal. And that I needed a proper weapon.

The new tech will fail you, same way it failed the world. A gun is your new best friend.

But my pistol was empty. Which meant I was about to put into action a plan my father would never have approved. Find a group of men, steal their weapons, bullets, or both, and be gone before they knew what happened. I wiped my hands dry, fished out my backpack, and started back up the steep riverbank. The squirrel's blood had dried beneath my nails, but I let it be. My hands had been stained by worse.

I pushed through the tall weeds until I found the overgrown trail that ran beside the river and the prints I'd found fresh last night. I remembered the trail; it had once been a mecca for young families, full of expensive houses and the flashy new tech machines my father hated. Out here, on the edge of the city, the lots were large and the massive houses were built right up next to the river, with backsides made entirely of glass. Now the expensive houses crumbled, and the Midwestern city once known for its hospitality lay still.

Yesterday a group of men had stopped here for water, then left the river behind and headed deeper into the city, where the buildings grew thicker. There were prints where they'd laid down heavy packs, and if I had to bet, one of those held a weapon.

There are no such things as friendly men, Ara. Not in this world. Not for you.

I tightened the straps of my pack and followed the tracks. The city grew slowly around me, as did the silence. No low drum of cars, no hum of airships, no voices. Only the wind and lonely birdsong. The plague killed females first and fastest, to the point I knew of no other female survivors. But even if a few men had been spared, it hadn't been enough to keep the world from falling apart. Gas stations and other businesses soon pressed in between the encroaching trees, signs faded, weeds and vines growing thick. I passed an abandoned airship lost in waves of billowing waist-high grass. The front half was crumpled, as if it had lost power and fallen straight from the sky. Growing up, almost every family I knew had the new, shiny airships that zipped through the skies, but my father had always preferred the older technologies: steel and oil. In the end, neither had brought salvation.

The driveway reflected the full heat of noon, and though the neighborhood should have been filled with the noise of laughing children, lawnmowers, and airships, it was quiet. Only my father's voice rang out through the dry, summer air as he loaded another jug of water into the back of the truck.

"Ara, did you put the matches in?"

"Yep, and two lighters."

"Good."

He tossed our backpacks on top of the other supplies in the truck bed. With them we could go three weeks in the Sawtooths, or even farther north into Canada. Bottled water, canned and dehydrated food, two containers of gasoline, two sharpened axes, our bows, and other supplies lined the truck bed. I'd never appreciated the supplies he kept until now. When news of the plague started just a few weeks earlier, the stores had emptied almost overnight. A week in, I'd heard Mother and Father talking late at night in the kitchen, and when I woke, she was gone. "A trip, to visit her sister," my father said, with eyes that couldn't meet mine. And then my sister Emma and I were separated. Under no circumstances were we to go into each other's rooms. My father brought us food and water. The first night I snuck out onto our rooftop and tapped on her window and her blue eyes greeted me with mischief. But three days ago, the day the electricity shut off, she answered my tap with white eyes weeping tears of blood. I nearly fell off the roof in terror.

The fear and silence when Father left with Emma that night made it hard to breathe. The world had fallen apart around me, but I hadn't cared or noticed till mine did. I sat on the roof all night, joined by the steady whine of cicadas, the distant sound of gunshots, and the steady thump-thump-thump *of earth as our neighbor dug two deep, long holes in his backyard.*

In the early dawn, they returned. Father carried her cradled in his arms. I could breathe again. He didn't tell me where they'd gone, only came to my room and told me to pack a bag. But I had a child's faith that she would be all right, that he had taken her somewhere that would make her well again. That was why we were leaving today.

Now Father's prized hunting rifle lay in the front seat, the pistol with which he'd taught me to shoot in the glove box. He'd changed into his hunting gear: a wool lined jacket, dark pants, a camouflage cap, and heavy boots. Unlike Emma, people always picked me out as his daughter. Same hazel eyes, same sharp cheekbones, same auburn hair.

He pulled the tarp over the truck bed and shut the tailgate. We were lucky he was a romantic who loved the old tech. While others had switched to airships years ago, Father kept his guns in a safe and the car under a tarp in the garage.

The leather squeaked beneath me as I climbed inside. Loki, our husky, whined from the back seat, unhappy at being alone. Usually he sat with Emma and me on either side of him.

"I could sit in the truck bed with Loki if Emma wants to sit here?" I said. "Then we'd still be separate?"

He started the car and began to back up, not meeting my eyes.

"It's just us, Ara."

~

The wrongness of the moment twisted my gut even now. It was a horrible thing we did, leaving her. A decision that has haunted me ever since. Maybe my punishment was that all I had now was an empty pistol and my father's final words: to go back to the beginning.

The tracks left the river path and moved west, pushing first through thick weeds and then following a dirt path that snaked through neighborhoods full of fading houses, shattered windows, and streets littered with cars and airships. Weeds, leaves, and dirt smothered all. I kept the rising sun at my back, and after an hour of walking came upon the remains of what I guessed was the men's fire from last night. The ash was still warm; if they'd started at daybreak, I couldn't be more than a few hours behind. If I could find where they camped tonight, I could steal the gun and be long gone by morning.

Rusted cars with grimy windows littered the roads and several times I passed collections of bones and dried flesh that I tried not to look at. The city grew thicker and I passed a dozen yellow buses, stationary, in front of a brick building. *FORGIVE US* had been spray-painted in white on the wall. It wasn't my school, but I stared anyway. It had been only three years since the world had ended, but I could barely remember the sixteen-year-old whose biggest problem was if she'd get back together with Sean Dennis, or if any colleges would offer her a track scholarship.

Funny, I'd once looked for others to race and now I spent my life avoiding it. My legs were thinner now, but just as fast. A fall breeze drifted between the abandoned houses, carrying scents of rot and decay. Most of the doors and windows had been boarded over, but some had been torn open, gutted clean as a fresh kill by scavengers like me. Only a few bore a red *X* painted across their front entrances. These were left untouched. The sun climbed higher, and I checked over my shoulder more and more often.

At noon, I came upon the second mistake the men made: a plume of smoke blackened the sky two miles west, dead on their current path. I scaled the largest tree I could find, a solitary oak with a tire swing attached, and surveyed the area. Trees and houses stretched as far as the eye could see. The farther I looked, the harder it was to make out the houses' missing shingles, faded paints, or fresh covering of vines. Nothing moved but the smoke drifting into the sky, all framed by the mountains rising in the distance. Why send a signal to the whole world? Stupidity? Overconfidence? Both? Part of me wanted to stay in the tree and wait till nightfall. I didn't know how many men still roamed the city. But I hadn't seen anyone else all day. Still, I was playing a dangerous game.

I left the tree behind and approached the fire slowly. The scent of burning flesh hit me well before I sidled up next to the bonfire, its warmth deceptively inviting against the chill of the day. It had been lit in the middle of a cul-de-sac, between a rusted Chevy and a blue minivan with no wheels. Buried beneath smoldering branches was the blackened body of a large animal. The scent of burning fur was almost unbearable, but even through the flames, I could see the white eyes. The animal had been infected.

The weight of the empty pistol felt suddenly heavier against my back. In the beginning, Father and I hadn't known that animals could get infected too. Then, in the mountains, we'd found an enormous bear with white eyes weeping blood; the same sign humans showed. Only this bear walked with jerky movements and charged at anything that moved. We tracked it for three days, before Father finally used two precious bullets to end it. Together we burned the body. After that we'd run into other infected animals, all grown far beyond their normal size with white, bleeding eyes, a jerky stride, and an aggressive nature beyond any I'd seen when they were wild. It made them easier to kill— they almost always charged—but the thought of meeting one now, without a weapon, terrified me. These men also must have known the dangers of the infected animals, as they'd burned the body. It made me wonder what else they knew of the plague. Not that I would ever get a chance to ask. The only thing more dangerous than an infected animal was a man.

Walking around the fire, I was unable to resist tracking the kill. A split heart, splayed wide. An elk then, and a large one at that. The tracks were spaced close where the first shot had taken him, then wide where he had run, a pool of blood where he had fallen then surged upward before the second shot downed him for good. I hadn't heard a gunshot, which meant they'd taken him with a bow. And one hell of a shot at that.

So, a group of four men, confident enough to light a bonfire in midday, armed and proficient enough to take down an infected elk. I rocked back on my heels, tracing the smoke still rising like a black flag.

They were good. But Father and I had been better.

Ara . . . I made a mistake, we all did. Go back to the beginning . . . go back . . . it's not too late.

I stood up and followed the men's tracks. Stray leaves blew across the street, catching flame and burning dangerously close to nearby houses. I didn't bother to stop them. Let the world burn; it had never done anything for me.

The tracks became harder to follow, crossing over into cracked blacktop in silent neighborhoods where thick brush had sprung up between buildings. A sense of wrongness prickled my neck as I passed into a section of trees cut through by an overgrown dirt road. The thicker covering made my heart pound and feet fall silent, the trees full of shadows. The road wound back and forth through the trees, and I stopped next to a rusted car and tilted the mirror to me. The glass was cracked, coated in dirt, but I didn't need more than a glance to make sure my auburn hair sat tucked beneath my cap. It was too long to pass for a boy's cut; I'd need to cut it soon. The mirror showed a face thinner than I remembered, my once-pale skin tanned from months of outdoor living. My clothes were faded and baggy, for warmth and protection only. Nothing to suggest my sex. Even if anyone saw me, they would mistake me for a boy.

Something moved in the mirror. I spun. The world stopped as he stepped out from the undergrowth, not twenty feet from where I stood. The first human I'd seen in months. *A man.*

Neither of us moved.

My entire body stiffened with fear. He was tall and well built, with curly hair and strange, green eyes, like the forest itself was watching me. In a different life, I might have thought him handsome, but now I saw only an enemy stronger than myself.

How the hell had he gotten behind me?

"Beautiful day for tracking, don't you think?" He had a slow smile, almost like a dare. He took a step forward.

I pulled out my pistol in one smooth motion, even as my hands trembled. His smile faded and seconds inched by as he took in my gun, my tattered clothes, my thin form. He lifted his hands slowly.

"Listen . . . Why don't you put the gun down? We can talk."

"I'm not much for talking." My voice was soft, but my heart was running itself ragged. Besides my father, he was the first human I had talked to in almost three years. And if I'd had a bullet, I'd have put it in him without blinking.

He took another step forward. "Look, I'm not going to hurt you. My name is Kaden, I live nearby. Let me help you."

"I said stop!" I shook the gun at him.

He stopped, but his eyes became hard. "All right, go ahead, shoot me. Can't say I don't deserve it." The gun trembled in my hands as he took yet another slow, measured step forward, his eyes locked on mine. "But see, here's the thing. I think if you were going to shoot me, you would have already. My bet? That gun is empty."

"You want to bet your life on that?"

He stopped again.

"How about this?" I took a step back, motioning with the gun. "You go your way. I go mine. No harm done."

He didn't move. His eyes flicked to the trees behind me.

It's a trick, don't look.

"How about this?" he said. "Surrender, and when we get back to the clan, I'll put in a good word for you. We could use a smart kid like you. We've got food there. You don't have to starve anymore. And my men won't hurt you."

Men?

Behind me, a twig snapped. My insides went cold.

Don't hesitate, Ara. There are no friendly men in this world. Not for you.

I pulled the trigger.

Click.

He flinched, but I'd already flung the pistol at him and vaulted into the forest. I dumped my backpack and sprinted through the trees. Better to have nothing if it meant my freedom.

Without my pack, I flew, adrenaline surging through me. They wouldn't catch me; I had the fastest 200-meter time in school as a freshman. A glance over my shoulder showed me the curly-haired man—Kaden—was still in the clearing. Another man raced parallel to my left, but he would never catch me. My feet barely seemed to touch the ground—

—until I slammed full force into a body. It was like running into a wall; a wall that wrapped its arms around me.

We went down hard and the forest became a blur of trees and grass. I caught a glimpse of red hair, long limbs. Kicking and thrashing with a vicious desperation, I gained my footing and lunged sideways when his hand caught my left foot. The forest floor rose up as I crashed forward with a flash of pain, fighting to rip my foot away.

Kaden's weight hit me, and this time the fight was different. He dug his knee deep into my back, crushing me. My fingers scraped against rocks and dirt as I struggled to throw him, but he only pushed harder, harder, until I buckled, my face grinding into the earth. I wanted to scream for Father, but I was alone, left only with the lessons he'd taught me. I got my elbows under me and tried to roll sideways, to throw him off. He pressed down harder. Black spots flickered in my vision. I couldn't breathe. A heavy hand pressed down on my lungs, making it impossible to move, to think. I thrashed, weaker now. Still, his body pressed. The harder I fought, the more the blackness filled the edges of my vision.

"Hey, hey, steady there!" He sounded concerned. "You're all right. Just calm down." His weight lifted a fraction.

He knocked the wind out of you. You're okay. Breathe!

"That's the boy who was following us?" A deep, slow voice from my left.

"Yeah, no wonder. He looks half-starved. Probably just looking for food."

This came from Kaden. God, he was heavy. But through the panic came a single thought: He didn't know I was a girl.

"Anyone with him?"

"No."

"You think he's part of a clan?"

"Nah, I mean . . . look at him."

The weight of their eyes was suddenly as heavy as the silence. I didn't like that I couldn't see them with my face ground into the dirt. Then—

"Jeb, come help me check him for weapons. He had a gun, might have a knife too."

My leg muscles tightened, screaming to run. What did checking me for weapons entail? There were a few things he'd notice if he checked too closely.

I readied myself for Kaden's weight to lift. My breaths came shaky and shallow, fingers tingling as I prepared for the race of my life. Instead, powerful hands grabbed my arms, and held me steady. For a brief moment the weight lifted as Kaden stood. I kicked wildly, making contact with someone, hearing a satisfying *umph.*

The satisfaction didn't last long. Sudden pain exploded across my lower thigh: one of the men had swung something hard against me. The pain radiated down my leg and I swallowed a whimper. Another set of hands held my legs now, and I was shaking, blinking back my tears.

What sort of pain would I endure if they found out I was a girl? Hands worked steadily up my leg, squeezing my thigh viciously. I jerked, but the hands kept moving. Maybe he would just search my back? When he paused at my waist, I allowed myself a feeling of hope.

The metallic note of a knife leaving its sheath broke it. Slicing upward, the knife cut through my shirt and cool air swept over my back. I closed my eyes.

"What the hell is . . ." I could almost hear him making the connection in his head at the sight of my bra. I was skinny, but even then, a woman's shape was still different from that of a man.

"Turn him over."

The pressure released. My window of opportunity. Like a viper, I flipped over, kicking the man who'd been searching me full in the face.

I should have aimed for Kaden. He tackled me and was sitting astride my waist before I could get to my feet. *Damn!* His eyes blazed into mine with a sudden understanding.

He reached forward and ripped my shirt away completely, not even bothering with the knife. Then he pulled the hat from my head. Tangled, auburn hair spilled down around my shoulders. My hair was one of the few features I was proud of; thick and straight, hinting at red in the light. I cursed myself now for not cutting it. Not that it mattered. I was trapped beneath a strange man, shirtless except for my bra, my pale skin exposed to the sunlight.

Kaden spoke first. "It's a girl."

He said it with such disbelief that, had I not been terrified, I might have been insulted. I resisted the urge to spit on him. The other men came closer. My eyes burned with humiliation and fear.

"I don't know how you were raised but sitting on a girl is not a polite way to introduce yourself." Or at least, that's what I probably should have said. What actually came out was a mix of profanities that amounted to, "Get off me. NOW!"

Kaden smiled, not at all cowed. Without taking any weight off me, he looked up at the others. "It's definitely a girl."

"Can't be. There's not any left."

This from the boy with red hair, freckles, and long limbs—the one whom I guessed had been running alongside me. His eyes seemed too big for his face, and they were filled with a sort of innocent longing, like he saw in me a lost mother or sister. I didn't want to imagine what the other men were thinking.

It didn't take long to find out.

"We should check, make sure it's really a girl, all the way," said the man with the drawl and the small, rat-like eyes, the one I'd run into. He was balding and had a rash across his arms. The left side of his face was an angry red, and I realized with satisfaction that he was the man I'd kicked. His eyes traveled down my body.

"No, it's a girl." This from Kaden. Somehow, I felt like he was the leader here. His green eyes trailed over me, and my face flushed. I returned his gaze with all the hate I could muster.

Then, suddenly, the weight was gone. I sat up slowly, surveying the men surrounding me. Besides the boy, Kaden, and the ugly one I'd kicked, there was a tall man with a hatchet strapped to his waist who hadn't been part of the fight. His deep bronze skin was contrasted by facial hair peppered with gray, a detail worth noting as I'd not seen anyone over thirty who'd survived the plague, besides my father. I stood, favoring one leg, still burning from the hit.

"Sam, give me your jacket," Kaden said.

The younger boy, Sam, took off his jacket and handed it over. He stared at the ground, face littered with freckles and hair unwashed. Kaden tossed the coat at me. When I caught it, I considered throwing it at his feet, but settled for glaring at him instead as I pulled it on. I was outnumbered, and my leg throbbed. In a foot race, I could beat every man here, except maybe Kaden. Even standing still he looked fast, with long legs and an athletic frame.

He caught me watching him and smiled. I decided I could outrun him;

but I'd put a knife in him first, to be sure. I crossed my arms. The jacket was well worn, soft, and still warm. When I breathed in the scent of leather, there was a metallic tang—blood, in my mouth. I had bitten my cheek when falling and didn't even notice.

"What's your name?" he asked. A simple question, but I hadn't been asked it for so long.

"What's *your* name?" I countered. Even though he'd already told me his name, I felt caught off guard, not sure I wanted to tell this group of men anything about me. Even my name.

"Kaden. That's Sam, Issac, and Jeb."

Sam, the youngest of them, gave me a soft, boyish smile, contrasted by Jeb's leer: he was the ugly one I'd kicked. Issac looked me square in the face and nodded, a quiet sympathy. He looked the oldest of the group, maybe even older than my father.

"Ara," I finally said. Short for Arabella.

Kaden picked up a rope from the ground, and I realized that was what Jeb had swung against my leg. He stepped forward, and I jerked back when I understood what he meant to do. "You're going to tie me up?"

He smiled, watching me through oddly long eyelashes. "Will you come with us if I don't?"

"No."

"Then it doesn't look like I've got much of a choice."

A cold breeze drifted through the trees, carrying scents of the forest, smells I'd spent the last three years in and had protected me—until now. He tied my hands in front of me with the meticulous movement of someone who knew what they were doing. I leaned as far as I could away from him, shifting the adrenaline, pain, and panic back with a plan. *They're just men. They die as easily as animals.* I could still steal a weapon. I could still make it home.

While he tied my hands, Sam ran back to the clearing and returned with my pack and my gun. He pulled out the magazine.

"It's empty," he said, sounding confused.

Kaden smiled knowingly, but I refused to acknowledge that he'd been right.

"You know," Kaden said as he gave the rope a final tug, forcing me a half step closer, "most people shoot a gun. But I like your style. Throwing one is much more sporting. Your aim is a little off, though."

"Give me the gun and a bullet and I'll show you how off it is."

He laughed. Then in a gesture that felt far too intimate, he stepped behind me and wound my hair into a bun. I tried to ignore the feeling of his hands in my hair as he pulled the cap back over my head and then picked up the rope.

"You know, princess, I don't think I will."

© 2021 H.J. Nelson